Waiting for Elizabeth

First published by Tangerine Publications 2013

Published by Tangerine Publications Ltd
www.tangerinepublications.com
PO Box 4135
Whanganui, 4541
New Zealand

ISBN- 978-0987664617

Cover design: Jellyfish Creative www.jellyfishcreative.co.nz
Cover concept: Gayelene Holly

Waiting for Elizabeth

For Sini

with best wishes

Joan Rosier-Jones

& thanks

Tangerine

appeeling books

Joan July 2016

Author's Note

The major events in this novel actually happened; many of the main characters were real people. However, I have woven these stories into a fictional tale with some fictional characters. Arthur and Morveen are figments of my imagination, as are the cook, the potman and many of the people Arthur meets. To avoid confusion for the reader, I have taken the liberty of eliminating the third Butler brother who was also called Piers.

I have endeavoured to recreate the world in which they lived as faithfully as I can, given the fact that their world existed over five hundred years ago.

There is a chronology of real events at the back of the book for those who are interested, and for further, factual reading I would recommend *The Ormond Lordship in County Kilkenny 1515-1642: The Rise and Fall of Butler Feudal Power* by David Edwards of University College, Cork. This is an erudite and readable account of the Butlers and I found it an invaluable research resource.

To the O'Carroll and Nevin families
who welcomed me to Ireland.

Introduction

Someone once said that the problem with Irish history is there is far too much of it. In this novel I focus on the period of Ireland under the Tudors. It is a relatively short period in historic terms, but it was seminal; the beginning of the end for the hope of a united Ireland.

It was a time when brother fought brother, the Norman earls fought against Irish chiefs when expedient and fought side by side with them when that was advantageous. Acquisition of, and maintaining, land ownership was paramount. As in-fighting continued, the Tudors brought devastation to Ireland. Even then it was not immediately realised that the real enemy was not a neighbouring chieftain or rival lordship, but Elizabeth and her settler troops.

Two of the many rivals were Thomas Butler, Earl of Ormond, known as Black Tom for his swarthy looks, and Gerald FitzGerald, Earl of Desmond. While Desmond was ambivalent about his allegiance to the Crown, Tom was steadfastly loyal. He was much closer to Elizabeth; a cousin on the Boleyn side, and he had been brought up at Court with Elizabeth and her brother, Edward. Elizabeth had nicknames for her favourite courtiers and Tom's was Lucas.

There were rumours that one of Tom's twelve bastard children was Elizabeth's son. This is possible. She was known to refer to Tom as her 'black husband'. Also towards the end of 1553, five years before she came to the throne, Elizabeth travelled to a house in the south of England with a few servants and Tom Butler as her guardian. In February the following year she was said to be pregnant. By May her condition had become more noticeable but when she was asked if she wanted to see a physician she said, 'I am not minded to make any stranger privy to my body but commit it to God.' Elizabeth was no fool. She knew that if she were to have a male child, it would both endanger her life and put paid to the possibility of her ever attaining the throne.

Elizabeth promised Black Tom that she would visit him in Ireland and he built a manor house onto his Carraigh-on-Suir castle to accommodate her.

Meanwhile battles raged, blood was let and Celtic, Catholic Ireland was in its dying stages. Time would see a renaissance but is yet to see a united Ireland.

PART ONE

Carraigh-on-Suir
February 1565

Chapter One

Young Arthur hobbled across the courtyard, lugging his gammy foot behind him. Step-drag-step-drag. The builders working on the new manor house were packing up for the day, and a couple of stable lads led horses to the armoury, from whence the clang of metal indicated that their day's work was not yet done. Step-drag-bump over the cobblestones. A boy he'd not seen before was mucking out the stables. Arthur dodged the dung that flew his way.

'Shite,' he muttered, meaning the boy, not the muck. The light was fading and puddles in the yard were icing over while mist drifted up from the river and oozed under the watergate into the inner court. The castle walls towered above him. Scrunch with his good foot, pull the bad behind him. He hated that leg as if it were a living person. If it weren't for that leg, born on him six years ago, what might have been? A crow sitting on the battlements cawed at him, and he picked up a stone, threw it at the crow, but missed. The bird flapped its wings and cawed again while Arthur limped on towards the kitchen garden.

Through the arched gateway the ground was soggy and his bare feet squelched in the mud. He took his customary wander, sniffing at the peat smoke in the air from hearth fires in the town, looking at the cabbages growing fat, round hearts on the cold earth, admiring the leeks, tall and straight almost ready for the pulling. No time to visit the mews and talk to the falcons. Around the neat bed of herbs he went until he came to the wood pile. His arms could not hold much, but he gathered some of the smaller pieces until the stack was so high he had to hold it under his chin. He steadied it and made his way slowly back through the garden, across the court and inside.

The candles had been lit and the kitchen was bright and shadowy at the same time. Arthur dumped the wood by the main fireplace. They were all there - the scullery man, the baker's boy, the boy who turned the spit and Cook himself, arms like hams, the head of a bull. Morveen was plucking sparrows for a pie and he cuddled into her kirtle. 'Good boy,' she whispered. 'My lord will be proud of you. Him away so with the men fighting the Desmonds. And you running the castle for the love of him while he's gone.' She giggled.

Arthur laughed, then said seriously, 'When will he be back?'

'When they have defeated those dribbling Desmonds.'

'I've heard tell those Desmonds are demons in the field.'

'Don't you go believing that shite. You know the Earl of Ormond, Black Tom Butler, is the finest man in all of Ireland. Fightin' or standin' still. You, of all people, should know that.'

'I do, Morveen.' He cuddled closer. 'Tell me again. Tell me my story.'

'We haven't the time.'

'Tonight then,' he said. 'Tonight,' and there was no room for argument.

*

'This all happened far across the sea...' Morveen took a breath.

'In the land of the English,' Arthur said. They were lying on a thin bed of straw under the long kitchen table, at the far end from the fire or the baker's ovens, cuddled together as much for warmth as out of affection. Grunts and snores came from the rest of the sleeping servants.

'Do you want me to tell the story?'

'Aye. I will be still now.'

'Well then,' Morveen paused for another breath. 'It was the blackest time o' night. The torch light… it flickered against the wall. It flickered and ran. The light ran. Someone far away was cryin', "Help." And the midwife ran as quick as her fat little legs could take her. It was a long run. Down the corridor, out into the light of the great hall, where some grand courtiers was leanin' against the wall tapestries. They looked away when the woman came a-running. Even then she held her hood close, not to be seen, so. Across the hall she ran, out into the dark again, clutching her chest when she ran out of puff. At the chamber door a manservant held a torch to guide her. A lady's maid opened the door and pushed the poor breathless soul in, then closed the door quick to stop the fierce din inside leakin' out to other ears.

In the middle of the room was the grandest bed you ever clapped eyes on. It was hung with gold-trimmed red damask curtains. The tester was embroidered with a coat of arms and the matching valances glowed in the flames of the roaring fire. It was fierce hot. The bed curtains were parted, and eight women stood by. The red-headed woman on the bed gave another screech and grabbed her belly.

The midwife pushed the other women back. "Breathe deeply," she ordered, still puffin' her heart out.

A final scream and the babby came out, plop into the midwife's out-stretched hands. "It's a boy," she said and the ladies clapped, politely like real ladies do. A boy. Just what they wanted. The mother groaned. The babby cried. The midwife put a hand over the babby's mouth to squash them cries. When he stopped she looked him over, sighed and began swaddlin' him.

"Let me see," the mammy ordered. "Before you wrap him." She held out feeble arms.

"Here's cheer," said one of the maids, holding out a glass of celebration. "We have the best glasses. Silver 'n gold goblets are not good enough for such…"

The ma struggled up. "No," she cried.

"It's your favourite…"

"No," the ma shrieked, and as her word was law, the maid put the glass down on the table beside the bed. "There is nothing to celebrate." The mother collapsed back on the pillows. "Get rid of him." There was a gasp, me'be in dismay, me'be in disappointment that they would not be gollopin' down mead distilled from herbs and honey, out of the finest glass you ever seen. "I will not have it."

Arthur nudged Morveen. 'Why did she..?'

'We go through this every time.'

'Was it cos…she was a-feared to have a…boy…' Arthur insisted '…or because of what the babby was…' Across the river an eerie howl came up from the wooded hills. Arthur shuddered.

'The wolves won't be after comin' for you here. Should I be goin' on?'

'Aye.'

'Then stop your blathering…The midwife bundled up the babby. She knew the boy was never going to live with his ma in any case. Plans had been made. "Is the wet nurse here?" she demanded.

The wet nurse came out of her corner.

"Take it." The midwife handed over the bundle and looked at the bed. The curtains were closed around the mammy and her favourite maid was trying to comfort her.

"Get rid of it," the mammy screamed from behind the curtains.

The mid-wife turned back to the wet nurse. "You know where to go?"

"Aye, Mistress." She lowered her voice. "But what is meant by gettin' rid of it?"

"Keep to the original plan," the midwife whispered back. "We'll be after taking care of things here." She waved at the bed.

Now it was the wet nurse's turn to run through them dark corridors. The manservant who had waited outside followed with his light because her arms were full. They ran and ran, causing a small stir in the Great Hall as they passed, then on until they rushed out into the bitin' night air. The babby whimpered. "Sh-sh-sh." The wet nurse rubbed the babby's back. The light led them down to the river. When they saw the wherry a-waiting at the water's edge, the light turned to go. "Godspeed," was all he said afore racin' back into the dark.

"You're in a big hurry." The wherryman leered at the wet nurse and her bundle. "We ain't going nowhere until dawn." He helped her into the boat and she sat herself down. The boy whimpered again. The wet nurse turned her back to the wherryman and took out a pap for the babby to suckle on. At first he turned his head away. Then he took her nipple in his tiny gob and sucked. She had good strong milk, the wet nurse did. Nothin' like the watery stuff newborns usually have. When he'd suckled a little she rearranged her clothing, lay the babby in her lap and turned to face the wherryman. "Will this boat get us across?" she asked. "I have heard that such boats bring danger of drownin'. I cannot swim...."

"That makes the two of us," said the wherryman drily. He pulled the flaps of his leather helmet tight over his ears and closed his eyes, as if to say, 'Enough talk, now.'

At first light the wherryman cast off and began paddlin'.'

Morveen looked at Arthur. He was asleep. '*Oíche mhaith*, good night, darlin',' she said softly before snuggling beside him. She was soon asleep herself, dreaming dreams nobody would, or should, believe.

Chapter Two

Arthur awoke to the clatter of horses on the cobbles, the Earl's bull mastiffs barking and the fearsome noise of men shouting and laughing. They were back! He crawled out from under the table and hobbled outside. Soldiers, kerne and gallowglass were everywhere, some astride horses, some on foot standing shoulder to shoulder, their swords sheathed, blood staining the hilts. Horses pawed the ground, obviously uncomfortable at being in such a crush. One reared onto its hind legs, but the men around it were fearless. More soldiers were in the outer court, trying to push their way in for a better view, and the noise of cheering men came also from the Great Park outside the castle walls. Even though he was standing on the door sill, Arthur could not see his Earl, Tom Butler, the Earl of Ormond, but knew he must be there somewhere. He would have liked to climb the battlements for a better look, but there was no path through. He looked up at the west keep and the splash of colour at the second floor window meant my lady, the Countess Elizabeth, was watching her husband's return.

'Into the oubliette with him,' someone shouted above the clamour and the milling soldiers parted to make a pathway. Arthur saw a man slumped over a horse. A gentleman soldier lifted him down, threw him over his shoulder and pushed a way across the yard.

'Where now the great Earl of Desmond?' a soldier from the crowd jeered.

The wounded man lifted his head. 'Where but in his proper place,' he shouted as well he could. 'On the necks of the Butlers.'

Morveen came out with the rest of the kitchen staff and stood with a hand on Arthur's shoulder, as if to protect him from the evil that was Desmond. 'That's the Earl's brother, Sir Edmund Butler,' she said above the noise, pointing at the gentleman soldier who was so remarkably tall and strong that the weight of his prisoner seemed no heavier than a small sack of grain.

Then the Earl of Ormond pushed forward, his mastiffs running behind, weaving in and out of the men who stood in their way. The Earl looked tired and his clothes were covered in blood. But he was handsome with his raven hair and striking black beard. No wonder they called him Tom Dubh, Black Tom. 'Take care,' the Earl warned. 'He's wounded. We'll get the physician to take the shot out ere long.'

'More than he deserves,' muttered a soldier close to Arthur.

The Earl's brother with Desmond still slung over his shoulder disappeared down the steps of the prison tower and the Earl turned to the troops holding up both arms to silence them. They quietened immediately. 'We have prevailed,' he said. 'We can afford the Earl of Desmond some charity.'

'Before we take the head off his shoulders,' a gallowglass called out.

The Earl smiled, white teeth against his black beard, and the men cheered, 'Butler a Boo.'

'Yes. Victory to the Butlers,' the Earl called. 'And now to your rest,' and he turned to follow Desmond into the dungeon. Morveen caught his eye. 'Well done, my lord.' She bobbed him a deep curtsy. *Conas atá tú?'*

'I am well. 'Twas Sir Edmund's pistol that done him,' the Earl said smiling. 'But it was a battle won fair and square,' and he slapped her bottom with the palm of his hand before marching off. His troops clapped, whistled and cheered his departing back. Morveen stood watching until the kitchen hands straggled off, and with a sigh she finally led Arthur inside.

Not all the soldiers had returned to the castle. Many of the kerne went to their homes, as had some of the gallowglass - those Scottish soldiers in the Earl's permanent employ with homes in Ireland. The other soldiers pitched tents in the Great Park and they needed to be fed. Richard Shee, the seneschal, came in to discuss the food with Cook, and the kitchen became as busy as on a feast day. Nobody seemed to mind. Black Tom Butler, Earl of Ormond, and his brothers, with four hundred foot and one hundred horse had beaten Desmond and taken him prisoner. It was a victory to warm the heart.

The rush in the kitchen came to a stop when the Earl's bard, Eoghan Mac Craith, a plump squinty man, came to see what to expect for his dinner at the hero's table. Cook showed him the roasting pig, the capons with oysters, the baked goose and the goose blood puddings. To honour the food the poet recited some of his new lines. 'My choice is Thomas, the choice and true love, of every fair-skinned young maiden…'

'That bears repeating,' Morveen whispered to the pot man.

'…The chieftain who annihilates rebels; I choose the Earl of Ormond – the potent earl…'

'How many bastards was it again?' the pot man whispered to Morveen.

'Six at last count.'

Oblivious the bard went on '…An earl of military troops; with Wyatt beyond the seas he made his first combat, the valiant sword-fencing lord.'

'He was but a child then,' Morveen said. Arthur scowled at her. He wanted to listen but the poet had finished and was on his way back to the great hall. He left behind him a small moment of silence, which the pot man soon broke. 'No mention of Desmond marrying my lord's mother,' he said. 'Nor that my Lady Joan's death has paved the way for this fracas.'

'Aye,' agreed Cook. 'Free of family ties, they are free to fight again.' He waved an arm. 'To work,' and the kitchen erupted into life again. They had a banquet to present, and little time in which to do it.

There was revelry that night all over the castle; much ale and wine was drunk. There was so much noise it drowned out the music of the Earl's harpers in the great hall, and to Arthur's relief, it also drowned out the howling wolves across the river. Morveen had vanished into the night by the time the candles were snuffed. 'She'll be out a-wenching with them soldiers,' said Cook when Arthur asked if he knew where she was. So Arthur found their spot under the table, blocked his ears of the noise and went to sleep on his own.

Next morning Morveen was beside him but he had a terrible time trying to wake her. 'Oh, me head,' she moaned. '*Níl mé go maith*. Oh, me gut. Fetch me water, Arty, there's a laddo.'

Arthur went to the pot man's bucket of clean water and filled a pannikin. 'Here,' he gave it to her.

She drank deeply. 'Off you run, so. We'll be busy here again and you get under foot. Fetch wood for the fire boy.'

Arthur went quickly through the court this morning looking behind him all the while in case Desmond had escaped from the oubliette and was after him. He knew that he was an eejit to think so, because the oubliette was a dungeon with only a trap door in the roof with no way for Desmond to escape, but he was so fiendish he might call some magic to his aid. In the kitchen garden he took his usual turn, and when he reached the weathering yard at the mews the falconer was there. Arthur turned to leave quickly, but the falconer said, 'Would you like to put her on your arm?' He pointed to a beady-eyed falcon sitting on the portable perch they used when they took the birds out. '*Tá sí go hálainn*. A real beauty. Been manned a year coming up. See how happy she is on the cadge?' He placed a piece of thick leather over Arthur's arm and pulled him closer to the cadge. 'Hold your arm out now.'

The bird fluttered and Arthur clucked to settle it, then the falcon stepped off the cadge onto Arthur's arm. She weighed heavy, but Arthur lifted his arm and supported it with his other hand. The falcon looked at him. 'Ttuck...ttuck,' Arthur clucked.

'You've a way about you, bucko,' the falconer said. 'I thought as much when I seen you in here afore. Not everyone can do that.' He nodded at the bird.

Arthur felt proud as he handed the bird over to the cadge again. He had a way about him! He'd held a falcon on his arm. Like a real gentleman. Smiling, he went to the wood pile, gathered an armful of wood and took it back to the kitchen.

He dumped the wood by the fire, and limped quickly outside again. It had begun to rain, but he did not care, a few drops of water never hurt a soul, especially not a bucko with a way about him.

*

Desmond was not long at Carraigh. A couple of days after his arrival he was taken in chains to Dublin Castle where his fate would be decided. Arthur was relieved. The inner court had not felt the same while Desmond sat in the castle cell. It was as if the evil of him seeped out just as the river mist seeped in. Once Desmond had gone he was soon forgotten. Far away in Dublin he could do no harm. The days lengthened and the weather warmed. Summer arrived, though it still rained a great deal. In spite of the weather the manor house was coming along. Where once there'd been a garden and the castle outer wall, now stood the north range. Two sides joined the east and west towers of the keep, and along the front it stretched right across between them. Arthur had watched it grow, looking down at it from the battlements. He had seen the wooden frames laid out on the ground in pieces; he'd seen the frames lifted to form the building's skeleton and watched the masons at work on the cladding. When that was finished whatever went on was done in secret behind the walls and Arthur would give anything to see inside.

Everyone knew the Earl was building the manor house so that the Queen, Elizabeth, would have a suitable place to stay when she came to Ireland on progress. And why would she not stay at Carraigh? The Earl was her cousin and a favourite at court. Everyone knew that. One rare sunny day Arthur finished mucking out the pigs and as he returned to the kitchen one of the household's miniature spaniels came running up and sniffed at him. Arthur laughed. 'All those porker smells, eh boy?' As he bent down to scratch the dog's ears a messenger galloped into the inner ward. He was finely dressed in a crimson cape and was riding so fast he had to pull his horse in quickly to avoid hitting the battlement wall. He jumped down, threw the reins at Arthur and ran into the keep. Everyone stopped work except for a stable boy who ran out and snatched the reins from Arthur. The spaniel barked, jumping up at Arthur in excitement. 'That's the messenger from Dublin,' Arthur heard someone say. 'He'll have a letter for my lord.'

*

Later they learnt it was a letter from the Queen herself. Of course nobody read it to the kitchen staff, but rumour took hold like a fire in thatch. There followed much tittle-tattle about the contents of the message. Some said it granted the Earl all of Desmond's lands, some that it was to inform him he had been made a duke, while others suggested that the Queen was finally coming on progress to Ireland.

'A foolish woman she'd be to do that,' the pot man said when they heard that piece of gossip.'

Morveen disagreed. 'She would be safe enough here, so. In my lord's care.'

'Mossa, she'll be going to Dublin,' Cook said. 'For sure she'd rather stay in the Pale.'

'Why send a messenger to my lord?' Arthur asked.

'Stop your gabby mouth,' said the pot man who liked to have the last word. He thumped a cauldron onto the floor just missing Arthur's good foot. '*Go hifreann leat.* Y' fecking dosser.'

Arthur went out and watched the smithy at work shoeing a horse. 'Do you know what the letter said?' he asked.

'Cheeky feck,' the smithy said. 'What has it to do with you, now?'

Arthur crossed the court and climbed up to the battlements. Across the river the wooded hills watched over castle and town, and he could smell the malty nose of the ale from the brewery not far off.

'Good day to you.' It was one of the pages. Arthur had seen him come and go in the privy kitchen where the Earl's meals were laid out ready for serving. Morveen had pointed him out: he was Piers, one of the Earl's bastard sons, born about eleven summers since.

Arthur looked with envy at Piers' two straight legs in their yellow stockings. 'Do you know what the letter from the Queen said?'

'I do,' said the page, sitting down on one of the stairs. 'It is not good.' He paused. 'Then again it might not be bad.' He frowned. 'It is hard to reckon.'

'What is it?'

'The letter has orders for Desmond to be freed from Dublin Castle.'

Arthur gasped. 'Why? After all the trouble my lord went through to capture him.'

'That battle at Affane did not have the Queen's approval. Both Desmond and my lord are to go to Court and answer to the Queen for their fight.' Piers paused, considering the matter for a moment. 'It could bode well. Or evil. It depends on her Majesty's mood I suppose.' He sighed. 'At the moment she is much displeased. Private wars are not allowed.'

When Arthur went back inside and told Morveen she said, 'Whoever told you that is codding you. My lord to London? In the same breath as Desmond?'

'The page, Piers, tol' me.'

'He should know,' Morveen agreed, and it was only next day that she came running into the kitchen. 'My lord's off on the morrow.'

'I knew it would come to no good,' cut in a scullery man.

'I never heard you say so at the time,' the pot man said.

'The Queen likes to say who can fight. And when,' said Morveen.

'And my lady?' Cook asked. 'Is nobody to tell me who we have to cook for in the Earl's absence?'

'I heard,' Morveen lowered her voice, 'the Countess will go as far as Waterford. Things are going badly between them.'

'That should be no surprise,' said a scullery lad. 'He has an eye that wanders.'

'Enough,' ordered Cook and a wave of his hand sent them back to work.

*

In the lull between dinner and supper, Morveen and Arthur sat together under the table. Morveen said she felt poorly and Cook said she could rest a while. 'Tell me,' Arthur said. 'Tell me my story.'

'Arty, I am not feeling well now. Leave me be.'

'Let her be, boy,' said the pot man. 'She's childing.'

'Shut your scabby gob,' Morveen shouted at the pot man. 'What is going on with me is none of your mind.' The pot man snorted derisively. 'And I'll tell the laddo what I choose. And say it when I choose.' She settled Arthur so his head was in her lap and began. 'After the wherryman had crossed them, they went on their way by land.' For all that she had stood up to the pot man on his behalf she sounded cross. 'They stopped in manor houses and keeps all along the way. The babby being sick all the time. All over the nurse's clothes. Drinking of her milk and puking it up again. The nurse had changed all the babby's swaddling clothes, and they both stank to the heavens by the time they got to Bristol. The stench was so great that the house they were to shelter in would not take them. It was a grange, the house, big enough for a hundred babbies.'

'Was it as big as my lord's manor house?'

'Not quite. Black Tom Butler's house is a marvel.'

'Have you seen inside it?'

'Aye,' she said.

'I wish I could.'

'Have I finished your story, so?'

Arthur shook his head.

'This grange, now, it was attached to a church but not belonging to it any more. The land taken by the old king for to give away to some noble or other. And oh japers, nothing holy about them owners. They told the nurse to take herself and her babby out to sleep in with the animals. It was hard to know who stunk most, the beasts or the babby or his nurse.'

'Tell me something nice,' Arthur begged. 'It was not like this last time you tol' it me.'

'Away with you if you don't like it. This is how it is today.' She drew breath and went on. 'Next morning the nurse stripped herself and washed under the pump in the grange yard. Then she took the babby and unswaddled it. She held it under the cold water, though it screamed an' screamed.' Arthur shuddered at the thought. 'When they was both washed and dried out the nurse wrapped the babby in her shawl and found her way to the dock. They went on board ship, went below and waited for to set sail. Soon they felt the ship moving under them. The sea was high. The waves billowed and the wind blew…'

'And, I know,' Arthur could not help laughing. 'They were all sick.'

'As dogs,' and Morveen laughed too. She ruffled his hair. 'My silly laddo. Enough. *Eistigi liom.* Listen,' she drew him closer. 'Tomorrow I'll feel better. Tomorrow will be our chance. With them away we'll see inside that manor house. I promise.'

Chapter Three

The courtyard by the watergate was busy. The gate was open and Arthur slipped through it to watch the barges lined up on the river waiting to be loaded with all that was needed for the Earl's trip to London and his wife's visit to Waterford. The Earl spent a lot of time at Court, often for a year or more at a time, and always at Christmas, but this was different. This time he had been summonsed in an angry letter from the Queen. Who knew how long he would be away? 'This could be the end of him,' Arthur overheard the blacksmith saying. 'One does not disobey the Queen lightly,' and he ran a finger across his throat to suggest what might happen.

The man he was talking with laughed. 'That will be Desmond's fate. Not my lord's.'

'They are both guilty of the same crime,' the blacksmith stated boldly as he walked away.

The River Suir was lazy and slow this morning, not like the flurry alongside it. A portable guarde was being lifted on board the nearest barge as Arthur found a spot for himself on the jetty. The smell of the doings from the guarde mixed with the smell of horse dung, as a stable hand encouraged a skittish mare up a ramp. Someone struggling with a large tin trunk pushed Arthur aside. 'Outta the way, boy.' He was followed by one of the Countess Elizabeth's ladies-in-waiting who waddled beside two page boys carrying a baggage chest, a handle each, between them. 'Put it down with care,' she ordered. When the trunk was safely on the jetty she sent the boys scampering back for more and turned to the next page. He held a bed cloth embroidered in gold and silver. It was Piers. 'Pick that end up,' the lady-in-waiting snapped. 'It's going to drag in the muck.' Piers, looking sheepish, gathered the bundle closer into his arms and Arthur felt a little less envious of his two fine legs.

Arthur stepped back into the courtyard and stood in the armoury doorway. The armoury was silent today; the smithy's job done for now. Arthur hoped the Earl was not in too much trouble with the Queen - but how could he be? He was the most powerful man in all of Ireland, so Morveen said, and he was completely loyal to the Crown. That was why he'd had to fight that traitor Desmond. And the Queen adored him. Morveen said that too. She had a pet name for him, Lucas, and only her favourites had pet names. Arthur watched from the doorway until, an hour or more later, everything needed had passed through the watergate.

Then came my lady Elizabeth with four ladies-in-waiting fussing around her, one of whom carried her favourite lap dog. Morveen said my lady came from the Berkeley family and married the Earl at Court in London, and everyone said she was the fairest of all the ladies at Court. Certainly today she looked fair in her popinjay blue gown with just a hint of her paps showing above the tight bodice. Her ruff was high and white and the caul on her head was made of gold thread laced with pearls. But her face was sour. Arthur wondered if she was sorry she was only going to Waterford; if she wanted to go back to Court where she came from, but perhaps she was just worried for the Earl, and he saw again the blacksmith's finger slice across his neck.

Lastly the Earl himself appeared, sword dangling at his hip. He swept through the courtyard with the usual sense of his importance to all around him, but today he looked worried and didn't nod his perky feathered hat at this person here, that person there; didn't slap anyone's backside or ruffle the younger servants' hair. Arthur tried to stand up straight, just in case, but the only things the Earl noticed were the two mastiffs held on chains by a stable boy. He bent down to pat them and say goodbye, then with a swish of the cloak thrown over one shoulder he was across the inner ward, through the gate and out on the pier without a glance at anyone.

Arthur wandered back through the gate and joined the group of servants and pages watching the final barge pull away. He was pleased to see Piers standing on the banks which meant he was not so favoured as to go with the family. On board, the Countess sat on a chair surrounded by cushions and her waiting women, but the Earl stood, already looking ahead, strong and brave as always. Arthur felt a tingle of pride as he watched the oarsmen paddle the barge into mid-stream, then turn it downstream so that soon it disappeared around the bend in the river.

*

Later with the watergate tightly shut and the castle all but empty Morveen found him. 'Where has everyone gone?' he asked.

'While the cat's away, the mice are at play, Arty.' She waved a hand in the direction of the town. 'They'll be candle-wasting at the ale tonight.'

'What about Mister Shee?'

'Ah, the seneschal. What he doesn't know won't grieve his heart. There are no men working today so he has no need of sticking his nose in.' She grabbed Arthur's hand. 'Come. This is our chance, me darlin'.' She led him running so fast that he had to hoppity-skip on his bodgey leg. They ran across the main courtyard towards the new inner yard, but when they reached the arched entry Arthur stopped and pulled Morveen to a stop.

'I've never been this close before,' he whispered.

'Don't you be fretting. You've got as much right as anyone.' She paused, 'More than some.' And she pulled him along again. They took a quick look in the downstairs entrance. Holes along the front were covered with boards, but soon there would be real glass windows and although the front door opening was only covered with boards, you could tell it, too, would look grand when it was finished. The grandest thing was the plaster cast of the Earl's head on the wall. 'The plasterer sez there'll be one of Queen Elizabeth opposite,' Morveen explained. She turned to leave. 'The paint-stainers are to put the colour on later.'

Out the entrance they went and in at a door on the western side of the court. 'Wait,' Morveen put up a hand to stop him before she ducked in, had a quick look and was out again. 'It's safe. I thought there might be a stray gentlewoman left. This is their room now when there's nobody at home. It's the new parlour,' and with a sweep of her arm she led Arthur inside.

She showed him the parlour, but quickly. That wasn't what they were there to see. She pointed at the winding staircase before running up the stone steps. Arthur followed as quickly as he could, but by the first turn Morveen had to stop and whisper down to him, 'Hurry up, you dribbling boy.'

It was all right for her, he was going as fast as he could. Morveen was right, he was a weakling, but it wasn't his fault. When he thought of whose fault it might be he had to stop. He couldn't blame those who had given him life. Nor could he blame God. That would be a sin. Could he blame the devil? But if he did that he would be saying that those who gave him life were in hand with the devil. And that was a sort of sin, too. 'Come o-o-on,' Morveen called again, louder this time. 'Time's a-wasting.'

At last he made the top. 'Beware. There's building going on yet,' Morveen warned as she stepped over a pile of wood. 'This will be the new banqueting room when it's finished.' She led him across the room, around carpenters' tools and plasterers' pails, then out into the brightest room he had ever seen. 'It's the Long Gallery,' Morveen explained. 'For all the lords and ladies.' Arthur stood in the doorway afraid to go further. The room was as wide as the yard below and seemed never to end. It was filled with light, and he held a hand to his eyes against the glow. 'They're windows,' Morveen said waving her hand at three of the walls. 'That's where the light comes from. It will be even better when it's finished. There'll be tapestries and paintings…And I heard they won't have rushes on the floor, but turkey carpet. It will be a foot carpet. Very grand.'

'Not on the tables and cupboards?'

'Maybe them, but on the floor too. Come.' She pulled him by the neck of his petticoat until he was inside the room and facing a huge fireplace. Above the fireplace was the Earl's coat of arms. There were the two animals with strange heads rearing up on both sides, some sailors' knots and the wine glasses he knew belonged to the family because they had rights over importing wine. Morveen had told him that often enough. Beneath that some marks were etched in the plasterwork.

'What are them marks?' he asked.

'They're words. All about Him.'

'My father?'

She nodded.

'What do they say?'

'I don't know.' Morveen sighed. 'I can't read no more 'n thee.'

Arthur sighed too and looked at the words for a long time as if just looking at them would make the meaning clear.

'But look here, Arty. This is important, too.' She led him away, her kirtle whispering across the wooden floorboards. At the next fireplace about halfway down the Long Gallery she stopped. 'There!' She pointed to the plaster form of a lady's face above the mantel. 'It's Her.'

'The Queen?'

'Yes,' she said triumphantly as if she had been personally responsible for putting her there.

'I've always wondered,' said Arthur. 'And ladies-in-waiting one on each side. Is that so she won't be lonely up there?'

Morveen hugged him. 'Silly.'

Arthur looked hard at the face. It was so high up he got a crick in his neck. There she was, and although her lace ruff was fine, and the stick she was holding looked important as did the crown on her head and her white face staring off the wall was pretty enough, it was the words he wanted. The words about his father. He turned and walked back to the other fireplace where he studied the words again. Funny, he was more interested in the words than he was in seeing Her, even though forever he had wondered; wished he could go to Court with the Earl and see Her for himself.

'Morveen,' he said, but suddenly she was upon him, hand over his mouth.

'*Bí ciúin.* Hush.' She held her head to one side listening. Yes, he could hear them now. Voices. Below. As they listened they became clearer. 'It's Shee,' she whispered. 'Run.' Arthur turned to run back down the staircase, but Morveen held him back. 'They're coming that way,' and she set off running along the Long Gallery, her kirtle flying behind her. He bolted after her, running faster than he ever had before. It was like running through the sun. So white and bright it was that it seemed to take forever. His heart pumped. His leg dragged. His breathing scratched. Then just as he thought the very breath of life would leave him they reached the end and escaped around the corner into another new room. They could hear the seneschal talking in the Long Gallery.

'It's a bad business. In more ways than one. My lord receiving the same treatment as Desmond.' They were obviously walking down the gallery towards them.

'We do not know that for certain,' the man with him said. 'Her Majesty still has to make a judgement on them. She holds my lord in high esteem.'

They were getting closer and Arthur tried to move further into the room where he and Morveen were hiding. 'Don't step back,' Morveen whispered urgently. She pointed to where the floorboards ended just steps away. Arthur went to the edge. Beyond was the darkness of hell. He knew they should not have come. God saw everything. They couldn't hide from him. Wobbly at the edge of hell he looked up at Morveen. She pulled him away, but there was nowhere to go.

'…Sir Edmund seems to think he can take over Carraigh while my lord is away. God save us! I am the seneschal. It is my…' Mister

Shee had stopped coming towards them, but it sounded as if he was standing close by. Morveen dragged Arthur further into the room, so they were both pressed against the wall. Arthur held his breath.

'He would not dare usurp…' the other man said uncertainly.

'Those brothers of my lord are trouble.' It seemed now as if Shee was walking across the gallery toward the windows. Arthur let the pent-up air out, but Morveen shook him to quieten him. Shee stopped again. 'Mark my words. And the Earl could be away for years. Who knows what the Queen has in store for him.'

'The gallery is taking shape,' the other man said, changing the subject.'

'There *is* a lot yet to be done, but aye it looks grand. Those mullion windows let the light in wonderfully well. Magnificent room, don't you say?' They were moving back along the gallery.

'Fit for a queen,' and the man laughed. He added something but his voice had become a mumble.

They waited until the voices faded to nothing. Then waited some more. Finally Morveen peeked around the door and beckoned Arthur. She put a finger to her lips, and they slipped silently down the gallery. Arthur took a quick look at the Queen staring from the wall as he passed. She seemed to nod her crown at him. Onto The Words. Another nod. How he wanted to be able to read.

Once they were back in the courtyard Morveen started laughing. She bent over and laughed and laughed. 'We fooled the aul' sot, Art. We did,' she said finally.

Then they heard a voice from the battlements. 'Stand!' The sergeant-at-arms was looking down and waving his rapier at them.

'Run,' Morveen shouted.

She had been shouting at Arthur, but the sergeant-at-arms ran too. He ran along the ramparts to the stairs and was almost at the foot of the stairs when they raced across the inner court.

'Stand,' the sergeant ordered again as Morveen flung the kitchen door wide and they scarpered in.

It wasn't long after that the man rushed in. 'I..you…' he began.

Morveen hitched her kirtle up and went to him.

'You and me, is it?' she laughed. She kissed him full on the lips and wriggled her hips against his hose.

He pulled away. 'Tonight,' he said. 'But let this be a warning to you.'

*

Later Morveen gave Arthur a plate of cold stew and a hunk of stale bread. It was cold without the fire, but Morveen told him the servants would be back on the morrow. Someone would be sent to drag them away from the ale, deboshed out of their minds. 'But we did a good thing, didn't we, Arty? You saw Her.' She wiped up the juices with her bread and smacked her lips. 'And you seen the manor house.' She cleaned her mouth with the sleeve of her bodice. 'An'it's grand.'

'And the words. I seen them too.' He picked a bit of mutton out of his teeth. 'But I was a-feared by the Sergeant.'

'Oh, he's nothing to be a-feared of. You leave him to me.'

'I think I was more a-feared when we couldn't escape. That black hole in the floor...

'You've a brave heart on y', Arty.'

'Like my father. When will he be back? Mister Shee said 'twould be years.'

'He's been away for years before. This time it's only for a telling off.'

'Good,' he said cuddling closer to Morveen and closing his eyes.

He dreamt he was slipping into a dark hole. The devil was waiting for him at the bottom, and the devil was an animal rearing on its hind legs, with a human face. A face he recognised as the face of Tom Dubh, Black Tom, his father. Then the words, the shape of them shouting at him, but he didn't hear what they were saying. And his father became the sergeant-at-arms, then he became God and God became the devil and Arthur cried into the night and woke. But Morveen had gone.

Chapter Four

The church was dimly lit with candles, a soft light came through the stained glass windows, and the priest walked up to the altar waving the censer. As he smelt incense and felt the presence of God, Arthur cowered into Morveen. God would surely see into his dark soul. Morveen bobbed at the altar and pushed Arthur down to do the same. '*Ave Maria, gratia plena*,' she recited.

'*Ave Maria*,' Arthur repeated.

The priest jabbered on in Latin and Arthur responded when Morveen did. '*Ave, ave.*'

Morveen left him while she took communion, and Arthur looked at the high vaults wondering what God was all about. The pot man said to Morveen as they left for mass it was all very well for the Earl to say they could worship how they chose, but there would be trouble in the end. Was there not talk that Elizabeth, Protestant Queen of England and Ireland, would be excommunicated by the Pope? And had not the Irish people cheered when they heard about that? Was not the Earl a faithful subject to the Queen? So where did she, Morveen, stand by taking the lad to mass and attending communion on her own account? Morveen said, 'A shroud on you and your heathen ways.'

If God was so almighty how could not people agree on how to

worship him? Arthur wondered. Surely he could force them to. But then he was dealing with the Queen. So who was most powerful? God or the Queen? Thinking about it made his head ache. The incense made him drowsy. He closed his eyes and only woke when Morveen shook him. Mass was over.

*

After mass Morveen was a-cuddling with the pot man behind the kitchen chimney, their religious argument forgotten, so Arthur went to play on the ramparts. Once at the top he looked down through the battlement. It was a long way into the stinking river and he'd drown if he fell; if he died they'd all be sorry; Cook and his ear-tweaking, the fire boy and his pinching; the stable lad holding his nose as Arthur limped by after he'd mucked out the pigs. They would all miss him. He looked into the river again. The current was slow and the smells of human and kitchen mess wafted up. It would be a foul place to spend your last moments on earth. And God. He'd snatch him out of the filth and fling him into hell: it was a mortal sin to kill yourself. But if it were an accident..? Arthur bent to pick up an old arrow head and threw it down into the water. Once he would have kept it in his hiding place under the loose flag stone in the kitchen, but today he could not care less. He hobbled carefully along to the corner of the battlement and looked out instead of down. A plasterer, dusty-white, appeared like a ghost in the doorway of the manor house. Arthur turned to the main court to see a groom saddling the Proctor's horse; a washerwoman balancing a buck-basket on her hip swaying across the yard. Arthur had followed her around often enough to know she'd be after finding the driest, windiest spot for to drape the washing. On the other side of the wall was the castle park and beyond that the town. He longed to go into the town. His world seemed to be getting smaller and smaller the bigger he grew.

He headed towards the east keep, arms outspread to maintain his balance. A lone lookout leaned against the wall. It wasn't the sergeant-at-arms so Arthur kept going.

'Stand,' said the kerne as Arthur approached. He raised his pike to his shoulder. 'Who advances?' His grin showed his front teeth missing.

Arthur knew he wasn't serious. 'Sir Arthur,' he said.

'Ah kind Sir,' the kerne played along, 'you've a-come to help me fend off those scurvy Desmonds.'

Arthur frowned. 'But Desmond is away to see the Queen with my lord,' he said forgetting the game.

'Aye, but there's plenty more of his sept left in Ireland. Won't they be wanting revenge for their defeat at Ormond hands?'

'Are they really coming?'

'They'll not be coming this way. Leastways not in broad daylight.'

'And after sundown?'

'Who knows? Can't trust those drabbing Irish.'

'Oh. How many men are here at night?'

'Enough.' The kerne grinned and resumed the game.' But if I were to tell you, Sir, you might betray us.'

'Not me,' Arthur cried, only half playing. 'Not me in a hundred years.'

'But, were not that you I spied a-coming out of the manor house t'other day?'

Arthur blushed.

'Best be gone,' said the sentry nodding down at the courtyard where Morveen arms akimbo was talking to the groom. 'I give you good day, Sir.' He bowed low.

Arthur spun about and limped quickly back to the battlement stairs, his petticoat fluttering in the breeze like a pennant. He turned and waved at the kerne who waved back. He was just about to go down the stairs when the page, Piers, came running up towards him and he had to stand back to let him pass.

'What are you doing here, boy?' Piers asked.

'Nothin'. I'm away now.'

Piers put an arm on his shoulder to stop him. Arthur ducked to avoid the expected slap. But Piers simply said, 'It's my birthday.

We're playing a hiding game.'

'How old are you?'

'Eleven. How old are you?'

Arthur took a quick look around the court for Morveen but she must have gone inside again. 'Don't know. Six. Me'be seven.'

'What? And still in your petticoats? Isn't it time you were breeched?' Piers sat down on the top step and looked down at Arthur. 'Why aren't you breeched? Can't live in petticoats all your life.'

'That's all Morveen gives me to wear.'

'Morveen the kitchen wench?'

'She's my nurse maid. Least, she's supposed to be.'

'Is she now? And what does she call you?'

'Arthur.'

'A right royal name! Was not the late king's brother, Her Majesty's uncle, called Arthur? And was not *he* called for Arthur of the Round Table?'

'What is a round...' but a group of children came running out of the west keep and spread out over the courtyard, and Piers put a hand up to silence him.

'There's something about you I like, boy,' Piers said, 'and we shall meet again.' He jumped up and side-stepped past Arthur, ran nimbly down the stairs and disappeared into the keep unseen by his hunters who were looking in all corners of the courtyard.

Arthur sat and watched a long while until the children had given up looking for Piers and gathered together by the watergate. They shrugged and went inside.

'Arthur. Arty!'

Arthur looked down at Morveen scuttling around the yard in search of him, and he smiled. Piers was not the only one playing a hiding game. Then, as if she had read his thoughts Morveen looked up and saw him. 'Arty. Get you down.'

Slowly he took the steps down and faced her. 'What?'

'Doesn't have to be a "what". Just come in.'

'What's a round table?' He looked up at her.

'Arty. You do ask some foolish questions.' She ruffled his hair.

Inside the kitchen smelt of baking bread and he suddenly felt hungry. He was about to go and see what he could snatch from the baker's end when he saw Piers standing by the door that led directly from the kitchen to the keep. He held a bundle of neatly folded clothes in his arms.

'You shamed me,' Morveen whispered, but she didn't look unhappy as she led him towards Piers.

'Here.' Piers thrust the bundle into Arthur's arms. 'You should take better care of him,' he said to Morveen before walking back to the door.

'I bid you Good Birthday,' Arthur called as he left.

'You loon. What have you been telling people?' Morveen was going through the clothes. 'Doublet, shirt...look at these tiny buttons. Oh, Art you will look the proper gentleman.' She held up one of the two breeches and a sleeve. 'They're embroidered, Art. Perhaps this means my lord is ready for you.'

'It's not him, Morveen. It was Piers. How would my lord know? He's at the English Court.'

'He might have sent a messenger.' Arthur opened his mouth to say something, but Morveen went on. 'Doesn't matter. You're going to look grand.' She held up a jerkin. 'Feel that soft leather. Oh. Let's get you clothed. That Piers is his father's son.'

'And his mother's if the tattle is true,' added the pot man.

'What tattle?' Arthur pulled one sleeve up his arm.

'Most royal blood, they say.' The pot man winked lewdly. 'Most royal mother.'

Arthur looked at Morveen who nodded agreement.

By the time Arthur had been dressed in all the layers the new clothes demanded he was still thinking about that nod. Piers had the same parents as he did, and that made them brothers. He was also thinking how long it would take him to get dressed in this finery every day. A petticoat might be a babbyish thing but it was certainly easy to don. 'Don't you go getting a fit above yeself,' the pot man said when Arthur strutted past him as proudly as his leg would allow. He marched on and out into the yard. The wind was chill, but he felt warm: this is what it was like to be a gentleman, one named after a Queen's uncle and a man with a round table.

*

Next morning he took so long to dress all the servants were in the kitchen before he'd finished. Cook laughed as Arthur pulled the doublet over his head. 'A grand wee fella we have here.' He tweaked his ear. 'Won't stop you having to muck out the pig sty.'

'He'll be mocked, Morveen,' the pot man warned.

'Leave him be. He looks handsome. He can't live in petticoats all his life.'

'That's what Piers said.' Arthur was struggling into a stocking, trying to get it to reach over the knee of his bad leg, smoothing wrinkles as he went.

The pot man ignored him. 'Least get him to take the doublet and sleeves off.'

Morveen turned away and bent down to help Arthur into his stocking. 'If you were a proper page you'd have someone to help you into this lot,' she said. 'Then it wouldn't be a bother.'

When he did go to muck out the pigs Arthur took the doublet and the soft leather jerkin off and worked in his shirt. He left the stockings on and although he tried hard not to get them messy some of the muck splattered over them and he spent more time trying to clean it off than he did on the pigs themselves.

Finally he had done his best for the porkers and he went back into the court and sat on the stairs leading up to the battlement. Piers came out of the east keep holding something in his hand. He walked over to Arthur. 'Pity is you have to work in those clothes,' he said.

'Sorry,' said Arthur.

'*You* are not at fault.' Piers sat down beside him.

'What's that?'

'A book.' He held it out for Arthur to see.

Arthur opened it. There were those words again. 'Can you read them?'

'What? The characters? Course. My tutor sees to that. He's a tough master.'

'Would you show me how?'

'It's not easy.'

'Could we try?'

'If you wish. Only girls in there anyway.' He pointed at the keep. 'Some girls are good at learning and some just want to embroider and dance.' So he took the book back from Arthur and read. '"Neither hath the eye seen nor yet the ear heard, neither yet hath it ever entered into the heart of any man, what God hath prepared for them that love him…"' He pointed to a word, then to his own eye. 'Eye….Ear…' he pointed to his ear. 'God…These are words Her Majesty wrote when she was not much older than I am now."

Arthur leaned over the book. 'That's "ear" again.' he pointed to 'heard'.

'You catch on,' Piers said with some admiration.

Arthur peered closer. 'God' leapt out at him from all over the page and he pointed the words out to Piers.

Piers read on, '"Faith joined with truth bringeth forth hope, whereby perfect charity is engendered, and charity is God as thou knowest."'

There was too much God in this for Arthur's liking. He changed the subject. 'Have you been inside the manor house?'

'One time. After they put the mullion windows in the Long Gallery. My lord says it is too dangerous for children.'

Arthur hesitated. 'I saw them windows too. And the picture of the Queen on the wall and her two ladies in waiting.'

Piers laughed. 'I think you mean Equity and Justice, *Equitas et Justicia.* You are lucky. I haven't seen the plasterwork yet. Those decorations are to go all the way around the room. And on the ceiling will go the Queen's monogram, and Tudor roses and the Royal coat of arms…and all manner of things.'

'How do you know if you haven't seen it?'

'I have seen the plans.'

'Did you see the words on the plan? Above the fireplace?'

'I did.'

The jangle of spurs and horses made them look below. 'My uncles,' said Piers.

'I have seen Sir Edmund,' Arthur said. 'He was the one who carried Desmond to the dungeon.' He pointed out the tall, strongly built brother.

'The youngest one, with the red hair, that's James. The other is Edward. I had best go and greet them.' Before he moved off, the seneschal, Richard Shee, came out to talk with the visitors, but his was no friendly greeting.

'You are not advised to manage my lord's castle here,' Shee shouted. 'I have been appointed and appointed I shall stay.' He hit one of the horses on its rump. It whinnied and shied.

'We are kin,' said the youngest brother.

'And who better than kin to look after your estate?' asked the one called Edward.

Sir Edmund interrupted, 'We come to offer assistance against the Desmonds.'

'Your assistance is not required. Be off.' The seneschal struck another of the horses and this time the three men wheeled the horses round and trotted out of the yard.

'Art.' Morveen made him jump up. He had only got as far as the pigs this morning. He'd better get a pace on.

Piers put a hand on his arm. 'If you wish I will bring you a copy of those words about my father. I know where they are. In a chest in his closet. This afternoon. Meet me here at four of the clock. My lessons finish then.'

*

Arthur was waiting the minute the town clock struck the four hours. Piers came soon after and sat on the step beside him. 'Look,' he said. 'I have copied it out.'

'Can you read it? Please.'

'At the top it says, "In the year of our Lord...anno domini 1565... In the seventh year of Queen Elizabeth."'

'When is that?'

'This very year.' Piers pointed a finger at the next words. '"Thomas Butler. Knight Viscount Thurles Earl of Ormond and Ossory…"'

'He is all of that?'

'There's more… "Lord of the Liberties and several Regalities in the Kingdom of Ireland had me made."' He paused. 'That means he had the plasterwork and the characters made. 'Here also is his motto, *Plus Pense Que Dire*.'

'What does that mean?'

'It is in French. It means, To Think Rather Than Speak.'

Arthur frowned. 'I *think* I understand.'

Piers handed Arthur the piece of paper. 'You can keep this.'

'*Sonas ort*!' Arthur folded the paper and put it into his jerkin pocket. 'My lord is the most important man in Ireland.'

'Some would say.' Piers nodded. 'But others would disagree and fight you for the right to do so.'

*

That night, cuddled next to Morveen under the table furthest from the fire, Arthur wondered who could be more important than his father. The brothers, Edmund, Edward and James? No, they did not have the earldom. They were minor Butlers. Desmond perhaps? And that reminded him that the Desmond clan might attack the castle in the dead of night. He wondered which was better – having Shee take care of them or the Butler brothers. He suspected the Butler brothers would make a better job of it and hoped there were enough guards above on the ramparts to fight off the Desmonds. He imagined a battering ram thrusting at the castle gate, men sneaking amongst the trees in the Great Park, creeping closer, closer until they were near enough to fire a cannon. The guards would fall in the river; Desmond's men would swarm the castle and capture them all. A wolf howled in the distance, disturbed perhaps by the creeping soldiers. Arthur shivered and told himself to say a prayer so they would all be saved. That reminded him about Piers and learning to read. He knew the word 'God' now, and 'ear' and 'eye'. He smiled. Things had changed. He was dressed like a gentleman. He could read. And he had paper with words on it in his jerkin pocket. The Desmonds were forgotten.

Chapter Five

It was not the Desmonds who were to cause trouble. It was the Butlers. Sir Edmund and his forces stormed through Kilkenny shire; Edward and James were warring in Munster. The very air was full of the threat of them. The Earl himself was still at Court. The Queen had forgiven him for the private battle at Affane, but put Desmond in the London Tower. The Earl had been away a year since and prattlers complained that he should be in Ireland sorting out the troubles with his kin.

Morveen had a babby of her own now, although nobody was sure who its father was. Aefe was born at Martlemas, as the weather turned for winter and Morveen was too busy lisping songs over her, and telling her fanciful stories to be bothered with anything else. Arthur didn't need her anyway, but he was outgrowing his gentleman's clothes and they had become so grubby and worn that he again looked like the kitchen boy he was, and since Piers had been fostered out to the Earl's Kilkenny castle for some months he didn't mind. None of the other pages took any notice of him, except perhaps to imitate his walk as he crossed the yard. He missed the lessons Piers sometimes gave him, but he could read quite well and was able to help himself. He felt more at home in his shabby clothes, especially as he had begun to spend time in the town.

The town was full of laughing boys and jesting women. He learnt much more of what was going on there than he did in the castle kitchen. His heart lifted every time he walked through the postern gate, along the high street past the craftsmen's houses, the traders' and merchants' residences. He liked to go right to the West Gate, slowing down to admire the grand stone house, Stokes Hall, as he passed. It was spring, the air gentle and the birds chirruping above the usual hubbub. Today he turned into New Street and stopped at the house of his friend, Donal O'Brennan. Donal's father was a thatcher, who built or mended roofs on the wattle and daub houses across the other side of town. And he seemed to know everything. It was from him, through Donal, that Arthur first heard that the Earl and his wife were officially estranged. 'No wonder,' Donal said, obviously imitating his father. 'He's never in Ireland.' Donal leaned closer. 'There's talk of a dalliance 'tween the Earl and the Queen. That's why he remains at Court. By her side. Why else would he be free as a sparrow while Desmond awaits his fate in the tower?'

Today Donal brought news that Sir Henry Sidney, the new governor of Ireland, was reported to be on his way to Kilkenny. 'He wants to take proceedings against the Earl's brothers. They are trying to take over the county in the Earl's absence.'

The town clock struck three bells. Arthur would have liked to know more, but he could not stay. 'I'd best be off,' he said. 'I've got to fetch some galingale for Cook's sauce and he has a foul temper on him today.' He moved away.

'Arthur,' Donal called him back. 'Come away with us tomorrow to Kilsheelan. My aul' fella has a gentleman to see there. He said you could come.'

'I'll try,' Arthur said, not feeling too hopeful.

'Meet us at West Gate at sun up. If you can.'

Back in the castle kitchen Arthur put the cloth of galingale powder on the table in front of Morveen. He watched her juggling Aefe on one knee whilst cutting the crusts off yesterday's bread and grinding them into small pieces for the galantine sauce. 'Oh Arthur,' she said when he asked if he could go away for the day with Donal and his father, 'you always want special treatment. You're not so special, hear you.' He held out his arms to take Aefe. She smelt warm and he kissed her downy head. Morveen continued chopping. 'You can't go, and that's an end to it,' she said finally.

He jiggled the babby up and down for a while, not wanting to look at Morveen, not wanting her to see the tears which smarted his eyes. It wasn't just that he couldn't go, that was hard enough, but each word of 'you're not so special' stabbed at his very heart. He *was* special. Morveen had told him for all his nine or so years that he was special, but now she had a pukey babby he was forgotten. He wished the Earl would come home and sort things out, or better still if the Queen would return with him. She would not stand Morveen's nonsense. No matter that the north range was not yet ready, the Queen could stay in the keep. He bet that if They were here Morveen would be banished from the kitchen with her babby. It had been different when he was a little 'un, he *was* special. He thrust Aefe back at Morveen and ran hobbling out. He could hear the babby wawling as he crossed the courtyard.

For a moment he hesitated, then ran on across the yard, out the gate that led into the house gardens and on to the postern gate. Once through the gate he stopped, knowing he couldn't get far enough away this night, but that tomorrow he would be on the cart with Donal and his Da. The castle would have to send a horse after him when they found him missing. He turned and shambled back to the kitchen where he pretended nothing was wrong. He brought in wood for the fire boy, and helped the pot man scrub the pans. He even held Aefe while Morveen ate her supper.

Arthur went to bed, as usual, beside Morveen. They did not touch these days, now she had Aefe and he was far too old for that. He lay stiffly, his head on the clothes he had removed for sleeping, and waited until Morveen was breathing deeply and the last of the men had settled on the floor and was snoring. Then he slid out from under the thin blanket they shared, took his pillow of shirt, jerkin and breeches and tip-toed to the door. It creaked as he opened it and he stopped. Someone stirred, someone else coughed into the dark, and he waited until all was quiet again before slipping through the gap in the doorway. Quietly he pulled the door to behind him. He would have to leave the castle tonight or he might be seen leaving come sun up. Up on the battlements he saw the shadows of two men sitting, backs against the keep tower. He had forgotten the watch! As he stared he realised they were motionless: they were asleep, fine guards they proved to be. Staying close to the shadows of the walls he pulled on the clothes he was carrying then worked his way towards the north range. The entranceway was open and he went in. The boarded spaces had their windows now, so there was enough light for him to see that, in the passageway, plasterwork of the Earl and the Queen looked down on him from either side of the wall, their white faces still wanting for a coat of paint, but they seemed to smile at him approvingly. You are no reel-footed kitchen brat, they seemed to say, you are noble born and noble you shall stay. As he crept on, the new boards creaked and he stopped and waited, then moved off. A noise behind stopped him again. He turned. It was just the sighing of the wind.

He touched the paper which he still kept in his jerkin pocket for the luck of it as he pulled at a board covering the door. It came away easily and he climbed through the narrow space and out into the night on the other side of the castle.

He knew the postern gate would be locked, but his plan was to follow the town wall around to the bridge mill where he would be close to the West Gate. Here he would wait outside until the morn. He had his jerkin, short though it was, to keep him warm and the weather bode well. The moon came out, an owl hooted, and he clung to the dark of the town wall, lest he be seen and thought a thief. Lest a wolf spy him from the woods. It did not take long to slink to the end of the wall. All was quiet at the mill except for the soft slop-slop of water against the wheels. He turned the corner, passed the mill pond and there was the West Gate. Gratefully he huddled in the shelter of its archway and waited for the sun to rise.

*

He awoke to the church bells ringing, and heard above them, 'Why here's the lad. Bright and early.'

It was Donal's father. Donal was steadying the horse harnessed in the dray. It was anxious to be off. Arthur rubbed his eyes. 'I bid you good day, sir,' he said as he stood.

'I'm no sir, lad. Just call me Bren, like everyone else.' He clapped Arthur on the back. 'Grand to see you. Now let's be gone.' He helped Arthur into the dray. Donal handed the reins to his father and hopped up beside Arthur. Bren flicked a whip and they were off.

They crossed the fair green, empty at this time of day, forded the river above the weir and took the road to Clonmel. Arthur had never been as far as this in the world before. Many a time he had watched longingly as members of the family set off for Kilkenny, or Waterford, or Cahir or London and he was left behind. Bren's horse trotted along, his hooves clip-clipping on the hardened soil of the boreen. Arthur looked back. The road was empty. It was still too early for him to be missed. Morveen would be up, but she'd be blathering with Cook, or offering a fat pap to Aefe. She would think him outside fetching wood, or mucking the pigs, and they should be well away before she caught on.

'See here,' Bren waved at the fields stretching out neat with new plants. 'That's Tom Dubh's land, laid out in corn. And yonder.' He pointed to a meadow where cattle grazed. 'He owns livestock beyond measure, Black Tom does. And land as far as the eye can see and beyond. And yonder that way,' he pointed again, 'there is the deer park. The only one in the whole of Ireland, so they say.' Arthur felt his customary stirring of pride. They passed a peasant cottage with a garden in front where a man was bent over a hoe tending his spring plantlings. Bren bid him good day as they passed. '*Dia duit*,' the man called in return waving his hoe at them. They followed the curves of the River Suir and in the distance wooded hills shone pink in the glow of the new sun. Arthur leaned back in the dray, and felt the wind in his hair, sniffed in the oaty, leathery smell coming from the trotting horse. This was living. But he still took a look behind him from time to time.

'What's troubling you, lad?' asked Bren.

'Nothing.'

'Always look ahead, lad. Never look back. A motto for life, I say.' Bren pointed to the mountains before them. 'Look now. There's Slievenamon, Mountain of the Women.' They had to duck to avoid an overhanging tree, then Bren continued. 'Story goes, Finn McCool wanted to take a wife from these parts. Beautiful women, they were. Still are. Your mother's a beauty, isn't she Donal?' Donal nodded.

'What happened? With Finn McCool?'

'He couldn't decide which beauty to wed, so he made them all run up the mountain. First one to the top won his hand.' He laughed. 'And his heart. Clever man that Finn McCool.'

As the morning went on and they got further away from the town, Arthur relaxed, enjoying the freedom. The river smelt fresh out here. Two swans drifted by and birds chirruped in the trees lining the boreen. With the sun high in the sky they stopped at a tower house. 'We'll sup here in the shade,' Bren said.

'Won't they mind?'

'Not at all.' There did not seem to be anybody about as they climbed down from the cart and sat on the grassy verge to eat the oatcakes and eel pie wrapped in a cloth for them by Mrs O'Brennan. A swig of ale from Bren's leather bottle each, then they packed up and were on their way again. Just beyond the tower house they turned off the boreen and onto a wider pathway. Ahead a band of riders approached. 'Careful lads,' Bren said.

'Too late to turn back, Da.'

'They'd give chase if we did,' Bren said. 'Say not a word.' There were about twenty men on horseback. They looked like soldiers. 'The Lord Deputy's men,' Bren sighed. 'So Sir Henry *is* paying a visit.' The sound of hooves became deafening as the soldiers came forward. Sun glinted off their swords. Some were in full armour, but the faces of those which showed were set and determined, as Bren pulled the cart to a stop and to one side to let them pass.

Instead of passing the lead horseman reined in his horse and held up an arm to signal the men behind. The horses halted sweating and snorting. The lead man drew alongside the cart.

'Are you from hereabout?' he demanded.

'Aye,' said Bren.

'What is your business on the Queen's Way?'

'Me and me sons here have work to do in Kilcash.'

'What's your name?'

'Con.'

'Con what?'

'Con O'Carroll.'

'Do you know any of the Butler clan?'

Arthur opened his mouth to speak, but Bren said quickly, 'Naturally we know *of* them, the knaves, but…'

'O'Bryns? Purcells? O'Brennans?'

'That pack of bully-rooks!'

'Where can we find them?'

'Heard they've all escaped. The rogues.' Bren spat on the ground.

'Pass by,' the leader said waving an arm. 'I'd stay away from Kilkenny if I were you. Don't want those lads of yours caught up with the rest of the riff-raff running amok there.'

Bren nodded, clicked his tongue and the horse walked off. Behind them the men kicked their horses into action, and with a sound like thunder they took off towards the tower. When the roar died away Donal started laughing. 'Bully-rooks, Da? Rogues and knaves?'

'Hush your tongue. Trees have ears.' And with a wink Bren turned to Arthur. 'Not a word, lad. Not a word. Even to the dead.'

'Your name's Bren O'Brennan. You told me so yourself.'

Bren tapped the side of his nose. 'Least said…'

'Are they the ones come to get the Earl's brothers..?'

'Aye.'

'But my lord would not stand for that. He is the most powerful man in the whole of Ireland.'

'I know he's taken you in, lad, with that wench that's your mother.

But there's more to all things than e'er meets the eye.'

'But she's...he's...' Arthur hesitated.

'I'll explain it to you, lad. But not here. Not now. Now we have business to attend to.'

Not much further on they rounded a corner and saw a grange beyond. Bren took the cart up the driveway lined with oak trees, and as they pulled up in front of the house a gentleman, who had been standing at the door watching, came down the steps to greet them.

'Here's the lad I was speaking of.' Bren helped Arthur down from the cart. So he wasn't just here for the ride, Arthur thought. But what could Bren and the man want of him?

The man watched as Arthur hobbled towards him. 'You did not mention that he was a capper,' he said. 'Look at the gatch on him.'

'He might be a capper, but he's quick on them legs,' Bren said. 'And he's got a brain or two in his head.' He turned to Arthur as he drew level with the gentleman. 'Arthur this is...' Bren hesitated. The gentleman shook his head. 'This is our host,' Bren concluded.

'I bid you good day, Sir.' This time there was no protest and Arthur could see by the cut of his fur-trimmed cloak and the size of his house that this gentleman was, indeed, a gentleman. The house was made of stone, but much bigger than the Stone House in Carraigh, though not as big as the castle and manor house. A set of grand steps led up to a wooden door with a huge brass knocker. 'Very progressive,' Bren said quietly to the boys, pointing at the house. 'No fortifications, no battlements. Here is a man with true faith.'

'Come inside,' their host clicked his fingers at the three of them standing in awe-struck silence. A stable boy came running seemingly from nowhere. 'Put the horse and dray around the back. So it cannot be seen,' and he hustled them inside.

The hallway was spacious and the gentleman led them down the length of it, over newly cut floor-rushes smelling of wormwood and sweet violet. To one side was a cupboard which displayed a collection of silverware and at the far end a long table with chairs set around it. 'Come,' the gentleman said. 'Sit.'

Arthur and Donal sat opposite their host and Bren. Arthur's feet could hardly touch the ground and Donal, though taller, did not seem to fare much better. 'Sir Henry Sidney's men are about,' Bren told their host as he settled into his seat. 'We were stopped on the road.'

Their host frowned.

'No need to worry. They let us pass and did not follow. For certain I did not give the gimps me name. They're after us all. O'Brennans, Purcells, O'Byrnes.'

Their host sighed deeply. 'So-o-o. Down to business it must be.' He turned to Arthur. 'Now lad. How old are you?'

'Nine. I think.'

'Almost a man.' Bren smiled at him and Arthur straightened his back.

Their host nodded his agreement. 'And you work in the castle kitchens?'

Arthur did work in the kitchens, he knew that, but he never felt like one of the workers. Somehow he had always felt he was filling in time. Till...till something happened to rescue him; until somebody came along and recognised him for who he really was. 'Yes,' he said finally, sadly.

'And you hear things? Prattle? Gossip?'

'Well…' he looked at Bren who nodded, say yes. Arthur could not quite bring himself to say the word, but nodded assent.

'I have heard that you can read, lad.'

'A little. The page, Piers, has taught me. A little,' he repeated. 'I have some reading here.' He fished into the pocket where he kept his precious piece of paper. The creases were black with use. He unfolded the paper and spread it carefully out on the table while Donal and the two opposite watched. 'Will I read?'

The gentleman nodded.

'"In the year of our Lord, 1565,"' Arthur began. '"Thomas Butler – knight – Viscount of Thurles…"' Before he could read further the gentleman snatched the paper out of his hand, screwed it into a ball and threw it into a corner.

'What tosh,' he exclaimed. '*And* you are reading by rote. That's not proper reading.' He slid another piece of paper across the table to him. 'Read that.'

Arthur swallowed hard. He looked at the paper. The words swam, they wriggled and he screwed his eyes tight for a moment. When he finally opened them the words formed themselves and he could make some sense of them. He cleared his throat and leaned over the page to get a closer look. Donal leaned forward with him, eager.

'Patrick Fyn, a lack…lackey late in the Earl of Ormond's live… live–ery now out of service was nailed to a post by the ear and whi…whip…whipped out of town nack…nacked…'

'Naked,' their host offered.

'…naked from the middle upwards.' Arthur sat back and looked at Bren for support.

'Clever lad,' Bren smiled at him again. 'You could be after giving my Donal a few lessons.'

Their host ignored the comment. 'That's what they do to those they don't like.' He folded his arms across his chest as if to protect himself. 'Nail them to a post by the ear and whip them out of town naked from the middle up. Those are Sidney's words, my lad. His words and deed. And a more partisan Lord Deputy Ireland has never seen. You mark those words.' His blue eyes stared into Arthur's own and Arthur thought that he had to mark the words because the Lord Deputy might be after hanging *him* by the ear and whipping him naked. He shivered under the gentleman's hard look.

Nobody spoke. The silence hurt. Donal coughed and finally Arthur could stand the empty air no longer. 'Who…who is Patrick Fyn?' he asked. 'What did he..?'

Their host took no heed of the question. 'I hear also that you are about the castle,' he said. 'In places you ought not to be.' He paused. 'From time to time.'

'How..?' But Arthur stopped himself, knowing no answer would come.

Their host took a small leather bag out of a fold in his robe and pushed it across the table towards Arthur. 'Look inside,' he ordered.

Arthur pulled the bag towards him and opened it. A gold coin lay at the bottom. He gasped. 'What am I to do with this?'

'It could be yours.' Their host put out a hand for Arthur to return the bag. Arthur closed it and pushed it back across the table. 'It could be yours,' the gentleman repeated, 'if you were willing to tell Bren here anything he might find of interest that happens at the castle.'

'Like..?'

'Like…anything to begin with. You're a bright lad. You will get the way of it soon enough. Your connections with young Piers could be useful.'

'But sir, Piers is in Kilkenny,' Arthur said.

'I hear he will be returning to Carraigh ere long.' He clicked his fingers and another boy appeared from nowhere. 'Ale and victuals for our guests before they journey home.' He stood. 'I will leave you,' and without looking back he swept across the hall his robe swaying behind him. As soon as he'd left the hall Arthur got up to rescue his piece of paper.

'Best not,' said Bren when he saw what he was doing, so Arthur left it and shortly after they left the house.

'I'll fetch the dray,' Arthur said, hobbling off quickly.

'Come back, boy,' Bren called. 'The stable boy will bring it.'

Arthur turned but not before he noticed three men walking through the side garden with their host. One had red hair, another was tall and well-built, and Arthur was sure he knew who they were.

*

On the journey homeward Arthur had so many questions, but he did not know where to begin. Bren said not a word, but smiled softly as if well pleased with the day's happenings. Arthur was sorry he had to leave his precious paper behind. He could see it in his mind's eye, lying lost in the corner of the hall. He also felt uncomfortable, as if he had been used, but he did not know why. The whole business smelt of trouble. As they drew closer to Carraigh he could see the castle ramparts on the skyline, set against the backdrop of the green hills over the river and beyond. They reminded him that soon he would have to face Morveen and trouble of a different kind. Perhaps he would say he had been kidnapped for a ransom. Word was about that his parentage was other than it seemed. But why did they let you go? he could hear Morveen ask. A snipe like you. You think you're such a dote. *So* special. He sighed and stared straight ahead. Donal was dozing beside him, but Arthur's mind was too busy to let him sleep. It had been a long night and day. And it was not over yet.

Chapter Six

An evening mist hung over the river by the time Arthur reached the castle. With as much courage as he could gather he walked into the kitchen as if nothing out of the way had happened. The place was its usual clatter. Cook looked up from basting the sheep spit-roasting over the fire. The spit boy stopped turning. Morveen had her head bent over Aefe who was suckling. She looked up when she heard Cook's heavy sigh. The pot man turned and looked at Arthur. None said a word, but they all watched and waited, while the fire spat and hissed. The fire boy poked his tongue out at Arthur and that small act seemed almost friendly compared to the awful hush that surrounded him.

Arthur did not know what to do; his excuses had disappeared, and he knew now he would be sent away. One did not leave the Earl's kitchen willy-nilly. Should he leave now? Just go? He could look for shelter with Bren and Donal. He walked over to Morveen. Touched Aefe's head lightly. 'I…' he started. Morveen looked at Arthur, then dropped her head to Aefe again. Cook went back to the spit. The boy started turning again. He heard the scratch, scratch of the pot man's scrubbing. 'I…' Arthur said again, but he had no idea what to say next so he shrugged, and left. It was dark outside now, the town gates would be locked. He did not want to spend another night outside, so he went to the wood pile, no dawdling, and gathered an arm full of wood which he took into the kitchen and set by the fire. Then he stood beside the pot man and handed him the dishes to be cleaned as he usually did, as if everything was normal, and the kitchen slowly resumed its usual pace and noise.

When supper had been delivered to the hall, the staff ate. Arthur sat in his usual place and Cook served him some roast mutton and parsnip which Arthur ate hungrily. Later that night he lay beside Morveen, but she was cuddled over Aefe with her back to him. He touched her shoulder. 'I am sorry,' he said, and felt like crying but he was no babby so he held his tears. Morveen rolled onto her back. 'So you ought to be,' she whispered. 'Where did you get to?'

'Kilcash.'

'There's talk about that Bren O'Brennan, Art. He's in with those Butler brothers. You be careful.' And she rolled over again.

Art! He never thought he'd be so happy to hear her call him that. Things would get back to where they were, of that he was certain.

*

The gold coin sitting at the bottom of the gentleman's bag haunted Arthur for the next few days. What would he do with it? Buy Aefe a beautiful babby's gown, perhaps. Buy Morveen something nice, though he could not think what. Buy himself a new set of gentlemen's clothes. Buy his own castle. At that thought he laughed out loud. How far did he expect a gold coin to carry him?

He was in the yard helping the brewer roll barrels of beer into the cellar. It was hard to believe how much beer they had been through in the time since the Earl left for Court last summer. As he waited for the brewer to come out for the next barrel Arthur noticed the Proctor waiting for the groom to saddle his horse. Shortly he would be out and about collecting the Earl's taxes. All that money, and the gold coin glittered in his mind. A castle. He smiled to himself. The sun was warm and he wiped his brow with the back of his hand. Then the seneschal, Shee, appeared followed by one of spaniels. Arthur moved a little closer and the dog came to him wagging its tail. Arthur bent to stroke its soft coat. After the usual pleasantries Shee said to the Proctor, 'We have news from Court. The Earl has pulled strings. Sir Henry Sidney won't be taking proceedings against the Butlers.'

'It took Her Majesty long enough to mete out his punishment, but I hear the Earl is in great favour with the Queen again,' the Proctor said. Arthur tickled the dog behind the ears, head lowered listening.

'Six months was a long wait. Nice royal touch, waiting until Christmas Eve to give him the news. A cheap Christmas box.'

'Hardly cheap at £20,000!'

'Oh, my lord will make sure to honour his recognisance to keep the peace.' Shee smiled. 'He won't be handing over his fortune in a hurry. Not even to the Queen.' The dog rolled over and Arthur scratched its stomach.

'When you consider Desmond's punishment, he got off lightly.'

'And Sir Henry is livid about his influence at Court.' Here Shee chuckled. 'According to my connections in Dublin, every step Sir Henry takes forward, the Earl sees to it that the Queen makes him take two backwards.' Shee paused, looked up and noticed Arthur kneeling beside the dog. 'What's with you, lad?' he asked.

Arthur stood, bowed and backed away giving the dog one last pat. He went back to the brewer's dray. No doubt the brewer was sampling his wares with the cellar man. As Shee left Arthur heard him say, 'Sidney's always been in Desmond's pocket and against the Butlers. The Butler brothers are only antagonising him. I do wish they would stop their rabble-rousing. It ill serves the Earl's reputation. Even if he can't see it himself.'

'Too far away for clear sight,' the Proctor agreed as he mounted his horse.

Arthur pushed a barrel and it rolled away, heading straight for the brewer who was coming from the dark hole of the cellar. '*Bí curamach*, young 'un.' The brewer jumped out of the way. 'You'll be after running me down.'

Arthur was pleased when Morveen told him later to go into the town to fetch some good powders for the red deer pie. 'And no dallying,' she ordered, handing him the coins he needed for the spice merchant.

He was panting fit to burst by the time he found Bren working on a hut near the West Gate. 'I have news,' Arthur puffed, looking up at Bren fastening down some straw ends. 'About Sir Henry.'

Bren rested his roofer's scallop on the ridge and climbed backwards down the ladder. 'What do we have, so?'

Arthur told Bren what he had heard. He watched Bren's face and noticed the smile die as he spoke. His last words were less confident than the first.

'We did say it would take time, lad.' Bren patted him on the shoulder when he finished. 'All that information you have there is well known by our people. We're all agin Sidney, as far as I know, but not everybody is with the Earl.' He tapped the side of his nose. 'He is too close to the English. His kin have right on their side. Understand?'

*

The gold still bothered Arthur. Having gone through the possibilities for spending it he worried about how he would hide the coin. Everyone knew about his hidey-hole under the flagstone, so it could not be there. It seemed that once he had begun to keep an ear out for information it was all around him, and just the next day he overheard Richard Shee talking to John Cantwell, one of the Earl's agents. 'The Queen has sent a letter to Sidney which is worrisome. She praises the Earl of Kildare and agrees to a provincial council in Munster. All of the one breath.'

'But I thought my lord was holding sway.'

'It seems not. At least not as soundly as we anticipated. The letter also suggested the time is ripe for an advance on Ulster and O'Neill.'

'Are you sure this is correct?' asked the agent.

'My sources are most reliable.' Shee smiled. 'The best to be found within the Pale.'

Arthur went through the items in his mind. Queen, letter, Kildare, Munster council, attack on Ulster. When the chance came to tell Bren he blurted out, 'The Queen praises the Earl of Kildare…'

'As well she might. He is in Sir Henry's pocket. Of that there is no doubt. Is there more?'

'She wrote that she agrees to a provincial council in Munster.'

'Now that won't suit the Earl. I thought he was in the Queen's favour.'

'Master Shee says my lord should be concerned.' He stopped, trying to remember what the last thing was. 'Oh, and she picks that the time is ripe for an attack on Ulster and O'Neill.'

Bren looked impressed. 'This *is* useful information, lad. Are you sure it is correct?'

'Best sources in the Pale, Master Shee said.'

'His spy in the Pale must be better than ours. To have access to Sir Henry's correspondence.' He sat thinking for a moment. 'Can't think who it might be.' He paused. 'But it matters not.' Turning back to Arthur he shook his hand. 'Most useful, lad. Most useful. Keep it up and that gold coin will be yours before you know it.'

As he limped away one word niggled at Arthur. He could not bring it out of his head, though. What was it Bren had said? Try as he might he could not catch it. That night he went to sleep with the sound of howling wolves haunting the distance, and he dreamt he had not one gold coin, but hundreds. They shone as if the sun had been caught in their leather bag. He tipped them out onto the river bank where he found himself and picked one up. On one side was the face of the Queen, the image that hung in the Long Gallery of the new manor house. On the other side a single word. Spy. He looked at another coin, then another, they were all the same, each one with the same word. Next morning he woke with a heavy head and an even heavier heart. For he finally knew what Bren's word had been. And what he, Arthur, was. A spy.

*

Countess Elizabeth, the Earl's wife, was coming to visit.

'But they are astranged,' Arthur said to Morveen.

'*E*-stranged,' she corrected. 'My lord is still at Court so she is free to visit. She must miss some of the pages.'

That afternoon Arthur stood near the watergate awaiting the arrival of the Countess. A fanfare of trumpets announced that the barge was in view. Pages and gentlewomen crowded forward. Arthur stood back to let them past.

Piers came rushing up. He stopped in his tracks when he saw Arthur. 'I have not seen you for some time. How is the reading coming?'

Arthur remembered the gentleman at Kilcash. Your connections with the young Piers could be useful. He felt suddenly awkward. 'Nicely. It is nicely coming along,' he stammered. 'You are returned from Kilkenny?'

'Aye. The Countess has decided to live in Kilkenny while my lord is at Court. And she is none too fond of me.' He grinned to show that it mattered not. 'I'd better go, though. Best to be seen in the welcoming party. But tomorrow… this time o' day we'll be falconing. Meet us at the mews.' He ran off.

The Countess looked as beautiful as ever when she finally came through the watergate. She was wearing a gown with pearl buttons down the front and an ermine collar, but her face was tight with anger. Without looking about her she strode across the court and into the west keep, her gentlewomen almost running to keep up.

*

Next morning Arthur went down to the mews and found Piers with a group of younger pages. 'We are training a new bird,' Piers said.

The falconer carried the cadge with the hooded bird on it into the garden. 'I unhooded her in the mews and she was nice and calm,' he explained, 'but just to be sure, Piers, you hold the aba at the ready.' He handed Piers a cloth wrap before taking the hood off the bird. The bird looked around. Piers lifted the aba slightly. The falconer clicked his tongue. The bird shifted on the cadge and lifted one wing. Then it settled. The falconer took the aba off Piers. 'Take the brail off,' he said. Piers untied the leather thong holding down one of the bird's wings. Released, the bird batted her wings then settled again. 'Good girl,' said the falconer before handing Piers a thick glove.

My lady and her maids appeared, and the falconer waited while they approached before taking the next step. 'I hope you are noting this, Arthur,' he said as they waited. Arthur nodded. 'It is good to let the bird get used to the surroundings. See how she is taking everything in.'

'Yes. She has beautiful eyes.'

When the Countess reached them she nodded at the pages and falconer. She looked at Arthur. 'And who is this?'

'Arthur,' said the falconer. 'For sure, he's a dab with them birds.'

She turned to Piers. 'When it is manned, that bird shall be mine. So man him well.'

Piers went to the cadge, put on the leather glove then he took the jess, the leather leash attached to the falcon's talon, in one hand and encouraged the bird to step off the cadge onto his other hand. Another page handed him a scrap of raw lamb which Piers threw into the air. At the same time he let the falcon go. The bird flew up and caught the scrap in mid air. Piers then pulled it back in by the rein.

The maids clapped. 'She's going to be a beauty,' my lady said. 'Do not get fond of her, Piers.'

Piers nodded and repeated the exercise. After a time Arthur's neck was sore from looking upwards. My lady was saying, 'A pardon. A complete pardon! Sir Henry is furious. Those Butler brothers are a law unto themselves.'

'Yes, my lady,' murmured the maid who was holding a parasol over her mistress' head to protect her from the sun.

'The blackguards get off scot free. Aaargh,' the Countess growled. 'And all because that black sod is simpering around the Queen. It is galling. It must have stuck in Sir Henry's craw. He can't know where he stands with the Queen. With that black-hearted buzzard pulling her strings. And who knows what else.' Arthur could not believe that one woman could talk so long and so fast.

'My lady,' a maid tried to calm her, 'don't fret so. None of this need worry you ere long. You sail for Bristol within the four week.'

'Only on account of the fact that I cannot attend Court. Not whilst *he* is there. If not for that I'd be gone beyond Bristol and back to my rightful place at the heart of the world.' She paced up and down as she spoke. 'And Lucas! What sort of name is that? The black-bearded, black-hearted...'

'*And* Her Majesty calls him her "black husband",' one gentlewomen whispered to another, although my lady had paced too far off to hear.

Arthur wondered if Bren knew of the pardon, and of the special names the Queen had for the Earl. Part of him badly wanted to race off and tell him. The other part was locked in the memory of the spy coins.

When the Countess had paced back to the group she looked towards the north range of the manor house. 'A further indignity!' she cried. 'An abomination. An insult.'

'Her Majesty would be foolish to make use of the manor house,' the gentlewoman soothed. 'I predict the Earl will never have his way in that respect.'

'He always gets his way!' Then the Countess sighed. 'It is all too great a burden. I shall probably die in Bristol.' She looked up at the falcon which was swooping on another piece of meat. 'I want that falcon in Kilkenny before we pack for Bristol,' she said to the falconer. 'She looks about the right size for me, don't you think?'

'Yes, my lady.'

She swept away with her maids trotting behind.

Arthur heard Piers sigh. The air seemed suddenly still and Arthur could understand Pier's relief. The falconer looked relieved too.

'Would the young 'un like a try?' he asked smiling. 'He's a natural with them birds, Master Piers.'

'So you've said,' Piers answered. He returned the bird to the cadge and Arthur stepped eagerly forward. 'Softly. Quietly.' Piers said. 'Don't startle her.' He gave Arthur the glove which was too big when he put it on, but he knew he was better with it than without.

Piers gave Arthur the jess to hold in one hand while Arthur coaxed the bird off the cadge and onto the other. As soon as the bird stepped off the cadge he thrust her into the air as he had seen Piers do. Piers threw a piece of meat and up flew the bird. For a moment Arthur thought he would leave the ground with her and fly too, but in a thrice she had taken the meat and was back on his hand again.

'Try again,' said the falconer, 'but take your time. Let her settle on your hand. Don't rush her, so.' Arthur tried again but slowly, more calmly. 'Grand,' said the falconer. 'Tomorrow we might be able to let her fly free.'

They took the bird back to the mews, and as they were leaving Piers said. 'I hope my lady will not be present tomorrow. What a loose tongue she has. Talking about the Earl in that manner. And the Queen. Especially the Queen. In front of her maids and the falconer…'

'And me,' Arthur offered.

Piers laughed. 'I should think you would be the least of the Earl's threats.' Arthur could not decide whether to be insulted or proud. 'Such talk is tantamount to treason,' Piers went on. 'My lady would hold her tongue or be deemed a traitor.'

*

The Countess soon returned to Kilkenny. No chance came for Arthur to go into the town to see Bren and he was both pleased and sorry. When the time finally came, Morveen was with him to help carry the parcels, and even though he caught a glimpse of Donal at the pie shop, he could not speak with him. He knew what

Piers said about the Countess being a traitor was true. A spy and a traitor were one and the same thing, and he decided to forget the gold coin and keep his mouth shut. From then on whenever he was called upon to go into the town, he went there and back as quickly as he could, looking neither left nor right for fear of seeing the O'Brennans. Once he saw Bren walking up and down outside the postern gate, but he kept well away. He wanted Piers' good opinion of him and would have hated it if Piers should perchance have cause to call him a spy and a traitor. The gold coin faded in his memory, although every now and then he took it out and spent it, mostly it seemed on pies these days. How many pies would a gold coin buy? he wondered. He was growing fast and was constantly hungry.

One morning he came into the kitchen with a bucket of fresh water from the well, proud that he had the strength to carry it without spilling any now he had grown so. Morveen was talking to Piers. 'What are you doing here?' Arthur asked.

'He wants you to go with him to Kilkenny to take my lady Elizabeth's falcon to her,' Morveen answered for him. 'It is an opportunity, Art,' Morveen said. 'I believe Kilkenny is a grand place.'

Piers nodded. 'The falconer suggested it.' And then he added quickly, 'And I agreed. It is a grand idea.'

'On the morrow,' Morveen said.

Chapter Seven

'You might like to reconsider,' the falconer said to Morveen who had come to wave Arthur off with Aefe sat on her hip. 'I am not certain that Kilkenny will be safe.'

'Art would be disappointed not to go,' Morveen said, 'Wouldn't you, Art?'

'Most,' he said.

'How bad are things?' Morveen looked uncertain.

'Sir Henry Sidney is on his way to make some sort of proclamation. There are many who won't take it kindly.'

'We could stay out of Sir Henry's way,' suggested Piers. 'Kilkenny is a big enough place.'

'And we must get the falcon to the Countess ere long. She wants her falconer to handle the bird before they leave for Bristol.' The falconer mounted his horse. 'Twould have been easier to take the bird directly to Waterford.' He looked at Arthur. 'But the boy? Is it an unnecessary risk? For both boys?'

'The bird is my responsibility. I must go,' Piers said.

'And I *want* to go,' said Arthur.

'Well, then,' laughed Morveen, 'I suppose you must. But,' she added more seriously, 'you are not to go to the castle. That's where the trouble will be.'

'Don't fret Morveen,' said the falconer. 'If you're agreed he can come, I'll look after both lads as if they was my own.'

The hooded falcon sat quietly in its cage. Piers handed the cage up to the falconer who balanced it between the saddle and the horse's neck. Piers mounted his own gray and pulled Arthur up behind him.

'*Go n-éirí an bóthar leat,*' Morveen followed behind as the horses walked out of the court and through the lodge gate.

'*Slán agat,*' Arthur called. He had never before been on a horse. It felt odd and he thought he was going to roll off, so clung tightly to Piers' back. 'You wait until we start galloping,' Piers turned to say.

'There'll be none of that,' the falconer said. 'We need a steady gait to keep this little girl calm.' He patted the cage lightly. 'And the horses have far to travel. We don't want to tire them.'

Arthur took a quick look behind him to see Morveen waving. She made Aefe wave her little hand as well, but Arthur could not remain turned about for long, and he faced the front holding tightly to Piers' back as the horses began to walk more briskly.

*

From the moment they entered Kilkenny, Arthur's mouth opened in astonishment. It was so big and busy and had so…much of everything. The falconer hurried them to an inn, dodging carts and dogs, horses and people. It was late in the day and the falconer said, 'It is too late to deliver our beauty today. We shall do it on the morrow. Piers and I. Arthur you must wait in the town.' Arthur was given the stables at the rear as his sleeping quarters, while Piers and the falconer slept in beds inside. How grand it must be to sleep in a bed. He shared the stables with the horses and the falcon, and once the other two had disappeared into the inn Arthur took the falcon out of its cage and removed the hood. She eyed the resting horses warily, then stared at Arthur as if looking at an old friend. Arthur felt sad that after the morrow he would not see her again. 'Hello girl,' he whispered. 'You are free for the night.' But the bird was content to perch on a railing just above Arthur's head and they both slept soundly until the cock crowed.

After their breakfast the falconer gave Arthur two pennies to buy something for his midday dinner in case they did not get back in time. He said they should be back before noon, but if anything happened to delay them Arthur was to leave town and wait at the Carraigh Road on Gallows Hill. 'As long as you don't go astraying too far from here, it's to your left at the corner.' Arthur said goodbye to the bird, and Piers and the falconer set off on foot for the castle. Arthur felt suddenly alone.

He wandered back into the stable, which seemed the safest place to be. He patted Piers' grey and the falconer's mount and fed them some hay, then sat down. Got up, sat down again. What was he to do all the morning? Then he stood up. Here he was in an exciting city and he was hiding in a stable at the inn. He hurried out and into the street before he could change his mind.

He had not gone far when he came across a throng of people. They had their backs to him, facing a platform at one end of what looked like the town square. On the platform stood a well-dressed man wearing a high ruff, a chain of office and a jewel-encrusted girdle around his waist which twinkled in the sunlight. For a moment Arthur wondered if his lost gold coin would have bought him such a girdle. Behind the man stood a row of officials and Arthur recognised the Earl's agent, John Cantwell, among them.

'As you all know, there has been a tradition in areas beyond the Pale of coign and livery,' the man shouted at the crowd.

'What about Kildare?' a voice from the crowd called out. 'Has not a blind eye been turned upon him and his coign and livery and is not he *within* the Pale?'

The questions were ignored and the official continued. 'It is feudal and unbecoming of modern English society…' Some in the crowd booed at that. This, too, was ignored '…to cause tenants to house, feed and pay for the soldiery of the local…local…' He was obviously searching for the right word. By the look on his face the word had a bad taste, and after a moment he carried on without it. 'Her Majesty Queen Elizabeth finds such a custom most displeasing.' This time someone shouted something in Gaelic which Arthur could not pick up. He pushed his way closer. 'As the Queen's Lord Deputy in Ireland I speak with her voice.' So that was Sir Henry Sidney. 'And I say, we are outlawing coign and livery and any similar exactions throughout Ireland.'

A cheer had gone up from the crowd. Some men slapped each other on the back, some clapped and others danced in circles of delight. Arthur supposed it was because these were the people who had to pay for the soldiery, and wondered how the Earl's victory at Affane against Desmond had been paid for. Sir Henry stood back and Cantwell clasped his hand enthusiastically. It would be much better, Arthur thought, if the Queen came to Ireland to deliver the messages herself, but, he supposed she was waiting for the manor house to be completed. It would not be long now, but in the meantime they would have to put up with this haughty, long-faced man passing on her instructions.

The crowd pushed closer, happy now to hear more. As Arthur looked back to see who was jostling him he saw to his right the gentleman from Kilcash, looking none-too pleased. Beside him, one on each side, were Donal and Bren. Bren saw Arthur and waved an arm, beckoning him to them, but Arthur turned and threaded his way through the crowd in the opposite direction. Sir Henry stepped forward, Arthur heard him say, 'Furthermore…' and when he felt he had enough distance between himself and Bren O'Brennan, he stopped and listened again, for now the crowd had turned sullen. Some people heckled in Gaelic and English. *Go dtachta an diabhal thú!* To the devil with you. *Damnú ort.*

Sir Henry held up a hand for silence. 'An act of the Irish Parliament has ordained this. It simply behoves me to enforce it. No rhymer nor other person whatsoever shall make verses to anyone except the Queen under penalty of forfeiture of his goods.' This was met with a stunned silence, and then a low rumbling. 'Accordingly,' Sir Henry raised his voice, 'my officials have been ordered to arrest the divers rhymers in Kilkenny. They will be divested of their belongings, whipped and ordered to leave the region.'

Some in the crowd moved away at that point. Arthur wondered if they were rhymers escaping before it was too late. He wondered about Eoghan Mac Craith, the Earl's rhymer. Surely the Queen would not agree to a law that stopped Eoghan from rhyming about her Lucas. He tried to remember the words he'd heard in the kitchen on the night of the victory. Something about the love of every young maiden. Well, then perhaps the Queen did not want her Lucas, her black husband, being rhymed about in that way.

Sir Henry had not quite finished. 'I hereby proclaim that according to the terms of the pardon made on the tenth of last month I have summonsed the Butler brethren and their followers to appear before me in the shire court to pledge their bond to keep the peace.' Sir Henry stood back again. This time John Cantwell did not seem so enthusiastic, but he led him across the platform and helped him down.

The crowd started moving off in angry swarms like wasps disturbed, a-buzzing and ready to sting. Arthur had lost his way in his flight from Bren and the gentleman and turned several times looking for a landmark to guide him. A hand rested on his shoulder. '*Dia duit.*' It was Donal. 'It is a surprise to see you here. My father would like to talk with you.'

Arthur tried to pull away, but Donal was the stronger and held him still. 'You must,' he said and he pushed him off with one hand firmly holding his jerkin so he could not escape.

'Ah, lad,' said Bren when Donal pushed him forward. The gentleman was nowhere in sight. 'It is a surprise to see you here.'

'I…I…came with Piers and the falconer. They are delivering a new falcon to the Countess.'

'You *are* close,' said Bren.

'In a way,' Arthur agreed. He took a breath. What could they do to him here? In a crowded square? 'I have decided I do not want the gold coin. I do not want to spy. I will not be a traitor.'

Bren smiled, in a kindly manner it seemed. 'I understand, lad. And good for you. It is noble of you.' He patted his shoulder in a friendly way. 'But who are you betraying?'

'My lord, the Earl of Ormond…'

'Hear me out.' Bren took Arthur by the arm and led him to the edge of the square. 'Then you will be free to go.' He pointed to the wall surrounding a well. 'Sit.'

Arthur sat down and Bren and Donal sat on either side. 'An interesting proclamation from Sir Henry,' Bren said. 'What did you make of it?'

Arthur thought for a moment. 'I wondered…I was thinking… how my lord paid for the battle at Affane…That was one thing.'

'Good place to start, lad.' Bren turned to Donal who nodded. 'The Earl does pay his gallowglass as a standing army. And he took the Queen's part on coign and livery. Until Desmond's men raided one of his richest properties in Tipperary.'

'Then,' Donal interrupted, '*your* lord called upon his brothers and they led an army against Desmond.'

'Funded by coign in Kilkenny and the re-introduction of coign in Tipp where he had previously banned it. Not the act of a man of principle, I suggest.'

Arthur was stunned. The Earl *was* a man of principle. Everyone knew that.

'It was almost his downfall,' Bren went on. 'But by God's grace the Queen was lenient towards him and hard on Desmond.' He paused, 'And that is our gripe. Ormond's relationship with the Queen. Yes, he is Anglo-Irish, and when he returned from court those years back he was welcomed as a son of the sod. He has many Gaelic customs. His rhymer, for one. His harpers.' Bren sighed. 'He allows freedom of religion and the use of the Gaelic tongue.'

The square was all but empty now. Arthur looked up at the sun. It was almost noon. 'I must go,' he said standing. 'I must meet the falconer at Gallows Hill.'

'A moment more.' Bren held him back. 'He might have Irish sympathies, but the Earl spends too much time at the English Court. Too many hours in the Queen's company. The English are the enemy, lad. Never forget that. The English army has already ravaged Ulster. They are trying to colonise Munster and the other Irish provinces. They have built forts all along the south-east borderlands and assembled garrisons. What do you suppose they are for?'

'For protection?'

'Don't be a dullard. They are there to enforce the reforms. And the reforms mean the end of our Ireland.'

'But we are English as well as Irish.'

'Pah! There is word that Sir Henry is going to grant powers of martial law to the New English! They are taking over our country. You, and Donal here, as Irish lads, will lose the very soil you stand on.'

'But I…' Arthur needed to say something, but could not think how to tell Bren what he knew about his parentage. 'I…'

'Whatever, you think lad, you are one of us.' Bren stood and turned to Donal. 'Now take him and show him the road home.'

Chapter Eight

At age eleven or so, Arthur was tall and strong in spite of his foot. He could read almost as well as Piers and even had his own falcon – at least until the Earl returned from court. He had been absent for two years now and there was scarce a soul who did not think it the Earl's place to be in Ireland controlling his brethren. Piers had out-grown another set of clothes and handed them down. The only thing that was missing was a pair of boots. Arthur's toes stuck out of the end of his old ones, but they would have to suffice.

The weather was as stormy as events around the countryside. All summer rain blighted the crops, fields were flooded, and much of the harvest swept away. Lashing winds stripped trees of leaves long before they had time to turn with the season. Fresh food was difficult to lay hands on. The only lovely thing was the completed manor house standing in all its glory waiting for Her Majesty, and life in the castle went on.

Since his encounter with the O'Brennans in Kilkenny two years back Arthur had seen them many times in the town. He liked them and was drawn to their Irish ways, although he kept any information he might have to himself. Oftentimes he would kick a pig's bladder around the street with Donal; other times Bren played a jaunty reel on his fiddle, or sang a haunting song about the auld days.

He loved to tell stories too, about the grand warrior-kings of old: Brian Bóruma, Cuchulainn, the O'Neills. Then there were Queen Medbh, Saint Patrick and the High Kings of Tara. Some tales were true, some myths, and when Arthur asked which was which Bren said, 'It's not easy to tell. Some myths are based on fact and some truths on lies; that is the way of history, lad, depending on the teller of the tale.'

Today was a soft day for a change. It was still raining, but the rain fell gently, straight from the sky, a mist hung over the hills behind the town and Cook sent Arthur to the apothecary in the high street for a powder to cure a headache. Privately Arthur thought it was caused by all the wine Cook had been drinking in the Earl's absence. Ale was one thing, but wine...that should only be drunk by lords, ladies and gentlefolk. Seneschal Shee was lax in such matters and the staff took advantage.

Arthur decided that Cook's head could wait and stole away to see if the O'Brennans were home. He could not imagine Bren working on a roof in the rain, soft though it may be and sure enough there the three were sitting at the fire. 'Weather's a mixed blessing,' Bren explained when they invited Arthur in. 'Roofs leak in the rain and that makes work, but it is impossible to mend them until the rain stops.'

'Da is worried, so,' said Donal. 'Some people are leaving their huts and moving off to live somewhere drier.'

'Fools they be. I don't believe there is anywhere dry in the whole county, so,' Bren said.

'Take your jerkin off, Arthur.' Bren's wife held out a hand for it.

'Dry it by the fire, Orlagh,' Bren said to her.

Arthur removed it and Orlagh O'Brennan hung it on a hook above the fireplace. 'Now, have yourself some prawkeen.' She fetched a bowl of raw oatmeal and milk and set it on Arthur's knee. 'For sure, we don't know how long the food for our bellies will last.'

'The harvest is a disaster,' added Bren.

'Then you should keep this...' Arthur said.

'Eat,' commanded Orlagh.

'What is new, so?' Donal asked.

Arthur hesitated.

'Sorry lad,' Bren said quickly. 'We're not prying.'

Arthur relaxed. 'I am sure everything I know, you know. And more.' He looked around the room. The only furniture was a settle by the fire, two other chairs and a small cupboard set against one wall. On it sat Bren's fiddle glowing rich in the firelight. Of such simple things they made happy lives. 'This weather is no good for the falcons either. Piers and I have been trying for days to get out. He's been waiting for a varvel for the falcon we've recently manned. And for the rain to stop.'

'I can't help you with the weather, lad, but I might be able to help with the varvel,' Bren said. 'Was it brass or silver he wanted?'

'I expect he would prefer silver, but brass would suffice.'

'I know where I can lay my hands on the very thing,' said Bren as Orlagh leaned forward to remove Arthur's empty plate. 'Tell him to come this time tomorrow. If I am back at my work, Orlagh will give it to you.'

'I shall see if he can get away from his lessons.'

'We'll see you tomorrow,' Bren said as he showed Arthur out into the street. 'Rain or no,' Donal called after him.

*

After his visit to the apothecary Arthur rushed back to the castle, pleased with himself on two counts. The first was that he had found a varvel for Piers. The second was this opportunity for Piers to meet the O'Brennans. The idea of spying on Piers was a faint memory and he knew that his agreement with Bren would hold, but when he mentioned the visit to Piers, he said the rector was coming to examine his Greek next day. 'I very much appreciate the man's concern. Would you please thank him and collect it on my behalf? When we know the cost I shall give you the money.'

So for the second time in two days Arthur went into the town. The rain was heavier today which meant Bren would still be away from his work. Arthur did not have a cloak to cover his new gentleman's clothes so ran as fast as his leg would allow. The streets were quiet, the only horse and cart in sight sat at the corner of New Street. The cart was covered so Arthur could not see who was driving it, but he felt sorry for the horse whose eyes were closed and rain dripped over its eyelashes and down its face. Arthur stopped to give it a quick pat. 'Poor auld fella,' he panted before running on. He was still panting by the time he reached the O'Brennan cottage. Water ran down New Street gurgling like a small river, and Arthur's feet were wet where it seeped into the broken seams of his boots. He knocked on the door. Silence. He knocked again, listening carefully. The rain was making such a noise, so. He would knock once more, then try the door, because he knew the O'Brennans would not want him standing out getting soaked to the very skin of him. He had his hand up to knock a third time when a noise behind him made him turn. Then everything went dark.

He was inside a sack. He could hardly breathe. 'Help,' he called, but his voice was muffled by a hand over his face. He kicked out at the person holding him, then heard men's voices. Someone picked him up bodily, threw him over his shoulder and ran back down the street. When they stopped the smell of leather and oats told Arthur they were at the cart on the corner, and this was confirmed when he was rudely thrown up into it. 'Help,' he tried again.

'*Dùn do bheal.* Shut up,' a man's voice said and the horse walked off.

Someone sat on him, curled up as he was inside the sack with his knees under his chin. He did not shut his mouth as instructed, but no matter how loudly he yelled, or how vigorously he squirmed there was no response, only the drumming of rain on the cover, and the clip-clip of the horse's hooves. That meant they had turned into the high street. He rested for a moment realising he needed to save his energy if he was to escape when they stopped. For sure, he knew he would not be forever clip-clopping through the streets of the town. The noise of cart wheels and hooves softened. They must have gone through the town gate, postern or west? He tried to remember how the turn was made, then he heard one of the men call out something and a faint reply seemed to come from below. Ah, that was the river. They had come out the bridge gate which meant they would be on the Waterford Road, heading into the hills beyond. The sound of howling which haunted his nights echoed in his mind: this was wolf country. He shuddered and struggled again. A foot kicked at him and hit him square on the back.

The road was bumpy which did not help the bruising he now felt. The men were silent as long as Arthur lay still and he hoped they might go to sleep. He waited. Eventually the person sitting on him got up, but kept a restraining foot firmly on his shoulder. Arthur waited some more. He thought he heard a gentle snore coming from nearby, so he tried to get out of the sack. This time the kick he received struck him in the head and he went into a faint.

*

When he came to, the cart had stopped, as had the sound of rain. The men were talking animatedly. They untied the sack and dragged him out. The sun was shining and he blinked. One of the men hauled him to his feet, and Arthur could see he was at a crossroads with five men standing in a circle around him, two with axes hanging loosely from their hands.

'Now Master Piers,' one of the men said.

Piers! 'But…' Arthur began.

'No buts you bastard son of a black bearded blackguard…'

One of the men lifted his axe to shoulder height and looked hard at Arthur.

Arthur knew now what had happened. What a fool he was to trust those O'Brennans. He looked around for help, but only an empty plain stretched before him. Now that his eyes had got used to the light he could see nothing but devastation. The land was covered in rubble. There was not a single blade of grass, not an animal. The only sign that the area was ever inhabited was the wreck of a single dwelling a short distance behind them. His gaze came back to the axe, and he hoped that it would not be the last thing he saw in his short life.

'They are a-coming here to get you, Master Piers. To take you for a ransom.'

'I am not Piers Butler,' he said, glad for once to be living the lie he lived every day. 'I am Arthur, the kitchen boy.'

'Dressed in your finest,' the spokesman said sarcastically.

'These are Piers' clothes. He gave them me. Look…' He pushed up a sleeve to show his dirty arms. Then he held out his hands. 'Are these the hands of a page?' He had another thought. 'And are these the boots of a gentleman?'

The man with the raised axe said, '*Shoneen*,' in disgust, but dropped his arm.

'You should be ashamed of yourself, so. Pretending to a gentleman,' said the spokesman. He turned to the others. 'This one is no good for us if what he says is true.' One by one the men climbed into the cart. Arthur went to climb in beside them thinking they were going to return him to Carraigh. The spokesman pushed him off. 'If you come with us you're a dead capper. You're on your own. If perchance you are lying we'll come back and cut the langer off you.' The driver whipped the horse lightly into action and they trundled off.

Arthur watched until the cart became a blur in the distance, then he looked around him. The road he was standing on was quite wide, but the intersecting road was but a boreen. He guessed that home was back the way they'd come. Maybe someone would come along and offer him help. Meantime he would start walking, so he set off following the cart's left wheel track and took a good look around. The wasteland showed patches which looked like crops burnt to the ground and razed pasture. As he got closer to the wreck of the cottage he could see through the broken walls to further devastation beyond. The shimmering outline of hills loomed in the far distance. Nothing for it but to trudge on.

He came alongside the cottage and saw how little was left, just the two side walls and a roof over a lean-to at the back. By now the sun was high in the sky and dark clouds loomed far ahead, but they were moving away and Arthur was sweating in his gentleman's clothes. He would shelter in the shade of the roof for a while and hope that someone chanced by.

He walked off the road and stood for a moment, it was so still and quiet he could hear himself breathing. Not even a bird sang; no skylark soared in the ceiling of the sky. He stepped into the shelter.

'I been a-watching you,' a voice said. He jumped and took a step back. 'I been watching you limp along.' He turned to see an old woman crouched in the shadow of the opposite corner. 'I seen them dump you off the cart. What've you bin up to?'

'Nothing. They mistook me for someone else.'

The old woman was bedraggled, her grey hair wild about her face, her smock torn and shredded at the edges, her feet bare. 'Glad of your company, boy,' she said. 'I am Bridie. Who are you?'

'Arthur…kitchen boy at Carraigh Castle…'

'You don't look like a kitchen boy.' She heaved herself on to her feet and moved closer for a better look. 'Look at them clothes.' She stretched out a filthy hand to feel the material of his jerkin.

'Those men,' he waved into the distance. 'They mistook me for the page who gave me these clothes.'

'Ah, and who would that be?'

'Piers Butler…'

'One of Black Tom's bastards?'

Arthur nodded.

'What is so with your reel foot?'

'I was born this way. It is a blight on me.'

'Aye. I would believe that.' Bridie clicked her tongue and shook her head. 'But you look stout enough elsewise. I like the looks of youse. We'll travel the road together. There's safety in numbers.' She cackled a phlegmy laugh. 'Think your earl will take me in?' She gave him a soft push out into the sunlight.

'He is still at Court.'

'Just me luck,' she said following him out.

'But Cook might take you on in the kitchen, so.'

*

They seemed to walk for hours in the heat of the sun along the desolate road. Arthur was aware of the flap-flapping of the broken boot leather, but soon lost himself as Bridie talked her way through every barefooted step. 'There was a young woman from Waterford,' she began. 'She was not beautiful but had charm enough to entrance a certain handsome young man who came to the town on market days with his milk and sausages. One day when the rain fell like sheets of ice from a heavy sky the young man asked the young woman to marry him. She said yes, and the day seemed to warm with the heat of their ardour.

'The young woman was very happy. For one thing she loved the handsome young man, for another the young man owned ten sheep and five head of cattle which made him a wealthy man by local standards. Oh, she did love her handsome young husband, but the sheep and the cows and the land they fed upon and the river beside them which provided fresh water were the jewels in the crown of their love. And soon further riches came their way. They had two beautiful children – a boy with hair as red as the sunset and, two years later, a golden-headed girl.

'The family thrived, adding four more cows and five sheep to their flock. Time passed and the babbies grew into children. The woman marvelled at the way the pastures grew green in spring and the corn glowed golden in the summer. She loved the smell of warm milk from the cows and the softness of their titties in her hands as she squeezed the milk out of them. And she did not even mind when the earth turned soggy with the rain and between whiles she had to drive the cows into the barn. Sure, weren't they lucky to have a barn? And was it not the good earth of Ireland that clung between the toes of her bare feet?' Bridie looked down at her own feet covered in mud before going on.

'Then something happened to take the heart out of her. The boy died of a fever. It broke his parents' hearts, but time passes and you learn to live with such things. Although she was no longer young the woman had another bairn to fill the space but it died at birth. The woman was nearly lost to the void. The golden-haired daughter worked hard. Only six and she was a-milking, helping bring the lambs into the world and calling her mother back from the edge of madness. One morning the woman cried, "Brigid arise. The cows are in agony with their titties full of milk." Finally, impatiently, she went to the crib where Brigid slept. She shook her but she did not stir. The woman knelt beside the crib and watched for the rise and fall of breath that did not come.'

Bridie stopped walking and wiped roughly at her eyes with the tattered sleeve of her smock. She sighed, and they set off again.

'The parents were bereft, but hard work dulled the pain. Seasons came and went. The winter wind seemed colder, the rain wetter; the summer sun not quite so warming. But time passes and you learn to suffer the loss of your little ones. And did they not have the sheep and the cattle and each other? Then one chill autumn day the couple were driving the cattle across the field towards the barn. The man was now a year off two-score, stooped with the toil of the fields. He fell. The woman ran to him. His face was still warm, but as she tried to coax him up he grew colder. She had now to run the farm alone.

'One day some years later, when there was finally hope on the breeze, an owl called early to the oak tree by the barn. "Leave, woman," the owl said. "Leave the land while you still have life yourself." The owl fluttered its wings. It landed on the ground at her feet and turned into a young man with wild red hair and bare feet. "Leave," he said. "Soldiers are on their way."

'As the shape-shifter left on the wings of the owl she heard the rumble of hooves in the distance.' Bridie's voice quickened as if she could hear the thunder yet. 'She ignored the shape-shifter's advice and stood mesmerised as the horde approached. Ahead of them were the cattle they had gathered on their way. Hundreds of animals all running for the life of them. The soldiers ignored the woman, but swept her stock before them and onward to the next holding. Behind them came more troops razing the harvest. The woman walked to the river and entered the cold water to avoid the flames. Betimes her land was a-blaze and the air thick with the smell of burnt corn. Even then the soldiers were not happy. Some soldiers moved ahead of the blaze and torched the dwellings and barns all about. The woman was left with nothing but the three scarred walls of the barn. She stood in the middle of the scorched land, lucky to be alive, but also sad to be so.' It was Arthur's turn to stop. He looked at the wastes about him and Bridie nodded.

'Time passes but you never learn to live with such a thing as losing the very Irish soil from under your very Irish feet.' Bridie looked down at her own feet again. 'So the woman made her way back to Waterford, the town of her youth. Here the townsfolk took pity on the poor Irish people of the countryside and allowed them in. Some came with lips green from eating grass which was all they had. The townspeople housed and fed them, but the town was full fit to bursting, so. Many had to leave.'

There followed a long silence which Arthur finally broke. 'And you were one who left?'

Bridie nodded. 'It was a long trake, and it wasn't worth it.'

'I'm sorry for your troubles,' he said.

'It is hard to say who is to blame. 'Twas the Butlers. Or the English.' She stopped walking and took Arthur by the arm to halt him too. She grabbed his chin with her dirty hands, and he squirmed out of her touch. 'Whose side are youse on?'

'The Earl's,' he said stoutly. 'The Irish have done me nothing but wrong.' He felt suddenly lonely. He longed to see Morveen smile at him; to have Aefe hold his hand in her fat little fingers, to call him, 'Uffer, Uffer'. To be in the garden with a falcon ready for flight; to hear Piers' delighted laugh when a newly-manned falcon took off after a pheasant. Could he trust this Bridie? She had suffered much and seemed kind, but so did the O'Brennans and look where trusting them had landed him.

'Like I was a-saying, 'tis the English at fault, now. Look you, there.' She pointed to land laid waste. 'That is all that is left of a forest of oaks. The English have stolen them for to make their grand ships, so. And your earl's as good as one of them.'

'But he was brought up at Court. The Queen is his cousin.'

'Be-dab to the Queen.'

'You should not talk so.'

'Aye. I won't be bad-mouthing when I'm working in that kitchen of yourn. But while your earl is jauncing with the Queen that Edward Butler is gathering the biggest army you ever saw. Sacking your earl's castles thither and yon. Laying waste to honest folks' land.' She started walking again. 'Giving that sherral Lord Deputy an excuse to interfere. Mark my words, young 'un. Henry Sidney will be giving Butler land to the English before you know it.'

Arthur's thoughts went back to Carraigh. He remembered the day he and Piers had watched Sir Edmund, Edward and the red-headed James Butler, try to bully the seneschal. What if they sacked the castle?

'They won't be attacking Carraigh,' Bridie said, as if she could read his mind. 'Black Tom is too powerful.' The wind blew her hair into her eyes and she brushed it aside. 'But he is of no use to anyone while he stays in England.'

Slowly the sun slipped down the sky, the air cooled and finally the distant hills became clearer. They were wooded, and that made Arthur happier than he had felt all day, they were getting somewhere. Bridie was quiet beside him now, her head down watching their feet as they trod.

The sun was setting when they started their climb up the hill. The woods would have been comforting except for… 'Are there wolves hereabouts?' Arthur asked.

'Not enough to worrit about.'

'One would be enough to worry about.'

Bridie cackled.

It was dark when they walked down the other side of the hill. The road widened and a space opened ahead. Candlelight shone from cottage windows. A wolf howled, a faint threat behind them, and an owl hooted nearby. Arthur's legs were sore, but he kept putting one foot in front of the other, and when he considered that Bridie had no shoes at all he was grateful for the bits of leather flapping around his feet.

They entered a small village with a river running alongside the path. They could hear it rather than see it.

'The Suir,' Bridie said nodding at it. Arthur smiled; his river. 'You will be home on the morrow, God willing. There is a boatman goes to Carraigh and beyond regular every day.'

They skirted round the houses and found a surviving, empty barn in a nearby field to sleep in. 'I've a fierce hunger on me,' Arthur said.

'Wait,' said Bridie. She left him in the dark too hungry to even think about wolves and when she came back she gave him a hard crust of bread. 'Where did you find it?' Arthur asked taking a large bite, then noticing Bridie had no bread for herself, 'And what about you?'

'Say the rosary with me, boy,' was all she said, taking a rosary from her underclothes.

He knelt beside her as she ran the beads slowly through her fingers, touching each one lightly. '*Ave Maria, gratia plena, Dominus tecum. Benedicta tu in mulieribus…*' When she had finished she kissed the cross and put the beads back within her clothes. 'In England we could die for doing such. But your earl is more tolerant.'

'And his brothers?'

'They are Catholic. All these shenanigans are as much for the Pope and the true faith as they are for Ireland. Why do you think Spain is coming to their aid?' Bridie asked.

Arthur yawned. He had no idea, but Spain seemed so far away it did not matter.

Next morning Bridie found a bleary-eyed waterman at the river with a load of green wood for Carraigh, and she arranged a passage for them both.

'It'll cost you a groat, so it will,' the waterman said grumpily.

'You'll get your groat at the castle,' she said. 'The lad is well in there. Youse just got to look at the cut of him in them clothes.'

The man agreed. He helped first Bridie, then Arthur on board and cast off.

Arthur smiled. He was going home.

Chapter Nine

'Where the feck have you been, you scullion snipe?' asked a red-faced Cook when Arthur entered the kitchen with Bridie.

'I was kidnapped,' Arthur explained. 'The waterman what brought us back needs a groat for our passage.' He looked up at Cook hopefully, but regretted asking for the money almost immediately because he realised Cook's flush came from anger, not the heat of the kitchen fires.

Cook ignored Bridie, as if she did not exist. 'You got away with it last time,' he shouted in Arthur's face. 'But not this time.' He swung at Arthur with a fist and hit him square on the jaw. 'Your hand out for a groat!' He grabbed a paddling spoon. 'You expect me,' he cried as he slapped Arthur on the head with it, 'to believe your lies. Kidnapped, huh.' He beat Arthur all about his body. When Arthur protected his head with his arms, Cook walloped his shoulders. Arthur tried to protect his shoulders with his hands, so Cook hit his head.

Aefe screamed, 'Uffer. Uffer,' and ran to Cook, battering him on the backside. 'Stop,' she demanded, but her little hands made no difference.

Morveen snatched her away, and cried out, 'Please,' to Cook, but he kept on. Bridie flapped her arms in front of Cook as if shooing at a flock of sheep, but still he beat away. When, finally exhausted, he stood a-huffing and a-puffing as if to draw breath to start again, Arthur ran off.

After dark with the kitchen settled for the night, he crept back into the inner court. He saw Bridie huddled in the doorway, but she was covered with Morveen's cape and she slept so he did not waken her. He went inside and slid in beside Aefe. Morveen was on the other side and she sat up when he came in. 'How do you fare?'

'Well,' he said lying. He was aching all over. But he wasn't dead. And he had not cried.

'I paid the wherryman his groat,' Morveen said. 'Else he would still be sitting on the bank waiting.' She laughed softly, 'Or taken over the castle as payment,' but Arthur was in no mood for jest, he whispered his thanks and turned his aching body over to sleep.

Next morning he went outside with a plate of bread and porter for Bridie's breakfast. He felt certain that once Cook's anger had subsided he would look more kindly on her. Even as he approached the doorway he could hear an altercation taking place. Gruff voices of the kerne and a woman's voice. As he drew nearer he could see Bridie cowed beneath the soldier's fist as he pummelled her. 'Who sent you?'

'I am come from Waterford. Of my own choice. I am no spy.'

Another kerne hit her. 'Do not lie to us.'

'Bridie,' Arthur shouted above the men's voices.

She lifted her head cautiously.

The kerne stood back. 'Are you acquainted with this wretch?'

'Yes, sir. She is come to work in the kitchens.'

'Work,' scoffed one of the kerne. 'She is too old. Look at the state of her.' He kicked her in the stomach and she doubled over.

'Enough,' said Arthur. For which interruption he got hit around the head with a flat hand. The impact made him drop the bowl.

Bridie tried to stand, but she fell back. 'I once…had ten head of cattle to my name. Fifteen swine and three sheep. I have lost them all.'

'May she pass?' Arthur asked the kerne. 'She has helped me and

I would like to help her.'

'How can a snotty scullion like you be of any assistance?'

'Aye strutting around in your gentlemen's clothes.'

'Let them go,' said a third. 'I can't see how either of these two can harm us.' The other two backed off.

Arthur bent down to help Bridie up, and to rescue the bowl although the contents were beyond saving. One of the kerne stood on his hand as he stretched it out. It hurt and he wanted to cry, not so much for the pain but because it was one of the Earl's men who had done it. And thrashed Bridie. He left the bowl where it was and half led, half carried Bridie to the kitchen. They stopped at the kitchen door while Bridie brushed herself down and straightened her bird's-nest hair. 'Must look my best.' Her laugh was weak, but Arthur laughed with her.

'What have you to laugh at?' demanded the pot man as they entered.

'Leave him be,' said Morveen. 'We are all miserable. It is nice to hear laughter from the young 'un, so it is.'

'We have nothing for an extra mouth,' said Cook, as if noticing Bridie for the first time.

'I will work hard,' Bridie said before crumpling to the floor. Morveen stopped what she was doing and went to her. 'Thought I'd be safe here,' Bridie whispered.

Arthur fetched some water and held it to her lips, but she could not take it.

'Leave her be, Art,' Morveen said. 'We have dinner to serve and the Proctor is here. You know how particular he is about meal times.' Arthur dragged Bridie as gently as possible so she was out of the way under the table, then joined the others as they went about preparing the noon meal.

When the meal was over they ate what little was left. Arthur saved some of his for Bridie and after the tables were cleared he took it to her. 'Bridie.' She did not stir. She did not stir when he gently shook her. She did not stir when he shook her harder.

Morveen had a look. 'She is dead, Art. God rest her soul.'

Cook could not wait to get rid of Bridie's body. He called in two kerne, but not the ones who had beaten her to death. They handled her gently. Arthur and Morveen followed as they carried her to the paupers' grave outside the town wall. As Bridie's wild hair disappeared under the dirt shovelled onto her by the kerne Arthur began to cry. Once he had started he could not stop. He cried for Bridie and he cried for himself, bruised and battered as he was from Cook's beating. Morveen put an arm around his shoulder to comfort him and he cried all the more, remembering the vicious kerne. The Earl's men. It had come to this.

*

It took a long time, but time passed, and each day Arthur's wounds healed. It took longer for his grief for Bridie to subside, and Morveen tried to comfort him. 'She was but an old biddy you met briefly. You hardly knew her. Why take on so?'

Arthur found it hard to explain. 'It was more than just Bridie. It was the way the Earl's men treated her, and she lost the land she loved so much…It all sorrows me… And,' he added emphatically, 'I *liked* her.'

'So be it, but time is the great healer, Arty. So it is.' And Morveen was right. Gradually he thought less and less about Bridie.

*

One evening in early summer the spit boy had been splashed with fat and Cook told Arthur to take over turning the handle. It was heavy work and Arthur felt a grudging respect for the spit boy who had to do this day in and out.

'You boy!' a voice boomed from the door. Everyone stopped work and looked up to see the Earl's oldest brother, Edmund pointing at Arthur. 'Come,' he ordered.

Arthur looked at Cook who nodded and took over the spit himself.

When Arthur reached the door Edmund Butler grabbed him by the neck of his shirt and dragged him outside. 'Who are you?' Edmund Butler demanded. His hair was dark like the Earl's, his eyes a burning bronze, and he towered over Arthur.

'I am Arthur, Sir. A scullion.'

'Why are you dressed thus?' He swept his arm over Arthur from breeches to collar.

'Piers gave me his cast-offs.'

'Why?' The eyes glowered.

'Because...because Piers is kind, Sir.'

'Black Tom's bastard, Piers?'

Arthur nodded.

'Do you know who I am?'

'Yes Sir. You are my lord's brother.' He hesitated, then asked. 'Have you come to take over the castle, Sir?'

Edmund laughed and called to his two brothers who were standing outside the east keep. Arthur had been too distracted to notice them. The brothers swaggered over, looking for all the world as if they owned the castle already. 'Who does he bring to mind?' Edmund asked when they stood in front of Arthur.

The red-headed James nodded his silent agreement.

'The image,' said Edward. He was the brother who most resembled the Earl, though his face was broader.

'So you've been mistook for young Piers?' James said to Arthur.

'Aye, I was, Sir. Some time back. Did you...did..?' He looked from one brother to the other.

Edmund clipped Arthur around the head. 'Did we what?'

'Nothing, Sir.'

Edmund and James laughed.

Arthur said in spite of himself, 'And Bren O'Brennan? He was in on it?'

All three brothers laughed this time.

'The thatcher?' Edward asked.

Arthur nodded.

'In a small way.' Edmund hit Arthur over the head again. 'An enquiry after a varvel for young Piers set the whole thing off.'

Edward put an arm around both brothers' shoulders to lead them away. 'We must keep an eye on that one,' he said as they walked off.

'Wait until my lord returns,' Arthur muttered under his breath. They disappeared into the kitchen and Arthur heard Edmund's booming voice shout, 'Now Cook. What's for our dinner? We are hungry.'

*

Arthur did not know how he managed it, but by morning Richard Shee had banished the Earl's brothers again. Their horses had gone, and when Arthur asked the stable boy about it, he just shrugged happily.

Some days later Arthur was approaching the postern gate when he saw Bren coming towards him. He turned to go back into the castle grounds, but Bren called out. 'Arthur. Arthur! I must talk with you.'

Arthur took off at a fast hobble, knowing that Bren would never be able to keep up. He could hobble like the wind…well like a good strong breeze at least. He hated Bren, holding him responsible for the beating Cook gave him when he arrived back from Waterford, hand out for a groat to pay the watermen, telling his wild story. He held him responsible for Bridie…

He had managed to avoid the O'Brennans since, but here now was Bren a-running after him. Arthur stopped suddenly. Why should he run? He was not a-feared of Bren, he would face him. Was he not of the bravest stock? He had withstood Cook's beating without a whimper; suffered the shock of Bridie's death and come out the other side. Moreover Edmund Butler said Bren O'Brennan had nothing to do with his kidnapping. Arthur turned to face Bren who came panting up. 'Ah, Arthur, lad. A word.'

'Of apology?'

'Of course, lad. Let's find somewhere to talk.'

'Here is as good a place as you will find.'

'Very well.' Bren took a deep breath. 'First thing. I did not arrange for the kidnap. My only error was to mention to those rogues and bully-rooks that I wanted a varvel for young Piers and he was a-coming for to collect it.'

'Tell me then. Who were they?'

'From Edward Butler's camp. There is much animosity for Black Tom amongst his brethren. A ransom for his…his bastard son…he has not a legitimate one…would cause concern in many quarters. I suspect it was more this matter than acquiring wealth that prompted the kidnapping' He paused, then added, 'Although, no doubt, the riches would abet them.'

'Those brethren have created havoc.'

'I have shared their passion in the past. The Irish people free of the English, free to worship as we choose, is my dearest dream.'

'My lord does not persecute Catholics,' Arthur said.

'Not yet.'

'Is that all?' Arthur turned to go.

'I want you to understand, lad.' Arthur faced him again, drew breath to speak but Bren hurried on '… not to spy, or even to take sides. Just to understand.'

Arthur shrugged. 'I think I do.'

Bren went on anyway. 'The Earl's brothers have some strange bedfellows in their enterprise. They have alliances the length and breadth of the country. They have linked their cause with the Desmonds. This unrest is as much anti-Ormond as it is anti-English. The Butler revolt could encourage the Queen to strip all the Butlers of their lands.'

Arthur remembered Bridie's cottage, or what was left of it; the barren surroundings; the felled oak forest.

'And the plantations. The English are encroaching on Irish soil everywhere.'

'So where do you stand?'

'At this moment I am torn. Many in the town are standing tall with Black Tom.' Arthur remembered Bridie's bruised body laying in its shallow pauper's grave. 'But for me,' Bren went on, 'he is too much in English thrall.'

'If only he would come home,' Arthur said. 'His men would not…' But he did not want to tell Bren about Bridie's death at the hands of the Earl's kerne; that would be disloyal. 'He should return to Ireland,' he reiterated.

'Aye, lad, aye.' Bren patted him on the shoulder. '*Go raibh maith 'ad*. Thanks for giving me your time.' And he walked away.

*

Summer passed into autumn and autumn into winter and the cold and stormy weather continued into spring. By Easter food was fast running out. Even the castle kitchen was on rations. There was a sense of gloom and foreboding like a dark cloud hovering above the castle, and just when they thought things could only get better, they got even worse.

Morveen came running into the kitchen one morning. 'My lord…the Earl…is dead,' she cried.

'Never,' said the pot man.

'How did it happen?' asked a scullion.

'I don't know,' sobbed Morveen. 'All I know is that the brewer brought the news from Waterford.'

'Happenchance he was poisoned like his father before him,' said Cook.

'Happenchance,' said Arthur, 'I can find out.' Piers was away, back at Kilkenny Castle, so he was no source. But Arthur did know someone who knew most of what went on. 'May I go into the town?'

For once Cook did not argue or give him a job to do on the way. Everyone was hushed with shock. Arthur ran all the way to the O'Brennan house, trying hard not to cry. He noted as he passed through the postern gate that the townsfolk were going about their everyday business, horse carts and hand carts headed towards the square, an onion seller called out, 'Who'll buy my fine brown onions,' three children kicked a pig's bladder from one to the other, and the pie man walked slowly by, his pies steaming in the basket on his head. These people were so unperturbed they could not have heard the news.

His knock on the O'Brennans' door was quickly answered. 'Da's at the Lundy cottage repairing the roof,' Donal said.

'The Earl is dead,' said Arthur. Donal gasped and went back inside to tell his mother. Arthur could hear him telling her, and she came to the door crossing herself. 'God rest his soul,' she said.

'You have not heard? Did Bren not have news?'

'No,' she said wiping her eyes. 'This puts a new light on everything. You boys had best tell Bren.'

They ran through the town to the Lundy cottage where they found Bren in the front garden talking to Michael Lundy. Donal got to him first and burst out the news. Bren looked at Michael Lundy who shrugged. 'Calm down,' Bren said to the boys. 'This could be a ruse. Sir Edmund wants us to believe his brother is dead, so we will fall in behind him and his Desmond cohorts.'

'You can't be sure of that,' said Michael Lundy.

'You are right, but let's not be too sorrowful until we know for sure.'

*

The cloud of doom hanging over the castle deepened. Opinion was divided between accepting the fact of the Earl's death, and considering the news a Butler ploy. They would have to wait for the foot post to arrive before they were certain one way or the other, but it made no difference, everything was in limbo. Life carried on, but with little enthusiasm. The question everyone asked was, if indeed the Earl was dead, who would succeed him?

One morning Sir Edmund arrived at the castle with a large retinue. He did not even dismount from his horse but spoke down to the seneschal who came out to meet him. His men surrounded Shee, horses pawing the ground. 'Prepare the castle for me. I shall return in a day or so.' Sir Edmund turned and left. The clatter of his men following was a threat none could ignore. The next day the red-headed James arrived. He was alone and when he tried to enter the west keep the Proctor and the seneschal barred his way until several kerne took him by the arms and neck and threw him out into the Great Park. They kept his horse and from the battlements where Arthur watched he could be seen walking towards the town, head down, humiliated. That would only make him the more determined to get his way, Arthur decided, but as the youngest brother surely he could not imagine he would succeed to the Earl's estates.

A captain of the gallowglass fortified Carraigh castle with what kerne and gallowglass could be spared from the fighting elsewhere. They brought from the fields what animals would fit within the castle walls. The night watch was intensified. The seneschal let it be known that until the matter of the Earl's demise had been confirmed there would be no changes at Carraigh. But dire news came from outside. Ormond plate and money were being stolen from all over. James Butler attacked the Earl's manor at Callan, terrorising the Earl's treasurer, Fulk Comerford, and stealing everything he could lay hand to. Desmond was still in the Tower but that did not stop his kin from joining the fray, sweeping through the English plantations and sending English settlers running for their lives. And still there was no direct word from Dublin or London about the Earl's death.

'There's talk of the Spaniards a-coming to fight against us now,' Morveen said one day when she returned from the town.

'But would not that be a good thing?' asked the pot man. 'They would restore us to the true faith.'

'Me'be. Me'be not,' said the baker who was up their end of the kitchen fetching salt. 'We of the Liberties might be done away with for being Protestants.'

That night, as happened most nights, Arthur tried to work out their escape should the castle be taken in the night. They could go by the Watergate, but, no, it was locked to keep the Butlers out. They could get out through the north range, but, wait, the Butlers would have the castle surrounded. He sighed and turned over. There was no escape. Butler men would come pouring in and murder them all before burning down the castle and the north range, that beautiful manor house. Arthur saw the long gallery, flooded with light, not from the windows, but flames. Burning, burning, devouring the plaster work, the Queen's beautiful white face blackened beyond recognition. My lord's coat of arms and his motto melting, dripping like candle wax to the Turkey floor rugs. Even if the castle was not sacked the Queen could never come to Ireland while it was in such a state. Nor would she come if her cousin, the Earl, really was dead, of that Arthur was certain. He turned over again.

Nothing had changed next morning, except that the sun was out. Perhaps that was God's answer Arthur thought. Sunshine to help the crops along for this year's harvest when last year's had been so dismal. But what was the use of the sun and a good harvest if the Butler men were going to come and destroy everything.

He took the opportunity of a quiet morning in the kitchen to go and see the falcons. At least they were not starving, not yet, and they gladdened his heart whenever he saw them. With Piers away in Kilkenny there had been no falconry of late, but at least he could go and look at the birds.

The falconer was in the weathering yard. 'Ah, young Arthur,' he said. '*Conas atá tú*?'

'I am well,' he said, then changed his mind. 'I am worried. Do you think the Earl is dead? Do you think the castle will be sacked by Sir Edmund? Do you think the Spaniards will come?'

The falconer laughed. 'So many questions. Would that I had the answers, laddo.' They moved into the mews and the resting birds batted their wings at them. 'They need exercise, and are certainly at their flying weight,' the falconer said. 'Let's lose our worries in these girls.'

Arthur felt better when they had finished with the birds and he was heading back towards the kitchen. No matter what evil occurred nothing could take away the beauty of a falcon in flight, the swoop, the dive and the pleasure of seeing the prey clutched in their talons. Better still he had a brace of partridges in each hand for Cook. There'd be a taste of partridge pie for supper this evening. As he crossed the court he saw Piers coming towards him. 'When did you arrive?' he called.

'In the dead of night.' Piers ran to him.

'How fares Kilkenny?'

'I am pleased to be out of it.' Piers clapped a friendly arm around Arthur's shoulder. 'The sheriff has a tight hand on matters with his martial law, but one can feel the current beneath.'

'What news of my lord?'

Piers shook his head. 'Nothing. We are a-feared of the worst.'

'Will you stay long at Carraigh?'

'They have sent me away because of the danger. But I am eager to take the field. My lord was a hero when he was but fourteen. I am a year older than that now.'

The jangle of stirrup and spur, and the rattle of hooves on the cobbles interrupted them. Leading the men were Sir Edmund and Edward Butler, dressed as if for battle, though their heads were bare. Behind them rode twenty or so horses. Arthur ran to the entrance between inner and outer court. There must have been at least another forty horse men there and behind them, milling in disarray, were foot soldiers. The leaders dismounted and handed their horses to the stable boys who were at the ready. They marched into the west keep. Arthur turned to Piers. 'This would seem to bode ill.'

'Aye.' Piers raced across the court and up onto the battlements with Arthur close behind. At the top Arthur put down the partridges and went to the side to look out at the Great Park. There were what looked like hundreds more kerne. 'That's James,' Piers said bitterly, pointing. 'They are all here.' He ran back down the stairs, calling over his shoulder, 'I'll be back presently.'

Arthur stayed on the battlements and watched the kerne. Some were pitching tents, others swam in the river, yet others were wrestling, while some practiced archery. The horsemen in the outer ward dismounted and led their steeds into the Great Park to graze.

They looked very much at home. Arthur looked down into the inner court. Morveen had come out with Aefe on her hip. 'Come up and look,' he called to her.

'Stop your foostering and get down,' she called back. 'We could be under siege ere long.'

Arthur didn't think the kerne looked as if they were readying for a fight, but one could never tell. There might be hundreds more on their way. He picked up the partridges and climbed down the stairs. As he did Sir Edmund Butler came out of the keep. 'You!' he pointed to a stable boy. 'Bring me a fresh horse.'

'But…' began the stable boy.

Sir Edmund marched over to him and before the boy had a chance to run picked him up by the legs and held him upside-down. '*Damnú ort.* Damnation on you!' He shouted before putting him back on his feet and pointing at the stables. The boy raced off and was soon back with a fresh horse.

'And we'll be needing more,' Sir Edmund said as he watched the boy saddle up. When the horse was ready he used the stable boy's cupped hands to help him mount, settled himself in his ornate leather saddle, kicked the animal viciously and galloped at dangerous speed across the court shouting something at his troops as he went.

He had only just left when Edward Butler and the seneschal Shee came out of the keep. 'Now if you will see to it that our troops are fed and watered we'd be grateful,' Edward was saying.

'There is not a great deal of sustenance in the castle,' Shee explained.

'It's the same everywhere. The weather…and the troubles… but we are fed willingly where ere we go. Why should it differ in the castle of our brother?' He paused, then added, 'Our *deceased* brother,' and he grinned.

'We have not proof of that,' Shee objected.

Edward ignored the remark. 'Especially when it is surrounded by two hundred kerne and fifty horse.'

'Is that a threat?'

'Take it as you will. Now to the kitchen.'

Arthur was closer to the kitchen than they were and he ran inside to warn Cook of Edward's approach. He threw the partridges at the pot man who caught them neatly, a brace in each hand, and hid them in a pot.

Edward Butler, followed by Shee, strutted in and began an inspection looking for food hidden in bins and boxes. 'There are nigh on three hundred mouths to feed.' Arthur was leaning against the stand where the partridge pot stood. Edward stopped in front of him and stared. 'You,' he said scornfully. 'Over-dressed snipe.' He moved on; opened one of the oven doors. The oven was empty. 'Do what you must,' he said finally before he marching out again leaving Shee behind.

'Yes, Cook. Do your best,' Shee said. 'He's threatening an attack. Best give them what food we can, sooner than lose everything.'

*

Cook did do his best. He stuffed several cabbages with a little minced spice meat. He boiled a cauldron of potage into which he threw all the leftover scraps from the two or three days gone past. He roasted what sparrows could be found and sent a boy out to catch some swans. Reluctantly Cook took the partridges from their hiding place. 'Sorry, lad,' he said to Arthur, and he spared him a wan smile.

Arthur helped Morveen pluck the birds, a job he loathed. Feathers flew everywhere and Aefe, who was under the table, gathered them up into piles of different colours, white, grey, brown and black. Morveen wanted her kept out of sight, because she was a-feared that one of the soldiers might be taken with her and steal her away. Piers came into the kitchen. 'I will be pleased to go hungry if it helps,' he said to Cook.

'Me too,' said Arthur.

'Me 'oo,' said Aefe and everyone laughed, except Cook.

'There will be no need of your hunger, Master Piers,' he said.

'We have much to be grateful for. We are not yet starving. Now off with you. We have work to do.'

That night after half a bowl of potage and a few shreds of cabbage, Arthur went to bed hungry. An uneasy night was spent while the foot and horse, camped in the Great Park, raided the cellars, roaring and deboshed. Arthur imagined the town would fare no better, and hoped the O'Brennans were safe. Into the darkest part of the night they waited for the worst to happen.

In the morning they awoke to silence. 'They'll be sleeping it off this morn,' Morveen said to nobody in particular, but when they got up the Great Park was empty.

'They came before cock crow,' one of the stable boys explained. 'Held a knife to me throat lest I make a noise.' He paused and looked around. Just in case. 'They said they were off to make war on the O'Carrolls.'

The Butler brothers did leave behind a handful of kerne who behaved as if they were protecting the castle. But from whom?

*

Several uneasy weeks followed. Daily they expected the Butler brothers to return. Then one day as Arthur was returning with the washer woman and an empty buck basket he found the watergate open and a barge sitting at the bank. A large man, grandly dressed in a fur-trimmed cloak, was coming down the plank. It was Oliver Grace, the Earl's closest servant. He was a man whose face rarely changed expression, so it was difficult to see how things lay. But he had been with the Earl in London so there would be news of some kind. Several pages were lined up beside Shee waiting on the bank with what gentlewomen were left in the castle. 'This is indeed a pleasure, Oliver,' Shee said to Grace as he stepped ashore.

'Aye,' Grace said. 'Call the town crier. I will go straight to the fair green to speak to the people.' He walked off, across the court towards the postern gate. Word soon spread and everyone in the castle down to the lowliest kitchen boy – Arthur – followed in his wake. They gathered townsfolk as they went and it was a strange band, with nobody knowing what to think. The question still hung over them – was the Earl dead or alive? The crier was by now running through the streets, and townsfolk left their work or came out of cottages, bemused at first, then eager to follow when they saw how large the crowd had become. At the fair green someone had placed a sturdy baggage chest onto which Oliver Grace now climbed. Arthur pushed his way to the front, leaving Morveen and the other kitchen staff in the middle of the swelling crowd. Oliver Grace held up both arms to silence the crowd. 'Good people of Carraigh,' he shouted. 'The Earl of Ormond lives!'

A cheer went up amongst the crowd. Olive Grace held his arms aloft again to quieten the people. 'My Lord is *very much* alive. He is, however, much displeased with his brothers for besmirching the good name of Butler with their treasonous acts.' At this there were murmurs of agreement. A woman beside Arthur said to another, 'Then best he return to Ireland to sort them out.' The other agreed. 'He dallies with the Queen, so.'

Grace raised his voice above the muttering. 'Sir Edmund Butler has agreed to go before an assembly of gentlemen and freeholders in Tipperary to apologise for his misdeeds.'

'I'll believe that pledge when I see it in the deed,' said a man standing behind Arthur. 'Aye,' said the two women beside him. 'Aye.'

Oliver Grace called for silence again. 'It pleases me to report that my lord remains one of the Queen's favourites.' A cheer went up at this news, but Grace stilled the crowd again. 'What is more, he has been admitted to Gray's Inn, the most illustrious inn in the metropolis. His coat of arms has been produced in glass and placed in a window at Gray's.' He paused and a few people clapped, while most were unsure if he had finished. He had not. 'What is more, Thomas Butler, Earl of Ormond, your lord, has been made a Privy Councillor for England.' This time he set his arms firmly at his side to indicate that acclamation was now possible.

The ensuing cheers began raggedly, but soon rose so as to

be heard as far away as Kilkenny. A young man ran off to the church and soon the bells rang out across the town. Morveen found Arthur and grabbed his arm as she went dancing across the green and onto the streets, Aefe sitting on her hip. They made a jolly little group, the kitchen folk skipping and dancing, dodging townspeople doing likewise. Already the tavern was filling as they passed. The pot man looked into it longingly, but Cook winked and drew him on. There was drinking to be done back in the castle kitchen, and none of your watered-down ale. The castle remained in Black Tom's firm hands, and they celebrated in style with some of the Earl's finest wines.

Chapter Ten

No matter that the Earl had sent Oliver Grace from the English court to try and control his wayward brothers, all through that summer the countryside was under siege. The Earl's closest manservant was powerless, although the castle was no longer under threat. Sir Edmund's kerne remained stubbornly behind at Carraigh, not so much to protect the castle as to sample the contents of my lord's wine cellar and the pleasures of the stews in the town. 'They'll be after getting the French pox from them strumpets,' the water boy said.

'How would you know such a thing?' the pot man asked, but the water boy just smiled a cocky smile, and went about his business.

There was scarce a soul who did not wish for the Earl's immediate return from Court, and then finally, finally word came that he was returning to Ireland to deal with his kin. Arthur was jealous of Piers who was going to Rosslare to meet the Earl when he landed. He watched the barge sail off down the Suir and walked disconsolately back into the courtyard. It would be days before they returned, and in the meantime the castle was open to attack, as were the Earl and his men: the Spaniards could get them at sea and the Butlers and Desmond once they had landed. At least Sir Edmund's kerne had crept away on receipt of the news.

Arthur picked Aefe up, put her on his shoulders and took her to meet the falcons. All was quiet in the garden and the falconer was not in the weathering yard. Aefe was frightened of the birds who batted at her, so Arthur took her for a turn around the garden showing her the leeks growing tall, ready for picking in a few weeks; the beets showing their heads above the earth. They would eat better this autumn, he hoped.

There was, in fact, little time. The castle had to be prepared for the Earl's return and the sleepy life they had been leading erupted into a storm of activity. The washer woman washed everything in sight. Cobwebs were brushed away, the old rushes burnt and the floor swept ready for fresh rushes on the day of the Earl's return. The Turkey floor carpets were beaten free of dust. Cook spent hours preparing sauces for to seep the fresh meat the farmer's butcher would bring when the Earl was nigh. Morveen and Arthur scrubbed out the kitchen, and Morveen was asked by one of the gentlewomen to help her clean the bed chambers. Arthur wondered what it was like in the keep and hoped Morveen might take him with her, but the gentlewoman hovered over her every movement so there was no opportunity.

The black cloud had lifted. The pot man whistled; Morveen sang, Cook even laughed. This was life as it was meant to be lived, it could not get any better, except that it did.

*

The staff gathered at the watergate to greet the Earl. There was not a soul left in the castle, while others had come from the town and further afield: Eoghan Mac Craith, a group of fiddlers, some pages and young gentlemen from the Kilkenny castle. They were all dressed in their finest, the rhymer in a tall beaver hat, the gentlewomen so brightly dressed that they competed with the bunting in the Earl's colours, blue and yellow, strung along the bank. The crush of people clamoured for the first sight of the barge as it rounded the bend in the river, and it was a wonder that nobody fell into the murky waters of the Suir. A cry went up, but at first all Arthur could see were the Earl's flags flapping above the barge, then he saw the Earl leaning on the front rail, dressed in the very height of London fashion, a tight doublet and short cape. Trumpeters on board heralded his arrival, the fiddlers on the bank struck up a jig and a loud cheer arose from the throng. The Earl waved as the barge drew closer and when it pulled in the young gentlemen on board threw the plank to the boatman waiting on shore, then stood in line while their lord disembarked. Behind came the barges carrying the Earl's necessities, his portable guarde, a new bed, his trunks and some livestock he had brought back with him, hounds, falcons and a couple of deer for his park.

The Earl marched down the plank and warmly shook Mister Shee's hand. 'Ah, but it's good to see you, Richard.' He took the seneschal's arm to draw him away and the crowd opened up to let them through to the watergate and on across the court to the battlement steps, where the Earl stood so all could see him.

Arthur wanted to see Piers, but the crowd pushed him along with it, so he had no choice but to follow. 'Thank you for your welcome,' the Earl said when everybody had made their way from the riverside into the court. 'It is grand to be back on Irish soil.' They all cheered, but the potman whispered to Morveen, 'Why did it take so long, then?'

'Order will be restored,' the Earl was saying. 'You may all go about your business in peace. God's peace and the Queen's.'

The crowd clapped.

'Now I have important business to attend to.' He laughed and the crowd laughed with him. They knew what business had brought him back. But it did wait. There was feasting that night with food brought from England. Grain and pickled vegetables; a salted cow and two pigs preserved the same way. It was just like the old days. When dinner had been served the staff had their own feast, the best meal they had had in weeks. Arthur took his first taste of wine that night, a special treat from Cook. 'Here is a toast to peace and good order in the countryside,' he said raising his tankard. After the third or fourth gulp, Arthur's head felt light, as did his body. He lifted Aefe into his arms and danced around the kitchen to the tune the pot man whistled. Morveen clapped, and Aefe copied her. 'I think the wine has been poisoned,' Arthur said to Morveen, as he put Aefe down. 'My head is going round and round.'

She laughed again. 'You are deboshed, me darlin'. Best sleep it off.' She helped him lie down in his usual spot, and tucked Aefe in beside him. 'Time for a little princess to go to sleep, too,' she said. Arthur wondered briefly who Morveen would be celebrating with that night. Then he slept.

Next morning he awoke with a sore head. He felt sorry for himself, but he was not the only one to suffer. Cook, most of the scullions, Morveen, the pot man and baker were all holding their heads. Just Arthur's bad fortune when he was feeling so badly for Piers to arrive in a great hurry. 'Arthur,' he said. 'My lord wants to see you.'

'What?' asked Cook.

'Are you certain?' said the pot man.

'Arthur?' Morveen's voice came out in a squeak.

'Yes. Before breakfast. He has a busy day ahead. He's away to tame his brothers.' Piers looked at Arthur. 'Better get yourself straightened though. You look like a scullion.'

'That's what he is,' said the pot man in a falsely patient tone.

Arthur was too stunned to move for a moment. Finally he asked, 'Why?'

'Because I have told him about you.'

Arthur washed his face and hands with water from the pot man's bucket. He straightened his hair, smoothed out his stockings and buttoned up his jerkin. 'That's better,' said Piers. 'Now make haste.'

At last, Arthur thought, I shall meet the Earl and see the keep from inside. They crossed the court and went in by the west door. It was dark after the bright light of morning, and it took a moment for his eyes to accustom themselves to the gloom. A little light came from the arrow slits in the wall. 'It is brighter on the floor above since the carpenters have put in the new oriel windows like those in the Great Hall.' Piers leapt lightly up the stone staircase.

Arthur kept pace holding on to the wall like a blind man feeling his way. Round and round they went, so fast that Arthur felt deboshed again. He hoped the Earl would not look into his soul and see what lurked there – guilt mostly for being in less than perfect condition. How should he address him? What does Piers call him? My lord! And Piers has been acknowledged as the illegitimate son. So, my lord, it is. And how to bow? A low sweep? A little bob? A flourish of the arms? There wasn't time to ask Piers. They were approaching the Earl's chamber. Piers knocked on the door which was opened by one of the Earl's gentlemen, who looked Arthur up and down disapprovingly.

The Earl was sitting on a straight backed chair at the end of the chamber, to one side was the biggest, most ornately carved cupboard Arthur had ever seen, and to the other side a studded trunk half open with clothes spilling out of it. The Earl's man was unpacking. Piers led the way.

'Ah, the boy,' said the Earl as Arthur bowed deeply before him, mimicking Piers.

'Arthur, my lord,' Piers said.

The Earl looked even more swarthy in his indoor clothes. He did not even wear a ruff and his chest which could be seen beneath his shirt was as black and hairy as his face. His moustache was not standing to attention as it usually did, but drooped over his beard. His dark eyes shone with…Arthur could not be sure… delight, amusement? Piers stood close to him and the Earl put an arm around his shoulder.

'Has he a tongue?' the Earl asked Piers.

'Yes, my lord. And a brain. For he can read, as well as his way with the birds.'

Arthur coughed. 'My lord,' he said bowing again. 'I…I am pleased to make your acquaintance.'

The Earl laughed. His man who was standing by laughed too, but not as heartily and you could see the laughter had not reached his eyes the way it had the Earl's.

'How is your reel foot?'

'It is much improved, my lord.

'That is good. Can you ride?'

'No my lord. Although I have been astride a horse. Behind Piers, my lord.'

'What are you most afraid of?' asked the Earl.

Arthur thought a moment. 'Wolves,' he said, not quite lying, and then sensing that the Earl would appreciate the truth, '...and your brothers, my lord. I am a-feared they will besiege the castle.'

'I think that fear can be allayed now that I am returned.' The Earl took his arm away from Piers and turned to his gentleman. 'Make the necessary arrangements. He has much to catch up, but I like the cut of him. Get him a set of new clothes. When do lessons start again?'

'The tutor is on hand awaiting the return of the pages, my lord,' the gentleman answered.

'Very well. Those who are not attending me at Kilkenny should get back to their lessons.' He stood. 'Now I must prepare myself.' He dismissed the boys with a wave of his hand.

Outside the chamber Arthur whispered to Piers, 'What is meant by that?'

'You are to join the household.'

'Amn't I already part of the household?'

'No.'

'What will happen?'

'You will leave the kitchen and come and live in the keep with the rest of the pages.'

*

So Arthur said goodbye to Morveen who kissed him as if he were going on a long journey. 'But I shall not be gone far. You'll see me when I come into the privy kitchen to collect the food for the great hall.'

'It will be different.' Morveen started to cry.

'I thought you would be pleased.'

'I am,' she sobbed. 'These are tears of happiness. It is no more than you deserve.'

'I'll miss you…and Aefe.'

'But you will be made a gentleman. Your life will be easier.'

Arthur reported to the Earl's gentlemen, and his life as a page began. He was given a new set of clothing, but as he well knew clothes alone did not make a gentleman. Neither did they make you happy. Piers had returned to Kilkenny now that it was safe from the Butler brothers, and Arthur felt very much alone. First came the lessons with the tutor, and Arthur was so woefully behind the other pages that his face flushed whenever he was asked a question he could not answer. The other pages ignored him, or worse laughed at his mistakes. There was Greek and Latin and the Gaelic, too. Only English was allowed to be spoken within the Pale and the Liberalities, but the Earl was most tolerant on this matter and even spoke Gaelic himself. Arthur spoke it fluently but had never seen it written down. On paper it was a most complex thing which made his head reel. Then there was the horse-riding, again the other pages laughed every time he fell off. Even sleeping in the attic was not as attractive as he expected, it was stuffy and overcrowded and he yearned for his sleeping space under the table next to Aefe and Morveen. He missed the pot man's sarcasm, and Cook's stony outlook on life. Even though he caught glimpses of them when he went to get the dishes to be served at the Earl's table, he never had a chance to talk. He felt a pang of deep regret as he remembered the night he danced with Aefe on his shoulders: he would never be permitted to do that again. Even with the food he was clumsy and spilt liquid if the dish was over full. The only time he outshone the other pages was when they took the falcons out. While the other boys seemed to be either afraid of the birds or indifferent to them, Arthur was in his element.

Nobody knew what the Earl said to his brothers, but they surrendered to him outside Kilkenny, and he was soon back at Carraigh. Whilst serving at table Arthur heard much more of the goings on in the world than he ever had from Bren, and in thinking that he felt bereft again that he would never more be able to visit the O'Brennans. He might have gained something by becoming a page, and he must not be ungrateful for the opportunity, but he had also lost a great deal.

This evening they were serving a supper of baked trout, roast rabbit, gammon pie and a salad with borage and hyssop. Arthur set one gammon pie at the bottom end of the table. 'Sidney's arbitrary rule is a concern,' the Earl was saying. 'Granting land to the English as he did Peter Carew. No wonder my brothers behaved like Irish rascals.'

'We of the Kilkenny gentry stood tall for the Crown, my lord,' said a visiting gentleman seated next to him.

'Yes, for now. But if Carew maintains his aggressive stance…'

'That adventurer!' said the gentleman on the Earl's other side.

'Yes, that adventurer, and others like him, no doubt. If Sir Henry gets his way. Where then Kilkenny loyalty?'

Arthur delivered his dish and took some empty plates down to the privy kitchen where he found Morveen. 'This is a surprise,' Arthur said smiling. 'You don't often venture here.'

'I have come to tell you that Aefe is going to be fostered.'

'Where to?'

'A Waterford family. They are very kind...'

'But you will miss her?'

'It is the Irish way, as well you know.'

'Hurry up there,' Cook shouted. 'The trout is getting cold.'

Arthur gave Morveen a sympathetic glance and took up the dish. When he got back to the Great Hall, the Earl was saying, 'I must spend more time in Ireland.'

'That is good news, my lord,' said a gentleman further down the table.

'Aye,' said the Earl, 'but I will miss life at Court.' He speared a piece of pastry on the end of his eating knife.

'Is there any chance Her Majesty will come to Ireland?' asked one of the men close to Arthur. 'Now that the north range is ready?'

'It is possible.'

Arthur began clearing empty dishes to make room for more.

'You certainly have a way with Her Majesty,' said another of the men.

'Aye and while Sir Henry is her representative in Ireland I shall have to find a way with him also.'

Arthur left the hall, his arms full of dirty dishes and the laughter brought about by the Earl's remark followed him down the stairs. He felt sad about Aefe, but Waterford was not so far away. Not like London. And one grand thing about being in the household, was that when the Queen did come to the manor house he would be much closer to her than if he were still in the kitchen.

PART TWO

Bristol, England
August 1574

Chapter Eleven

Five years would pass before Arthur had his chance to see Good Queen Bess. Finally he found himself at Quay Head in Bristol as part of the Earl's entourage to honour the Queen who was on progress through the Western Counties and due to arrive in Bristol on Saturday. The Earl was already with her at Bath, and his retinue had two days to settle into Bristol, the second largest city in England after London.

So this was England. Two and three-storey merchants' houses towered over the opposite side of the harbour. The quay was lined with ships, their masts tall, sails furled. It was a-jostle with pack horses and people. Merchants supervised men unloading goods, customs officers kept a tally of bales of wool on their way out and barrels of wine on their way in. The *Redcliffe,* the ship they arrived on, carried carpets, tapestries, cushions and coverlets woven in Kilkenny with the help of imported Flemish weavers and the goods sat in divers trunks beside the ship. Arthur sat on a trunk while they waited for the cart that was to carry them to their lodgings. A man with a strange animal on his shoulder pushed his way past. 'What is that?' Arthur asked Piers who was standing nearby, a foot on one of the trunks.

'That's a monkey. Her Majesty is most fond of monkeys.' Arthur would have liked a closer look at the odd creature, but the man was soon lost in the crush. Ducks and geese quacked and cackled from a crate, and a donkey brayed close by. At least Arthur knew what they were. It was not so much the noise or the throng that bothered Arthur, it was the smell. It was an indescribable mix of dung, salty water, rotting food, the stench of sweating men. A rat ran out from behind a barrel and scuttled up the plank into the *Redcliffe* completely unafraid of the people about, and obviously in its element.

Also on the wharf was a band of players brought by sea from Swansea for the Queen's entertainment. They wore suits of yellow, blue and red and did a little turn as they waited for their stage and props to be off-loaded. Arthur stood and joined the others to watch them juggle, tumble and dance, but the Earl's young men turned away as soon as one of the players took off his cap and held it out in the hope of payment. The young men had little money to spare for watching such antics, and Arthur hoped the Queen would reward the players well.

He preferred not to dwell on his voyage across the Irish Sea. He was no sailor. Just as well most of the Earl's young men fought on land. He had yet to see battle, but with the ongoing troubles in Ireland he knew it would not be long. Piers had been fielded many times and told him tales of glorious battles well fought. Only last year he had fought with Piers Butler of Butlerswood, one of the Earl's faithful kin, at Ballymack, where they killed Shane McOwen McHugh, who had seized the attainted property of the rebel Thomas Comerford. Here, too, they captured Moriertagh McArt Boy, a notorious traitor who led the kerne in the Butler revolt. They sent McArt Boy to the Lord Deputy in Dublin for his execution, and Piers was promoted to horse. Arthur both admired and envied Piers these experiences, what must it be like to look such evil in the eye, and overcome it?

Arthur was now seventeen and had conquered all the manly arts, standing tall, if sloping slightly to one side, amongst the other young courtiers at the Earl's court. He was accustomed to travelling between Carraigh and Kilkenny and some of the other twenty-five castles the Earl owned. He acquitted himself well at tilts; had a special way with the horses and rode now as if born to the saddle. He excelled at archery and of course falconry; he could read somewhat in Latin, Greek and Gaelic; was competent in English. He had long since read the stories of King Arthur and the Knights of the Round Table, and bore his name with pride; a thorough gentleman with little trace of the scullion he once was, but that did not mean he had totally turned his back on Morveen and Aefe. He saw them when he could and was looking forward to telling them about Bristol and the Queen's visit.

'The Quay is exceptionally busy,' Piers said. He had been to Bristol before, so he would know. 'It will be on account of the Queen.'

Their cart arrived at last and some hefty local men loaded it with their trunks and chattels. Like the merchants of the Earl's estates, his young gentlemen were freemen of Bristol, and as part of the Earl's retinue they would be treated with great respect. There were ten of them and they climbed into the cart with some excitement. 'Is that where we are headed?' Arthur pointed to a castle high on the hill ahead.

'I fear not. The castle is in disrepair,' Piers explained. 'Nobody has lived there for a hundred years.'

'The Queen is to stay in the Great House at St Augustine's Back,' offered one of the other young gentlemen. 'I suppose my lord will reside there too as a member of her Court on Progress.'

'John Young built the house especially for her visit,' one of the others said.

'Just as my lord has done at Carraigh,' said Arthur. 'Do you think she will come to Ireland?'

Some said, yes they did, and others said no, it was not a safe place for the English monarch. Piers remained silent and Arthur wondered if he knew something the others did not.

They had not far to go. Their lodgings were not the most comfortable, but the city of Bristol was full to overflowing and they had to make the most of what they could get. There were two saving graces, one that they were on the Quay just across the river from the house where the Queen and their Earl were to stay, the other that their landlord, Giles Codrington, required no payment. It was an honour, he told them, as he greeted them, to have the Earl's young gentlemen lodge with him. 'He has interests in Ireland,' Piers said in an aside to Arthur, 'and is no doubt looking for some concession from my lord. He owns a store on the quay and comes each year to the fair in Kilkenny with a miscellany of goods for sale. No doubt at great profit.' Piers grinned.

The young gentlemen settled in and waited with barely suppressed excitement for the Queen's arrival.

Saturday dawned cool and fine, but by the time the young gentlemen of the Earl's retinue were ready to make their way to Lawford's Gate to greet the Queen the sky had darkened and the sun shone fitfully between the clouds. The young men were accompanied to their welcoming position by an assistant to one of the Common Councillors, a fussy little man dressed in the city livery with a copatain hat perched precariously on his head. Arthur was excited, but his excitement was dampened by the grumbling assistant who moaned breathlessly as they walked. 'Corporation's spent a fortune on this visit,' he puffed. 'No,' he contradicted himself, 'it's the people of the wards who have paid. Paint and gild for High Cross, Newgate…and the rest.' He put a hand up to make sure his copatain was still in place.

'The good people of Bristol are to be congratulated,' said Piers. 'The city is looking very smart.'

'And how much sand do you suppose has gone onto these streets to level them?' Then without pause the councillor's assistant answered his own question. 'Fifty-two lighter loads. Not to mention the cost of the gun powder, the cannons and city uniforms for four hundred infantry.' One hand on his hat, he spat his disgust into the sandy street.

'Somewhat treasonous talk,' Piers said softly to Arthur.

'That gun powder has already killed ten men at the Pelican this morn. There is talk of a plot against the Queen.'

'Twill be the Irish that gets the blame,' Piers said in another aside, 'if that piece of gossip is true. Be wary.'

The streets were thronged with excited people. Arthur had never seen so many people in the same place at the one time, and he dodged around a group of country folk obviously dressed in their best smocks, as the councillor's assistant cut a swathe right through them. Not everyone was going in the same direction, but all were obviously looking for a vantage point. Arthur heard one poorly but neatly dressed man say to his companion, 'No use heading for the Gate, all the gentry will be there and we won't see a thing.'

'Try Frome Gate,' someone suggested. 'The Grammar boys have rhymes for Her Majesty a-waiting there.'

A clutch of youths who obviously had had too much strong ale for breakfast sang bawdy songs. 'Hie,' one of them called after the councillor's man, 'you look like you know the best spot. Wither goest?'

'Lawford's Gate. Where else? And we'll get there too late if we can't get through this mob.'

'We shall follow thee,' the youth said.

And so they arrived at the gate, not with the decorum the occasion demanded, but with a raggle-taggle band of followers. A considerable crowd had already assembled, held in check by the city's pike men whose weapons rested against their shoulders. The councillor's assistant elbowed himself to the front amidst curses and moans. But it was obvious from the young men's clothing and the official dress of the assistant that they were important so the crowd reluctantly made way, and by the time they struggled through they had left their followers behind.

Theirs was an ideal position in the front row of the seething crowd, just inside the city gate through which the Queen would enter. The gate gleamed in its new paint and gilt, opposite were tiered seats where the gentlemen of Bristol sat, and a little further beyond was a dais set with a throne-like chair piled high with cushions. Her Majesty should be at St Lawrence's Hospital by now,' the councillor's assistant said. 'She is to change out of her travelling dress there.' He looked anxiously towards the town. 'Mr Thomas Kelke should be here. He's the mayor.' The crowd pushed forward, sending the pages stumbling into the backs of the infantry. 'Steady, steady,' called the councillor's assistant. 'Else you'll feel the tip of yon lance,' and the crowd took a communal step back.

A cheer went up, and soon the mayor, aldermen, members of the Common Council and the Recorder, Mr John Popham, as their guide was quick to tell them, came into view. The mayor indicated with an imperious wave of his hand that the men were to sit. From beyond the city wall a cannon fired and they heard the sound of musket shots and trumpets faint at first, but growing louder. All heads turned towards Lawford's Gate and a hush fell over the crowd. She was coming.

Arthur was shaking. It had been years since he last heard Morveen's story of his arrival into the world, but he had never forgotten it. Surely the Queen would stop and talk with him, and Piers who was in the same situation. Arthur glanced at him to see his eyes shining and a broad smile on his face. Arthur held one shaking hand with the other to calm them. Aye, Piers had the right response, it was a joyous occasion.

There came the sound of horses and ragged cheers from those who were forced to wait outside the gate. The trumpets grew louder still; with them now the rattle of drum rolls and, as if on cue, the sun came out from behind the clouds. First through the gate were page boys strewing rose petals in the Queen's path, then some of the infantry, wearing the Queen's coat-of-arms on their black and red coats, carrying gilt halberts with their heads held high. An escort on horseback held the Queen's ensign aloft, followed by three gentlemen, conveying the royal sceptre and sword. The crowd became restless but took their cue from Mayor Kelke and did not applaud.

Then there she was, sitting sideways on a white horse, the bright blue saddle beneath her trimmed with silver. Cheers erupted from the crowd, people cried out, 'Good Queen Bess' and 'God Bless

You, Your Majesty.' Trumpeters blew their loudest, drums rolled and the clamour was deafening, but Elizabeth's horse, led by a page, was calm and steady and the Queen smiled down at her people, waving and nodding. She was dressed in red and gold, a high ruff around her neck and a small crown perched on her red hair. Her face was white as plaster and she was much smaller than Arthur had imagined her to be. She looked like a child perched atop the charger.

Men took off their hats and threw them in the air cheering. Piers doffed his hat, and Arthur belatedly followed suit, willing the Queen to look at him. She looked right and left, hand raised in a salute, but did not meet Arthur's eager gaze. In her wake, flags flying like sails on a ship, came her retinue of nobles. The Earl was close behind her and he *did* notice the men of his household, giving them a knowing nod as he passed. When the last of the entourage was through the gate the councillor's man led Arthur and the other young men in his charge to a spot almost in front of the dais. Courtiers helped the Queen dismount and climb the dais. In spite of her size she was a magnificent presence as she sat on the wide, cushioned makeshift throne and smiled at the assembled company.

With a gracious gesture she beckoned for the mayor to step forward. His former dignity seemed to have deserted him and he went before Elizabeth nervously, bowing almost to the ground before handing her a gilt mace. Another cheer went up; more hats in the air. One hat fell at the feet of the Queen's horse and it made to shy, but the page holding the horse pulled it down, and Arthur wished he could have been in charge – then the animal would never have shied. The crowd held its collective breath for a moment, the horse stilled and the Queen handed the mace back to the mayor. Another cheer rose into the air and the mayor knelt at the Queen's side. The city Recorder stepped up onto the scaffold and addressed the Queen. 'Your Most Royal Highness, the Mayor, Councillors and good people of Bristol bask in the glory of your presence...'

The Queen seemed a shimmering apparition, scarcely mortal. The sun glistened on the jewels and the gold and silver thread on her bodice which made it hard to watch her for any length of time. As the Recorder droned on; the apparition shone and Arthur thought he might faint from the heat and the push of the crowd. What an embarrassment that would be. It was one way to get her to notice him, but what would she think of him then? She had said seventeen years ago – take him away I don't want ever to see him again, and if he fainted now that would prove her right. He took a deep breath, stood taller and listened again to the Recorder's oration. He was presenting the Queen with a splendid purse of silk and gold containing, he said, £100.

'I thank you, Mr Recorder.' The Queen's voice was strong. 'And I thank the City of Bristol for this right and royal welcome.' She nodded at the Recorder. The welcoming ceremony was over and he was to help her down from the dais and back on to her horse. Once she was seated on the charger again, Mayor Kelke led off. Then came the Queen, the Common Council, the trumpeters, nobility on horseback and lastly those on foot. Behind then followed the spectators, jostling for a good position. Arthur lost the Councillor's assistant, and soon lost sight of Piers and the others. A lad about his own age fell into step beside him. 'You are one of the Earl of Ormond's gentlemen, are you not?'

'Aye,' Arthur responded 'Are you acquainted with my lord?'

'Not at all, but we see his livery around these parts when he's rushing off to London to visit the Queen. It is indeed an honour to have you here.'

Arthur remembered the talk of an Irish plot. 'Yes, my lord is one of Her Majesty's most faithful subjects,' he said loudly hoping that others around would also hear.

'I believe so,' said the lad. 'Did you hear this morning's explosion?'

'I did not.'

'Some say it was a papist plot.'

Arthur wondered if the good people of Bristol knew of the religious leniency which held in Ireland. An Irish plot and a papist plot might be deemed one and the same thing. 'I heard on excellent authority that it was gunpowder stored for Her Majesty's entertainment gone off early. Sadly some men were killed.'

'Methinks if you scratch any man hereabout you would find a papist not far beneath the surface,' the lad said.

Arthur kept his silence.

'Then again,' the lad continued, 'there was much rejoicing here when the Queen was excommunicated by the pope those four years back.'

The procession stopped in front of them. Ahead, on horseback the Queen turned to face the crowd. She looked down at someone standing below her. 'Oh dreary me,' said the lad. 'This is High Cross. Methinks we are going to be treated to some of the most awful twaddle from Thomas Churchyard. The City has paid him a mighty sum to create orations and poetry for Her Majesty.'

'I had better find my other gentlemen,' Arthur said.

'Wait a while, and have a laugh with me. A gentleman like you would find Thomas Churchyard amusing, methinks.' But the pressing crowd swallowed the lad up and Arthur was on his own again. The lad was right, the poetry was dreadful although the Queen smiled sweetly all the while. Eoghan Mac Craith would have done better. Arthur tried to locate the Earl. It was easier to spot the nobility on horseback, but as they all had their backs to him Arthur could not tell one from the other. The interminable poetry finished and they moved on to the Frome Gate where a platform had been erected at the entrance to the Grammar School. Three fresh-faced grammar schoolboys representing, they said, 'Salutation', 'Gratulation' and 'Obedient Good Will' began their poetical orations in what turned out to be far too many rhyming couplets. When Obedient Good Will stepped forward for the fourth time and took breath to begin anew, the Queen held up her hand and cut him short. She gave a stony nod as an indication to the mayor that it was time to move on. Perhaps she was hungry, for soon after the procession reached the Great House on St. Augustine's Back. Cannon and musketry saluted her arrival with deafening peals and filled the air with acrid smoke. The people coughed and flapped their arms, but Her Majesty smiled and waved to the crowd, before she was led inside and the gates were firmly locked.

The crowd began to disperse, slowly at first, as if hoping for a reappearance, but when it became clear that the show was over for now, they walked off.

'They'll be at their supper now.' It was Piers 'And I must say I am ravenous myself. Come,' he held out an arm to Arthur. 'Our guide and friend tells us that we are to dine quite royally ourselves in honour of the occasion.'

'What…what did you think? Of her?'

'She is just what I expected,' said Piers confidently.

'In what way?

'Ah…Royal, I suppose.'

'But how is that different? From…the Earl, for example?'

'Well, they *are* cousins…but she…she…shines.'

'It's all the gold and precious jewels. Anyone could shine dressed like that.'

'Arthur,' Piers reproved. 'She is the Queen…'

'And your…'

'Monarch.' Piers clapped an arm around Arthur's shoulder. 'Now let's go and partake of this right royal feast promised us.'

'All I can say,' said Arthur as they joined the rest of their retinue, 'is I am glad I am not royal if it means having to listen to endless twaddle such as that Thomas Churchyard presented. Or the Grammar school boys.'

'Poor ducks. You could see the wind taken out of their sails when the Queen stopped the lad in mid-breath.'

'I suppose she has a surfeit of such rhymes,' Arthur said.

'Yes, and as an accomplished poet herself it must have been agony for her to hear the language tortured so. Oh look.' He pointed at a procession of slow moving carts rattling past. 'Her Majesty's baggage train. See there is her oak bed. I've heard over two hundred carts come in her wake.' They counted them as they passed, but had only got to forty-nine; they were still coming in a long slow line, when one of the other young men ran back to hurry them along, and they all sprinted to their lodgings.

A feast indeed awaited them. Mr Codrington had spared not a penny. The young men ate fish, quail, crab, and a spit-roasted lamb, washed down with wine. And more wine. Their host joined them and he also drank freely.

'It's hard to think,' he said raising his glass in yet another toast to the Earl, 'of another noble man so blessed as your Black Tom Butler.' He took a long pull at his tankard. 'He has, with Her Majesty's approval…' which words he heavily emphasised '…overcome an act of attainder and thus saved the skins of his traitorous brothers. Who else could do such a thing? He is a powerful man amongst men and you, my dear guests, are lucky to be so closely associated with him.' With that he drank another toast. This one to the young gentlemen entrusted to his care. The supper lasted most of the night. Some of the party drank a great deal. Arthur, wary of wine since he took too much with Morveen those many years back, remained relatively sober. It had been an exhausting day but when Arthur finally went to bed that night he could not sleep. Bright in his mind, as he tossed and turned, was the image of the Queen sparkling in the sun. Somehow he must meet her.

*

The Queen spent a week in Bristol and during that time there were plays, sumptuous feasts and visits to churches. The Earl's retinue followed the entertainments as faithfully as the Queen herself. They were there when the Queen described St Mary's as the fairest, biggest, most beautiful parish church in the land; they were there for every mock battle staged under the military theme that was the prominent form of entertainment. There were mock battles on land and water; so many of them that finally even the glitter of the Queen seemed to fade. A scaffold of strong timber had been built at The Marsh as a box for the Queen's comfort while she watched. 'No doubt at great expense to the city,' Piers noted laughing to Arthur. The Marsh was a-flutter with flags. The mock-warriors, on horses sporting red and white caparisons emblazoned with the city's crest, wore tunics of the same design and carried lances striped in like colours. Common spectators stood or sat on benches according to their station, while courtiers sat in the Queen's box. The Earl was often at Elizabeth's side. She would lean over and whisper something softly in his ear, but he was not the only one to receive her attention. The rivalry amongst members of her entourage was apparent in the thunderous looks bestowed when she favoured one of her nobles over the other. The ladies-in-waiting were hardly to be seen, as she fluttered her fan at the men, and Arthur thought such coquettish behaviour would not be accepted from anyone else, though he felt disloyal thinking so. He had given up all hope of an audience with the Queen, and that left a dark stain in his heart.

*

While they were at their midday dinner on the fifth day of the Queen's visit the Earl strode into the room, waving a hand to indicate they were to remain seated. He took a chicken leg from Piers' plate and sat on the one empty seat. As he chewed he spoke to them in Gaelic, 'I see they are feeding you well.' Arthur looked around to make sure nobody was listening. Gaelic was an almost treasonous tongue, but the Earl seemed to get away with a great deal under the Queen's gaze.

Then the Earl said in English, 'My lads. You are to attend the tilts this afternoon. Her Majesty has agreed to see for herself just what fine young gentlemen Ireland breeds on her soil. Present yourselves at The Marsh at two of the clock. I will select our team then. Mr Mayor is none too happy, he has men trained at the expense of the Common Council to impress the Queen, but we will not hog the Queen's light too long.'

'And do we not have the freedom of the city, my lord?' Piers said. 'Is there not some obligation?'

The Earl stood. 'The obligation, my lad, is to your Queen. If she wants to see her loyal Irish subjects at the tilts, she shall.'

'My Lord, is it a traditional tilt?' Arthur asked. 'Or one of those silly mock battles.'

'Traditional, of course. We will leave the silly mock battles, as you call them to the mayor and his infantry. Do your utmost.'

Chapter Twelve

When they reached The Marsh that afternoon the Queen was in her box and yet another mock battle was in progress. How tenacious the Queen was sitting through the same thing day after day, smiling and clapping delightedly as if each new clash was the first. Arthur had the nerves on him hoping he would be chosen to joust. It would perhaps depend on the horses and armour available, and he knew others were better jousters: Piers for one. But what he had over them, and he was sure the Earl knew this, was that he could handle a new horse better than any. The Earl was on the dais with the Queen and eventually she leaned close and whispered something to him. He nodded, stood and stepped down from the scaffolding, then went and spoke to the blacksmith standing by with the armour.

Arthur held his breath as the Earl strode towards them. 'Piers,' the Earl said, signalling for him to stand to one side. 'Charles. John. And...Arthur.' They stood together, a small select group. Arthur looked over at the Queen to see if she was watching, but she was laughing with one of the noble men. 'The blacksmith will give you what armour they have available. And the cavalleria will provide horses,' said the Earl. 'Make me proud,' and he walked back to the scaffolding to join the Queen.

The four young men walked across to the tilt yard. As this was an entertainment there would be no blood drawn. In fact it would be like another mock battle, with the English pitched against the Irish, but this time with the regulations required of modern tilts. Arthur determined to show the English, and the Queen, just what Irish mettle was made of, and that his heroic name befitted him.

But when they reached the yard Arthur was disappointed to find they were to run the *quintain*. Even fighting the Earl's own men would be better that pitting himself against a dummy, although the *quintain* could give you a head wallop fit to knock you dead if you did not get out of its way soon enough after impact. The keeper of the horse led out two horses, a medium-weight charger and a more solid destrier. He tethered them to a pole, then went back to the tent for two more. As Arthur approached the charger shied; the other animal stood placidly. Unlike the horses they had watched through the mock battles, these two wore caparisons of plain blue. Arthur wished they could run with the Earl's colours, but their inclusion in the Queen's spectacle had been unexpected, so they would have to make do. The horses had no need of the *chanfron* because their heads would not need protecting from the swinging *quintain*. The counter weight was set so that the dummy hit the rider, not the horse. 'That charger looks like the horse for you, Arthur,' said Piers joining him. He put out a hand to the charger. It tried to rear but was held down by the tether. Arthur took the rope and loosened it. 'There, boy,' he said calmly. The horse stood still but looked at them with wild eyes.

The armourer came up with two lances fitted. 'Try these for weight,' he said, and they sorted out the order of run accordingly. Arthur and Charles were to use the lighter lance, while Piers and John would take the heavier one. That meant that Piers would go first and Arthur last.

The keeper brought out two more horses, both the heavier war horses. "Who is the best horseman?' he asked the young men.

'Piers,' the three said in unison.

'Ah,' said Piers. 'I might be once I am in the saddle, but Arthur is the one to tame that charger.'

Arthur approached the charger again. It shied, then steadied and allowed him to stroke its muzzle. 'You are a grand boy,' he said quietly. 'Will you let me ride you?' The horse eyed him suspiciously.

'Has this horse been fully broken?' he asked the keeper.

'Aye, but not for long. He is still chary of strangers. He be a good test of the young Irish gentleman's skills. And,' he paused, 'it will add to the spectacle.'

Arthur turned back to the horse. 'Her Majesty is waiting,' he said softly. He mounted. The horse reared, but Arthur held it firm. It whinnied and pawed the ground. Arthur leaned over and whispered, 'I will not hurt you.'

Piers and the other two mounted the destriers, and lined up. Now they could look towards the Queen, who glimmered in the sun, her white face a mask. She waved her fan and Piers took off. It did not take long for him to reach speed. The crowd roared, although Arthur could not be certain what they were roaring for – Piers' success or his failure. The hoof beats echoed through the earth and the horse kicked up clouds of sand as it raced towards the target. Piers struck it and spurred the horse onward as the *quintain* spun around. He escaped, pulled the horse in and rode past the Queen, to whom he bowed before trotting back to the others. Charles' horse was the heaviest mount and much slower to build up speed. He struck the target but the horse was not quick enough and the swinging *quintain* hit the young man on the back and threw him to the ground. There was a pause in proceedings while a steward went to help Charles. It had looked like a vicious strike, but Charles stood, dusted himself down and walked back to the Queen's box. He bowed low, but she was not looking at him, and he walked, head down, to the area where the Earl's men were seated.

After John's clean run came Arthur's. When he kicked the horse it bucked almost unseating him. He settled himself again and held the horse steady. He waited a moment more before kicking the charger again. It raced towards the target. Arthur hit the target square, hoping the impact would not frighten the horse further, but it hesitated and the *quintain* swung around and struck Arthur in the back. Arthur heard the gasp from the crowd almost before he realised he had been hit. The horse bolted with Arthur clinging on in a most undignified manner. They were at the line of trees that edged The Marsh before he managed to rein in the panicked animal, and almost into the river before it stopped. He settled the horse then dismounted and walked it back to the tilt yard. There would be no victorious walk past the Queen.

The other young men were unhappy that they had not been allowed to joust. Piers had a word with the Earl, and next day, the Queen's last, he said that tilts would be held and they could all take part. It was to be an open joust, without a tilt barrier.

'I'll take the same horse, if I may,' Arthur said to the keeper when they arrived at The Marsh.

'No. I'll take him,' said Piers. 'You must make good at the tilts, Arthur.'

'That is not fair to the horse. He was getting used to me. We must not frighten him with a new rider,' Arthur insisted. 'Albeit, one of the best riders in Ireland,' he added quickly.

'If not all of England,' Charles offered.

Piers laughed. 'Flattery does not flatter the flatterer,' he said. Then he turned back to Arthur. 'If you are certain.'

'Aye. I am.'

Their lances this time were fitted with a coronal. They were given some light armour designed to break apart on impact, and a helmet. Arthur preferred to joust without a helmet, but the armourer insisted he wear one.

'It protects the eyes,' Piers said. 'Ride low and lean forwards. Straighten up just before you strike.'

Arthur was glad of another chance to prove himself before the Queen. This time they were to joust against each other and the two best would go to tilts against the finest of Bristol's men. Away from the spectators the Earl's men practised with the ring, riding past the dangling hoop with the intention of spearing it. Piers did this every time. Arthur missed the first few times because he was trying to ride with the helmet, and the horse was still skittish, but soon he could recognise the right moment to straighten up and spear the ring. The horses were wearing the protective *chanfron* and the charger became calmer because it could only see what lay ahead of it. Arthur hoped he would be matched with Piers, but found himself against Charles with mixed feelings. He would like to see his opponent win today, but not at *his* expense.

Just before the tournament began the Earl strode over to his men. 'Remember you are doing this for your Queen and the pride of Ireland.' The charger was behaving well, but as they lined up, one at each end of the tilt yard, it reared again, surprising Arthur and nearly throwing him. He settled it before the signal to go, and prayed to God for the best outcome.

His charger was much quicker than Charles' mount. He could feel the earth pounding beneath him as the hooves thudded measure for measure with his heartbeat. He could hear the horse breathing and the crowd baying. They were well past the halfway mark when the two horses crossed. He lifted his head, pushed the lance forward and struck Charles to the ground. He galloped on a pace then pulled the horse in and rode sedately past the Queen. She nodded at him, and he rode back to the others.

Piers won his tilt, but there were several other rounds to go before both he and Arthur were announced the Earl's two champions. Surely the Queen must be pleased that her two were the finest. All that remained was to beat the Bristol men. While they waited for that elimination to take place, Arthur stayed with the charger, taking him through his paces patiently and quietly building his trust. 'Don't let me down, now,' he said as the horse let him rub his muzzle. 'This is important, so.' The horse was tiring and Arthur did not want it worn out before the final joust but he was glad that some of its anger had dissipated with the energy.

The keeper of the horse took the charger off him not long before the final joust. Arthur followed him to the tent, not quite trusting him, but was delighted when he saw that the keeper was changing the caparison for the Earl's colours. Arthur remembered the Earl's words. 'You are doing this for the Queen and the pride of Ireland.' He mounted the horse and rode proudly out of tent in the Earl's regalia. 'You might be an English horse,' Arthur leaned down to whisper in the charger's ear, 'but you have the heart and spirit of an Irish one.'

Piers, too, fought in the Earl's colours, and they defied the patriotic cries of the crowd and beat their English opponents soundly.

The spectators applauded half-heartedly, but the Queen clapped merrily as Piers and Arthur rode up to her box. She smiled down at them, fondly, it seemed to Arthur as he bowed. The Earl stood and walked to the edge of the scaffolding. 'Your Majesty, may I present Piers, gentleman of my chamber.' Piers bowed deeply.

'Well done, young man,' the Queen said, waving her fan at him.

'And,' said the Earl, 'this young gentleman is Arthur.'

'You managed that lively horse well,' said the Queen. 'It took courage to ride it a second time.'

'Your Majesty.' Arthur swept a low bow, so low his face rested in the horse's mane. So she had noticed; he had made an impression, but when he lifted his head the Queen had lost interest and was flirting with another courtier. The audience was over.

Arthur kicked the charger into action and without waiting to be dismissed rode it back to the keeper. Piers hesitated, then followed him. 'Well done, Arthur,' he said as they dismounted. 'I thought the horse had the better of you for a second time earlier. But you have ridden him like a hero.'

Arthur did not answer. He handed the reins to the keeper and strode off in as manly a way as his foot would allow.

Chapter Thirteen

The voyage home was no better than the voyage out had been: Arthur was seasick all the way, but when they finally reached Waterford he felt as if he had grown up. Bristol had changed his outlook on the world. He was ready to go into the field.

Arthur's heart lifted when he saw the castle at Carraigh ahead of him as the boat rounded the bend in the river. The Earl's other young men were also excited to be home and as the boat arrived at the watergate they set up a cheer.

Morveen was on the pier, and with her stood a tall young girl with dark ginger hair tied back with a ribbon. 'Art. Arty,' Morveen called. 'You have grown much. Say hello to Aefe.'

'Aefe?' Arthur ran down the plank towards them. She stood shyly to one side. 'You are very pretty. And how you've grown!'

Aefe walked slowly towards him. She quickly pecked at his cheek before withdrawing again. He tried to work out how old she now was...ten...eleven..?

'You are handsome, so you are,' Morveen said as she finally came close. 'Aye, you are,' she said as if she could not quite believe it herself. She took his arm and led him through the watergate. 'Come and let the kitchen see how you have changed.'

'I had better get my trunk,' he said pointing to it sitting on the pier.

'You are a gentleman. Let someone else pick it up,' and Morveen pulled him across the court. Aefe followed. 'We've all missed you,' Morveen said. 'Even the falcons, so the falconer says, does he not, Aefe?' She laughed and it was such a beautiful sound that Arthur laughed too and Aefe joined in.

'So our gentleman is back,' said the pot man.

'We have not the time to be admiring young gentlemen, handsome or not,' said Cook. 'We have supper to prepare,' but Arthur could see that he was not displeased.

'Could you spare Aefe?'

'For a short while,' Cook growled.

'Then come with me to the battlements, Aefe,' Arthur said. They left the kitchen and crossed the yard to the battlement steps. The girl was halfway up before Arthur reached the steps, and he quickened his pace to catch up with her. When they were both standing on the battlements Aefe turned to Arthur.

'I love it up here,' she said and Arthur thought it fitting that those should be the first words this new, pretty Aefe spoke to him.

'There is not a place fairer in the world,' he said and for a long time they stood without speaking, watching the light die over the castle park and the town.

'What is it like?' Aefe said finally.

'Bristol?'

'No. Being a member of my lord's retinue.'

'There are good times and bad. I would rather be my own master, like Bren O'Brennan, but the food is good.'

Aefe laughed, her laugh not unlike Morveen's. 'When will you be fielded?'

Arthur hesitated. He did not want to accentuate his reel foot to Aefe. 'Some time, soon, no doubt.' He could see that Aefe would be impressed if he were a soldier. He would just have to make the Earl see that he was as good as any man on foot. Besides Piers had been promoted to the horse, so Arthur was sure that he would not be a reel

-footed soldier for long. He was as good a horseman as any.

Aefe was looking out across the river and the wooded hills beyond. 'Will you still come and see us in the kitchen when you have won glory in the field?'

'Of course. No matter what happens I would never stop visiting you. You...and Morveen.'

'Good,' she said and turned to go.

'Aefe,' he called to her retreating back 'I am very pleased to see you. Come and visit the birds with me.'

'I must go back. Cook will be displeased.' She was at the bottom of the stairs looking up at him. 'Anyway, I visit the falcons every day.'

'Do you? I remember they frightened you once upon a time.'

'No longer. I saw them this morning.' She took off across the court. 'They are grand.' She threw the words over her shoulder.

Arthur went to see them. They were grand, and he was happy.

*

Two evenings later Arthur went down to the kitchen. There was nobody to talk to in the keep. The Earl had wasted no time in taking his young men into the field and all except Arthur had left the day before. Arthur had to stay and tutor the pages. Aefe was already asleep under the table, but Morveen was still awake. 'Come let's sit by the fire,' she said, leading him away from the sleeping girl.

'*Dún do bheal,*' someone grumbled as they knelt by the dying coals. So they sat closer and whispered.

'What is Bristol like?

Arthur told her a little about the city and then he looked across at Aefe. 'She is indeed beautiful, Morveen,' he said. 'I've a mind to marry her once she is of age. That is only two or so years to wait. I will be fielded by then.'

Morveen was silent for a moment, then she said, 'No.'

'But I am determined to be fielded. When my Lord returns I will persuade him. And as for Aefe, it would not be a love match, not for now at least, but it would be a good catch for her in my present position.'

Morveen shook her head. 'You can't marry Aefe.'

'Why not? I would do it as much for you as for her. It would better your position. I do not mean that I will marry her tomorrow.'

'Nor the next day.' Morveen stood up. 'You...you...are a gentleman and she is but a scullion wench.'

'I am sure my lord would allow it. He is quite fond of me...'

'Consider her then. Do you think she would want to be a soldier's wife and never know if her husband would come home dead or alive; whole or in pieces?'

'The Earl's men always return alive. It is the traitor's who arrive home in pieces.'

Morveen stood. 'There is no question of you marrying Aefe,' she said forgetting to whisper.

'Ah, shut your gob,' the same man said.

'But,' Arthur said.

'But nothing,' hissed Morveen, and she walked away.

*

There was little time to fret over what Morveen had said, and in any case Arthur had other things on his mind than a distant marriage; it had been but a fanciful notion, and he was surprised Morveen took it so seriously, especially as he had only said he had a *mind* to marry, and the thought had been as much for Morveen as it was for Aefe, lovely though she was.

The Earl came home briefly from his skirmishes. Desmond was back on Irish soil, living peacefully in Munster, but there were other rebels to be brought into line with the Queen's wishes for Ireland. There was no great fanfare at the Earl's arrival this time. He had come back with the bodies of four of his kerne killed in the field. The unthinkable had happened, but as some of the Earl's gentlemen who were with him said, they were not the first and would not be the last. They never lost as many as the traitors, but lose men they did, and in a strange way this made Arthur all the more determined to be fielded. It was not right that Piers and the others had to endure such risks while he stayed at home, his hands blackened with nothing stronger than ink.

Next day an intimate family dinner was held in the new parlour and Arthur felt honoured to be a part of it, albeit at the far end of the table. At the top were the Earl and his brothers Edward and Edmund. They had been forgiven, but the Earl kept a close watch on them. A few of the Earl's men were also at table. The first course of raw oysters and barley bread was set before them. 'Young Arthur down there,' the Earl pointed, 'did the Ormonds proud at the Bristol tilts for Her Majesty.' His brothers looked at Arthur and smiled. Neither appeared to recognise him as the boy they dragged out of the kitchen those many years ago. They treated him in the same way as they treated all the Earl's other young gentlemen, except Piers, in a lukewarm manner that scarcely hid their disdain.

'I hear Piers is to wed,' said Edward.

'It is a good match, is it not, Edmund?' the Earl said.

Edmund nodded. 'Margaret Fleming is the daughter of the Baron of Slane.'

'But is not the Baron a papist?' Edward asked. 'That is an heretical stance since Her Majesty was excommunicated,' Edmund said, although the look he exchanged with his brother belied the sentiment.

Edward nodded, 'You yourself, Tom, have always been tolerant of the old faith.'

'But I am a Protestant,' the Earl said firmly. His voice softened. 'As you know, it is becoming increasingly difficult to be openly Catholic.' He paused, thinking. 'Piers will show them sense,' he finally assured them. 'He will win both his wife and father-in-law over to the reformation cause.' He wiped gravy from his mouth with the back of his hand, and changed the subject. 'Piers is to take the house at Duiske.'

One page arrived to clear the dishes and another to place a dish of roasted larks and bacon in front of them. Conversation stopped while they were served hearty portions. Arthur felt betrayed. Piers had not mentioned marriage or houses to him. How long had it been since he went back to the field? Six weeks, or more. Arthur supposed that a lot could happen in six weeks, and the Earl was obviously making the arrangements.

The Earl was asking, 'What news of Sidney, Edward?' This brother shrugged, his mouth too full to reply. The Earl sighed. 'I was sure Her Majesty would appoint Essex to the post.'

Edmund pulled a lark bone out of his mouth and set it on his platter. 'And here we are stuck with Henry Sidney again.'

Edward finally swallowed his mouthful and added, 'Who is tenfold worse than he was last time.'

The Earl nodded. 'Those trumped-up charges against you, Edmund.'

'Not to mention the allegations against me.' Edward waved his hand in the air.

'Which also impugn me,' the Earl added. 'Sidney is in no hurry to clear you. He is deliberately dragging it out. How long has it been now that you are waiting for the investigation to tell of its findings?'

Edward paused, counting on his fingers. 'Six months,' he said finally. 'At least six months.'

'And all of that in spite of the fact we received accolades from Dublin for our service against the rebels.' Edmund took another mouthful.

'That insult at Durrow Castle. The Fitzpatricks steal my castle and Sidney allows them to keep it!' The Earl paused, his head bowed over clasped hands as if in prayer. Then he looked up. 'I await word from the Queen for a bloodless outcome to the Durrow affair. For now we must stop further incursions into the north east.'

'And what word from the Queen about us?' asked Edward. 'We are still attainted. When shall we be restored to the blood?'

'The Queen has promised she will attend to that.'

When the table was empty of food and they were preparing to leave the dining chamber, Arthur said, 'Might I have a word, my lord?'

The others left and Arthur and the Earl sat at the table again.

'But what about the tutoring?' the Earl asked when Arthur told him what he wanted.

'Could you not appoint someone else?'

The Earl smiled. 'Then what about your…' He nodded at Arthur's foot.

'If you would like to put it to the test, my lord, I will run a race with anyone you name. And wager I would beat them.'

'Wager?' The Earl's eyebrows were raised. 'Did you pick up bad habits whilst in Bristol? Many young gentlemen have wagered their lives away. Believe me. I have seen much of that in London.'

Arthur feared they were moving away from the subject in hand. 'I used the term figuratively, Sir.'

'Good,' said the Earl. 'Now what am I to do with a reel-footed soldier?'

'Try him in the field. If I fail, I die and I am prepared to do that in your service.'

'But you might jeopardise my other men.'

'Then you could put me in the horse at the first opportunity.'

The Earl laughed. 'We shall see.' He thought for a moment. 'How old are you now?'

'Nearly eighteen, my lord, I think.'

"Ah. I was but sixteen when I was first fielded.'

'I have heard tell, my lord.'

'Fifteen-forty-seven. King Edward's army against Scotland.'

'My lord...' Arthur feared again that they were straying from the subject in hand.

'The Battle of Pinkie. They called it the "Rough Wooing" because His Majesty was...'

'My lord?' It was hard to keep the pleading out of his voice.

'Very well,' the Earl sighed. He looked Arthur up and down briefly, then stood. 'If you are determined?'

'I am, my lord.'

'Be ready at first light.'

*

Later that day Arthur went down to the kitchen to say goodbye. He had not seen Aefe since the day he came home: she was always in the village. It was the same this evening, but he did not deign to ask why she was out so late. The gates would be closed and she would not get back again until after his departure. Morveen's doing he surmised. He was cool with her when he bid her farewell. 'Arty,' she said. 'You take care o' yourself.' She stepped forward to hold him, but he moved away to speak with Cook, then turned his back on her and walked out. He heard Morveen call, '*Beannacht Dé leat*,' after him, but ignored her. He did not need God with him anyway.

At sunrise Arthur was kitted out in standard kerne uniform; a tabby weave woollen jacket, kilt, helmet and sandals. He was given a long bow and quiver of arrows glad that he had been well trained in archery as a page. They marched out of the castle just after sun up, the cold air striking Arthur's bare legs which until about an hour before had been warmly clad in stockings. They were a small group of kerne but destined to join the much larger contingent already waiting instructions at Kilcollan.

Arthur found the first part of the journey easy. The pace was steady but not too fast, and he swung his arms in time with each step. As time passed and the sun climbed the sky he began to sweat. He willed the men to slow, but they kept the same pace, up hill and into the vales, across meadows and through forests so thick the kerne in the lead had to hack their way through with their swords.

All day, one foot in front of the other. The sun had gone and now a cruel, unseasonable wind blew right through him. The kerne bent their heads against it and marched on. Arthur was looking forward to seeing Piers. He wondered how he felt about his upcoming marriage. He thought about Aefe, briefly. There was plenty of time to win that argument with Morveen, as if Aefe could afford to turn down an offer from a gentleman such as he! What was the alternative, the pot man's spotty lad? He may even find another suitable candidate ere the time came for betrothal, first things must come first, he decided as they reached the summit of a long but gently sloping hill: he must acquit himself bravely in the field.

By late afternoon the pace slowed. They walked around Kilkenny's walls, crossed a bridge and set up for the night in a field on the banks of the River Nore just north of the town. Arthur took his sandals off and rubbed his foot. 'You did well, young master,' said the kerne who had marched beside him all day. '*Maith thú.*' It was their first exchange of words. Arthur stopped rubbing his foot and began work on the good one. It was either that or put his sandals on again. 'The march will not be long tomorrow,' the kerne went on. 'My lord wants us fighting-fresh on the morn.' It was warm beside the fire they cooked on, but less than a foot away it was cold. Arthur's old fear came back to him. They would make a grand meal for a hungry wolf lying out in the open. Sleep was difficult. His legs and feet were cold. The sound of water whispering over the stones in the river made him think of Carraigh. During the night the fire went out and by dawn a soft drizzle was falling which meant there would be no warm food or hands at breakfast. They arose, took up their weapons and marched on.

By the time they reached the rest of the Earl's troops at midday the rain had stopped and all was quiet. This was a more permanent camp with tents set around the camp fire, and they were fed with bread and beer. The Earl was already here having travelled by horse. He had decided to delay the fighting by a day to allow another contingent of horse and gallowglass to reach them.

Arthur knew Piers was in the camp somewhere and after wandering around asking for him he finally found him in a tent with another horseman. He looked ill and was not his usual self. 'What is wrong?' Arthur asked.

'Nothing.' Piers said. 'I fare as well as can be expected when in the field.' He nodded at the other soldier who immediately left the tent. 'Arthur,' Piers held out a hand to him. 'It is good to see you. But I would rather you had remained a tutor than come out to fight. It is a bloody business. The more I see, the less I like it.'

Arthur looked around the tent. Just the pallet beds with Piers' boots sitting neatly beside his and the small stool on which Piers sat.

'Dead men on both sides.'

'Better a dead traitor than a live one.'

Piers sighed. 'You are such an innocent, Arthur.'

'I hear that you are to be wed,' Arthur said changing the subject.

'That I am.'

'Are you pleased?'

'It is grand. Or it will be when I get the time to be a husband.' Piers smiled sadly.

'I have a mind to wed Aefe once she is of an age. And I am in the horse.'

Piers sat up. 'I don't think...that is not possible...'

'I am as good as any man with a horse. I shall not be on foot for long.'

'That is not what I meant. Your marriage to Aefe is not possible.'

'Why not so? Morveen is against it, but she does not have agency in this. I do not love Aefe as a man should do...yet...but I am sure we will grow into that.' Piers was about to speak again, but Arthur rushed in. 'I shall ask my lord.'

Piers shook his head. 'Do you not know?'

'What should I know?'

'I should not be the one to tell if you do not know. But I cannot believe you are in ignorance of this.'

'Of what?' Arthur's voice rose alarmingly.

'Whisht,' Piers put a restraining hand on Arthur's arm. 'Aefe is your sister.'

'My lord is her..?'

'No,' Piers laughed at the suggestion. 'Morveen is her mother.'

It was Arthur's turn to laugh. 'Of course she is. I was there when Aefe was born under the table...'

'But don't you know?' Piers sounded astonished. 'Morveen is also *your* mother.'

Chapter Fourteen

Arthur felt an absolute fool. Of course Morveen was his mother, she was free and easy with her favours. The surprising thing was that there were only two off-spring - that they knew of. Why had he not seen it all this time? Then there was the story of his birth; Morveen could not have known any of that without experiencing it. The night was cold, but he strode out of the camp and down the dark and lonely boreen ahead of him, arguing with himself backwards and forwards, about the identity of his father - many people had commented on his dark good looks; about why Piers had taken such an interest in him if they had no blood ties and why the Earl had taken him into his household if he was base born. He walked and walked, not caring where he finished. He could walk into the arms of traitors for all he cared. His bare legs were cold and he drew his woollen jacket close to his body for warmth. A fitful moon came and went, and he felt the same sense of indecision, his mind going in an endless cycle over the same points. Finally, with a helpless sigh, he turned and at a much slower pace made his way back to camp.

The camp was not heavily guarded. Two gallowglass holding lighted torches stood talking some distance from where Arthur stepped over the low wall into the meadow again. The camp itself was in darkness, the only light the flickering flames of the dying camp fire on the far side. He crossed the grounds heading towards his tent. He wondered if the kerne he shared with would have notified someone of his absence. They were aware that he was one of the Earl's household and that earlier he had been looking for Piers. They might assume he was spending the night in Piers' tent. As he drew closer to the fire he saw two eyes reflecting in the glow. Then the shape emerged from the shadows. It was a wolf. Arthur stood still, as did the wolf. The wolf presented a fine figure, alert ears, sturdy body, strong legs and a long tail. Touches of white on its fur shone in the flickering firelight. The moon slipped from behind a cloud and for a brief moment the animal was more than a shape. It was the most beautiful creature Arthur had ever seen, much more attractive than the Earl's stocky bull mastiffs and the lap dogs that wandered the castle. They watched each other for some time, and Arthur's reaction surprised him, because after the first heart-stopping moments he was unafraid. '*Mac tire*,' Arthur whispered. 'You are indeed a son of the land. We both are.' They continue to stare until finally the wolf threw back its head and howled, then turned and loped away. The sound echoed long in Arthur's head. How he wished he could howl with such abandon.

He would not disturb the kerne in his tent. He lay down beside the fire, not caring about the cold now, not worrying about the wolf's possible return. He dreaded the morning and having to face Piers, but his last thought before sleeping was of the magnificent creature he had just confronted.

Next morning there was no time to worry about anything except the battle to come. They were to march north to the Earl's tower at Kilmocar and take it back from Tirlagh Ftizpatrick. Before they left the Earl rode up and addressed them. 'My good men,' he shouted. 'It will be but a skirmish this day. It is my belief the tower is lightly defended. The kerne and gallowglass will approach directly. The horse will surround it. We shan't waste the battering ram or the cannon, on a rogue like Tirlagh, we shall simply lay siege to the tower, and maintain that position until the enemy surrenders.

It is imperative that we regain the territory. We cannot let those Fitzpatricks gain a strong foothold in the north-east of Ossory.'

'Thence to Durrow?' a gallowglass called out. 'The Fitzpatricks have held that Ormond castle too long.'

'Not to Durrow.' The Earl shook his head vigorously to emphasise the words. 'I am to petition the Queen for that. I intend to act the part of the injured party that I am. An attack on the castle would undermine my position.' He waved them off. 'Make me proud of you this day,' he called as they turned to leave.

The kerne were armed with pike staffs and long bows. Arthur was pleased he had a bow. It would distance him from his target. He did not relish the thought of sticking a pike through a man. In front of them on foot were the gallowglass, wearing light coats of mail, a few carried firearms, the rest held two-handled axes and claymore broadswords. They marched off ahead of the horse, striding steadily over the rolling hills, some in pasture and some wooded, the trees bright with spring green. A mist drifted softly over the tops, and the only sound was the tramp of feet on the soft earth and the warble of a lark. It took them two hours to march the distance to the tower at Kilmocar, during which time the weather cleared and the sun made even their marching feet sound more cheerful.

When the tower came into sight they halted. It was eerily quiet and nothing stirred while they waited for the horse to catch up. They heard them first and then the horse came galloping, lances glittering in the sunlight, forward to the left and right of them to surround the tower. The Earl's pennant flew from several standards, and the noise of the flapping competed with the thunder of hooves. Gallowglass spread out across the rise, their spar axes and broadswords at the ready. The kerne followed suit, bows drawn and pikes pointing ahead. The kerne drew closer to the tower, so close that Arthur could see the arrow loops clearly. The battlements looked empty. Tirlagh and his men must have retreated already.

And then they heard the sound of horses behind them again. All heads turned to look, assuming it was more of the Earl's men, but these horsemen rode bareback and were bearing down with broadswords and longbows. Behind them, running at speed in close formation, came what seemed like hundreds of foot soldiers in rough Irish garb. Their hair was long, their beards wild, and brutish cries erupted from them, as they spread out to surround the horse as well. As a man the kerne turned to attack. The enemy came on relentlessly. Some kerne turned again and ran, others stood their ground but there was little room to manoeuvre the pikes. Success rested on the archers.

Arthur hesitated. Then he aimed his arrow and shot. He made a direct hit and the horseman closest fell to the ground, the horse shied and ploughed on through the ranks of the kerne, knocking some over. Beside Arthur one of the kerne knelt to make room for the man behind him to lower his pike from his shoulder. There was just enough room for him to stick his pike through the fallen horseman and when he pulled it out half the man's guts came with it. Arthur made another direct hit, and another. Hesitating again, he looked at the blood seeping into the soil from men dying around him: the entrails, bits of brain, all his work. A horseman was bearing down on him, and in trying to avoid him Arthur tripped and fell. A huge hoof rose above his head and he just managed to roll out of the way before the hoof hit the ground and the horse pounded on. Arthur stood and gathered up his bow and quiver only to be confronted by another horseman and his steed.

Surely the Earl would bring in the ram and cannon now. He reloaded his bow, shot, struck the horseman in the leg, but it did not stop his approach. Arthur ducked as he swung by. The horseman struck off the head of one of the Earl's kerne just ahead of Arthur. It flew through the air and Arthur dispassionately noted the blood spurting from the body before running zig-zag through the mayhem. He had to get away or he would die.

There was a copse at the perimeter of the battle field and he headed towards it. A horseman swiped his broadsword at Arthur's head. The blow glanced off and yet another sliced at his arm. There was no pain and he just kept running. Blood ran down his face making it difficult to see and he dropped his bow. Arrows fell from his quiver as he ran. By the time he reached the copse he was aware of the deep wound on his right arm and a gash on his head. Panting he hid behind an oak. He sat down, leaned against its broad back, bent over and vomited into the earth. The sound of battle seemed to fade, he wiped his left arm roughly across his face tasting the blood on his lips. Then it struck him: he had run away from battle. He was sick again.

He stood and ran back into the fray, picking up a dead man's lance on the way. Bodies from both sides lay everywhere, their blood mingling in death as it never could in life. Arthur stepped over the head of a dying foot soldier and lunged at a horseman. He hit the horse, and it toppled over crushing its rider. For a brief second he felt sorry for the horse, then leapt forward again.

He was a madman, waving the lance in the air and thrusting it wildly, pulling it, covered with blood, out of one man and thrusting it into the next. A blow struck Arthur's shoulder and a swipe passed down his face. He had no idea where he was. All he knew was that he had to kill as many of the bareback horsemen and the uncouth foot soldiers as he could. The Earl's men were in disarray, but Arthur kept fighting. He saw Piers on horseback ahead of him fighting sword on sword with the enemy. He received another heavy blow from behind and staggered forward looking for something with which to steady himself. There was nothing. He slid to the ground slipping in blood and innards, landed on the body of one of the enemy and gratefully fell unconscious.

*

The air was still. He could hear voices. '...brave young gentleman...' '...heroic' '...fought like a tiger...'He wondered who they were talking about. He would like to meet him. Maybe it was Piers. The voices drifted in and out of his head. 'Heroic...brave...' He felt sick again at the thought of his own behaviour, he had deserted. He groaned. 'He's coming round,' a voice said.

Arthur opened his eyes to find a concerned face looking at him. He tried to sit up, but fell back. It was so quiet he could hear the wind soughing through the trees. He groaned again. 'Go...go...' he wanted to tell them to go to the brave young gentleman they had been talking about, or had he dreamt that? Someone wiped his brow and someone else lifted his jacket. 'Go...' he tried again.

'Hush,' said the man who was wiping his brow. 'You are injured, but you are safe.'

Arthur fainted again, and next time he came to he was on a litter, looking up at a sky where clouds hung ominously. The litter bearers stepped around corpses and wounded men. He turned his head to see the Earl's men finishing off those of the enemy who had survived their wounds. Quickly, quietly. Their own men were being helped to their feet or slid onto litters. The smell of blood was nauseating and Arthur closed his eyes again.

Away from the battle field the bearers had room to break into a trot, and the pain set in as the litter bounced up and down, it was a pain both physical and in his spirit. He had deserted. What would the Earl think? He would never be allowed to join the horse now. Then he remembered what Piers had told him. He gave a long moan. 'Twill not be long, young sir,' said one of the bearers. 'We are nearly there.'

Back at the camp site they delivered Arthur to a tent. Rain had begun to fall, Arthur could hear the drops on the skin of the tent. The bearers were lifting him onto a pallet when he heard Piers ask from outside. 'Who have you there?'

'One of the kerne,' the first litter bearer said.

'Your name?' the second asked of Arthur.

'Ar...Arthur.'

He heard the thud as Piers leapt off his horse, and then he rushed into the tent. Arthur turned his head away.

'Arthur,' Piers said. 'I have heard of your courage. What a fighter you have proved yourself to be this day. My lord will be proud.'

'But...' Arthur started.

'Whisht,' Piers ordered. Then to the bearers, 'Prithee bring him to my tent.'

'No. I am comfortable here.' Arthur tried to sit up.

'Very well, I shall fetch the physician.'

While Piers went in search of the physician Arthur listened to the rain and thought of all the men dead in the field. He saw again the rivers of blood and viscera and felt the pang of guilt. The rain could not wash any of it away.

'Will he live?' were the first words Piers asked when he and the physician came into the tent.

Arthur tried to smile but fancied that it came across as a grimace. He had not considered dying, although that would be a way out of this mess: the desertion, confronting Morveen with her lies. But that would be cowardice. He had been a coward once, and not much liked it. He would live. All the while the physician was looking at his wounds. 'He has lost a lot of blood, young sir, but he is fit and healthy. I don't think we need bring in the priest just yet.'

'Good.' Piers said. 'What treatment will you serve on him?'

'I think some styptic on the wounds. I have a special one on hand. I will dress the wounds. That is all. Then get him away from the field. Home is the best place for a cure.'

*

'Art. Arty.' Morveen's face was white. 'You are alive.' In spite of the pain he had insisted on entering the castle on foot, and Morveen rushed to help him. 'For sure now you know what I meant about being fielded.' She put out a hand and softly touched the dressing cloth around his head, but Arthur pulled away and made straight for the keep. Nonetheless the lady's maid who helped him up to the bed chamber allowed Morveen in to see him when he was settled, although he pretended to be asleep. He felt her fingers touch his hand gently, and turned over, away from her.

The Earl came in to offer his congratulations. 'I was wrong in my thoughts of you,' he said. 'You are a warrior. As soon as you recover I shall arrange for you to join the horse.'

'Did you...did we lose many men?'

'Not near as many as the Fitzpatricks.' He patted Arthur's hand. 'It is not good to lose any man in battle, they leave behind mothers, fathers, wives, children. But sometimes the greater cause makes the means worth the end.'

Arthur nodded, but he did wonder what cause could justify so many lives lost. And did not the enemy have mothers, fathers, wives and children? Did not the enemy have a cause?

*

The day arrived when Arthur was allowed out of the bed. 'Where to?' asked Piers who had come to help him.

'I would rather like to see the Long Gallery.'

'So you shall,' and Piers helped him out of the room and down the stairs to the manor house extension.

The Long Gallery, bright and spacious, startled Arthur after the weeks of lying in the dim light of the small keep chamber. Followed by Piers he hobbled over the Turkey carpets to the Earl's fireplace to look at the effigy of the Queen. It bore little resemblance to the real woman. Flanking her on either side were Equity and Justice. Arthur wondered what justice there was in keeping the Earl's brothers attainted since they had been pardoned. He read the inscription. 'Viscount...earl...Lord of the Liberties...' Out the windows opposite the sky was blue with just a few summer clouds. He turned to Piers. 'I'd like to see the birds.'

'Are you well enough for that?'

'I am fighting fit. I can scarcely wait to go back to the field. I would not mind another turn at routing those traitorous Fitzpatricks.'

Piers sighed. 'I thought you understood,' he said. 'The Fitzpatricks are not traitors. They are as loyal to the Queen as my lord. They were simply expanding their territory at Sidney's bidding, and it was our task...is our task... to save both my lord's reputation and his lands.' He sighed again. 'Not everyone my lord goes to battle with are traitors.'

Arthur rubbed his hands together thinking of something to say which would not make him seem such a ridiculous innocent. Nothing came to him.

'Ah my dear friend,' Piers took his arm and led him down the stairs. 'Let us not dwell on such matters. Let's go and see those birds.'

But they did not get to the birds that morning. They came across Morveen who was draping wet bed sheets on the bushes in the kitchen garden.

Arthur stopped. He was not sure whether he was ready to speak with her, but he knew he had to sooner or later. He nodded at Piers. 'I will be grand,' he said and Piers walked away leaving the two of them alone.

'You can bring Aefe back from the town,' were the first words he said. 'She is in no danger from me.'

'She is not in the town. She has returned to the foster family in Waterford.' Morveen paused. The silence grew, until finally she added, 'Cook said that one woman in the kitchen was enough.' She tried a laugh but it did not quite work.

'Is she content?'

'Well enough, I hear.' She picked up a sheet from the washing basket.

'I know she is my sister.'

Morveen dropped the sheet back into the basket. 'How? Who told you?'

'Piers. He did not want to, but I forced it out of him.'

'Then there is nothing more to be said.'

'I beg to disagree.'

'Arty, you have got uppity since you joined the household.'

'That maybe so, but that is not the subject under discussion here.' He realised he was sounding pompous. 'If you are my mother, who is my father?'

Morveen picked up the sheet again and hung it over a bush before answering. 'I am not rightly certain.'

'The probabilities?'

'A gallowglass. Or...or...my lord.'

He let that rest for the moment. 'How did you know all that nonsense you filled my mind with? The castle, the river, the wherryman, the red-headed queen.'

'My lord...'

'You see I have remembered it all, so stuck in my head has it been.'

'My lord used to tell me how it was. He likes to talk about such things. He told me, too, about a birth in the castle that he knew of.'

'Piers?'

'He would not say.'

'But why? Why did you make me believe those lies?'

'I wanted you to grow up thinkin' something of yourself. To make up for that foot of yourn.'

'The lies have not achieved that.' The next question came quickly. 'Does my lord know about me?'

'He was somewhat uncertain at first. But when you grew and showed how clever you were and what a natural skill you had with the birds. And horses. And your hair grew darker...'

'But my reel foot? He would not have been impressed with that.'

'Was not his father, the ninth Earl, called James the Lame?' She reached out to touch the scar that sliced across his cheek.

He pulled away. 'Do not expect me to call you Mother.' He walked off.

Chapter Fifteen

Arthur limped into the high street. His foot was bad again after the battle and he made his way slowly. He was feeling much better, but at a loss with nothing to do. He had been replaced as tutor, all he had done while sick abed was read and he had tired of that. He could not even hope to see Aefe in the town now that he knew she was well removed to Waterford, and now that he knew she was forbidden he could not see the point in seeing her, except as a sister and that bond seemed fragile at best. At the Stone House corner he stopped to smell the bread baking in the town oven down the lane. It brought back memories of the castle kitchen on a cold day, snuggled into Morveen's kirtle by the fire with bread warm on the hob. Even that memory was tainted now, spoilt by her deception.

'Master Arthur,' a voice called and there was Bren O'Brennan thatching the apothecary's roof. Arthur crossed the road and Bren slid to the side of the roof and climbed down the ladder. 'I heard you had been wounded,' Bren said as he approached. '*Conas atá tú*?'

'I am in excellent shape. It is nothing more than a nuisance.' Arthur stood straighter as if to prove it. 'What news of Donal?'

Bren was obviously trying hard not to look at the scar on Arthur's face. 'The lad was apprenticed in England, but is coming home soon.'

'Has he finished his apprenticeship already?'

'No. He...he is tired of the English. And I would not have him stay where he is out of place.' He looked back at the roof he was mending. 'I had better get on. I have much to do and only one pair of hands. At least until Donal returns.'

'Perhaps I... I am fit enough to climb a ladder, if you showed me what to do. Life is tedious with idle hands.'

'The work might look easy...' Bren thought for a moment. 'But... here is an idea that might be workable. You know your figures?' Arthur nodded. 'That is where I find little time. In figuring the accounts to be rendered. And the payment of accounts owed by me.'

Arthur grinned. 'I would be glad to help.'

'But what about the Earl?'

'My lord is preparing to go to Court. He is to petition the Queen in the case of Durrow Castle.'

'I heard he was to take a high moral stance against the Fitzpatricks.'

'He must surely win...but he will have no need of me until I can go into battle again.'

'And we must make sure that does not happen for a long time to come.'

*

Arthur began work the next day sitting in the O'Brennan cottage with the accounts book balanced on his knee. The figures were easy to work with and by the time Bren came in for his dinner Arthur had several accounts written in his neat hand. Donal's mother smiled fondly at him, as she placed a partridge pie in front of him.

'Don't be after asking where the birds came from,' Bren said, winking at his wife.

'You will stay on this evening, Arthur?' She ignored her husband. 'The storyteller is coming and half the town will be here listening.'

'That I would like.'

*

Indeed, it did seem like half the town was crowded into the small cottage when the storyteller arrived that night wearing a cloak of fine wool, a yellow doublet and woollen cap. The chatter dwindled to silence as he stepped into the cottage. Bren came forward to welcome him. '*Céad míle fáilte romhat*.'

The storyteller doffed his cap and made his way through the people to the fireplace. He stood on the settle so he could be easily seen and said how pleased he was to be there. He began his story slowly, softly so they had to strain to hear in the crowded room. 'In days not so old, an Englishman invited three hundred Irish fighting-men to a grand party at the fort at Mullaghmast.' He described the preparations for the party in the kitchens and it took Arthur back to the days in the castle kitchen when all was a-flurry cooking mountains of food for a large party of guests. 'Finally the guests arrived and gathered around the fireplace in the grand hall. And,' the storyteller paused, 'it was a very fine hall indeed, with Turkey carpets on the walls and silken cushions lain about for the folk to rest upon. They danced jigs and swords while the fiddler sawed his bow fit to kill. The night wore on. Food was eaten. Drink taken. They had never seen such a feast in their lives. And never would again. For some the dancing became more frenzied, for others it slowed as they drooped their drink-addled heads on the banquet table, or slid sleepily onto the silk cushions.' He paused again, himself to take a sip from the tankard handed up to him by one of the listening men, then he continued. 'There was one young man who did not eat the food or take of the drink or kick his heels up in the dancing. He stood to one side somewhat in the shadows and watched. He watched until finally the only people left standing were the hosts who seemed strangely unaffected by the excess. He watched in horror as the hosts took each sagging head by the hair, pulled it back and cut its throat.' There was a gasp from some of the women. 'The blood flowed freely. The host's men slipped in it and had to watch their step as they moved from one Irish guest to the next. Some of the revellers woke and saw what was happening. They staggered to their feet and slipping through the blood of their fellows tried to make an escape, but there were guards at the door all too ready to lop off their heads or stick them through with a pike. Soon the only Irishman left standing was the young man in the shadows at the edge of the great hall. One of the host's men noticed him. With a cry he leapt at him. He too slithered in the blood now smeared across the floor. He picked himself up, and slid towards the shadows. But when he was close enough he saw there was no young man. Just a grey wolf with bright eyes and fangs bared. It snarled and the host's man ran for his life. The wolf did not follow, it padded its way around the bodies. It sniffed at the blood-red silk cushions. It walked across the hall and out into the night where it threw its head back and howled to the moon.' At this point the storyteller did just that. His howl was so like a wolf's that Arthur wondered if he was the shape-shifter himself. There was silence for a long time afterwards. Then the man next to Arthur whispered, 'The O'Mores.'

'Aye,' the storyteller said. 'That was the massacre of the O'Mores.'

'Not more than a month back,' the man next to Arthur whispered again.

'There is a great broad-armed tree in Stradbally,' the storyteller said loudly above the talk that had begun. 'It does not bear telling of in a story, but it bears the bodies of the men, women and children of Leix. Francis Cosby, the host at Mullaghmast is a man with unusual tastes in entertainment. His delight is to string the innocent women of Leix to a branch of the tree which sits outside his house and use their hair to string their children beneath them.' A woman listening let out an anguished cry and others sobbed. 'Those women,' the storyteller continued, 'have committed no crime, except that of worshipping the true God. And when the tree sits in winter branches with no fruit there upon, Cosby talks to it kindly thus, "My tree, you look sad. You are too long bare, but I shall soon adorn your branches with dead bodies."' The sobbing lifted, and the storyteller's voice rose above it. 'No Irish tree on Irish soil should be weighed down so. But,' and this time he shouted, 'the wolf watches still. We shall take our revenge!'

*

The story of the massacre haunted Arthur. Next day he asked Bren about it. 'Aye,' Bren said. 'The story is true. It was Cosby, plantationer and general of the kerne of Leix. With help from his English friends.' They were in the yard at the back of the cottage and Bren was cutting wadds into the right length for the next stage of the apothecary roof. Arthur was helping by whittling a spar.

'And the tree? Surely that cannot be a true account.'

'Sadly it is, lad.'

Arthur remembered Bridie, beaten to death by the Earl's kerne. 'But the Queen. She cannot condone such behaviour.'

'There are those who say she encourages it. Especially now she is so determined to reform her English church. All Papists are traitors.' Then he added, 'Not that all wish to be.'

'Then who is the wolf? The shape-shifter?'

'He is no shape-shifter. He is Rory Oge O'More.' Bren looked up from the bale of straw he was untying and said, 'Ally to Desmond.'

'But Desmond has been lying low some time since.'

'Aye, but this will surely bring him out fighting.'

*

The Queen was a vain woman, but Arthur could not believe she would grant her agents cause or permission to commit such acts as those described by the storyteller. He would have liked to talk with Morveen about it, but could not bring himself to do so.

That evening back at Carraigh castle several of the Earl's most powerful men had gathered. The brothers were there, and were reated affably by the seneschal. They dined in the Great Hall and the supper conversation was lively, more so in the relaxed atmosphere of the Earl's absence. Sir Edmund's voice rumbled above the rest.

The harper played while they ate, jaunty music that set feet a-tapping under the table. It was a pity there were no women present to dance with.

Eoghan Mac Craith was also present, eating and drinking heartily. Obviously Sidney's prohibition on rhymers had been ignored, for when he had finished eating the poet stood. The seneschal hushed the harper and the men so that Mac Craith could recite. 'I speak of Thomas, Earl of Ormond. The blood-shedding Earl of Kilkenny, who twice set Glen-con-cadhain on fire, this wealthy and tender-hearted chieftain. One time he made an onslaught on the Geraldines. He administered to them a purging dose which worked with violent dire effect. He stormed, demolished and burned Dunlo. After his visit to Ibh-Rathach shepherds were left in want of employment. I speak of Thomas, puissant lord, renowned for gracious deeds. A comely royal cousin.'

Arthur felt nauseated by the poem in praise of the Earl. It seemed indecent, especially in the light of the massacre at Mullaghmast and Cosby's despicable tree. The contradictions in the poet's description of his subject might have been amusing in another context, but Arthur could only think of sheepless shepherds wandering land laid waste as Bridie's was. He could only think of innocent women and children slaughtered. For what? Because they stood firm for their own lands? Because they stood firm for Ireland? He stopped listening to the poet's droning and looked at the wood grains on the table. How old an oak was cut down to provide a table for the blood-shedding Earl?

The door opened and Piers strode in. He nodded at Arthur as he made his way to a seat closer to the seneschal. He leaned forward to say something to the seneschal, then sat back and listened as the Earl's deeds and misdeeds continued to be glorified by Eoghan Mac Craith.

With the poem finally over and the meal eaten they took their goblets of wine and wandered into the Long Gallery. Piers waited for Arthur and pulled him towards one of the window alcoves to talk. Piers explained his lateness. He had been stopped by Sidney's men out of Kilkenny. 'They had nothing with which to reproach me, so they had to let me go.'

'Were you not afraid that Sidney might have trumped up a charge?'

'I am but a minnow in Sidney's ocean.' Piers took a sip from his goblet.

'He is not in the Queen's favour.'

'Someone,' Piers tapped the side of his nose to indicate that the someone should remain anonymous. 'Someone intercepted a letter to Sidney from the Queen advising him to be friend, not foe, to my lord on pain of losing his position.' One of the seneschal's men had moved within hearing distance. He stood apparently looking at the fading sky out the window. 'Enough of Sidney,' Piers said changing the subject. The seneschal's man moved away with a brief nod at the two of them. 'How are you entertaining yourself? It must be dull with my lord away...' He took a book out of his jerkin pocket. 'This may amuse you.'

'*Utopia*', Arthur said looking at the cover. 'I have long wanted to read this.'

'I have the second volume for you when you have finished that.'

'I hope not to have too much more time for reading. I am eager to get back to the field.'

'We are all on leave. My lord is lying low until the Durrow castle affair is resolved by the Queen.'

'Then things must be dull for you, too.'

Piers laughed. 'Would that they were, but I am supervising the restoration of my house at Duiske...and doing some wooing. Margaret is a fine young woman.'

'Is it true she and her father are of the Catholic faith?'

Piers put a finger to his lips, and nodded.

*

Next morning he took Piers' book and sat comfortably with his feet up, in one of the alcoves in the Long Gallery where the light from the windows was good to read by. He sat for a while looking out the window, trying to work out where he stood. He was disillusioned with the Earl's territorial campaigns. Who were the traitors, and what were they traitor to? Elizabeth, Ireland? He could not decide which cause was the nobler. If it was treason to follow the Catholic faith, as had now been proclaimed, what business did the Earl have in marrying Piers off to a papist?

He opened the book and read the first page. *Henry VIII, the unconquered king of England, a prince adorned with all the virtues that become a great monarch...* Arthur looked up. There was no getting away from the question. This was the prince who decided to take Ireland for his own. But Arthur trusted Piers. If he suggested he read *Utopia*, read it he would. He had not got much further when he heard voices from the other end of the gallery. One of them he recognised as Sir Edmund's bellow. Arthur was about to show himself when he heard his name being spoken.

'What about the lad, Arthur? Where does he fit into the succession?' That was Edward.

'Nowhere. Tom accepts the bastard, Piers...for obvious reasons, but not that capper...'

'Our grandfather was James the Lame, remember. Couldn't get more of a capper than him. God rest his soul.'

'But he was not a wench's son. Tom should be more careful who he beds.'

'And is the lad true?' Edmund asked. The men seemed to have moved a little closer, but their voices were slightly muffled. They must be sitting at one of the windows. 'Remember when our friend in Kilsheelan enticed him with a gold coin. Snipes like that will do anything for money.'

'But I understood that he would not do it'

'Tom won't have him in the field again.'

'Why not?' Edward sounded surprised. 'He came home a hero.'

'Tom said it was not heroics. It was madness.'

Arthur knew that was true, but it hurt to hear it, especially from one of the Butler brothers.

'If this Arthur is so worthless, why then, did Tom take him in?'

'To please Piers. He's the bastard we have to contend with when the succession comes. Bah!' Edmund's voice roared. 'Everything is done to please the bastard son.'

'Sh-sh-sh,' Edward warned. 'Come away now. Someone will hear you.'

Their voices faded and Arthur was on his own again, but he was not the same young man as the one who had sat down so contentedly with a book just half an hour earlier. He had never expected to succeed. That was unthinkable, but to have the Earl think so little of him. That was unbearable.

Part Three

Munster
1578

Chapter Sixteen

'So you are one of Ormond's bastards?' The wild-haired Desmond eyed Arthur up and down. He had changed much since Arthur saw him being bundled off to Dublin in chains. He looked frail, but his wife, Eleanor, standing beside him looked ready to strike anyone who did not take his side.

'I suspect I might be.'

'No mistaking those dark looks. What brings you to Munster, now? Are you come as a spy? There is little fine feeling 'twixt Tom Dubh and the Desmonds, as you well know.'

Arthur considered whether he should tell Desmond that he thought his cause a more noble one than Black Tom's. 'I was much troubled, Sir, by the massacre of the O'Mores at Mullaghmast,' he said finally.

'Your father would not feel so.'

'I don't know what he feels, Sir. He is at Court. I come of my own bidding. And Bren O'Brennan was kind enough to arrange this meeting.' He nodded towards Bren and Donal, who were sitting around a fire some distance away eating mutton chops with Desmond's men.

'What now, so?'

'I would like to join your cause. It is just.' They had travelled across an empty plain into the foothills of the mountains where Desmond had been in hiding since the English had threatened him with imprisonment again. The English had tried to tame the wilds; they had planted English garrisons throughout the flat farmland, but in creating them had slashed and burned so that no Irishman would be able to make a living off the soil. Stock was driven into the hands of the English, cottages and crofts were burnt to the ground.

Only in the small defended towns were there any signs of civilisation and those were few. Mostly occupied by soldiers, the towns were as unruly as the countryside was devoid of life. The three had tried not to attract attention in the towns and Bren's cart stacked with straw gave them good cover. When halted, as they frequently were, they said they were on their way to the next town to do some thatching.

Desmond was looking at Arthur waiting for more. 'I have fought for my lord...for the Earl in the kerne.'

'You would be hindrance to my kerne. Look at the state of you.' He looked contemptuously at Arthur's leg.

'I am a fierce good horseman,' Arthur offered.

Desmond laughed, his laugh belying his frailty. 'We have no spare horses.'

'I have money. I could buy one.' The more questions there were, the more determined Arthur became.

'And give cause for gossip? An unknown young gentleman bearing a strong likeness to the Earl of Ormond wanders into the town. Out of nowhere. To buy a horse,' Desmond spluttered. 'How can I trust you?'

'My word is all I have.'

'Apart from being troubled by what that devious Cosby did to the O'Mores, what else troubles you about the state of affairs in Ireland?' This time it was Eleanor's turn to question him.

'The English, my lady. They are cruel and heartless. Look at what they have done to the countryside hereabouts.' He waved an arm.

'They will not be happy until they have taken the whole of Ireland for their own.'

'Mossa, but your earl has not been entirely innocent of such acts himself.'

Arthur recalled his embarrassing discussion with Piers about traitors, and the words of Eoghan Mac Craith. He said nothing.

'I must admit that he treated the O'Mores fairly when he tracked them down at New Ross those years back,' Desmond said. 'But then his mistress of the time was O'More kin and they submitted to the Lord Deputy for her sake rather than his. But since then your lord has changed bed mates and we have changed our minds.' He laughed again. 'On the matter of religion?'

'I don't think it matters how a man worships his God.'

'His God? What about your God?'

'I am not sure I have one. But I do not agree with persecuting a man for not worshipping in a certain way.'

'Oh aye.' He flicked his hand as if dismissing a fly. Arthur was to return to Bren and Donal.

'So?' Bren raised an eyebrow, and licked the mutton fat off his fingers.

'I have offered my services.' He sounded surprised at himself.

'Ah, you are to join Donal in the fight against the English?'

'Donal is to do this also?'

'Aye,' Donal said, his eyes shining.

'Methinks Desmond mistrusts me. And I cannot say I blame him for that.'

'Wait and see.'

'I need a horse. I would be no good in the foot I fear.'

'That can be arranged.'

*

Arthur's life as a rebel horseman began. He was pleased that Donal was with him, otherwise he would have felt out of place. The life was hard and Donal always managed to help keep Arthur's spirits up. They slept out most nights and were constantly on the move, sometimes just hours ahead of the English. Desmond's men were cruel themselves when it came to the English, they thought nothing of hanging, drawing and quartering them. 'Like your precious majesty does to those she considers recusants,' one of the executioners told one Englishman about to be strung up.

Arthur did not enjoy watching these proceedings, but did not want to cause Desmond to suspect him, so forced himself to watch and cheer with the rest. To the disinherited Irish Desmond was kindness itself. He gave them food when it was available; he retook sheep and cattle for grazing on the mountain slopes. His men helped protect the stock and assisted the Irish and their animals to escape as soon as word came that a raid was imminent.

Their forays were more annoying than disastrous for the settlers, but they were constant and the settlers lived in fear. Desmond fought with the men and Eleanor was never far from his side, a magnificent horsewoman who often outran the men. After his experience at Kilmocar, Arthur was determined that he would rather die than run from a battle, and he gained a reputation as a ferocious warrior, but from time to time he was troubled, and was pleased to have Donal to talk matters over with.

'I have absconded from Carraigh and the Earl's patronage. What am I doing here in the wilds of Munster fighting for my lord's arch-enemy against him?'

'But you are not fighting the Earl's men. The fight is agin Sidney's men. And in doing that you are helping the Earl's cause. If we can keep the English out of Munster his own territories have a better chance of remaining intact.'

'Ah, Donal,' Arthur sighed. 'You have a way with you in mending my guilt. But Ormond troops are not far away. What if I came face-to-face with Piers? I have no fight with him.'

'As rebels we must look at each day as our last. So what purpose is there in worrying about tomorrow? Or the next day.'

'You are right, Donal, as always.' Arthur put an arm around his shoulder. 'Do you believe the stories from the village men that the

Queen is to come to Ireland?' He gave a hard laugh. 'I remember well as a child waiting for her to visit the manor house at Carraigh and now it seems I am still waiting, but this time for to kill her.'

'The Queen's visit is nothing but a fairy story. Elizabeth is not a stupid woman. It would mean her death if she came.'

'Aye. And we would be fighting each other to be the agent of that death.'

*

As the old year tipped into the new, terror spread amongst the Irish throughout the countryside. The new chief governor, Sir William Drury was scouring the land for those who disobeyed English law; any law, it did not matter and the legal proceedings were but skimmed like a stone across water. The easiest English law to break in Ireland, though, was the law pertaining to religious observance. Court hearings in Kilkenny saw many hanged and heard Drury crowing of his deeds.

For Desmond and his men the summer had been bearable sleeping under the stars, but when autumn set in and the wind came from the north it was fierce cold. Some of the older men got sick and died of exhaustion and exposure. Arthur and Donal dug their share of shallow graves, and stood heads bowed while the Jesuit, Father James Archer, who travelled with them, said the funeral mass over the fresh damp earth. Desmond himself looked ill, limping badly from the wound in his thigh sustained at Affane. Often his hands shook and he could no longer mount his horse unaided, although Eleanor tried as best she could to help him.

*

The trek to Desmond's seat at Askeaton was long, but the sight that greeted them was worth it. The castle sat atop a rocky island above the Deel River but a mile or so from the Shannon River estuary. The upper ward was like a crown on the rock whilst below, the castle was built around it. When they had marched in, the seneschal, who had been taking care of the castle in Desmond's absence, showed some of the men around. 'No wonder Tom Dubh is anxious to get his hands on the Desmond heritage,' Donal whispered to Arthur. 'This castle is a marvel.' They thought the upper ward magnificent enough, but when they were led downstairs they saw an even greater wonder. The banqueting hall with its vaulted ceilings and nearby kitchens and chambers brought a long silence from the men.

Life at the castle required little of the men, except to maintain a watch. It was good to spend nights under cover and to eat well. Harpers came to entertain them and the music and merrymaking lasted into the night. One night some weeks after their arrival, Eleanor proposed a toast to her husband which was gladly given. 'Aye,' Desmond sighed as the cheers died down. 'We have been through much together, my faithful wife, and I.'

She laughed. 'Remember your escape from Dublin?' She turned to the men at the table. 'Your lord was no sooner on the right side of the Pale than we threw our English clothes from our backs and dressed properly again.' She ran her hands down her rough woollen kirtle to show what 'properly' meant. 'And what a welcome, my lord, when you returned to Munster.'

He laughed, pleased with the memory.

'But my lord,' Eleanor went on, 'you must needs go to Dublin again and talk to the Council. If we make our peace with them they will allow us to keep Askeaton and your other properties. They will take your side against your kin. It is a small price.'

Desmond thought for a while. 'My wife,' he said to the assembled company, 'is hand-in-glove with the Queen.'

'Only so much as to keep your lands, privileges and power in your hands.'

Arthur looked at Donal across the table from him. Donal shrugged. Was there no honour in the whole of Ireland? Here they were thinking the fight was to rid the land of the English and here was Desmond, no better than the Earl of Ormond. But what a fine woman Eleanor was, so loyal to her husband. Arthur wished he had a woman so true, no, he simply wished he had a woman.

Desmond was looking at Arthur. Could he read his thoughts as Bridie had? 'You're a tough fighter, Butler,' Desmond said. 'If we must to Dublin I will leave the castle in your hands. Daniel Caech, the seneschal, will look after the running of things as usual, but you will be responsible for its safe-keeping.'

Desmond and Eleanor left two days later with a small contingent of men. Arthur was pleased to be staying put for a while longer; to be sleeping not just under cover but in a bed, not a truckle bed, a real one with curtains and a red canopy. Being accountable for the safety of Askeaton and its occupants was a huge responsibility but he relished it, and with Donal's help arranged a water-tight defence with short round-the-clock watches so that no man would be so tired as to be found asleep when an attack came. Daniel appointed a lad called Michael as Arthur's manservant. He brought him water for washing in, set out his clothes and kept his chamber tidy and clean.

Eleanor scorned the idea of maids and for that Arthur was grateful. It was easier to defend a household of men. Only three women were required to help in the running of everyday affairs. Two were older women, almost past their usefulness. They reminded him of Bridie. The third, Meadhbh, a comely redhead of about sixteen, reminded Arthur a little of Aefe, but the more he saw of her, the smaller the resemblance became, apart from the colour of her hair. The girl bobbed him a curtsy on his first day as protector and he said, 'No need for that.'

'Sorry, my lord,' Meadhbh whispered.

'I am not your lord. Master Arthur will do.'

*

Life at the castle ran smoothly. Arthur began to feel as if he was at home with the River Deel a cleaner, faster running version of the Suir. Most days some of the men left the castle in a skiff to catch fish in the Shannon estuary, others prepared the ground outside the walls for planting at Candlemas. Some sheep and cattle lived within the castle walls but were taken out to graze from time to time. People from the village called in now and then, mostly family of the staff and always well vetted before allowed entry. They brought provisions, and news. Baltinglass of the Pale had repelled the English at Glendalough, the first Palesman to revolt. Things were looking grim for the English.

When the weather had warmed, a messenger from Desmond arrived. They knew what he had come for. The winter break in fighting was over, and all bar a skeleton staff must return to the field. Arthur was to stay, and Donal to go. It was a sad day for both when they said goodbye, but life continued as it had done, a little lonelier, but there was always something to attend to.

Candlemas came and the three kitchen women seemed unusually animated. Arthur watched them at the long kitchen table making crosses out of straw. '*Feill Bhride*,' Meadhbh explained.

'It might be the Feast of Brigid, but we can't eat crosses of straw,' Arthur laughed.

Meadhbh smiled shyly at him. 'This is for women. We drink milk today. You men will eat as usual.' Arthur went outside and climbed the parapet. A raven flapped his black wings and settled on the battlement. Arthur watched it for a while knowing that this was a good omen for the weather to come. Later, after supper he took his customary walk around the castle defences, and was astonished to see three lights moving around the battlements. 'Guard,' he called. The watch appeared from the shadows. 'What is happening here?'

'It is the festival of First Light. They are lighting the way for Brigid,' the watch explained.

'Who are they?'

'The women, Sir. It is *Feill Bhride...*'

'I know. But they can't... Look man, they are providing a target. Get them down.'

The watch grumbled something into his hefty beard. Arthur did not hear, but he did gather its drift. 'Now!' he ordered. He waited and watched while the guard went and spoke to the women. They did not immediately douse their torches, but walked slowly back to the battlement steps, silently passed him and stepped down. Only the older woman, Roisin, looked at him. Was that malice that shone in her eyes? Meadhbh and the woman called Fainche looked straight ahead, their torches held high. He went in search of Daniel Caech, but was told he had gone to the village and would not be back until the morrow.

Arthur spent an uneasy night. When he finally he slept he dreamed of crops withered in snow. Then a raven flew and sat on his shoulder. '*Fitheach moch, feannag anmoch*,' it whispered in his ear. 'I was early to come. The weather will be bright.' The snow melted as he watched and the corn grew green and tall.

Next morning the women acted as if nothing had happened. There was still an undercurrent of excitement, but Arthur thought little of it as he ate his breakfast with them at the kitchen table. When he was called to a knock at the castle gate, he jumped up and ran to the entrance. The portcullis was down as always, but the gate up. Anyone could have shot an arrow or fired a musket through the ironwork. He must have a word with Daniel. Before him stood a small girl dressed in white. The women had followed him from the kitchen.

'The Brideog,' said Meadhbh.

'Let her in,' Roisin begged. 'You must allow her. She is Brigid.'

'She could be a decoy...a spy...'

'Look at the size of her,' said Meadhbh and the other women cackled at his stupidity.

Somewhat reluctantly Arthur told the guard to lift the portcullis.

'Bride is come,' cried Fainche as the child walked slowly into the castle.

'Bride is welcome,' Roisin chanted. 'Bride is welcome.'

'We must give her butter and cake,' Meadhbh whispered to Arthur. 'If we do not the crops will fail.'

'I dreamt the crops will flourish. I saw a raven yesterday, and last night one spoke to me in my dream. It said, "I was early to come. The weather will be bright."'

'*Fitheach moch, feannag anmoch*,' Meadhbh smiled up at him.

'Come.' Roisin took the girl by the hand and led her down to the kitchens. When Arthur went to follow Fainche held him back. 'Womenfolk only.'

Later Roisin asked for permission to take the child in white to the nearest cottage, so that they too could be blessed. Arthur agreed, reluctantly again, but he felt helpless against the power of these women. When he returned to his chamber he was surprised to find Meadhbh pouring water from a jug into a bath which sat in the middle of the floor. He was not expecting to bath for weeks and surely it was Michael's job to draw the water.

'Shall I be sending someone in to help?' Meadhbh asked.

Arthur laughed. 'No. I am quite capable.'

Meadhbh left the room and Arthur undressed, but before he could step into the bath Meadhbh had returned. She shut the door behind her and leaned her back against it. Arthur stood by the bath with not a stitch of clothing on him, too shocked to hide his nakedness. She moved towards him; came closer than any woman except Morveen had ever before. When she ran a finger the length of the scar on his face, he pulled away. 'No,' she said. 'I like it. It shows how manly you are. And for that I shall bathe you.'

She helped him into the bath. The water was warm, but not hot enough to stop Arthur from shaking. Meadhbh took a washing ball out of her sleeve and lathered her hands with the suds. She spread the lather on his back and slowly worked it into his skin, then she took the jug, scooped it full of water and washed the soap off. Next she turned to his front, smiling as her fingers rubbed the suds through the dark hair on his chest. She smiled even more broadly when her hands reached below the water level. 'Ah your *bod* is risen.' She put more soap on her hands and began work on that, but had not been long at it before Arthur was relieved of his pent up lust. She smiled again. 'Do not waste it all,' she said as she helped him out of the bath. She wrapped the drying cloth around his shoulders, and Arthur felt like a child, not that he had ever had a bath as a child, but Meadhbh's ministrations were almost like those of a nurse with her charge. Was it not time for the child to become a man? He felt his cock arising again, so let the drying cloth slip and lifted her smock over her head, but was dismayed to find yet more clothing underneath. He ran a hand into the top of her bodice and caressed her breasts. When he touched her nipples she shuddered. He looked at her face, her eyes were closed and she wore a blissful smile. The bodice was loosely tied and easy to unlace, even though his fingers fumbled at the task, and soon her breasts were free, pert and creamy in the candlelight. She let her kirtle drop to the floor and there they stood for a tense moment naked together. Then Meadhbh pulled him into the bath with her, making a huge splash across the floor, and they rolled over trying to grasp each other, but there was little room and the water was cooling, so as one they rose and stepped out of bath. Meadhbh's nipples stood on end and as they dripped water all round them she pulled Arthur's head towards one breast and set his mouth down upon it. He lifted his head and looked into her green eyes. 'Suck,' she ordered, and he obeyed, just like a babby, but a babby would never have felt the blood course as his did now.

He was never sure quite how it happened next, whether she pushed him, or he pulled her, but betimes they were both lying on the bed and he was ready, slipping into her and pushing his cock, hot in the depths of her until he was lost. Several times he was lost. For a time he found himself, then was lost again. When they were finally spent Meadhbh ran a finger down his scar again and said, 'That is good. Our coupling too will encourage the crops to grow a-plenty.'

'And the bath? Was that part of the encouragement?'

'It is good to come to Brigid cleansed of the world.' She kissed him and Arthur wondered if that would be that then; a yearly bath and mating ritual to encourage the crops to flourish. But for now he did not mind. It was a worthy cause.

'The Queen's men. The Queen's men,' Daniel's voice rang out through the corridors. 'They are on their way.'

Arthur leapt up. Good, he thought, the Queen's men, not

Ormond's. He kissed Meadhbh quickly on the top of her head and dressed. She lay on the bed watching him and smiling. He ran from the room leaving her lying there still smiling. At least, he thought, she has faith enough in me not to fret about an invasion.

Arthur ran up to the battlements. The men were in a line at all corners shooting arrows and firing muskets. Arthur wondered if anyone would go into his chamber to help the defence and find the smiling Meadhbh lying naked on his bed. He did not care, he was a proper man now, fielded *and* bedded. He grabbed a bow and shot several arrows striking at least two of the Queen's men.

The Queen's men did not stay long. They were small in number and suffered several casualties without getting close enough to the castle to climb the parapets. Their own shots had fewer targets and generally hit the castle walls and fell to the ground impotent. Arthur regretted the two horses killed in the river, but the attackers retreated and the castle returned to its normal routine. But there was no doubt they would be back and Arthur sent word to Desmond by messenger that they would need more supplies to withstand a siege.

They would have to wait some weeks, Arthur knew, before the supplies arrived. He hoped the English would take as long to prepare themselves. They would certainly need extra men if they wanted to succeed. In the meantime his evening with Meadhbh at the Feast of Brigid proved to be the first of many. At first he wondered if she might be a strumpet, so free was she with her favours, and so easy had she been to penetrate. Surely she could not have been a virgin, and he wished Donal was there to talk the matter over, although he was probably no more knowledgeable about womanly wiles than Arthur himself. As time went on he began to realise that she loved him, as he loved her, although he could not exactly say what love was, except this scorching desire for the exquisite experience of being inside her, sometimes riding hard and fast with sheer lust, others rising and falling gently with soft desire.

Meadhbh still worked in the kitchen and in the absence of pages, served at table, and he had to be wary not to be so lax as to let castle security suffer, but every night, when he was not on watch he took her to his bed. Many a time afterwards he just looked at her, admiring the way her breasts glowed creamy in the candle light; the way her red hair spread out over the bolster. Sometimes afterwards they talked, then he enjoyed being able to teach her the ways of the world, telling her about Bristol and Bridie. And Carraigh. 'Miss you Carraigh?' she asked stroking his scar.

'Aye. But I am happy here.' He kissed her.

But it was not the world, or even Carraigh, Meadhbh was most interested in. It was the ways of the flesh, and Arthur could not get enough of her.

*

One night Desmond and Eleanor arrived under cover of darkness, with supplies enough for twelve days. 'Mossa. That was a fine day,' Desmond said when Arthur told him of the skirmish. 'It warms the very heart of me to have Tom Dubh Butler's son fighting off the Queen's men.' He put an arm around Arthur's shoulder and led him into the banquet hall.

Eleanor followed. 'Would you acquit yourself so well if it was Butler blood you were spilling?' she asked.

'I believe I would.' As long as it was not Piers, Arthur added to himself. 'What of my friend, Donal?'

'He is fit and well, last I heard.' She paused to help Desmond into a chair. 'We met Ormond on our journey from the Pale,' she continued. 'Ormond told my lord to become a loyal subject.'

'And that I am. I do not want to fight the English. I just want to retain what is rightfully mine.'

Eleanor gave a hard laugh. 'And that after we had to give up Castlemaine in order to be pardoned.'

Desmond looked uncomfortable at the reminder of the loss. 'And what's this I hear about you and the child Meadhbh?' he asked changing the subject.

'She is no child. She is sixteen. Four years and more above

marriageable age.'

'And do you intend to exchange vows with her?' Eleanor asked.

Arthur looked at the floor. 'It…it is a responsibility I have not considered,' he said at last.

'Whack to you.' Desmond slapped him on the back. 'You are wed enough as you are.' He took Eleanor's hand and kissed it as if in apology for not pursuing the marriage theme. 'Women maketh the man.'

Eleanor smiled. 'Aye,' she said. 'We do.'

Chapter Seventeen

Desmond and Eleanor left after a few days, and the threatened siege never took place. Munster was in an uproar, but still the castle at Askeaton remained untouched.

Arthur enjoyed the rhythm of the seasons and the ancient rituals the women, Daniel and the other men liked to observe. Thus they celebrated the spring equinox, 'time of the winds', then came Beltaine at the beginning of May when they celebrated the sap rise. Now the bees were loud in the summer meadow. Obviously Arthur's coupling with Meadhbh had done the crops a power of good. Life at the castle went about its normal routine, interrupted only by the occasional messenger. Then one dark night Desmond and Eleanor returned, dishevelled and tired, and Arthur's great joy was that Donal was amongst their small retinue.

'Should I go back into the field?' Arthur asked Donal when they had a quiet moment together over a goblet of wine.

'The *field*?' Donal laughed. 'There are no fields left. We fight in the streets and anywhere there are English or Ormond troops. Tom Dubh has been appointed military governor of Munster. He is fighting rebels on all fronts.'

'Do you see him...or..?'

'Piers? No. But they are losing some of their staunchest

supporters. English treatment of innocent Irish folk has disgusted many.'

The latest news was that Ormond and the Queen's man, Pelham, had joined forces and were rampaging through the shire killing, burning and looting. 'They have sacked castle after castle and left nothing behind them.' Donal took a drink from his goblet. 'I fear Desmond will have a time of it trying to keep a hold on Askeaton.'

'I have done my best here, but I would like to be out in the world of men again.' Arthur sighed. 'I enjoy my life here with Meadhbh...'

Donal laughed again. 'From the little I have seen that is understandable.'

'…but castle life is unbecoming of a man,' Arthur continued. 'It lacks vigour...and companionship.'

'Aye,' said Donal. 'I have missed you, too.' And they both laughed.

'Eleanor has put marriage into my mind.'

'It is a good Christian custom.' Donal took another sip of wine and appeared to be considering just how good.

'If we were betrothed before I went off to fight, Meadhbh would know I intend to return.'

Supper the following night was held in the banqueting hall, although the size of the party was such that they were swallowed in the vastness of it. 'The Lord Deputy goads us,' Eleanor said as they began on the roasted venison. 'He *wants* us to rebel. Then the English can have all our lands.'

'We are pressured on all sides.' Desmond wiped his brow with a shaking hand.

Eleanor took his hand in hers to still it. 'There is news that the papal flag is flying in the South. While my lord is being pushed into a corner by the English he is compelled by his kin to consider joining their rebellion.'

Arthur wanted a chance to talk with Eleanor without Meadhbh's hearing, and waited until she had left the hall with empty platters. 'What of me?' Arthur asked. 'Should I go back into the field?'

'What is your wish?' Eleanor asked. 'You have acquitted yourself with honour here.'

'Then I beg leave to join the men when they return to battle.'

'Ah,' said Desmond, 'There are to be no battles. I have been bound over to keep the peace. I have lost my taste for rebellion.'

Eleanor held Desmond's hand. 'My lord is unwell. He's needs to rest,' and so life at Askeaton carried on with its lord and mistress in residence.

Arthur felt disappointment, mixed with relief; he would not have to tell Meadhbh he was leaving. He could, though, ask for her hand, then when Desmond and Eleanor set off again, and he with them, she would know for certain that he would return – unless death intervened which he doubted very much.

There would need to be a full moon on the rise. He'd heard the women talking in the kitchen about a villager who wed on a waning moon and what bad luck she was bringing down on herself. Of course, this was a betrothal, not a wedding, but best to be sure. He bid his time until the propitious night and after they had coupled, he kissed Meadhbh deeply, then lifted his head to look at her. Her eyes were closed and she looked sweetly contented. She should really be below helping Roisin and Fainch, but they did not seem to mind his favouring her. They encouraged it, in fact. 'I shall return shortly,' he said, and as he did most evenings he left her for a few minutes to climb the ramparts, check the watch and look out over the river and the countryside. The moon was just on full, high and bright in the sky, illuminating both castle and countryside. Not an auspicious night for an attack; a wise adversary would creep up in the dark, but a most auspicious night for a betrothal.

When he returned to the bed chamber Meadhbh was asleep. He had worked himself up to this point, going over in his mind the words he would say, and now all he could do was stand looking down at her pale face framed by her red hair; her strong-boned limbs and taut breasts. He pulled a cover over her naked body and sat on the bed, took her hand and she stirred. 'Meadhbh,' he whispered.

'Mmm?'

'Are you awake?'

She nodded, but added, 'Tired…'

'Will we get married?'

She sat up then, her eyes wide. 'A handfasting? Oh, aye, Arthur.' She put her arms around his neck and kissed his lips, his face, his neck, his ears, at which point he felt the familiar stirring in his loins. 'We will seal it in a minute. When should we wed?'

'A betrothal is a year and a day, but May is not good. It will have to be June.' She was babbling in her happiness. '*Gráim thu*,' she laughed, kissing him again.

'And I love you,' he replied, 'Dearly.'

She began kissing him again, her hand stroking his thighs and creeping towards his loin, then suddenly stopped and asked seriously, 'Does my lord know? Has he granted permission for us to handfast?'

Arthur hesitated. He had not thought of that. Desmond seemed pleased enough with the arrangement, and Eleanor had asked if they were going to exchange vows. 'My Lady Eleanor has sanctioned it,' he assured her.

She jumped out of bed and threw her smock on.' I must away to tell Fainch and Roisin. They will be happy for us.' She turned at the door and said, 'Get into bed. I will return.'

Return she did with the two women behind her laughing softly. They pushed Meadhbh into the chamber and to Arthur's dismay followed her in. Meadhbh threw off her smock and climbed into bed beside Arthur, and for a moment Arthur thought they were meant to couple in front of the two older women. His ardour left him as they came to the bedside. Meadhbh took Arthur's hand in hers and held their hands out to Fainch who tied them together with a green cloth. 'Green for fertility and good luck,' Meadhbh said, as the women left the chamber laughing. His bod has risen again and eagerly he took her, plunging deep within the cave of her; his cave, his betrothed, his beloved.

*

Next morning the whole castle knew and Desmond and Eleanor were quick to congratulate Arthur and Meadhbh on their betrothal. Donal was enthusiastic in his greetings. 'It is a wonder.' He slapped Arthur on the back. 'A wonderful wonder, and I wish you both health and happiness.' But there was little time to dwell on this wonder, because Daniel Caech came a-running with news of a messenger at the gate.

'I have a message from the priest, Nicholas Sander,' the man said when Arthur called to him through the portcullis.

'He is English?'

'Yes, but Catholic.'

'Is the message written down?'

'Aye.'

'Leave it on the ground and we will collect it from there.' Arthur held the musket while Donal went out to fetch the letter. The seal looked genuine enough. 'Wait,' Arthur instructed the messenger and he handed Donal the musket while he took the letter to Desmond.

'It seems true enough,' Eleanor said after she had read the message to Desmond. 'So the rumours of help from the Pope and the King of Spain hold.'

'Bring the messenger in,' Desmond ordered.

What transpired Arthur did not know, but soon after the messenger left. It was not the last time they saw him; he came every three or four days with letters from the priest outlining the plans and encouraging Desmond to join in the crusade against the heretical Queen.

The troubles drew closer until one night the watch called, 'Fire.'

Arthur told Meadhbh to go with him and they both struggled into the clothes they had abandoned in haste an hour or so before. As they left the bed chamber Donal was running out of his quarters pulling on his jerkin with some of the other men behind him, and they pushed past Eleanor who was helping Desmond up the steps to the battlements. 'Put the men on guard and watch all corners,' Arthur ordered. Roisin, Fainch and Daniel were already at the top looking at a sky alight with flames. Askeaton Abbey was on fire. Arthur instructed the men to arm themselves, but to try and save the abbey would be foolhardy. 'See yon line of horsemen,' Desmond pointed to the silhouettes on the far bank. 'They are just a-waiting for us to fetch water from the river for to dowse the flames.'

'Who else will be out there?' Donal said, not expecting an answer. There was nothing to do except stand and watch while the abbey burnt almost to the ground.

Eleanor stood beside Desmond holding a cloak around his shoulders. 'They will be after desecrating the grave of the late Countess,' she said. 'The castle will be next.'

'I imagine Tom Dubh will be none too pleased at this insult to his dead mother. Her tomb lies in there.' Desmond turned to Daniel Caech. 'Prepare a messenger to ride. If we are to stay loyal we must call on Tom Dubh's help. Sander said in his last despatch that Ormond is camped but two days' ride away.'

The messenger was despatched and they waited. A week went by, but the messenger did not return and no other answer came from Tom Dubh, although Sander's messenger arrived again. Without Elizabeth's permission, the Lord Chief Justice in Dublin had proclaimed Desmond a traitor. Eleanor read the message out to the men then said, 'We have decided. There is no alternative but to turn to Nicholas Sander. We shall join the rebellion in the name of the Pope.' Desmond's hands seemed to shake more than ever and his limp was more pronounced, and Arthur wondered how he would fare in the wilds of Munster again.

'I would like, my lord, to fight.' Arthur turned to Eleanor to see her response. 'Would that I could join you?'

She smiled at him. 'What about your betrothed?'

'Is it not a woman's lot to wait at home while her husband fights to keep her safe.' Then Arthur smiled at what he had said to a woman who never left her husband's side. 'Unless, my lady, the woman is a mighty warrior herself.'

Eleanor laughed. 'I think we can make other arrangements here.' She turned to Desmond. 'My lord?' He nodded his agreement, and

Arthur felt with that nod the first chill of loss. He would miss Meadhbh, but did not Desmond and Eleanor return to Askeaton frequently? He was sure they would accommodate his desire to see his betrothed when circumstances permitted.

Some days later he and Donal were kitted out with a band of about fifty men. He was not to go with Desmond as he thought but to join Richard Butler, bastard son of Sir Edmund. In the meantime Desmond would gather more troops before setting off.

'Support is strong for the Spanish invasion.' Eleanor was looking more cheerful as she waved the men goodbye. 'My lord and I shall join you at Ard na Caithne. We are promised six hundred foot and two hundred horse.'

Arthur's last night with Meadhbh had not been as he expected. She wept at the thought of his departure, refusing to be comforted. 'But I shall be back ere long. You know how frequently Desmond and Eleanor return.' Meadhbh sniffed and began crying again.

'We'll be wed in June,' Arthur tried.

'That is many moons away,' she wailed, and because Arthur felt some guilt about leaving her, and his mind was already elsewhere, his manhood hung as limp as a flag on a windless day. If he was honest with himself he was happy to say goodbye to Meadhbh's needless grief. He would return, of that he was sure, but for now he was pleased to be away from the confines of the castle. So as he set off in the soft light of morning with a small group of Desmond's men and their escort, Conn, his heart lifted and he rejoiced to be back in the real world.

*

It was Samhain, Festival of the Dead, by the time they reached Cloghane on the Dingle Peninsula where they were to wait for the rebel Butler kin to join them. The veil between the upper and lower worlds had thinned, and the villagers would not go anywhere until they had celebrated All Souls. Some of the lads they had gathered on their journey practised the old ways and on their last night in

Cloghane they sat around the fire telling stories of how the dead left their *sidhs* and drifted over the countryside haunting the living. As they listened the flames made shadows which waved and whispered like the very ghosts themselves.

'It is madness,' said one woman of the village. 'To begin battle at Samhain. It is too late to be fighting. Any sensible man, Spanish or Irish, should be sitting by a turf fire be now.'

'Aye,' Donal said. 'I remember Desmond telling me that in the old days the best time was Beltaine, halfway between spring equinox and summer solstice. At Samhain they all came in and made peace until sap-rise.'

'Methinks,' said Arthur, 'it's a plot to catch the English off guard,' and they all laughed. But it was no laughing matter. Several of the men were reluctant to leave the village and join the fight.

'Tis a risky time to be abroad, so it is,' said their guide, Conn, 'but you cannot leave the Spanish stranded at Ard na Caithne.' He paused, 'Even if the others are delayed by some mishap there remains the small garrison left behind at the fort from the landing last year.'

'What happened to their comrades?'

'James FitzMaurice was first to go. He was killed whilst at his prayers at the Holy Cross. The others fought valiantly and well, but alas they fell to the sword.'

'All of them?' asked Donal.

'All, except the priest, Nicholas Sander. He is at liberty yet.'

'Ah, Nicholas Sanders,' commented Arthur dryly. 'He seems more like a juggler of people, than a priest. His man was back and forth to Askeaton begging Desmond to join the fray.'

'And now he has,' said Conn as if that was all the answer that was needed.

Arthur changed the subject. 'Would you take a letter for me. To Askeaton.'

'Aye, I will, but it might be some moons afore I get back.'

It was better than nothing. Arthur knew that Meadhbh could not read either the Gaelic or English, but Daniel Caech would read the letter to her, in which case he would need to maintain a formal approach. One of the villagers had quill and ink and a small piece of parchment to spare on which Arthur wrote: 'My dearest beloved. I miss you more than I can say…' That was not quite true. He had been enjoying the company of men, and the outdoors, cold though it may be. 'I trust that you are well and those at the castle. I will be home ere long. The Spanish ships should be here…' That last was crossed out with thick, black ink strokes; it would implicate Meadhbh and the castle in the invasion if it should fail and the letter got into the wrong hands. 'All bodes well here, chilly but we are in good heart. *Gráim thu,* Arthur.'

Next day a lookout from the village came back from climbing St Brendan's Mountain which offered views for miles across the peninsula. 'Sails,' he said. 'On the horizon.' If they did not move now they would miss the action. Perhaps Richard Butler had mistaken the rendezvous point. Desmond with his eight hundred should arrive any day and there would be too many men to manoeuvre into place at once. It was an opportune time to go.

Four curragh were required, but it would be relatively safe to make this voyage by day. In spite of Conn's words of encouragement, several young men stayed behind, afraid of fighting at such an inauspicious time. Conn had others to guide elsewhere so he bade Arthur and the men farewell as they headed out towards the open sea.

Out at sea, but closing fast, was a small fleet of galleons, square sails billowing, their sea castles high above sturdy hulls. They were still too far away to distinguish which flag flew from the masts. Arthur counted them. 'One...two...three! I expected more. 'Maybe this is the vanguard,' he suggested, but he did not feel as optimistic as the words allowed.

As their curragh came into the harbour they saw but a single man on the beach watching their arrival. Where were Butler and his men? They pulled up on the beach and began unloading the boats. Soon after the galleons entered the harbour, and the men stopped to watch them for a moment. It was with relief they noted the red flags with the yellow cross. These were indeed Spanish vessels. They had only three masts, but a swing canon was clearly visible while light guns sat on the main deck. Sailors were trimming the sails and, satisfied, Arthur and the men with him returned to the task of off-loading the curraghs.

When the boats were empty the oarsmen climbed back in and pushed them out again. The lone onlooker came forward, picked up a small box of ammunition and led the way up the beach to a point where it was easiest to climb to the cliff top above. They scrambled up. 'It is a three-mile walk to the fort,' their guide said. 'Take with you what you can and we will send others for the rest. We will need all the hands we can get when the Pope's men come ashore.'

'Has Richard Butler arrived? Arthur asked.

The man shrugged. 'Not to my knowledge.'

'We expected them at Cloghane.'

'I expect he's a-waiting Viscount Baltinglass. He is the author of this plan and is to join us here also.'

'Baltinglass of the Pale who revolted at Glendlough?' one of Desmond's men asked. The other man shrugged again as if to say, who cares which Baltinglass, and kept walking.

'Look,' Donal cried and they turned to watch the galleons turn about and sail out of the harbour. All hands stopped work and there was a general sigh of disappointment, but almost immediately the men went back to the task.

'Tide's too low,' said the man leading them.

'They may prefer to come in under cover of dark,' suggested Arthur.

As they approached the fort Arthur wondered how anyone could inhabit such an abandoned shell. A swarthy man came forward to greet the band of new-comers. 'I am Pedro. Welcome to Fort Dún an Óir.' He spoke with an accent, but he was easily understood. He shook as many hands as he could manage. 'Welcome. Come and eat while we await the arrival of the Pope's men,' and he led the way into the fort.

'He'll be one of the men from last year's attempt,' Arthur surmised and Donal agreed.

'I am afraid we can offer little shelter, but the first task when the men arrive is to rebuild our fortification. They are to show us a new Italian method.'

It was not until nightfall that the galleons returned and anchored in the bay. The men on shore watched for signs of movement, straining their eyes to see through the dark. The moon rose and they could more clearly see the ships resting in the bay. The sails were furled but there was not a flicker of light from aboard. 'Why are they waiting so?' asked one of Desmond's men.

'Who knows who is lurking in the hills and vales quietly a-waiting their chance,' said another. 'Those English could have learnt some Irish ways be now.'

'We know not what they are thinking,' Donal said. 'But it's a beautiful sight, so it is.'

They watched for some time, then certain that nothing would happen until the break of day they huddled into sheepskin cloaks and sheltered from the worst of the wind in a corner of the castle shell. The night was cold and the sky clear but they slept and when they woke the galleons looked as if they were on fire in the glow of the reflected sunrise. 'What a sight,' Arthur said, as he ate the dry bread they had been given. 'We had best make our way down, Donal.'

They had to go back along the peninsula some way before they could climb down and onto the sands of the bay. By then the first of the skiffs had been rowed ashore and several of the garrison's men were running to welcome the foreigners. Although they spoke different languages the warmth of the welcome was clear by the smiles on both sides. Arthur and Donal helped unload the skiff so the oarsman could row back for more men and goods. There were several skiffs in the water now, and they were kept busy all morning running trunks and building materials up the beach. They left them at the foot of the cliff at a spot where the sand was dry and access easier and other men took them on up to the old fort.

The wind off the sea was cool, but they were sweating by the time the sun told them it was noon. So they were pleased when a band of local men, women and children appeared over the ridge of the hill, marched down to the harbour and immediately began helping with the unloading. By now, too, there were many Spanish hands to help.

Last ashore was the captain of the ship. Arthur had lost Donal in the melee but he, himself, was there to help the captain out of the skiff. 'I am Sebastiano di San Giuseppe of Bologna,' the captain said taking Arthur's hand and stepping out of the boat.

'Welcome to you and your brave Spaniards,' Arthur said.

'The ships are Spanish, but we are not all Spaniards. I am from Italy and many of my men are Italian also. We fight for the same cause,' and he crossed himself slowly, deliberately, unlike the quick and illicit crossing that went on in public in England and Ireland. He took another look around. 'The Earl of Desmond? The Viscount of Baltinglass?' he asked. 'Where are they?'

'We still a-wait them, Captain.'

The captain turned to another man stepping out of a skiff. 'This is Colonel Don Sebastian.' He gave a short laugh. 'He *is* a Spaniard.'

The colonel gave Arthur a brisk nod and moved up the beach.

One of the leaders of the kerne pushed his way forward and took over. 'We are fortifying the old garrison up there,' he said to the captain pointing to the cliff top.

The Italian shrugged. 'We have much to do.' He walked up the beach and began organising the men in carrying the building materials they had brought up onto the cliff top. Arthur was disappointed to note that most of the newcomers were boys, but he did not have time to dwell on this. If he thought dragging the goods up the beach was hard work, it was a day's holiday in comparison to getting the building materials up the cliff. But there were many willing hands. They worked through the dusk and only gave up when there was not enough light to see their footing. The villagers did not bother going home, It would waste time. If they stayed in the fort they could start work at daybreak on the morrow.

Bread and porter was served and Arthur and Donal settled down amongst the crowd in the corner of the castle shell. A small boy approached and sat beside them. 'Are you here to fight, so?' Donal asked.

'My father says I am too young. But I don't think I am.'

Arthur looked him up and down. 'Maybe next year,' he said. '*Cad is ainm duit?*'

'My name is Eamon.'

'Well, Eamon,' Donal said, 'do you want to share a sheepskin?' he nodded and they settled, the three of them under two sheepskins.

The moon came out. '*Attenti!*' called the captain, and the word was passed along to the exhausted people trying to sleep. Donal and Arthur left the boy, Eamon, sleeping and began work again in the moonlight. They finally finished when the moon had set. And slept, but not for long, at dawn they were at work again, aware of the urgent need to create the fort before the weather changed, and more importantly in case their arrival had been noted and the Queen's men were on their way. The work was difficult even for Donal who was used to hard labour. The new Italian method required the men to dig squares of earth and put them in place on the fort's remains. It was doubly difficult for Arthur whose hands had grown soft during his stay at Askeaton, but he, like those around him, gave of his all to build a strong fortification as shelter and protection. There were many hands – local men and children, Eamon amongst them, bent to the work with the Irish faithful, Spanish and Italians. A priest walked amongst them and spoke words of encouragement.

Arthur straightened his back from lifting yet another slab of earth for the bulwark, and in spite of the hard work he felt proud, life had a purpose and the fort was in an ideal position. At its back was Mount Brandon and to the fore it commanded a great view of harbour and coast. He looked out to sea. Clouds were gathering on the horizon. The anchored ships rose with the swell. They would need to hurry even more to beat the storm. Cut, bend, lift, pass along. Cut, bend, lift, pass along. Cut... There was no time to think of anything else.

Local wives, daughters and sisters cooked the meals. Food was brought from the village and the women also used food brought from Spain although it was a mystery to them how to cook some of it, and the Spanish boys had to explain what to do, as best they could. They all ate heartily at dinner time that noon and Arthur was almost asleep on his feet. There was shelter enough now for them to sleep under complete cover, but the fort needed much more work. He put his back into it again, longing for nightfall and a dark, moonless night. They could not work in the dark, even rain would be welcome.

Finally the day was done. The light faded and the clouds grew blacker. They ate by candlelight, their hunger so deep they could not wait for the priest to bless the food. They huddled together men, women and children; Irish, Italian and Spaniards. It did not matter; they were working for a common cause, the liberation of Ireland and the restoration of the true faith. Arthur's last thought was of Meadhbh. He wondered what she would be doing. Probably with the castle almost empty the three of them would be sitting on the bench at the kitchen table gossiping about some village lass, or... and his thought made him smile...planning Meadhdh's nuptials. With that thought he slept and soundly for a good part of the night. Just as dawn was breaking he woke, but was so exhausted he fell asleep again. He dreamt he was on a ship at sea in a gathering storm, with waves booming against the hull, crash, boom. Bang. The passengers screamed, and he awoke to the screams of women and children: the fort was being bombarded and he leapt up.

Some of the women ran outside to escape and ran straight back in. 'We are cut off,' one cried.

'The red coats are out there,' another shouted.

The Captain passed the message down through one of the Italian commanders. They were to stay calm. The fortifications might not be finished but they had food enough for two weeks, including the locals who were also trapped there. They would withstand this onslaught with God on their side.

Arthur went to the seaward side of the fort and pushed his way through the men to a place where he could see over the bulwark. An English ship lay in the harbour. As he watched, it fired a cannon at one of the three Spanish ships. And another. Then another. The ship caught fire in the hull and soon the blaze had spread up to the fore castle. Then the Spanish galleon tipped forward and quietly, almost gracefully, sank. Cannon balls flew into the fort. Some fell short while others hit the end which was empty of people. Arthur went in search of Donal and Eamon, but a Spaniard handed him a musket before he had the chance to find either. He fired shot after aimless shot, the English were too far distant to be in any danger and soon the men in the fort saw their error in wasting ammunition thus. They must wait until the enemy drew closer before firing any more.

The enemy appeared over the hill, a long line of them which seemed never to end. They dropped down into the bay until there seemed to be as many of them as grains of sand on the beach. Futile to hope that Desmond and his eight hundred would appear. Or Richard Butler and Baltinglass. The walls of the old fort were stout enough to withstand much of the impact, but the new earthworks were too soft. They had not had time to harden in the sun. They were breached in several places, and men rushed to mend the gaps. Still the enemy was too far away to aim at. Several men fell and a quick look told Arthur they were beyond hope.

It was a long day and Arthur had not time to eat. He caught sight of Donal once but they were both too busy trying to mend the fortifications to talk. When the sun set the pounding stopped and he went in search of food, Eamon and Donal. He was starving. The women had done what they could but the meal of Spanish rice and tough boiled chicken was disappointing. He ate it nonetheless, then pushed his way through the tired men, stepping around the dying. Here the priest was busy. '*Per istam sanctan unctionem*,' he chanted over one man. He moved on to a young woman. '*...et suam piissimam misericordiam...Indulgeat tibi Dominus*,' Arthur heard him say as he blessed yet another casualty.

At last Arthur found Eamon and Donal leaning against one of the standing walls talking to a group of boys from the village. Donal was finishing a story which made the lads laugh. It was such a sweet sound that Arthur could have cried. 'For sure, won't our own men be creeping up a-hind the English this very night?' he said trying to add reassurance to the laughter, but the words did not ring true. Baltinglass and Desmond would need thousands of men to out-number the enemy on the beach and surrounding hills. And there had been no sign of them.

The men took turns on watch. Nobody seemed to stray from the camp fires lit amongst the English tents. The captain held council with the priest and some of the senior officers. He included Arthur and Donal as the only English speakers amongst the Irish band. 'We could try an ambush, but I fear we are outnumbered,' the Captain said.

'Best to wait them out,' the priest offered. 'They cannot last long with so many mouths to feed.'

All agreed and with a watch set up they settled down for the night. Arthur slept fitfully. In his dreams he saw a parade of people from his past: Piers, Morveen, Aefe, the Earl, Bren and Bridie. And Meadhbh whom he watched from afar with longing. As she drew closer he could see that she was crying, but Bridie was smiling as she beckoned for him to join them. Arthur woke with a start. It must be time for his watch. Stars shone hard in a dark blue sky, but provided none of the joy they usually did. All was still, the only sound someone sobbing quietly. No doubt there would be more losses with daybreak. Arthur's watch was the final one for the night. At the sentry post he nodded at the Spanish soldier to tell him to go, and was glad of something to do as he stood hands clapped under his armpits for warmth.

Slowly the sky lightened. With the first rays of the sun came the first volley of gunfire. The fighting at sea was renewed and another Spanish ship went down. The walls of the fort were breached in several places. Many dead lay about the old fort while the living moved away from the damaged areas, leaving their dead behind.

They would be easy targets if they were to bring the dead in during daylight. The whole end of that wall was completely exposed, and Arthur remembered the toil that had gone into building it only a day or so before. So many hands, so much time and all destroyed in a flash of cannon fire.

Amazingly they survived another day, although with losses, but they were now huddled uncomfortably in what was left of the old fort, and that night there was no let-up in the attack. Eamon found Arthur and Donal.

'*Conas atá tú*?' Donal asked and the boy began to cry.

'Your mother?' Arthur asked.

Eamon nodded.

'Your father?'

The boy nodded again. 'Gone to God in heaven,' he said and he clung to Arthur's legs in terror.

'Come. We will find you somewhere to rest,' Donal said. 'Where are your little friends from last night?'

'A cannon got them, too,' Eamon said simply.

The three spent the night, sleepless and afraid. Arthur thought about Meadhbh and wished he'd had the sense to stay at Askeaton. He longed for her arms about him, to hear her whisper, '*Gráim thu*,' and to whisper back, 'I love you too', but it was torture to think. He had chosen this path; he had only himself to blame for cutting himself adrift from her. This was God's punishment on him for failing in his duty. He shut his mind to such thoughts and concentrated on the present; looking after Eamon and getting through the bombardment.

With dawn on the third day a runner went out with a white flag to surrender to the English leader, Lord Grey de Wilton. He was followed by Captain di San Giuseppe, Colonel Don Sebastian and an Italian officer. The surrender was accepted. The firing stopped. And the nightmare began.

Chapter Eighteen

'We are to be taken prisoner,' the colonel said. 'Gather arms and ammunition ready for collection and wait in the fort.'

The priest gave the last rites to the dying who could not be moved, and men gathered the bodies of the dead into one area where the women keened over them. There was much to prepare for their upcoming journey under guard. Some gathered food while others relieved the dead of warm clothing and boots, if they had them. Beakers of soup were passed around and drunk, if not lustily, then out of practicality. They would need some sustenance before marching off to their captivity.

'Where is Donal?' Eamon asked Arthur.

'You take this into you and then we will find him.' Arthur handed Eamon a beaker and watched to make sure he drank every last drop. 'Now,' he said, 'we look for Donal. But we must be quick for we have work to do.'

They found Donal in a dungeon below. The door had obviously been used for fire-wood as all that remained were the hinges. It was dim, the only outside light coming from a small slit high above in the stonework, and they could see several children huddled around him.

'We have surrendered,' Arthur explained. 'We are to prepare to march.'

Donal had taken a shot to the leg but insisted he was well enough to travel and hobbled a few steps as proof. 'Eamon, you must keep close to us,' Donal said. 'Mustn't he, Arthur?'

Arthur nodded. 'All you children must stay close.' He turned back to Donal. 'For the moment, you stay here. You will need to save that leg. I shall go and find clothes for the children.' He held out a hand to some of the older boys. 'You...and you...and you, come with me.' They hesitated. 'On my word,' Arthur said. 'The firing has stopped. And things should get better once we are away from here. At least in a prison they do not fire cannon at you all the long day.' The boys moved towards the door. 'Eamon, you take care of Donal, and these three young ones. We will be back soon.' He and the boys left the dungeon and ran up the steps.

At the top Arthur sent the boys to collect muskets, broadswords and other weapons and put them on the heap that was growing by one of the entrances, while he went to look for suitable clothes among the dead. It was a distasteful job, but it could save lives. The best bodies to plunder he decided were those with the least blood on their clothes. He found a young Spanish sailor, with a woollen doublet and sturdy boots, who had been shot through the back of the head. Arthur felt sick as he lifted the boy to remove the doublet, but the clothes were a find and would serve some prisoner well. Children's clothing was going to prove more difficult because none of the poor dead innocents were well clad and were either bare-footed or wearing worn out pieces of badly stitched leather. A villager about Donal's size provided a coarse but warm woollen cloak, and Arthur had just added this to the clothes in his arms when the first of the enemy troops stormed in.

With swords swinging and muskets a-blaze the enemy shot and struck at everyone in their way. 'You traitorous bastard...' one shouted as he lopped off a man's head.

'You Godless woman...' cried another.

'You detestable Irish bastard of a bastard father.' Another struck out at one of the boys Arthur had brought up from the dungeon. The boy fell and was stabbed for good measure. Another fell beside him. Arthur turned and ran back down the stairs. Above, absolute panic reigned, and he knew as he ran into the dungeon there was no escape. This would only delay things. Donal was helping Eamon into a woollen jerkin. 'What is it?' asked Eamon.

'Massacre?' Donal did not require an answer.

Eamon and one of the younger boys began to cry. Arthur took Eamon's hand. 'Sh-sh-sh,' he said. 'They will not find us here.' Why, he asked himself, did he have to keep lying to the boy? Of course they would be found. It was only a matter of time. Meantime the four boys, Donal and Arthur sat in a huddle in a dark corner. If someone took a cursory look inside they might be safe. They spoke not a word. Arthur could feel the quivering bodies beside him and felt utterly helpless. Screams and the raucous cries of the attacking men came from above.

Finally the noise abated. Only the wail of a babby was heard, rising and falling like a keening woman. Then, a grunt of effort and that, too, was silenced. The voices retreated and a deathly quiet fell upon the fort. They waited. The dim light gave them no idea of the passage of time, but it could have been an hour they waited. Maybe more.

Arthur said, 'I shall venture out. You stay there.'

'No. I'll go,' said Donal.

'It must be me,' Arthur said. 'If they catch me I will tell them I am Tom Dubh's son.' Without a backward look he left.

At the top of the steps an English soldier was searching one of the dead for valuables. He looked up as Arthur appeared. 'Halt,' he called.

Arthur stood still. He might get away with it yet. If he could entice the soldier into the dungeon between them they could overcome him. It would be nasty for the boys, but already they had seen terrible things.

The soldier came closer, his sword at the ready. 'So we did not get the lot of you.'

'I am the son of the Earl of Ormond.'

'And I am the son of Her Majesty. Here,' he shouted. 'Here,' he called even louder, and some other soldiers came running. ''E says he's the son of Ormond.'

'Let's be seeing you then,' said one of the other soldiers.

Arthur stepped forward. 'I am the son of Black Tom Butler, Earl of Ormond.'

The soldier looked at him. 'I ain't never seen the Earl of Ormond.'

'He looks black enough,' a third soldier laughed.

'Could be a trick,' said the first.

'But if it ain't,' said the second, 'we could be in trouble.'

'And, there might be an 'andsome reward for rescuing 'im.'

'True. Put 'im with the other 'ostages.'

The first soldier took him by the arm, then suddenly pointed to the steps. 'Have you been down there?' he asked the men.

'I ain't,' said the second soldier.

'Me nee-va,' said the third.

'What's down there?' The soldier asked Arthur this time. 'If you be an earl's son you would not lie, now would you?' The other two soldiers were on their way down the steps.

'My friend,' Arthur called after them. The word 'friend' was out before he could check it. He should have said, 'my brother...my son...'

He was turned about and marched away as the remaining soldiers ran down the steps, muskets at the ready. He knew Donal would not think he had betrayed him and the boys. His intention had been to save them. Even now all was not lost, because the English soldiers would certainly think twice about murdering a friend of the Earl's son. And his child. He hoped Donal had the presence of mind to fabricate some story that would link their bloodlines with him.

He was led, stepping over dead bodies, sliding in lost blood to the entrance of the fort. A chill north-west wind bit into him. There were more bodies outside; those who tried to escape had fallen straight into enemy hands.

'We surrender,' he said to the soldier leading him, 'and this is what you do to us.'

'We? I thought you were the Earl's son. Are you one of them?' He waved a hand at the bodies lying on the ground.

'I am,' Arthur said proudly. 'But that does not alter the fact that I am the Earl of Ormond's son. And...and... he is fond of me.' They clambered down the cliff face and wove their way around the tents on the beach. 'What happened to our reinforcements?' he asked the soldier.

'Whose man are you?'

Arthur did not answer and the soldier pulled him along until they arrived at a large heavily guarded tent. One of the guards pushed Arthur in. A group of men obviously of some value to the enemy were gathered waiting silently. Arthur looked around. 'The Captain..?' he asked one man.

The man shook his head. 'I know not what happened to the Captain and his officers,' he said. 'I am Oliver Plunkett from Drogheda, and this is Father Laurence O'Moore.' Arthur introduced himself emphasising the name Butler.

'A familiar name,' said Plunkett.

'On both sides,' the priest added.

'What happened to our support?' Arthur asked.

The priest shrugged. Another man was pushed into the tent. Arthur recognised him as one of the villagers. 'You have been spared.'

'It was not my wish. I had to watch my wife and children slaughtered. But I am Eoghan O'Suileabhain, chief of the clan. They thought my life worth saving.' He grabbed his long unkempt hair in two hands and pulled hard. 'It is not, so,' he wailed.

'There are several village children still in the fort. I am hoping they will be saved. I have contrived it.' Arthur explained about the dungeon and sighed, 'Where is our God now? He appears to have abandoned us.'

'Never say such a thing.' Eoghan O'Suileabhain crossed himself.

Later soldiers came in and herded twenty or so of the Spanish and

Italian officers together. 'You are free to return to your homelands,' one of the soldiers told them. 'You are to tell your people about the poverty and infidelity of your Irish friends.' Arthur wished he had known that was going to happen, he would have risked sending Meadhbh another letter, via Spain, to say he was alive. News of the defeat would reach Askeaton soon enough - but the foreigners had been led away as soon as the thought had arrived in his head.

'Infidelity?' O'Moore managed a chuckle.

'Let's hope they tell the truth about this betrayal,' said Plunkett. 'May this not be the last fight for the Catholic faith on Irish soil.'

Later that day the same soldiers returned. They pushed Oliver Plunkett and Father Moore into a corner and onto the ground. Two soldiers sat on a man apiece to keep them down, while two others held fast to one arm each. The remaining solider drew out a single-edged backsword and rested the tip under the priest's nose. 'Do you accept the Queen as the head of the church?' he demanded. The two men said nothing. The soldier asked the question again. This time O'Moore cried, 'Long live Pope Gregory!'

'That fancy Nancy boy!' The soldier with the backsword laughed. He nodded at the men holding fast the arms. They lowered their captives' arms to the ground, and before anyone knew what was happening the soldier had cut off the thumbs of the two Catholic men who endured the torment stoically, not uttering a sound.

'Now what do you think?' the soldier waved his sword threateningly. 'Who is the head of the church in England and Ireland?'

Blood was dripping from the men's hands. Plunkett of Drogheda lifted his head, and said simply, 'The Pope.' Enraged the soldier cut off both their forefingers. It seemed he would not be happy until he had all digits lying on the floor, but when there was not a cry or a whimper from the Catholic men, although Arthur could see by their faces that they suffered, the soldier nodded at his companions and they left. Later still more soldiers came and set about them, making the same demands. The weight of the silence in the tent as the soldiers awaited an answer was heavy. Arthur was certain he would not have the same resolve under similar circumstances. In the matter of religion he was indifferent, but he admired the courage of these two.

'Rightho,' said one of the soldiers, as the silence lengthened, and they pushed the two men outside. It was not long before they were back. Now they were carried in. 'Obliging that blacksmiff,' said one soldier as he threw Plunkett into a corner.

'Handy 'ammer 'e's got,' said another, dumping Moore beside him.

'Broke both their arms 'n legs,' said the first. 'Most obliging he was. Now who is the head of the Church in Ireland?' Silence. The soldier kicked both men in the stomach and left them in disgust. 'Fink about it,' he said as he was leaving.

Arthur knew that everyone else in the tent must be feeling as he did – would they be next? Dinner that night was an unappetising cold soup accompanied by stale bread, both of which Arthur recognised as coming from the fort. But it was nourishing - and they would need nourishment for the long march ahead, if they were indeed to be saved. He ate it out of a sense of obligation to Meadhbh, although he could not conjure up her face as he thought of her, and he was too worried about Donal and the boys, to be able to swallow readily. He was also concerned for the two men lying in the corner of the tent, guarded by soldiers so that none of the other hostages could comfort them. But what could one do?

He was shamed to realise on waking next morning that he had slept the night through. It had been five days since he had been able to sleep beyond an hour or so. No wonder he had slept, but the day ahead was daunting. After breakfast of dry bread and weak ale Oliver Plunkett and Father Moore were carried outside, not to be seen again. Twenty-five or so hostages remained and they were inspected by some gentlemen officers. The Lord Deputy's secretary, Edmund Spenser introduced himself. He had a long face, high forehead and bulbous eyes. Around his neck he wore a lace turned-down collar. His companions, Admiral Sir William Winter and Captain Walter Ralegh of the Foot, wore military breastplates and high ruffs, and Ralegh, wearing a cocked hat with a feather in it, sported a small, pointed beard. The hostages were lined up and interviewed, and when Ralegh came to Arthur he raised an eyebrow at his reason for being spared and called Spenser who looked hard at Arthur. 'You have a brother?' he asked.

'Yes,' said Arthur. 'Piers Butler of Duiske is my brother.'

'Uncles?'

'Sir Edmund...James, and Edward.'

'And your mother?'

I...I know not where she is. The Earl of Ormond took me to his court and educated me.'

'Where would that be?'

'At Carraigh on the River Suir. But he has many castles, Kilkenny…'

The Captain of the Foot raised a hand to stop Arthur from going further. He and the admiral whispered quietly together before Ralegh returned and told Arthur to wait outside the tent. Here he was joined by the O'Suileabhain chief. Ahead they saw the priest and Plunkett hanging from a makeshift gallows. Two more men were brought out of the tent and taken a few steps away before being shot. By the time the three officials had made their choices twenty men remained with the guard. 'Hup,' called one of the guards. 'Form in twos.' They moved off expecting to be advanced to their permanent place of imprisonment, instead they were marched around the harbour and up the hill to the foot of Mount Brandon and forced to walk past row upon row of bodies. The air was heavy with the smell of blood and decay. Some soldiers had bodies propped against a tree and were using them for target practice. Arthur recognised many faces – the women who served their meals, the Spanish solider who handed him the musket, the man who had greeted them the first day. He looked for the priest, not wanting to think about who else he might see.

Moving along the rows ahead of them English soldiers beheaded the dead. They hurled the bodies wide out across the cliff top and into the roiling sea below, the heads were thrown onto a pile. The whump, whuff and faint following splash below beat a macabre rhythm.

Then there they were. Side by side. Donal and Eamon. Arthur turned away. He could still hear the splash of the bodies hitting the water. Bending over, he vomited on the ground in front of him. His guard pushed him forward. Another solider intervened. 'Someone you know?' he asked.

'Aye,' said Arthur.

'Then you've no need to look,' said the soldier.

*

They were a tragic group that stumbled out of Ard na Caithne, the prisoners forced like mules to pull the cart carrying their provisions, food for all and two barrels of ale for the soldiers. It rained every day of the long trek back to the Pale. Sometimes Arthur felt as if he was swimming, not walking. The whole country ran with water. Bogs became oceans; mountains waterfalls. Bare trees shone black and bleak, and all the while the rain dripped relentlessly on the forlorn bunch of hostages. It ran over their heads into their eyes; it dripped down the back of their jerkins and soaked into their shoes.

Before too long Eoghan O'Suileabhain had fallen and was left where he fell to die. Arthur opened his mouth to protest but nothing came out. He was numb with cold. And it got worse. The rain turned to sleet and the sleet to snow. For two days they sheltered in an abandoned hovel, not so much for the prisoners but for the benefit of their guards. There was a stream nearby for water, but there was no great comfort to be found in the hovel. Water dribbled down the walls and the ground was damp.

The hostages huddled together for warmth in one of the driest corners and whispered prayers together. *Pater noster qui es in coelis, sanctificetur nomen tuum.*

The soldier who had been kind to Arthur before they left on their march came across with the bread and water that had to suffice as their meal. 'Be careful,' he warned. 'They,' he nodded at the other guards who were quaffing ale from tankards, 'they know the Our Father as well as you do.'

'Hey John,' one of the guards called to him. 'Come and get your fill.'

Arthur nodded his thanks, and the hostages sat in silence while they ate. Then one shivering man began softly, '*Ave Maria, gratia plena, Dominus tecum, benedicta tu in mulieribus, et benedictus fructus ventris tui Iesus.*' The guards were now too busy carousing to be bothered with their captives. When they got to *in hora mortis nostrae* Arthur wondered just how close 'the hour of death' might be for some of them. The hostage who began the prayer had slipped into an exhausted sleep. Next morning he was dead. The guards threw his body into the swollen stream.

Arthur lay on the hard ground that night and began to believe that he would be next. He had not thought about Meadhbh for days, but dreamed he was holding her, and her soft voice, warm on his ear, whispered, 'They are calling you, but go you not,' and he heard Donal and Eamon calling, 'It is safe here. There is nothing to worry you. Come.'

*

They could not wait indefinitely for the rain to stop else they would run out of food, so on the third day they were marched off again with only a piece of stale bread to sustain them. The damp was now deep inside their bones. The stream had become a river, the willows that had once wept at its edges, marooned like islands. There was no way around the water so they had to wade waist deep through it. The cart had to be left behind and the prisoners carried what they could of what little was left. Two of the hostages slipped, fell and tumbled downstream, one of them became caught against a willow tree. 'Egads,' said one of their keepers when they reached the far side, 'We'd a-got an 'andsome price for him.' But they made no attempt to rescue him, if indeed he was able to be rescued. A guard tripped and was swirled away. Arthur was too cold and tired to feel any of the pleasure such an accident might have induced, but somewhere deep inside he was sustained by Meadhbh's call to him. 'Go you not.' He kept a firm footing and struggled on.

There were only fifteen hostages left. Once they reached the settlements they were given food and shelter and even a change of clothing. The weather took some time to improve, but the sun was shining the morning they walked into Dublin.

Dublin was a scruffy town; narrow muddy streets lined with merchant stores. This was the Pale and the place was alive with soldiers, some bearing the Saint George's cross, their red and white uniforms dirty and tattered, others dressed like the poorer townsfolk, only distinguishable by the muskets they carried. A handful of gentlemen officers rode past in their feathered hats and pleated pantaloons, but there would be no escaping them, for they carried both swords and pistols. Livestock, pigs, sheep, and a rooster wandered aimlessly in the streets, and Arthur could not imagine an Irish farmer leaving such expensive animals to their own devices. An English soldier came running out of a tavern chased by a serving boy, but as they ran in the opposite direction to the one the prisoners were taking they never did find out why. Arthur presumed it was a matter of a groat or two. Two young boys who painfully reminded Arthur of Donal and himself when young, dodged past them kicking a pig's bladder between them. After the cold but fresh country air, the city was fetid and it turned Arthur's stomach so that he retched into a gutter streaming with water and piss. One of the guards kicked him to move him along.

As the motley band of prisoners trudged up the hill to the Castle the ordinary folk stopped to watch them, some spitting as they passed, but many looking with sympathetic eyes. The cobblestones leading up to the castle, no doubt considered a luxury compared to the other streets of the Pale, were uneven and the men staggered over them in their fatigue. Forbidding though they looked, the gates to Dublin Castle were a welcome sight; they had arrived.

Up to this point the hostages had been treated the same. Now they were divided into groups - those who could fetch a ransom, those who might have information useful to the English and Arthur. He was not worth a ransom because they would have been charging their own leader. 'What about Desmond? Would he pay for him?'Arthur overheard a guard ask.

The guard called John said, 'We can but ask.'

'I doubt it,' Arthur chipped in from his position slumped against a cold stone wall. Now the journey was over he was too tired to even stand. 'He will not want to be seeing me again.'

'Get up,' ordered the first guard kicking him. Arthur did not move.

'Let's kill him,' said a second guard. 'He's of use to nobody.'

'But what about the Earl?' asked John. 'I am sure he'll want to see his son again.' He lifted Arthur and propped him against a wall. 'I hear the Earl is coming to Dublin to collect some of these ransoms. What say you to meeting with him? If he wants to release you, well be-it. If he wants you dead...then I am afraid...' He let the unspoken words hang in the air.

Arthur recognised there was no choice in the matter. Life or death. He was uncertain about the Earl, if what his brothers had said about his indifference was true, but one thing Sir Edmund had said stuck in his mind. Tom Dubh might do it for Piers, and sure enough that evening word came that the Earl was asking for Arthur. John told the others the Earl was coming to reclaim his son, and Arthur was separated from the other prisoners. Although still kept behind a locked door, he was made comfortable with a truckle bed, clothes as befitted a gentleman, good food and the best wine. His health improved daily, he would be fit for Meadhbh on his release. But the Earl did not come.

Two weeks later John came and took him to a dungeon.'Sorry I am,' he said, 'but they are preparing the rooms for someone more important than you. Maybe when he's gone they'll let you back to your soft bed.' There was none of the rancour which characterised the other soldiers' behaviour.

Arthur was placed in a cell with a pallet of straw and stinking air. Here he watched the sky through the arrow slit in the outer wall high above his head. The cell was damp and cold. He was fed little and often forgotten at meal times. When the food arrived it was usually thrown along the cell floor at him, as if he was a wild animal. Only the guard whose name was John treated him with some respect. But worse than the conditions were the noises, all through the long days men cried out, screaming in pain and it was small comfort to Arthur that he was not being tortured. The weather was fierce cold, and the sky through the arrow slit constantly grey, so Arthur knew they must be getting close to the winter solstice. Keeping track of time seemed to be the only control he had. 'What day is it?' he asked John one morning about a week after he had been in the cell.

'Tomorrow is Christmas Day.'

Yes, that would be right. It was Samhain, the end of October, when they arrived at Ard na Caithne and that was all over in a matter of days. They must have been several weeks on the road to Dublin. When John left, Arthur scratched a cross on the far wall of the cell with a fingernail. He would keep a tally of the days starting from Yuletide.

On Christmas Day the guards were too busy celebrating to remember Arthur, and when John delivered his breakfast on St Stephen's Day Arthur was shivering with cold and hunger. 'I was allowed to have Christmas Day to myself,' John said. 'Did they give you some special victuals for to celebrate the birth of Christ?' Arthur shook his head. 'Well, that is a damned pity.' John left the cell but was soon back with an extra bowl of oats and a sheep skin. 'Call it a present,' he said, gruffly, tucking the skin around Arthur's shoulders.

'You must feel lonely so far from home on a feast day,' Arthur said sadly, realising how lonely he, himself, felt. He remembered a winter solstice spent with Meadhbh when the drummers came from the village to welcome the turning of the season and Meadhbh had danced with abandon to their beat before they took themselves off to his bed chamber.

'I am lonely, but needs must. We were employed by Her Majesty not for a wage but on the understanding that we'd be able to settle in the plantations and become landed gentlemen.'

'How did you come to be here, so? In the Pale?'

'The land is infested with rebels…' He hesitated '…begging your pardon.' He sighed, 'In any case the land is laid waste and…I have not the heart for it. With the Dublin garrison busy fighting rebels within the Pale there was work here.'

'What is happening out there?' Arthur waved a hand at the cell wall.

'Many Palesmen of high and low standing are upset at having to pay taxes to support the thousands of soldiers, their wives and servants. Even the Old English are in revolt. And the Desmond rebellion continues beyond the Pale.'

'How fares Desmond? Do you know?'

'Only what I hear from returning soldiers. His wife tried to divorce him...'

'Never! She is devoted to him.'

John laughed. 'So it seems, sir. The Lord Chief Justice would not allow the divorce at which she promptly ran back into her husband's arms. 'Twas but a ploy so she would be free to present Desmond's case to Her Majesty. Now they are both in hiding.'

'What happened to our reinforcements at Ard na...Smerwick?'

'They were ambushed long before they reached Dingle...'

'Who is being tortured?'

John hung his head. 'I know not. That is not my department. God be praised.'

'Any word from the Earl?'

'Not a one,' John shook his head sadly. 'He has not been at the Castle for many a month.'

'How long am I to stay here?' Arthur tried to keep the pleading out of his voice, knowing that John had no say in the matter.

'I cannot say.'

'Could you get word to my brother, Piers of Duiske?'

John said he would try, but he had no means of getting word out of the castle and the wall became full of scratches, an x marking the beginning of a new month and a single line denoting the days, which lengthened into Candlemas, the Feast of Brigid. He remembered his first evening with Meadhbh, and realised how naive he had been to imagine he would return to Askeaton and live life as before after the rebellion. He held his hands over his ears to drown the tortured cries. All he had were his thoughts, and he remembered much. Sleeping under the kitchen table with Morveen; the joy of watching a falcon rise, seeming to float on the air in that moment before swooping on the prey; his travels through the countryside with Bren…that thought led to the only thing he refused to think about – Donal and Eamon. He was relieved to have a distraction when John brought him some books. 'They are taken from the Castle library, so you must treat them with care,' he explained, and Arthur appreciated the risk John was taking on his behalf. The least appealing of the books was Foxe's *Book of Martyrs*, but the primitive persecutions under the Roman Emperor, Nero and the account of the Inquisition in Spain proved compelling. Another book was Pliny's *The Secrets and Wonders of the World*. Arthur was particularly taken with the Oliphants. At first he could only read by standing under the arrow slit to get enough light, but one day John brought him a lighted candle and thereafter each evening when he delivered his supper he brought a candle by which Arthur could see to both eat and read.

The books and broadsides John slipped into his cell helped while the hours, the days, the months. Spring came, then the summer solstice. Arthur watched the sky through the tiny gap to learn the state of the moon. A year and a day of betrothal was over and when one night the moon shone brightly through the slit he knew that night would have been his wedding night and ached at the thought, but determined to get a letter out to Meadhbh. When John came next he said, 'Could you get me quill and paper?'

'Aye, I can,' said John, 'but I doubt it will do you much good. Everything and everyone, in and out of the Castle, is checked; all the guards and soldiers. There's a terrible fear of conspiracy about, and it would not be worth my life.'

Arthur sighed. 'I would not put you in jeopardy, John. You have been good to me. Instead I will comfort myself with the reading matter and my thoughts.' He wrote many letters to Meadhbh in his head: they all amounted to the same thing '…I love you, *á tá mo chroi istigh ionat*...my heart is within you. I was a fool to leave Askeaton. I am sorry and will understand if you have broken our pledge. I am alive, but I am a dead man…'

The year turned again at Samhain, and yet again a second time and still the Earl did not come, and still Arthur languished. He had been forgotten.

Then one evening some time just before Beltaine, more than two years after the massacre at Ard na Caithne, the door was unlocked and in strode the Earl.

Chapter Nineteen

'Arthur,' he said, his arms outstretched. 'I have wanted for this day.'

'My lord.' Arthur bowed his obeisance.

'I have been at Court these last many months.' The Earl was slightly stooped and some of his dark hair was greying.

'How is Her Majesty?'

'She is well. We are friends again. She finally realised that I have done my duty. And more. But whatever were *you* up to? Surely you could have got word to me that Desmond had you hostage.'

'Well, my lord...it was not quite like that.' Why, if that is what you thought, Arthur wanted to ask, has it taken you more than two years to get to me? 'I was...I was there of my own volition.'

'So why did they not kill you along with the other traitors at Smerwick?'

'I am afraid, my lord, I traded on your name.'

'Fools.' The Earl turned on his heel and left. The key turning in the lock sounded particularly ominous. Arthur waited all night and all next day, but nobody came near him. There was no food or drink, and all he had were his unhappy thoughts. Arthur was sorry for causing the Earl pain, and the full impact of his disloyalty hit him. He owed everything he was to the Earl, yet, it had not been

Black Tom he was fighting, but what he stood for: allegiance to the English crown. What a dilemma. Why had the Earl taken so long to attend to his case? He was convinced now he would be executed for his tyranny.

At noon on the third day the door was opened again. This time the Earl had Piers with him. Arthur stepped forward eagerly, then hesitated. Piers looked unwell, but stern and unapproachable. 'Arthur,' he said finally and sadly. 'What became of you?'

'I...' He knew he could either prevaricate and be humble, or stop being apologetic and tell the truth. 'I did not like what the English were doing...are doing...in Ireland. And the massacre at Ard na Caithe...Smerwick as you no doubt refer to it...has only confirmed my belief.'

'Her Majesty was most disturbed to hear of Grey's summary executions at Smerwick,' the Earl said.

'But,' it was Piers' turn, 'the Desmonds themselves are the most fiendish of men. They take no prisoners. Surely you saw them in action; all the Irish septs are cruel beyond compare.'

Arthur noticed that Piers held one hand to his stomach as he spoke. He had seen too many fighting men with wounds not to know what that meant. He turned to the Earl, after all it was he who would hold his life in his hands. 'I think the English have set a fierce example, my lord.' Then by way of conciliation for his outburst he said, 'I am sorry I cannot offer you a chair.'

The Earl sighed. 'Let us talk of other matters.'

Piers nodded, then said brightly, conversationally. 'My lord has a new bride.'

'Oh,' said Arthur. 'And the Lady Elizabeth in Bristol?'

'She is dead,' said the Earl. 'At last.' He stroked his beard. 'Elizabeth Sheppard is most comely, is she not Piers?'

'That she is.'

'And she is with child,' the Earl added. 'I am to have an heir.' He looked apologetically at Piers. 'A legitimate one.'

'Good tidings, indeed, my lord,' said Arthur sincerely.

Piers nodded his agreement. 'Sadly my lord will not have long to spend with the Countess. He has returned from Court with four thousand fighting men.'

'And sadly,' the Earl added, 'Piers will not be joining me in routing that Desmond out of the fastness of Aherlow.'

'You are wounded?' Arthur asked Piers who waved a dismissive hand..

There was a silence which Arthur fought to fill, but he could think of nothing to say, after the long months with only John to talk to and his thoughts to torture him. At last the Earl spoke. 'It has been decided. You will stay with Piers at Duiske.'

'How stay? As a prisoner?'

The Earl looked at Piers who said, 'As a prisoner in kind... But you will be as free as you wish whilst on the estate. My wife, Margaret, is looking forward to meeting you.'

'And I,' added the Earl, 'shall be glad to see you, like a stray sheep, back in the fold. I will negotiate your pardon once I have despatched Desmond.'

*

Piers' house at Duiske was on land belonging to the old Cistercian Abbey. The church had fallen into misuse after the old King Henry had dissolved the monastery and the land and buildings passed into Ormond hands. The house was spacious and comfortable, some of the crumbling stone had obviously been replaced and there were new tiles on the roof. Inside there was mullion glass in the window frames and the wainscoting was new, the framework of each panel in red and the infill in silver. The white ceilings were decorated with both the Earl's coat of arms and the Queen's head, and instead of rushes, turkey carpets covered the floors.

Piers' wife, Margaret, was comely with more of an Irish look about her than an English one, although her heritage was mixed. She had a broad and kind face with a ready smile, enough to warm your heart. After his long absence from women Arthur had forgotten how soft and comforting their presence could be.

'Come,' she said greeting them at the door, 'we have prepared the best chamber for you, Arthur. You have suffered much.'

'Aye.' He could not argue with that.

'And your friend, Donal from the town. What of him? We heard he left Carraigh with you, and his father returned alone.'

'You have spies?'

She laughed. 'No. Just gossips.' She looked at him for an answer.

'Dead.' He would spare her the details.

'That is sad,' Margaret said. 'But these are sad times, are they not? Every time my Piers goes into the field I wonder if he will come back to me.'

'He is a capable solider,' Arthur offered politely.

'Margaret knows full well that makes no difference.' Piers took his wife's hand.

'We say our prayers and hope that God is on our side,' she said.

'But God is supposed to be on everyone's side.' Arthur could not help himself from objecting. 'He can hardly satisfy every single one of us.'

'I am talking personally,' Margaret said simply. 'Now,' she changed the subject. 'You must both take a bath. There is nothing like a bath to soak the trouble out of your bones. Your tubs are filled and ready for you.'

Arthur was thankful for the way she refrained from pointing out just how filthy he was in his prison clothes, and later as he soaked in the wooden tub set up in his bed chamber he thought how simple life would be in wedded bliss with Meadhbh. He recalled the words of his dream, 'Go you not.' At least he was alive and comfortable, but as a house prisoner was in no position to find his way to Askeaton. In any case, Meadhbh would have found someone else to share her rituals with by now: it had been three years and more. He could write, there were quills and papers a-plenty is Piers' home, but what use would a letter do - raise Meadhbh's hopes, or make her feel guilty? He did not know when, if ever, he would be free to go to her.

A clean set of clothes was placed on the bed, obviously belonging to Piers and they reminded Arthur of his first set of gentlemen's clothes, also provided by that generous soul. When Arthur went downstairs again Piers said, 'It is our habit to say the rosary before we sup.'

Arthur hid his surprise. 'Then I shall be happy to join you,' he said. Certainly, he thought, an old Cistercian Abbey is an apt place for a couple of papists.

Piers took Margaret's arm and led the way to a small chapel which was decorated with the statuary so noticeably absent from Saint Nicolas in Bristol. Margaret pulled a rosary out of the little purse she carried on her wrist and only then did Arthur notice that Piers had his rosary wound around the wrist of his left hand. They knelt in front of the small altar, Arthur kneeling beside Piers, and had just begun their Hail Marys when they heard horses galloping into the court, followed shortly by a loud banging on the door.

Piers stood, helping Margaret up with him and calmly they left their rosaries on the altar. Piers beckoned Arthur to follow and they left the chapel, Piers pulling the door shut behind them and sliding a cupboard over it before Margaret placed a painting of a stern looking man over the upper hinges. 'We had this especially made,' Margaret explained. 'Matters are only going to worsen for those of the true faith.' As they left the room Arthur looked back and realised that nobody would ever know the chapel was there.

They need not have worried, the visitors were Margaret's father, the Baron of Slane and another man. They were invited into the chapel to say the rosary, and afterwards dined in the hall. As Arthur's first proper meal in a long while, the food was particularly wonderful. To begin with there was a full-bodied stewed broth, followed by roasted capons with cabbage and turnips, and finally gingerbread and plum tart. Arthur savoured every morsel.

The conversation began safely enough. 'Francis Lovell is making meat of his new position,' Margaret's father said.

'Do you remember Lovell, Arthur?' Piers asked. 'He was Sir Henry Sidney's secretary.'

'I am not sure I do,' said Arthur. 'What is his new position?'

'Sherriff of the county,' said the other man. 'My lord, the Earl of Ormond, was forced to appoint him.'

'Earl Thomas wants him prosecuted for murder, so vicious and meaningless have been his executions in Kilkenny,' Margaret offered.

'What chance does my lord have of that?' asked Arthur.

'I would not mind betting that the Dublin authorities will grant Lovell a royal pardon before proceedings take place.'

The small page who offered Arthur the salt ornate, which was almost too big for him to handle, reminded Arthur of his own days serving platters of food to gentlemen, and trying to find out what was going on in the wider world. This young one seemed to linger unnecessarily long, but Piers took no notice. Margaret whispered something to him when he went to remove her platter, and he left.

'So you were at Smerwick,' Margaret's father said to Arthur. 'Was it the massacre of rumour?'

'Unimaginable,' said Arthur.

'We share your sympathies...' Margaret's father began.

'Let us talk of better things,' Margaret interrupted, and so they discussed the weather and the price of cattle.

It was still light when they had finished eating and whilst Margaret took her father and his friend for a walk around the garden, Arthur broached the subject of religion with Piers who said, 'I was born a Papist under Mary and I hope to die a Papist. As you know Her Majesty *was* happy to accommodate the Catholic religion as long as it was quietly observed.'

'You think she has over-reacted to the excommunication?'

'I think she fears for her life. And rightly so. There are those who would prefer Mary Queen of the Scots to be Mary Queen of England also.'

'And you are with them?'

'No...'

'You have heard what happened at Mullaghmast? And how Francis Cosby took his fun at Stradbally?'

'Aye. Loyal as I am, I am not with the Queen and her persecution of the Irish because they are Catholic.'

Arthur hesitated before responding. Then he said, 'You and Margaret would surely be among them if it were known.'

'Aye,' Piers said again.

'But Her Majesty would not go that far with her kin?'

'The Earl's influence has its limits.'

'I was not referring to my lord, but to you, Piers. Rumour has it that you are the Queen's son.'

Piers sighed deeply. 'And I know that to be the truth, but for Her Majesty's sake and my lord's I have forgotten it. There are those who would like a male heir for the Crown, even a bastard heir is better than none, for was not the Queen deemed a bastard at one time by her father and Queen Mary? And I am doubly attractive to some as one of the Catholic faith. We are loyal to Elizabeth and would never endanger her life. So the tale remains gossip and rumour and I am entrusting it to you as such.' He pushed his chair back from the table. 'Come with me,' he said.

Arthur stood. 'How do you fare, Piers?' he asked. 'I see you holding your wound, so.'

Piers did not reply; he simply took his hand away from his stomach and strode ahead down the stairs. It was gloomy in the kitchen, but the far end was lit by a fire with a standing torch on each side. Beside the fire sat two women with their backs to them. One of them jumped up when she heard the men enter. 'Art,' she screamed. 'Oh Arty, my Art.' And Morveen came flying at him. She threw her arms around him and held him tight.

'You have these two to thank for your life,' Piers said, 'Not that I wanted you dead.'

'Morveen,' Arthur said. 'I have missed you, so I have.' He had not realised just how much until he admitted to it.

The other woman was Aefe, grown into a beautiful woman.

'Hello Arthur,' she said quietly.

'Oh Arty, What did you mean by it? Running off. Becoming a traitor?'

'Ma, that is enough,' said Aefe firmly. 'He is here with us now.

And that is all that matters.'

Arthur turned to Piers. 'This is a wonderful surprise. How long…'

Piers waved a hand to stop his question. 'I shall leave you here,' he said, 'and you can catch up with everything there is to know.' He turned to Aefe. 'Pour your brother a goblet of wine and have a sup or two yourselves.'

When he had gone, Arthur said, 'What luck to have you two here. How did it happen? Have you just arrived?'

Morveen laughed. 'Still my same old Arty. Questions, questions, questions. Now sit down and we'll tell you everything, so.'

Aefe fetched the wine and they drank and talked. Aefe and Morveen had been at Duiske since Arthur left Carraigh. Piers and Margaret were kind to them. When they heard that Arthur was in Dublin Castle, they begged for mercy, and here he was!

'You have grown so like my lord in looks.' Morveen held his face in her two hands for a moment. 'And Piers. They call him Piers Dubh, so, after his father.'

'You shall be Arthur Dubh,' Aefe laughed.

'Are you happy here, Aefe?' he asked. 'Surely a beautiful young woman such as you should be wed.'

'She is wed enough,' said Morveen.

'I…am…' Aefe began, but before she could continue the small inquisitive page came running into the kitchen. 'Mama,' he held out his arms to Aefe. 'Papa said I might come and meet my uncle.'

'Give your uncle a kiss,' said Morveen. 'And then if there's one to spare you can give it to your poor auld grandmother.'

The child obeyed, and then stood, legs apart looking intently at Arthur. 'I have never seen a traitor before,' he said.

'Edward!' said Aefe. 'Do not make such talk.'

'No,' said Arthur. 'It must be confusing for him. There is good and bad on both sides,' he said to the boy, 'and I know not which side to take.'

'There should be no question,' Morveen said. 'My lord and Piers have saved your life. Your loyalty lies with them.'

'One day I will tell you my story,' Arthur said.

The boy clapped his hands, but Arthur shook his head. 'Not to you, Edward. You are too young to hear what I have to tell. When you are a man will be time enough.'

'Now to bed,' Aefe shooed him away.

When he had gone Arthur said, 'So Piers is Papa?'

'Aye,' said Morveen in a way that said - there will be no discussion of that.

'How...how does Margaret take this…this child? She seems a nice woman...'

Aefe said, 'She tolerates Edward. For his father's sake.'

'And you? How does she take you and Piers?'

'Piers is his father's son,' Morveen said laughing. 'My lord sent us here to help with the household and things...happened. While Margaret was childing and unwell, and unable...'

'Her babby died,' said Aefe.

'But you and Piers..?'

'No more. I am in my place in the kitchen.'

'And this is the best life for all of us.' Morveen was being emphatic again. 'It is a small household, just a few fostered pages, close-knit with kin.'

*

For a brief moment on waking next morning, Arthur could not decide where he was. For so long he had awakened to his shadowy cell; to the clang of the keeper's keys and the crash of his bowl being set before him on the floor as if he was a hound. It was late and he dressed quickly. Margaret was the only one taking breakfast, although there were used tankards and bread crumbs on the table.

'They said to bid you farewell, but they could not wait.'

'You should have woken me.'

'Not on your first morning of freedom,' she laughed.

'And Piers?'

'He has gone with them. There was a matter to attend to.'

'Is he well enough to travel so?'

'Aye. He is a strong man.'

'At least he's not back in the field,' Arthur said.

Margaret smiled, somewhat sadly. 'Aye,' she said after a pause. 'For now. Methinks he is eager to return.' She sighed. 'Such is man.' She was silent while Arthur helped himself to some salted fish.

'So you met Aefe and Edward last night?'

'Aye. I...I was surprised...Piers and...'

'Such is man,' Margaret said again. 'He is a good husband.' She filled a tankard with weak ale. 'We have no son of our own.' She sighed, then said, 'No doubt Edward will be fostered out shortly. 'Tis the Irish way, as you know. Then Aefe and Morveen will return to Carraigh.' She handed him the tankard.

'Why is he not fostered to you? Then you would have the child, but not the mother.' He took a long pull at the ale.

'I do not want the boy. I am a Christian woman and I must forgive, as Christ instructs us to, but I am all too human.'

Arthur decided to change the subject. 'I must say I was surprised to find you both remain recusants.'

'My lord, the Earl, often quotes the Queen. How does it go? "I refuse to make windows into men's hearts and secret thoughts…"'

Arthur took another pull at the ale before responding. Then he said, 'You and Piers are in mortal danger.'

'Aye,' she agreed. 'Either way. For our souls, if we become Protestant and for our lives if we stay true to our faith.'

'Is it her Majesty, or the English authorities in Dublin, at fault?'

'A touch of both, methinks. But you must remember the territorial imperative drives us also. Both my father's and the Ormond estates and titles are safe while we fight on the side of the Queen.'

'It is a truly complex situation.'

'Aye, and we would be deceiving ourselves if we did not admit to more than a degree of self-interest within it. The Queen herself expects much revenue from Ireland.' Margaret refilled Arthur's tankard. 'Alas, so far it has done nothing but cost her money. Piers said that last year she garnered three thousand pounds from Ireland

and spent eighteen thousand on her defences.'

'What do the New English fear most?'

'A Catholic invasion.'

'If my experience at Smerwick is anything to judge matters by they have little to concern themselves. Desmond was a reluctant rebel, and the whole enterprise was very badly put together.'

'Ah my dear friend,' Margaret took his arm and led him out into the morning sunshine. 'We are much too serious. Now I shall go and let Aefe and Morveen know it is only we two for dinner this noon.' She set off back into the house, but turned and said, 'They may as well dine with us, or we with them in the kitchen.'

'I would like that.'

Margaret made for the house again, then turned once more. 'While you are here would you tutor some of the younger pages? They are missing their lessons with all the troubles.'

*

Piers returned from escorting his father, to remain home until his health was completely restored. Life settled into a pleasant rhythm. Arthur's days were spent tutoring the boys who for the most part were eager to learn, evenings were spent listening to Margaret play the lute. Sometimes Piers sang with her, sometimes a harper came in to entertain them, and there was dancing. Piers, Margaret and their local friends did the intricate courtly dances imported from Italy, but more often than not they danced the English country dances. Piers explained that the Queen liked her aristocracy to perform country dances because it brought them closer to her people. Arthur wanted to point out that they were *English* country dances, and were not the people of Ireland also the Queen's folk deserving of being brought closer to her with an Irish Hey or *Rince Fada*, but he held his tongue.

Storytellers visited and told the tales of old. Even Eoghan Mac Craith called in on one occasion and recited his epic poem about the deeds of 'the earl of the Suir...the warlike hundred-wounding chief'. He had added to it substantially with several verses in praise of the manor house at Carraigh. Arthur inwardly shuddered at such lines as: 'He stormed, demolished and burned, Dunlo the fiery famed of old for heroes; after his visit to Ibh-Rathnach shepherds were in want of employment.' The words stirred his old hatred, but Mac Craith only came the once and the hatred in Arthur's stomach settled to a dull ache soon after he left.

By March a visiting physician proclaimed Piers well enough to return to the field. Arthur understood Margaret's anxiety but she hid it well as the household stood in the courtyard waving him goodbye, and God's speed. The pages jumped up and down and cheered, dreaming, no doubt, Arthur thought, of their own glory days to come. Aefe held Edward's hand and cried. Morveen called, 'God be with you,' and Margaret crossed herself and went immediately to the chapel on her own. After that moment of apparent weakness she kept her spirits up – for Piers' sake, she told Arthur. She told Aefe to be brave and stand tall. There was no room in the household for moping. Arthur felt guilt along with sadness at seeing Piers ride away, but he knew that neither Tom Dubh nor Piers would trust him to join them. That, too, left a pang, not that he wanted to be fighting the Desmonds, but he missed the camaraderie of belonging. Somewhere. Anywhere? He thought, perhaps not *just* anywhere, but he did not know where his belonging was at that moment, except with Meadhbh and he had closed that door in his mind.

The seasons came and went. He missed the old ways of celebrating as they had done at Askeaton. He could not summon the enthusiasm Margaret had for the rituals of the church, Lent, Easter Day, the annunciation of the Blessed Virgin, All Souls. Fasting on Ash Wednesday and Good Friday was particularly difficult. His stomach complained all day, and he could not help but compare the church's emphasis on denial with the old ways as he remembered the feasting and frolicking at Askeaton. Occasionally a fugitive Jesuit called in and took mass with them in the little chapel. Arthur appreciated the risk the clerics took in these disjointed times and took part because of it. He also wanted to be as obliging as he could, given Piers' and Margaret's kindness to him.

All Souls, or Samhain as Arthur preferred to think of it, had just passed and winter was truly upon them. Lessons were over for the day, but it was too wet to be outside and Arthur was teaching the boys to play primero and other card games. Of course they did not play for money but put acorns down as they bid. Margaret came rushing in waving a letter in the air. 'The Earl's men,' she cried. 'They are returning home.' The men had been in the wilds of Atherlow for eight long months, and while Sir John of Desmond was dead, Garret Fitzgerald, Earl of Desmond, and his wife Eleanor had escaped to furthest Kerry. They would flush him out in the spring and meantime winter in comfort.

The Earl, Arthur thought, would be particularly anxious to be home. The Countess had given birth to a son, James, in September. Ormond losses had been few and there was much for which to be thankful. Piers' household seemed to sing with joy at the prospect of a battle-free winter.

Chapter Twenty

Arthur was in the meadow beside the house supervising the boys in a friendly game of fight. Edward, his cheeks red with exertion and the cold, had the box-ball in his arms and was running as fast as his little legs could take him towards the mark at the house end of the meadow. As one of the older boys grabbed the child from behind and pulled him down Arthur heard the sound of horses in the yard and saw two horsemen arrive. The boys leapt up and ran to the courtyard. Arthur followed. 'Papa!' he heard Edward cry.

He walked slowly across the meadow to allow the boys time for their welcome. As he entered the court he saw Piers helping someone down from the second horse. 'A hand if you please Arthur,' he called and together they helped the man into the house.

It would be two days before Arthur saw the visitor again, his food had been taken to his chamber by either Aefe or Morveen. In the meantime over supper that night Piers explained that he was the Archbishop of Cashel, Dr Dermot O'Hurley. 'Until the excommunication of the Queen the Protestant Archbishop, Miler MacGrath tolerated Dr O'Hurley's presence in Kilkenny. Now...' He shrugged.

Margaret took up the story. 'He recently returned from France. For some time he has been hiding with my father at Slane, but a few nights ago my father had Sir Robert Dillon dine with him….' She sighed. 'I don't know what possessed him. He sat O'Hurley amongst his guests and Sir Robert…he's one of Her Majesty's judges…recognised him. The Archbishop has been on the run since and Piers has brought him to sanctuary here.'

'And what of the war against Desmond?' Arthur asked Piers as he helped himself to a large portion of baked swan.

'It would have been good to have Desmond's head on a pike, but we did manage to reduce his numbers considerably. When we began he had about two thousand men. Now there is less than four score.' Piers was chewing on a wing bone with gusto. 'Now the poor wretch is being hunted like an animal by a handful of the Earl's kerne. Rather him than me in this weather.'

'Does his wife remain with him?'

'No. She has surrendered. Desmond said she was a hindrance, but that is hard to credit.' He laughed. 'She is a wild horsewoman that one. Often times she would be riding like the wind away from us. My lord's men would follow and Desmond would escape in the opposite direction.'

'Perhaps she wants to plead his case as she has done before,' Arthur said. 'Desmond tried hard to stay loyal. He was pushed into rebellion on all sides. He even asked for my lord's help, but none came.'

'I recall that occasion,' Piers licked the baking juices off his fingers. 'We thought it a trick to entice us into an ambush at Askeaton.'

'Does Askeaton remain in Desmond hands?' Arthur tried to keep his voice steady.

'No. It fell to Pelham.'

'What of the staff?'

Piers shrugged. 'I know not. It was being cared for by a band of Spaniards while Desmond was on the run, and sadly they set about its ruination so that none would benefit from the capture.' He turned to Margaret. 'Askeaton was a most impressive castle.'

'Aye,' agreed Arthur. 'That it was.'

*

On the third evening the archbishop appeared in the chapel as they were about to say the rosary. He was a large man with kind eyes, although his face looked worn by his troubles, dressed in a collarless shirt, a simple black doublet and black breeches; around his neck was a large cross which he held in both hands, perhaps for comfort. He gave them Holy Communion, then joined them for supper. It was Friday so there would be no entertainment and fish was served. It was a whole turbot and Edward could not resist poking at its round, black eye as it was set on the table. His father laughed and one of the older pages pulled his hand away. Another page, attending to the wine, set in its bucket of cold water under the cupboard, poured two glasses and presented them to Margaret and the archbishop, then went back for Piers' and Arthur's. When all the glasses were filled Piers stood and raised a toast to the archbishop. Then the archbishop stood and raised his glass. 'To His Holiness the Pope.'

The fish was served. 'Your Grace,' Margaret said, 'do tell us the significance of the fish. It is important that the children know why we observe the meatless Friday.'

'Easter Friday is remembered every week in this way,' the archbishop began. But before he could explain further there was an insistent knock at the door. They had not heard horses approach so whoever it was had arrived on foot. The adults crossed themselves and said a quick prayer.

'Hush,' whispered Piers. He beckoned to the archbishop and silently they left the room. The knock came again and they heard men's voices loud above Morveen's. Margaret swooped the Archbishop's plate and eating knife off the table and hid it under her kirtle. As she sat down, the door burst open and three men strode in, with Morveen protesting behind them. Then, thankfully came Piers. 'Where were you?' he snapped at Morveen. 'Does it take you forever to open the door?'

Morveen bobbed at him. 'I am sorry Sir. I was a-washing of the saucepans. They make such a clatter I did not hear at first.'

One of the men pushed forward and looked at the plates. 'Fish, I see,' he said. 'And it is Friday. Such Papist practices are punishable…'

'By death…' said another man.

Morveen started crying, and Edward and another page joined her. 'I am sorry Sir,' Morveen said to Piers, 'but we have no meat. With the men away fighting for Her Majesty, we have only the fish caught in the weir by a page this morn. 'Twas that one,' she pointed at one of the older boys.

'I did not know it was Friday,' he said. 'Else I'd have caught a hare.'

'Neither did I,' Morveen sniffled. 'Else we'd have had eggs.' She wiped her sleeve across her nose.

'Stop snivelling woman,' said the last man. 'Come,' he ordered the other two, and they left the room. Piers moved to join them, but was stopped at the door. 'You stay here.'

They sat in silence and listened to the footsteps stamping around the house, upstairs and down. The boys stopped crying and listened intently. 'I hid Doctor O'Hurley's trunk,' Morveen whispered. 'But only in the cupboard. There was not time.'

'You played your part well,' said Margaret. 'Now we can but wait.'

'What about Aefe? And the meat?' Morveen ran out of the room before anyone could stop her. They heard her calling. 'Aefe. Aefe.' And a response came, 'Shut up bitch'. Then Morveen laughed and the man laughed with her. Silence and they waited. Then the feet began marching through the house again. They were directly above in the Archbishop's chamber. They did not stay long there, but moved on out into the hall again and on to Arthur's room. Doors banged, footsteps ran down the stairs again, into the parlour where they seemed to spend an age and it felt as if everyone in the room had stopped breathing. Out again, and out the front door without comment.

Piers went to the window. 'They are leaving,' he said. 'At least for now. We must be more careful in future. The least we can do is keep Doctor O'Hurley's trunk in the chapel. It is inconvenient, I know but for now…'

The door opened and Morveen came in. 'Clever girl, my Aefe,' said Morveen. 'She hid the meat in the bread oven.'

Margaret lifted her kirtle and set the Archbishop's plate and eating knife back on the table. 'Better get him out,' she said getting up.

'Edward,' said Piers nodding at the plate and knife. 'Kindly get a clean plate for Doctor O'Hurley.'

*

That evening Piers, the Archbishop and Arthur sat by the fire in the parlour. 'They will be back, of that I am certain,' Piers said. 'We must get you away from here, Doctor.'

'I fear I am outstaying my welcome in Ireland,' O'Hurley said. 'There are not many places left to hide.'

Piers thought for a moment, then said, 'Arthur, you will take the Archbishop to my lord at Carraigh.'

'But what about the boys' lessons?'

'Margaret can continue as she was before you came. She does not have the Greek or Latin, but is more than adequate at reading and writing English and the Gaelic. And you should be back within the seven days. It will be good for you to see Carraigh again.'

'What about my imprisonment?'

Piers shrugged. 'My lord will see the sense in this, of that I am sure.'

*

That was how Arthur found himself riding with Archbishop Dermot O'Hurley, taking the least travelled roads back to Carraigh with a letter in his pouch which begged the Earl to give O'Hurley shelter. They had several hard days' riding ahead of them journeying through the by-ways to avoid meeting any of the Queen's men.

They did not dare use the rivers. The horses walked in single file because there was so little room on the boreen, but later as the path widened the archbishop draw up alongside Arthur and they rode side by side in silence for a while. The archbishop seemed so meditative that Arthur thought he might be praying, but when he spoke he said, 'You do not strike me as a particularly religious young man, Arthur. What sent you to Ard na Caithne?'

Obviously tongues had tattled at Duiske, but Arthur did not mind answering. 'Who, is a more likely question, your Grace. I did as Desmond bid me.'

They rode in further silence until the cleric asked, 'What made you turn to Desmond?'

'I heard about the massacre at Mullaghmast. I was disillusioned about my life...I did not like what the English were doing in Ireland... do not like it.'

'But, my boy, there is no Ireland. It is a country of septs and lordships, Gaelic and Normans fighting for their share of the land. If the chieftains and the lords would only join forces instead of fighting against each other...now *then* you'd have an Ireland.'

'But the New English are overtaking us with plantations and massacres.'

The archbishop was lost in his thoughts again. Then he said, 'So your stance is more political than religious?'

'Aye, though I must confess to being a little confused at the moment. My lord and Piers have been so kind. They saved my life.'

'And why do you suppose you are sent to guide me to Carraigh?' Arthur did not respond, but the archbishop continued. "Who in the household is most dispensable?'

'Are you saying it is a sham? That my brother and his wife do not care for me, as they appear to?'

'I am sure they are fond of you, but this is a matter of expediency.'

'Aye,' was all Arthur said.

'Just as I am a matter of expediency, and if the wind was to turn I would be as dispensable as you.' They were forced to ride in single file again. This time Arthur took the rear, and when the path widened he did not hurry forward, but the cleric slowed his horse and waited for him. 'Now let us return to matters political,' he said when they were side by side again. 'Do you know what is happening in the Pale?'

'Only what one of my gaolers told me…he was a kind man...' He paused remembering him... 'called John.'

'And what did this John tell you?'

'The garrison has many soldiers and the Palesmen are unhappy with the additional cess required to keep them.'

'And on the other hand the English administrators are fearful of a Spanish invasion…a *successful* invasion. They see conspiracies everywhere. They think the Old English Catholics are conspiring to destroy them. That is why they are so afraid of me.' He laughed at the thought. 'Now your earl…about to harbour me. Is he part of the conspiracy?'

'I know not.'

They stopped by a stream and ate the bread, Holland cheese and fruit tart which Morveen had packed for them. They washed it down with ale which had warmed and soured a little in the leather bottles. Again there was silence, the only sound the gurgle of water over the stones in the bed of the stream. Eventually Arthur stood, brushed the crumbs off his jerkin and went to his horse. The archbishop followed. They mounted and rode on. 'So to the Pale,' said the archbishop. 'There are other young gentlemen in the Pale who share your idea of a country called Ireland. A country without the English. If you were so inclined I would put you in touch with them.'

'That would mean my having to desert the Earl again.'

'It may. It is up to you young man.'

*

For three days hard travelling the conversation never swerved from the political and religious implications of the English presence in Ireland. When they finally arrived in Carraigh Arthur was delighted to see everything was as he remembered. There were two things he wanted to do. The first was to visit the O'Brennans; the second to see the falcons. It was after dark when they arrived, so he had to wait to do both, but he did call into the kitchen to give them news of Morveen. The pot man was not there. Died of a fever, Cook said when Arthur enquired after him. They were busy with the Earl's supper and Arthur left. Next morning he went to the kitchen garden and was pleased to see the falconer in the mews. He was bent now with age. 'Jesus and Mary,' the falconer crossed himself. 'Is it young Arthur? But you are the spit of my lord. No mistaking your parentage. It is right good to see you. Come and see the birds. Some of them are getting on in years, but they still hunt well.' Arthur dallied with the birds as long as he could. He had somehow always associated them with his being taken into the household.

Much as he wanted to see Bren and his wife he was fearful of the visit. How much should he tell them? How much could he tell them without his own weir of grief spilling over? He had kept his last sight of Donal and Eamon hidden even from himself, suffering in the deep recesses of his mind from a mixture of guilt and sadness.

Finally he had to leave the mews. The morning was wearing on and he wanted to arrive on the O'Brennan's door sill at dinner time because Bren would be home and he did not want to face Donal's mother on his own. He said goodbye to the birds and the falconer and made his way through the arched gateway, back into the court and out the postern gate. Slowly, softly, dragging his bad leg as he had not done for a long time.

The door to the cottage was open, and Bren was inside taking off his work boots. 'Arthur,' he said. 'Orlagh,' he called. 'It is Arthur. Come in, lad, come in.'

Little had changed inside the cottage, but Arthur noted Bren's fiddle leaning against a corner wall covered in dust. There was a pot of stew on the fire and Orlagh O'Brennan stopped stirring it to rush at Arthur and kiss him on both cheeks. She waved the stirring spoon in the air.

'It is good to see you, so,' said Bren. 'Now eat and drink with us and tell us all there is to tell.'

'Donal is…is…'

'Aye, we know of that,' said Bren.

'I…I…I am at a loss.' He turned his head away so he did not need to look at them.

'Just tell us word for word what happened,' begged Orlagh.

Arthur gave the details straight and true, including Donal's kindness to the boys, particularly Eamon, but the tears came when he had to talk about his march past the bodies of the massacred. 'There,' said Orlagh, patting his hand. 'There. There's a time for weeping. We have done ours. And prayed for Donal's soul.'

'And he died for a cause,' Bren said. 'He believed in what he was doing for Ireland.'

'Aye.' Arthur sniffed hard and sighed.

'What will you do now?'

'I could go back to tutoring the young ones, but I have another opportunity to do something for Ireland.' He told them about the conversation with the archbishop.

'There's the heart of it,' said Bren. 'The Pale. But have you not done enough for the cause?'

'I have nothing else to occupy me. I was betrothed at Askeaton…'

'Well,' Orlagh lifted her skirts and sat down eager to hear more, and Arthur told them about Meadhbh. 'You must write to her now that you are out and about. Bren would get a letter to her, would you not?'

'For sure I would,' Bren replied.

'But,' Arthur interrupted, 'Askeaton is destroyed. I know not where she is.'

'Leave it with me. I'll find her if I can. Give the lad the means with which to write, Orlagh.'

Arthur wrote the words which he had practised so long, finishing with the Gaelic, *Tá grá agam duit*. He folded the letter and handed it to Bren. 'My heartfelt thanks, though I admit to being a-feared that she will have found another.'

'At least you will know.' Orlagh stroked his hand for comfort.

Bren stood up. 'I've got to get back to work. I have a roof to finish thatching before nightfall.

'I could help you,' offered Arthur.

'No lad. You go away and consider what the Archbishop has said.' He was pulling on a boot and he looked up. 'But don't take a step until the letter has time to reach its target.'

The Earl asked Arthur to stay a while at Carraigh. He sent a messenger to let Piers and Margaret know and Arthur felt a pang of regret. He suspected his prolonged visit was at the Earl's new wife's insistence. She seemed to like his easy way with the pages and there was no doubt the Earl doted on her, especially now with the birth of his son. If she had asked for the moon, the Earl would have gone to any lengths to fetch it for her. However it happened, here he stayed and here he considered his situation.

The archbishop was lodged in the town, and was on an understanding with the Earl that he would confine himself to the borders of Tipperary and would not make contact with rebel elements. The Earl sent him food daily, and at times Arthur went to fetch him to the castle. Here the archbishop and the Earl sat for hour on end discussing matters of faith and virtue, and on one occasion the Earl asked the archbishop to baptise his son. The ceremony took place in the little chapel in the keep with only a handful of people present. As water dripped over the crying baby's head and Dr O'Hurley pronounced, '*Nomine Patris, Filii et Spiritus Sancti*', Arthur wondered what the Queen would have to say if she knew. Was this a window into the Earl's heart through which she did not want to look?

When Arthur walked him back to his lodgings that evening, the archbishop said, 'Come in for a moment. I have something for you.' They climbed the stairs to the archbishop's chamber and once inside he handed Arthur a sealed letter. 'Use this if you will. Or must. I say no more.' He held the door open for Arthur to leave. 'It is up to you whether you act upon it.' After the discomfort of Dublin Castle Arthur was not in a hurry to sleep in the rough again which without a doubt would be the end result of Dr O'Hurley's offer. As yet there had been no word from Meadhbh, but there was still time and Arthur hoped that, with the intercession of the Countess, the Earl would pursue his pardon, and he would be a free man. Once he was free, if he knew where to look for her, and she had no other… 'obligations' was how he liked to consider it… he would collect Meadhbh and they could join Piers' close-knit household. So he stayed put and lived in hope.

*

One rare fine day before Christmas the men were in the court giving the boys an archery lesson. Arthur was demonstrating his prowess; the Earl was holding one page's bow in the correct position against his shoulder and the archbishop wrapped warmly in a cloak sat on a stool watching with benign amusement. The Countess stood at the window of the ladies' parlour with her baby in her arms also watching with enjoyment. A messenger galloped into the court and ran to the keep door where one of the Earl's servants stood. The Earl looked up then went back to the boy. The servant pointed to where the Earl stood. 'Now pull it back,' the Earl instructed. The boy did so and the arrow dropped to the ground not far away. 'Tension. You need more tension on the bow before you let it go.' The messenger approached running, thrust a letter at the Earl, who turned from the boy to read it, frowned and read it again. He dismissed the messenger with a flick of his hand, and walked over to the archbishop who was clapping the success of the page's second try. 'Your Grace,' the Earl said, 'I am afraid…the baron has, of necessity, given away your whereabouts. I must beg you to give yourself up to the authorities. Some Dublin men are on their way to take you.' The archbishop stood. 'You see how badly this will fit with my position,' the Earl added. 'Shall we say you came here to hand yourself in?'

'Of course. I am grateful for your help thus far.'

The Earl led the archbishop inside, indicating to Arthur that he should carry on.

The light finally faded. Arthur gathered the boys and told them to put their bows and arrows in the armoury. As he walked towards the keep he heard horses approaching at a gallop along the path in the Great Park. He was nearly run down by the first horse into the court. He stepped aside and watched as five more men galloped in. How many men did it take to capture a harmless old prelate?

There were no niceties, the men ran into the keep and shortly after came out with the archbishop bundled in chains. They slung him over one of the horses, while the Earl was noticeable by his absence, but the pages came running to see what was happening. Arthur waved wanly at the archbishop, a gesture in vain, for the horsemen left with the same speed at which they arrived. The archbishop's head, the only free part of his body, was rocking hard to the gait, and Arthur wondered if he would live to see the inside of the Castle. He drew the pages into the keep and shuddered, knowing only too well what discomfort imprisonment in the Castle meant. And if they decided to torture Dr O'Hurley what cries and screams would emanate from his cell?

Arthur felt uncomfortable supping with the Earl that night. What had Margaret said, they all had a degree of self-interest? The Earl's behaviour that afternoon had displayed absolute self-interest. There were no guests, so some of the older pages were allowed to sit at table. Silence hung low over them until finally the Earl put his knife down and said to the pages in general. 'Know you who Arthur is?'

Of course they knew, but the Earl went on. 'He is a man of principle.' Arthur could not detect irony in the tone but it seemed as if the Earl had taken of too much drink earlier. 'I admire that in you, Arthur. It is a commendable trait. That and loyalty.'

The Countess gave a small gasp, and the Earl put a hand on hers before taking a gulp of his wine. 'I mean what I say. But principles are difficult things to keep in hand.' He paused. 'Take the good archbishop as an example. He is an admirable man, a man of virtue.

But expedience sometimes has to outweigh principle. Had I let Dr O'Hurley free, it would have brought the full weight of Lovell and his men down on the whole county.' He waved his goblet in Arthur's direction to indicate that this speech was intended particularly for him. 'And we all know there are many Catholics among both the gentry and the base born hereabouts.'

'Do you mean, my lord,' one of the older pages asked, 'that the archbishop's capture was for the greater good?'

'I do,' said the Earl taking another deep draught. 'Indeed I do.'

Shortly afterwards the Countess said, 'My lord, I think it is time we retired. Let us leave the boys to make merry of their own volition,' and she led him away to his chamber.

*

Arthur kept the archbishop's letter with him. It seemed to burn his fingers when he touched it tucked inside his doublet. It had the disturbing weight of something from his youth. What was it? He thought over what had been said about expediency overcoming principle for the greater good; he thought about self-interest and how great the good was for the Earl, but also for his people. Lovell was a vicious man, so they said. Then he remembered the gold coin he had been promised if he became a spy. Ah, he thought, what an innocent I was. Now I know so much more, I realise how little I do know. He envied the Earl his certainty.

Disturbing news came from Dublin. The new Lord Justice of Ireland, Sir Henry Wallop, had written to Walsingham, the Queen's secretary, in London complaining about the excessive power the Earl of Ormond wielded. 'I would not trust that Walshingham,' the dinner guest said. 'Queen's Secretary. Pah. He's her spymaster.'

'And very good at it, too,' said a second guest. 'He has his nose into everybody's business.'

'I hear,' interrupted the first guest, 'that Walshingham has given permission for O'Hurley to be tortured.'

Arthur, who had only been half listening at that point, staring into his goblet admiring the rich red glow of the Burgundy, looked up.

'The aim, as I understand it,' the man went on, 'is to get him to reveal information that will implicate you, my lord, your son Piers and his father-in-law. What was it they called you?' he paused, thinking. 'Ah yes, Romish runnagates.'

'They are determined to discredit you, my lord,' said a third man who had been quiet to that point. 'My suggestion is this. We gather the lords and gentry of the south somewhere, say Kilkenny, and get them to sign a petition to Her Majesty outlining your exemplary conduct in the war in Munster.'

'Excellent plan.' The Earl clapped his hands. 'Isn't it my dear?' He turned to his wife.

So it was done, and when the Earl returned from Kilkenny after the rally, he was looking pleased. 'That should show 'em in Dublin and London,' he said at supper that night.

*

For weeks Arthur waited for a response to his letter. Bren said he had placed it in safe hands and if it was going to get to Meadhbh it would. Although Arthur thought of Meadhbh by day, he did not dream of her; his dreams were haunted by Dr O'Hurley's screams, but the prelate did not fail the Earl and Piers under torture. Their gentlemen who had an ear at the Castle said when next he dined at Carraigh that the Lords Justice had asked permission for O'Hurley to be killed. 'They can make up what they like about his confessions with him dead,' the man suggested.

'I must to Court,' the Earl said.

'Will you tell of the archbishop's torture?' Arthur asked.

'I will tell of my own good deeds,' said the Earl. 'I have my petition. I will take it by hand to her Majesty.' He turned to look at Arthur. 'And a misguided sense of loyalty to the man who christened my son means I will speak for his release.'

Within the week he had gone. It was spring and the boys were full of energy which Arthur helped them expend, making mock battles in the Great Park and riding far and wide. They practised their archery and ran races one against the other. One day they returned to the castle to find a messenger there, which was strange because messengers rarely called when the Earl was absent. When Arthur looked into the ladies' parlour the Countess was there with three of her women comforting her. 'What is it?' he asked from the door. 'Can I be of assistance?'

'Come in Arthur,' the Countess said. 'It is a letter from the Queen telling my lord not to go to Court. What a blow this will be to him.'

'But he should be there by now,' Arthur said. 'Once he is there the Queen will not rebuke him.'

'Of course, my lady,' said one of the gentlewomen.

'He will show his petition and in any case the Queen will take his word against those in Dublin,' another assured her.

'But,' the Countess said with less confidence than her ladies, 'the Queen appointed Lovell, when my lord expected the appointment as sheriff himself. That is not a show of confidence.'

'But with him at her side, she will see things as they really are.' Arthur knew he was prevaricating. The Earl had harboured a Catholic archbishop.

'Quite so,' said a gentlewoman.

'Aye. It is true he is a favourite,' said another.

'Don't worry,' Arthur said, 'I am sure my lord has overcome greater obstacles,' but secretly he wondered if the Queen was piqued with Tom Dubh, her Lucas, her 'black husband' for being so contently married to a beautiful woman.

*

At the beginning of June Arthur asked permission to visit Piers, which the Countess granted. He thought it expedient to hide the archbishop's letter rather than carry it with him in case Lovell's men stopped him, so before he left the Carraigh keep he found a loose brick on the fireplace surrounds and tucked it in behind that.

'I know you won't let me down,' the Countess said as she saw Arthur off.

It was good to be back in the more relaxed atmosphere of the house at Duiske. Piers, though, was worried about the Earl. 'It seems Lovell has begotten himself to Court and is besmirching my lord's name everywhere he goes, particularly in the Queen's presence. And Her Majesty will not let my lord attend.'

'It is a truly terrible state for him,' Margaret said. 'He has travelled all that way, only to be rebuffed.'

'Lovell has managed to justify his indiscriminate use of the death penalty,' Piers went on. 'He is strutting about as the very model of a fair sheriff, restrained and reliable.'

'The Earl has set home for Ireland without so much as a glimpse of the Queen. He will be so upset.' Margaret was close to tears.

'At least,' Piers comforted her, 'he will be back in time for the new Lord Deputy's swearing in on the twenty-first.'

The Earl did return in time for that event, and for one even more momentous. It was summer solstice, a bright summer's day and Arthur remembered running after Meadhbh who was chasing a fire wheel down the hill one midsummer eve. When he caught up with her, they slipped into the bracken to celebrate the descent of the sun from the heavens in their own passionate way. He sighed. There had been no word from or about Meadhbh and he now accepted that all was lost.

A messenger finally arrived at Duiske, and the household ran out to greet him. Aye, he said, there was news of the Earl's ship landing at Dublin. He would be back at Carraigh on the morrow. There was further news. He paused to gain full effect. 'Archbishop O'Hurley was hanged this day at Hoggen's Green, outside the city walls.'

Piers looked stunned for a moment, then regaining his composure, said, 'We must to Carraigh to welcome my lord,' and he sent the messenger off to the castle to say they would be there shortly after the Earl's arrival. 'He will be doubly upset at his return. Poor O'Hurley.' Margaret turned and went sobbing quietly into the house. Arthur was eager to go back to Carraigh and retrieve the Archbishop's letter. It would not do for the Earl to find it. But more importantly, Arthur thought, now was the time to honour Dr O'Hurley's death with deeds.

Chapter Twenty-one

It took several months to get away but Arthur turned his back on Carraigh for the last time just after Samhain. The Earl had not seemed overly upset by O'Hurley's death. He was more anxious to go after Desmond in the south, so for a time Arthur was left at Carraigh, not in charge of course, but the Countess enjoyed his company so he had not the heart to leave until the men came home when the weather turned. All the while his anger at O'Hurley's death bubbled beneath like a pot just off the boil.

The day was cold as he drew near to Dublin, remembering the last time he approached the city, five years before. This time he had a purpose stronger than self-preservation. He carried the letter from the Archbishop martyred some months earlier. It was sealed with Tom Dubh's seal, though the Earl knew nothing about it. He also had an address, with instructions on how to locate the meeting place, so he did not have to ask directions. It mattered not how he dressed. Gentleman of the Pale or Irish peasant alike were all suspect these days. There were soldiers and spies everywhere; to speak to anyone could mean death, and Arthur was only too aware that he was a fugitive again. So he was dressed in clothes of middling quality, which bespoke of a gentleman a little down on his luck.

He found the street in Dublin city and the house reputed to be a safe haven for rebels. Here he would find Tibbot O'Toole. The door was ajar and when he pushed, it opened. Arthur checked the street up and down, nobody was about to see him so he entered quickly. In the front parlour men sat around tables drinking ale from pewter tankards. There was a fire in the grate. A serving man came to him and asked what his business was. 'I come in search of Tibbot O'Toole,' Arthur said. 'I hear he frequents this tavern.' The man smiled knowingly. 'This is no tavern sir, but if you have the address and the name of O'Toole on your tongue you are in the right place, for sure you are.' He sat him in a chair at an empty table. Some minutes later a swarthy-looking man approached. He turned to the manservant. 'A jug for two,' he ordered as he sat down opposite Arthur.

'Did anyone see you?' he asked Arthur.

'I was most careful.'

'Do you know who owns this house?' Arthur shook his head. 'Tis Gerald Fitzgerald, Earl of Kildare.'

'I thought the Earl of Kildare was a loyalist.'

'Things are not always what they seem. There are some who would agree with you, there are others amongst the New English who are set dead against him. Only the Earl himself knows what he is thinking, but he has been a grand friend to the O'Tooles.'

Arthur felt vaguely uneasy.

'You have a letter of introduction?'

'Aye.' Arthur handed over the letter. Tibbot O'Toole broke the seal and read it.

'*Ard na Caithne*,' he said admiringly. He folded it and gave it back to Arthur. 'Burn it,' he said pointing at the fire. Arthur got up and went to the fire. He was tempted to read the letter now the seal was broken. O'Toole noticed his hesitation and waved a hand to say – throw it in, and this Arthur did. He stood and watched the seal melt into an indecipherable lump of wax, then become liquid and the parchment turn to ashes. He went back to O'Toole.

'Now you will follow me to your lodgings,' O'Toole said. 'We must not appear to be together. You are a wanted man. And I am also high on the list. It will be up to you to follow close enough without arousing suspicion.' He inclined his head towards Arthur's foot.

'That won't be a problem. I can do a day's march with the best of them.'

'Oh, aye,' said O'Toole as if he did not believe him. 'Oh aye.' He nodded at the serving man and left. Arthur waited a few moments before following. Out in the street O'Toole was disappearing around a corner. Arthur all but ran to catch him, but O'Toole must have slowed because he was not too great a distance ahead by the time Arthur himself turned the corner. They did not have far to go. O'Toole stopped in a doorway halfway along this street. He knocked and walked on, and by the time Arthur got to the door it was open. He stepped in.

His lodgings were comfortable enough, and the landlord told him he was to stay in his room until instructions came. Two days went by and Arthur thought it almost as bad as being held in the Castle, no knowing what the future would bring, but on the third day a message came that he was to meet O'Toole at Kildare's house. No time was stipulated so he went as soon as he got the message. Nobody spoke, except the serving man, who bid him good day and seated him in the same chair as before. People mysteriously came and went, either through the entrance or out towards the back of the house, and Arthur waited a long time, uncertain of what was expected of him. He ordered a tankard of ale, but took his time drinking it.

He thought of Meadhbh with some longing, he had not had another woman since; he thought with pleasure about Morveen and Aefe. They were happy and relatively safe. What he was doing was to make Ireland a safer place for young Edward and the other youngsters both at Carraigh and Duiske.

Finally the door swung open and O'Toole walked in. Nodding at Arthur he ordered a tankard. Arthur waited for him to approach but instead he went to sit with a group of men who had arrived not long before. The door opened again and several English soldiers burst in. One nodded at O'Toole and the men rushed him, but not quite quickly enough, as O'Toole took off out the back. The soldiers followed and while they were out of the way Arthur calmly stood and walked out, relieved to find no soldiers outside. At an even pace, but with his heart beating wildly, he walked to the corner, turned it and walked up the street. Several people were about so he ignored the door to his lodgings and kept walking. He knew his walk was unmistakeably unsteady so he stopped for a moment and rested. People passed him but nobody took particular notice, and eventually he went back to the lodgings, and told the landlord what had happened. 'The Earl of Kildare will not be happy about having his house assailed,' the landlord said. 'I would feel in a better frame if you left.'

Arthur had no idea where to turn. For a small moment he considered going to the Castle and asking for John, but that would only lead to his imprisonment again, according to law he was still under house arrest to Piers. He had work to do, and the only course he could take was to return to the Kildare house, there must be someone there who could tell him what he was to do.

The street was quiet. He checked it for signs of the militia and satisfied there were none about, he knocked sharply on the door of the house. There was no reply, so he tried the handle. The door firmly locked. Arthur knocked again, louder this time, but no answer came. He was determined and walked around the block to the back entrance, where a snarling dog was tied to a post. Arthur walked past it. The back door was open and he walked in. The serving man sat at the kitchen table, and was angry when he saw Arthur. 'Get thee gone,' he cried. 'You are a danger to us all.'

'Just tell me. What should I do?'

The serving man sighed. 'O'Toole had you set for London. There is a plot to kill the Queen. You were to play a part.'

'How was I to get there?'

'On the *Thomas Cog* which sails for Bristol at high tide tomorrow. Wait,' he said, and he went into the interior of the house and shortly came back with a packet. 'All may not be lost. Here is money, your ticket to sail and an address.' He handed the packet over and pushed Arthur out the door which shut firmly behind him.

*

If Arthur thought Waterford big and Bristol bigger, London was enormous. The streets were narrow, houses built one upon the other, and they were crowded with people who cared not if they pushed you over with their creaking cart, or ran into you in their hurry to get somewhere. Men in rough country smocks and gentlemen in cocked hats, and poor jostled together and Arthur very quickly learnt to step around those in his path. He jumped over what could either have been mud or excrement, only to be faced with an oncoming barrel rolling towards him. It hit a stone and reeled to one side, and narrowly missed. The man pushing the barrel shook a fist and shouted something in a foreign language, as if Arthur were the one at fault. Even at midday the many taverns were doing excellent business. Outside one a strumpet leaned against the wall and lifted her kirtle to show Arthur her wares. 'Wotcha dah-ling,' she called after his hastily retreating back. It felt as if disease was in the very air; not just the French pox which no doubt the strumpet passed on along with her services, but the flux, the ague, the plague even; the stench of them came off the streets and the river which rivalled any port. He hoped his mission would be a speedy one.

His letter was addressed to a Sir Anthony Babington, a zealous Catholic who stood on the fringes of the English Queen's court. It took Arthur some time to find the inn where Babington was reputed to spend a great deal of time.

A serving wench smiled at him when he asked and pointed to a young man, about Arthur's own size and age who was holding court beside the fire. He was fashionably dressed with an embroidered, hip length cloak hanging off one shoulder. As Arthur approached and coughed to attract attention, Babington stopped talking, looking a little annoyed, but once he had taken the letter which

Arthur held out to him and read it, his expression changed. 'I bid you welcome to London,' he said. 'I hope you enjoy your stay.'

Arthur said, 'I am eager to do what must be done and return to Ireland.'

Babington drew Arthur to one side of the fire away from the others. He sat on the settle and indicated for Arthur to sit next to him. He spoke in a low tone. 'Are you not a fugitive from Ireland?'

'I am so, but I have places to turn,' he lied. 'Much of Ireland is as yet free of the English.'

'We must be patient nonetheless.' Babington took a pipe and pouch out of his trunk sleeve. 'You shall stay as my guest.' He waved his spare hand as Arthur protested. He pulled some thin brown strands of tobacco from the pouch, put them in the bowl of the pipe and tamped them down firmly. 'I have money a-plenty.' He took a taper from the fireside, lit it and then set off the pipe. 'Some say more than is good for me.' He drew deeply then blew the smoke out into the room. 'I must say you are the spit of the Earl of Ormond, in spite of the scar on your face. It gives me an idea for a means to achieve our ambition.'

'How will that help?' Arthur watched the smoke swirl to the ceiling.

'Once the Queen is dead and gone, the throne belongs to Mary Stewart.'

'But how will that help Ireland?'

'Mary will return both England and Ireland to the true faith. There will be no need of Spanish invasions. We will all be our own people again.' He took another puff at the pipe.

'Can Mary be trusted?'

'I was a page in her household when a child. I know her dear, sweet nature well. If there is anyone in the world we can trust, it is her.'

'*We* can, but not the Queen. Does Mary guarantee that she will put a stop to the plantations?'

'I am certain of it.'

'I would like to see that in writing.'

'I will send a request by the next post.' He coughed. 'Would you like to try some tobacco?' He waved his pipe as inducement.

Arthur shook his head. 'Will a letter be safe?'

'We have an ingenious method of getting the Queen of Scots' mail to her via the weekly beer barrel.'

'Does not the mail get wet?' Arthur laughed.

'It goes in a water-tight bung hole. It is as safe as houses. Nay,' Babington laughed too, 'safer.' He stood, adjusted his sideways cloak so that it sat squarely on his shoulder again, and pulled Arthur to his feet. 'Now come and meet our friends.' They returned to the group at the other side of the fire. 'How sounds this?' Babington looked around at the group of his fellow conspirators. 'We have an Irish rebel in our midst.'

Babington's house in Shoe Lane was comfortable, if not palatial. 'My family estate is Dethick Manor in Derbyshire,' he said by way of apology for Arthur's lodgings. 'My wife, Margery, awaits me there, but needs must that I am close to both the Court and the French embassy at present.' He left Arthur to settle in. 'We sup at six,' he said as he shut the door behind him.

Just before six Arthur made his way down the stairs. He could hear male voices and when he entered the room he found two of the men who had been at the inn earlier. Babington had divested himself of cloak, jerkin and doublet. He sat, resplendent, in a blue waistcoat. The men were introduced simply as John and Chid. 'Least you know, the better,' Babington said. 'We are preparing a letter for Queen Mary.' He waved a parchment at Arthur.

'Are you a literate?' the man called John asked.

Arthur smiled. Such prejudice, he thought. 'Do I look like an illiterate?'

'Apologies,' the man called Chid said. 'We have been led to believe that all the Irish are peasants.' He pushed his blond curls back off his face.

'But what of my lord, the Earl of Ormond?'

'He is more English than the English,' Babington laughed.

Arthur laughed too. 'And in Ireland they say he is more Irish than the rest of us.'

'Is not Arthur like The Queen's Lucas?' Babington asked the other two. 'And therein lies my plan.' He turned back to the parchment. 'But to the business in hand. How sounds this?' he asked reading aloud from his parchment. '"For the despatch of the usurper from the obedience of whom we are by the excommunication made free, there be six noble gentlemen all my private friends..."' He stopped. 'I may change that to seven.' He read on, '"Who for the zeal they bear unto the Catholic cause..." Now what else should I write?'

John suggested '...and your majesty's service...'

'...will undertake that tragical execution,' Chid took up.

Babington wrote both down and blotted the ink carefully. A sweet smell arose from the blotting paper. 'Mmm,' he said, 'I like that latest perfumed paper.'

'Perhaps,' said John, 'we should make suggestion of our reward...'

'...in the nicest possible way,' added Chid.

Babington wrote some more, blotted it again, then read it out. '"It resteth that according to their good deserts and your majesty's bounty their heroical attempt may be honourably rewarded."'

'Very good,' Chid said and John nodded his agreement.

'Does it go thus?' asked Arthur. 'Do you not use a cipher?'

'Of course,' said Babington. 'One of the six attends to that.' He folded the paper and slipped it into his vest pocket. 'Tomorrow we shall deliver it. But now we must sup.'

After supper Babington and Chid sat chewing on their tobacco pipes. John refrained, and the other two kept offering Arthur a puff, but he could not abide the smell and could only imagine what the taste was like, given the foul breath coming from the smokers. The air in the house became fuggy and he felt like vomiting with the stench of it. So, the next day Arthur was pleased when Babington said, 'You will join us on our walk.' The time had come to take the message to the cipher, and an outing in the fresh air, even if it was the air of London, sounded good. They were to show Arthur the river first. He had seen it, of course, you could not enter London without seeing it, it seemed, but he humoured them.

Arthur's enthusiasm for the outing was dampened, though, when they came to the Puddle Wharf and ahead lay London Bridge. On poles hung above the bridge were the heads of the latest criminals and traitors. 'That one will interest you,' said John, pointing to the highest pike. 'That is the Irish rebel Desmond.'

'Nay,' said Arthur. 'He has been in hiding so long…'

'Desmond stole cattle from some untamed Irish peasant or other.' Chid was so short he had almost to run to keep pace. 'And by way of retribution they found and killed him.'

So, 'twas not the Earl who did him. 'I must say,' Arthur added as they walked on, 'you English can be untamed yourselves when circumstances allow.'

'Come,' said Babington, 'we must be of one heart and one mind.'

So Arthur let it be, but he was still annoyed at the arrogance. He purposely dragged his bad foot to slow the others down and did not have a mind to speak with them during the whole expedition. And Desmond gone. No doubt it was a blessing given the state of the man's health. It could have only gotten worse while he was on the run, but it was the final blow to his estate. He recalled how hard Eleanor had fought for Desmond both diplomatically and physically. In spite of their separation he was sure she would be bereft.

As they passed through Holborn and left the mansions and houses behind Arthur did admit to himself how pleasant the air became, and how splendid was the cloth of red and yellow strung out in the tenter grounds. They watched washerwomen spinning while their clothes dried on the moor, men practising archery, and stopped at an inn for a tankard of porter. Arthur wondered when they would deliver the parchment to be ciphered, but it was not until they strolled back through Holborn that they stopped again. Babington pointed to a brick house opposite. 'There,' he said. 'You wait here. If I am not out shortly disperse and leave for the safe houses immediately.'

'We have little to worry about,' said John to Arthur as they waited. 'Spymaster, Walshingham, is in complete ignorance of what we are doing. Our tracks are carefully covered.' Indeed soon afterwards Babington left the house and they made their way back through the streets. 'It will be ciphered this night and delivered on the morrow,' he said as they fell into step again. Arthur was sorry to be heading back towards the more densely peopled part of the city. He turned and looked back longingly.

'They were but a few apostates and cobblers, to quote Campion,' John was saying.

'Who was that?' asked Arthur who had not been listening to their chatter.

'The Protestants eliminated by Mary Tudor.'

'So it was legitimate for Mary to kill for reasons of religion, but not her sister?' Arthur asked.

'It is the sister who is not legitimate. That is the reason,' Chid said. 'Elizabeth's mother was not legally married to the old king.'

'We are discussing the fact that Calvinism is no religion for a gentleman,' Babington said.

'But are *you* a gentleman?' Chid turned to Arthur.

'I am the son of an Earl,' he said hating himself for the defensive way in which he said it.

'We understand you have a half-brother said to be born of the Queen,' John said.

Babington laughed. 'But we know even a Protestant Queen would not lower herself to bed with the Irish.'

'The Earl of Ormond comes from good Norman stock.' Arthur was indignant. 'He is high born.'

'Chid is high born but would rather be called a poet.' Babington was obviously trying to calm the waters which were becoming increasingly turbulent.

'I heard an English poet once.' Arthur's mind went back to the Queen's welcome in Bristol. 'He wrote such gross rubbish as to make your innards groan.' He was embarrassed by his own bitterness, but their remarks about the Irish chaffed him dreadfully. He fell silent again.

'The poet Spenser has written some verses about Ireland,' John said. 'Named *The Faerie Queen* for our Protestant bastard.'

'He was one of those in charge at the Smerwick massacre,' Arthur ventured, not wanting to start another argument, but determined to press a point.

'Well, he has certainly *captured* Ireland,' Chid said making a play on the double meaning. 'I can recall some of the lines…' He paused, thinking, then began, '"Out of every corner of the woods they came, creeping forth upon their hands because their legs could not bear them…They looked like anatomies of death…"' He waved his arms dramatically to emphasise the point. '"They did eat dead carrion…and if they found watercress they did flock to it as if to a feast…they spoke like ghosts crying out of their graves…" or some such,' he petered out, his memory exhausted, but then recovered himself to reach his point: 'This is the Ireland you are so proud of, Arthur!'

'Have you no heart, man. This is the Ireland the English have made.' Arthur's voice was sharp with rage, but he stopped himself and walked on ahead of the other three, not caring that they would be snickering at the Irish gatch on him. He walked so quickly he had to wait outside the door in Shoe Lane for the others to be let inside. When Babington finally arrived and opened the door, Arthur was glad to retire to his chamber when the pipes came out.

*

The days passed slowly. Time seemed to hang over them while they waited for Mary's response to their letter. They played gleek and primero although Arthur merely watched because he had no money to stake. Babington read aloud to the group. He had a fondness for travel books, his favourite being *The Voyage and Travail of M. Caesar Fredericke, Merchant of Venice into East India*. 'When this task of ours is over, gentlemen,' he was fond of saying, 'we shall follow in that merchant's footsteps.' They spent some time at the inn where Arthur had first found Babington, where they drank, caroused and listened to a blind harper who put new words to old melodies, not all of which were suitable for a lady's ears. Sometimes Babington and Chid took themselves off to Court where they sat on the margins, ignored by Her Majesty but happily picking up tit-bits of useful information from some of the lowlier courtiers. It was in this way that Arthur learnt how the assassination was to be effected.

Eventually a reply arrived from the Queen of Scots. Several of the conspirators gathered at Babington's house to hear it. 'Is it safe?' Arthur asked, 'to congregate thus?'

'Nobody is aware of our intentions,' said one.

They lit their pipes and sat around the small fire. It might be July but the London wind was not aware of it. The air filled with smoke from the green wood in the grate and the pipes, as Babington, in his customary blue waistcoat, read: '"Affairs being thus prepared, and forces in readiness both without and within the realm, then shall it be time to set the six gentlemen to work..."'

'What does she say of Ireland?' Arthur asked.

Babington waved a dismissive hand and read on, '"...taking order, upon the accomplishing of their design..."'

Arthur went to the window. Down in the narrow street a man stood opposite looking upwards. When he saw Arthur at the window he moved away. Babington was saying, 'There is a postscript here. She asks for the names of the six.'

'Is that safe?' asked John.

'It is sensible,' Babington assured him. 'She will want to know of our credentials.'

'But what of Ireland?' Arthur's voice had risen. 'What does she say of Ireland?'

Babington gave him a long look. 'Nothing,' he said finally. 'Nothing.'

'I am to play the greater part in this enterprise and she says nothing of Ireland?'

Babington turned back to the letter, ignoring Arthur. 'Then I shall play no part in it,' Arthur shouted. 'She offers nothing and I shall offer nothing in return.'

'But you are the key to it,' Babington looked up again. 'An invasion is imminent. We must strike now. I have bribed the Master of the Tents to loosen the stays at the rear of the Queen's tent at the Court Gate tilt yard.'

'The current Master is but an underling,' Chid put in. 'Eminently bribable.'

'His own master returns next week,' Babington added. 'We must attend on the morrow.'

Arthur gave a sardonic laugh. 'And I am to crawl into the tent... beguile Elizabeth, standing no closer than pistol range...'

'Yes.' Babington nodded. 'Her eyesight is poorly. And you are the spit of Ormond. Ain't he?' He turned to the others who murmured their agreement, content, no doubt, Arthur thought, to be usurped in the role of assassin.

'Then I shoot the Queen and such lady's maids as are with her. And run?'

There followed an uncomfortable silence.

'What if I am found? Caught? There is every likelihood.'

'You will beg for mercy.'

'I will not do it unless for Ireland,' Arthur said finally.

Babington's voice hardened. 'You must. Else risk being struck by the same pistol.'

'If he is to pass as the Earl,' John said, 'we must needs dress him in some suitable clothes. Those Irish rags will never do.'

Arthur did not rise to the bait. He knew when he was defeated.

Chapter Twenty-two

Arthur heard the rumble of hooves and the roar of the crowd. Babington and Chid had gone ahead to check the state of the tent. If the Master of the Tents had done his job they would nod at Arthur on their way back through the Court Gate. He was dressed up like an earl, a cocked hat with feather, the highest ruff he'd ever worn, and a short velvet cape with gold trim over a red doublet; all of them Babington's, so it was as well that they were much of a size. The pistol weighed heavy inside his jerkin as he scanned the crowd for a sign of his co-conspirators; passing courtiers in brightly coloured silk netherstocks, and velvet doublets intricately embroidered, who strolled arm-in-arm, or with ladies whose clothes were equally dazzling. Arthur could not see the Queen; she would be sitting in the red and white pavilion watching the tilt. There was no mistaking her tent, though. Her colours flew over it and it was as big as a house. Another roar went up, so loud it could only mean that the Queen's favourite had won.

Jousters in jerkins emblazoned with family crests stood around the back of the tilt yard watching their horses being groomed and caparisoned. Beyond where the horses were tethered, a line of chest armour stood at attention waiting to be donned, some engraved, others gilt, more decorative than protective. Finally there they were:

Babington gave Arthur an exaggerated nod as they passed, while Chid looked the other way. Arthur moved on, nerves taut now, recalling how as a child he had waited for Elizabeth to visit the Earl's manor house, and now he was waiting for her again, only this time to kill her.

He made his way to the outskirts of the tilt yard, and there was Elizabeth sitting on a dais surrounded by her closest courtiers. She glittered as always in the sun, but her usual alabaster white face could not disguise that she had aged, and her lips painted as red as her hair only added to this impression. The victor rode forward and bowed low before her, and Elizabeth handed over a yellow sleeve which she must have had at the ready beside her, because she still wore both her own white sleeves. The victor bowed again, was dismissed and rode off. Then came a pause in proceedings while Elizabeth spoke to the gentleman sitting next to her. He gave her his hand, helped her out of the cushions, down from the dais and across the yard to her tent.

This was the moment they had been waiting for, but Arthur had not counted on her being accompanied by a man. He would probably have a pistol too and Arthur would be dead before he got the chance to fire a shot. Guards stood either side of the tent opening, muskets at the ready, but as Arthur watched from a distance, the gentleman came out closing the flap behind him, least prying eyes should catch the Queen at leisure.

Arthur stole around the back, and sure enough the stays were loose and the skin of the tent slack. It was a tight fit but he managed to crawl inside the tent. A lady-in-waiting attended the Queen. Arthur had not supposed there to be anyone else inside and his heart beat a little faster. They both had their backs to him.

'It is too hot in the sun,' Elizabeth was saying. 'I cannot abide this vexatious thing a moment longer,' and she took her hair off. Beneath the wig her head bore but a sprinkling of hair. She seemed to sway where she stood. The maid set the wig on a table next to her and helped the Queen sit in a chair. She then turned her attention to powdering the Queen's face, but the Queen slapped her hand down. 'Not that. I want another secke.' Arthur watching from behind stood and brushed himself down. He felt the solid shape of the pistol stuck inside his jerkin. The Queen's attendant filled a goblet from a flask and handed it to her. Elizabeth drank deeply before setting the goblet on the table. She hiccoughed. 'Fetch me another,' she said to the lady's maid, 'and do not let a soul enter here.' She patted the wig to show why. 'So many guards. They quite suffocate me.' The maid left. Arthur removed the pistol and stepped forward.

'Your Majesty. It is I, Lucas.'

'I knew not that you were at Court.' Her words were slurred. 'Did I bid you come?' She peered at him, then remembered her hair and hastily replaced the wig so that it sat askew.

He kept well back, glad that her eyesight was obviously not as sound as it once was. 'No Majesty, I...I...' The pistol was warming in his hand.

'Well, now you are here, tell me. How goes Ireland?'

'O'Hurley is dead.'

'I know. I permitted it.' She sighed, 'But it was Walsingham who sanctioned the torture. Poor man. They burnt his feet and tortured him most cruelly. The pain your monarch has to bear! It is no wonder I need secke to quicken my spirits.' She held out a hand so he could kiss the ring on her finger. 'But I knew dear Lucas that you were blameless in the matter.' She shook the hand at him. 'Come. You are looking uncommonly well for a man of your years.'

She looked so pathetic with her wig awry, so vulnerable, on her own without a soul to save her. Here he was fighting for the Queen of Scots and the Catholic faith when at heart he was a pagan heathen. He had lost his taste for the undertaking. He turned, crawled under the skin of the tent and ran.

He pushed past a lady's maid and just missed a gentleman in armour grooming his horse. 'What the..?' the gentleman said, but Arthur did not stop. He ran faster than he ever had before, ducking around bemused people, diving under arms held aloft until he was out of sight of the crowd. He found a gap in a hedge big enough to crawl into. It was a quiet street off a main thoroughfare, nonetheless he looked behind him to see if he had been followed. There was nobody, so he crept into the hole and stayed, stiff and silent, until the curfew bell rang. He set off in the dark for Babington's house with an eye out for the watch on one side and ne'er-do-wells on the other. The streets were uncannily quiet and his footsteps echoed as he walked. He saw a brazier burning at the far end of the Strand. If the Watch was about he would surely be caught, so he ran down one of the lanes that led to the river and took the bank as far as Fleet Ditch. As he walked he decided what he would say to his fellow conspirators, he would make some excuse for failing: a guard came in, perhaps, or a courtier drew a pistol on him, perchance the ladies maid recognised him. The lanes past Bridewell Church were clear and he sighed with relief when he arrived at the house undetected.

Silence greeted his knock at Babington's door. No candlelight slipped under the curtains. The house was empty and he had no way of getting in. If the conspirators had escaped to safe houses, they had not taken the trouble to tell Arthur where these were. He felt sorely used. Where should he turn? The only possibility that presented itself was the house at Holborn. Again he set off into the quiet streets, not knowing what to expect at any turn. A light wavered at the far end of Chancery Lane, so he crept into the gardens of Lincoln's Inn, climbed the far fence and stuck to that until he reached the Holborn High road again, and so came to the brick house.

There was a flicker of light in the front window so he knocked quietly on the door. When that brought no response he knocked more boldly. And again. Finally a face appeared at the window, and obviously satisfied with what it saw a few minutes later opened the door. A man stood in front of Arthur with candle held high 'Forsooth, sire. I beseech thee stop your knocking.'

'I am a friend of Babing...'

He had not time to complete the name before he was pulled inside and the door shut resolutely behind him. 'There is danger in naming names.' The man held the candle closer to Arthur's face to see the better.

Arthur apologised. 'I am not adept at conspiracy.'

'So you are Arthur? The others got word of a raid by Walsingham's men. Robert Poley has been a-spying and they are doomed if caught. Queen Mary's letters have been intercepted. The plot is out.'

'Then I must not stay here and implicate you.' Arthur turned to go.

'I am but a servant here. I know nothing of the arrangements but what I overhear. I have been instructed to stay and look after the house on my master's behalf. Until...until such times as...' He could not bring himself to speak the necessary words. 'But after your courageous attempt methinks you must be given some hope. Come with me.' He took Arthur into the interior of the house and gave him victuals. 'Your clothing,' he said when Arthur had finished eating, 'must needs be changed.' He opened a trunk and pulled out an assortment of clothes such as a common man would wear. 'Farmer? Soldier? Watchman? What's it to be?' He held up different jerkins and cloaks as he spoke. 'I suggest a farmer. That will allow you to roam the countryside freely without raising suspicion.'

Arthur agreed and soon changed Babington's clothing for the simple garb of a farmer; smock, woollen netherstocks, for comfort and warmth a waistcoat to be worn under the smock; a pair of ankle boots, a wide brimmed hat...'the better to disguise you,' the man said, as he added a waist length cloak, shabby but warm. 'Tonight,' he said, 'you must sleep in the stable. The horses have been taken, but there is plenty of hay to hide beneath should the need arise. Take this bread and porter for your breakfast and be on your way at break of day.'

It was a restless night, but next morning Arthur was away from the house as quickly as possible. He had been given the address of a Mrs Bellamy at Harrow and he set off, skirting the city so as not to look out of place in his new attire.

It was nightfall before he reached Harrow and a serving man

opened the door almost immediately to his knock. When Arthur asked for his mistress he was told to wait outside and the door was closed in his face. Soon, though, the man was back and he ushered Arthur into a parlour where four men sat at cards. They looked up somewhat startled when Arthur walked in, and turned for a suitable response to a woman sitting on a high-backed chair nearby. She waved a hand at them to continue their game as the servant led Arthur towards her. 'Our friend, Babington, is at his prayers,' she said.

'Pass,' said one of the men at cards.

'Numerus thirty-two at two crowns,' said the man to the left of him. Mrs Bellamy nodded knowingly at Arthur as the man put his stake on the table in front of him. The man was bluffing. From where they were Arthur and Mrs Bellamy could see he held a queen of clubs, ace of spades, seven of hearts and a four of diamonds; a primero with a point total of 61.

'Pass,' said the next man.

Mrs Bellamy turned to Arthur. 'You obviously did not succeed in your mission, but it was a valiant try.' She lowered her voice. 'One of these gentlemen newly come from Court has suggested that the Queen had taken of too much wine. It is a known fact that the Earl of Ormond is in Ireland. He is too good a subject to disobey his Queen and return to Court unbidden. She is presumed to have been having a fit of the vapours, a vision caused by too much heat, too much secke...' She paused briefly and looked at him. 'There is a strong resemblance. We shall get that beard cut.' She called the serving man and gave him instructions to feed Arthur, shave his whiskers and then take him to the room where their other guest stayed. Arthur hoped Babington did not have his pipe with him. He would suffocate if he did, and it would be a give-away if Walsingham's men got word of his whereabouts.

'Primero, forty-nine at three crowns,' one of the men said. Mrs Bellamy dismissed Arthur and turned back to watch the game.

In the kitchen a well-dressed visitor sat on a bench by the ovens. He looked up as Arthur came in. 'This is Arthur, Sir,' said the servant. 'He has come to stay with our other guest.' He spoke loudly as if explaining something to a simpleton. Arthur realised in an instant that it was not the well-dressed visitor who was a simpleton, but himself. The visitor left rather too hastily. The servant held out a hand for Arthur's cloak and hat. He would shave him before he supped. 'Forgive me,' Arthur said, 'but I need the jakes first.'

The servant opened the door and showed Arthur the outside privy set close to the house. He watched while Arthur stepped into it. Arthur spent some time in the unpleasantly smelling closet hoping the servant would go inside. When he could stand the stench no longer he opened the door a little. The man had gone in but lamplight shone out the open door. He took the risk, feeling badly about abandoning Babington, but knowing he could do little to help him except risk his own life. Had it been someone like Donal or the boy Eamon he would not have hesitated, but Babington had proven to be no friend to Arthur or Ireland. He crept around to the rear of the closet, paused to listen, then ran across the meadow in front of him.

He had not gone far when he heard horses approaching the house. The moon was rising and he made for a field of hay stooks. He ducked low behind one and watched, his heart beating at his chest so hard he could scarcely breathe. The men leapt off their horses and forced their way into the house and shortly came out with Babington. Mrs Bellamy and the card playing men remained inside and Arthur could only wonder at their treachery before creeping away into the night.

*

Arthur was drawn against his better judgement to St Giles Field. He had been living rough for six weeks, stealing food where he could, drinking from rivers and streams. Always on the move. His aim had been to make his way across country to Bristol, but he had been thwarted at every turn. The city and surrounding countryside was swarming with soldiers. After nearly being caught a third time trying to cross the river he had stayed on the outskirts of London waiting for things to settle down after the Babington trial. The last act was to be played out this day. He pulled his wide-brimmed hat down over his face. His farmer's clothes were getting shabbier by the day, but he did not look out of place in this crowd of spectators. He thought it ironic that the place of execution should be so little removed from the house in Holborn where the men confidently delivered their lethal letters to the cipher. People had obviously travelled for miles to be here, common folk stood on the ground in the four corners of the square, held in check by ropes strung between beer barrels. They pushed and jostled for a better view while children escaped beyond the rope and played catch until sent scuttling between the legs of their elders by a pikeman. A dog jumped up on Arthur, provoked into barking by the excitement of the crowd. The more well-to-do hung from the windows of houses situated around the square, some opportunists balanced on window sills. Summer had been short and this September day held more than a touch of the winter to come. Even though the sun shone in fits and starts it was cold and Arthur was glad of the cloak that had been added to his wardrobe.

Around him the spectators were oblivious to the weather. The occasion had the air of a fete. A pie seller marched up and down selling his wares. Arthur wished he had some money to indulge. The smell was tantalising. A juggler stopped in front of Arthur and threw several balls in the air until someone in the crowd threw him a penny. He swooped it up without missing a single ball. The crowd clapped. Another penny came flying and the juggler repeated the performance before moving along. Next in the parade was an ale merchant, a spectator passed his tankard over Arthur's shoulder to have it filled.

So the carnival continued and Arthur had to look at the hangman checking the noose on the scaffold to remind himself what this occasion was really about. Also on the same raised platform was a trestle in readiness for the next stage of the punishment, and a brazier in which a fire burned. 'A n'istorical moment, this,' said a man next to Arthur. Arthur simply nodded and the man obviously dissatisfied with the response turned to the woman on his other side. ''istorical moment, ain't it?'

'Yerse,' she said. 'Such a loverly lot of 'em this time. Seven this day and seven termorra.'

'Them executioners should be able to drag it out for 'ours.'

'I go to 'em all,' the woman bragged. 'All the hexecutions. But this is bound to be the best one yet. Don't often get the drawing and quartering. That 'angman will be a *proper* butcher no doubt. 'e'll need his butchering skills ere today.'

'They saves that butchering business for traitors,' the man said. 'Don' they?' He turned back to Arthur who shuffled out of his way.

A wild roar went up amongst the crowd. 'Here come the traitors.' People spat and jeered. A chant went up, 'Traitors, traitors, traitors.' And on the other side of the square, 'Kill them, kill them. Let's see their blood.' A line of seven horses pulling seven hurdles walked into the square. On each hurdle was tied a man. It was hard to distinguish one from the other, but Arthur recognised Babington by his blue waistcoat. He was on the first hurdle which meant it would be over quickly for him, and he would not have to suffer the anticipation of the others. Next came John Ballard, easy to identify because of the colour of his hair. Was that Chid Tichborne behind him? Slowly the horses pulled the hurdles across the square. They were in no hurry, the crowd was enjoying every moment, and Arthur tried to imagine what the men were feeling, thinking back to the days they had spent together with a nostalgia deeper that was deserved. That they should end like this! He turned his head, tempted to leave, but to do that with this baying crowd would only invite suspicion. Now he was here, he would have to stay. And watch.

Finally the first horse arrived at the platform. Babington was untied and pulled to his feet. With a guard on each side of him he was escorted up the steps to a spot exactly under the hangman's noose. The crowd bellowed, people shook their fists in anger at him; an official climbed to the scaffold platform and held up his arms for the crowd to be quiet. He turned to all four corners of the square and slowly the crowd quietened. 'Anthony Babington,' he shouted, although he did not look at the prisoner but at the now silent crowd. 'You have been tried in Court and found guilty of conspiring to assassinate our beloved Majesty, the Queen Elizabeth.' He paused and there was a murmur of assent from the crowd. 'The punishment accorded you by Her Majesty and signed by her at Westminster Palace on the 17th day of September reads thus...' He took a parchment from beneath his cloak and read. '"You are to be led from the place of arraignment and taken to the Tower and thence to the gallows at St Giles in the Field."' The official waved an arm about as if to say, and here we are. '"There to be hanged and being half dead to be cut down and the bowels to be taken out of the belly and fed into the fire."' Here the man pointed to the burning brazier. '"The head to be cut off and the body divided into four parts."' He nodded at the hangman and stepped back. The spectators broke their silence with a deafening cheer.

A gentleman standing beside Arthur said to his companion, 'I believe Her Majesty wanted something more severe.' Arthur did not look at them. He watched his feet and listened.

'And so she should. These supporters of Mary must be stopped.'

'None more so than Mary herself.'

Arthur remembered the Queen as he had last seen her, bald headed and in her cups. What did she imagine could be a more severe punishment than being hung, drawn and quartered?

'And to think that knave offered the Queen a thousand pounds for his pardon...'

'Pardon! Bah. He admits to the plot.'

'But at his trial... Were you there?' The second man did not reply and Arthur assumed he had shaken his head because his companion went on, 'He brought up that old saw about the legitimacy of Queen Anne's marriage.'

'Refuge of a scoundrel.'

The crowd whistled and screamed. Arthur looked up. Babington was hanging now. The crowd shouted, 'Take him down. Bring him down while he has breath. Take him down before he dies,' and eventually the butcher did just that. Assisted by the escort he lay Babington on the trestle and tied his hands and feet to it. Babington was limp but he still lived and at the first incision of the butcher's knife into his stomach he let out a scream that pierced Arthur's heart and set the spectators into a frenzy of delight. Then there was silence, until another thrust of the knife, another agonised cry brought on another cheer. So it went on with the crowd leaving space in the air for to hear the agony before setting up a clamour again. Arthur longed to cover his ears against the screams. Finally the drawing was done, and Babington's innards held high for all to see before they were thrown into the fire. The butcher came into his own in the next part. First the head was cut off. This too was held up for the crowd to see. 'Take a good look at us you traitor,' someone called. 'See how we hate you.' The quartering was deftly done and all five parts of what used to be Babington put in a basket and trundled off on the sled on which he had arrived. The butcher slapped his hands together. 'Next,' he called but Arthur could stand it no longer. The consequences mattered not, he pushed back through the crowd and walked away.

*

Now that was over he could make his way home to Ireland, but he would need a better disguise. No farmer would set sail alone in smock and cloak for Ireland. Perhaps if he took the offer of a soldier's uniform he would better pass inspection. It was a faint hope, but a hope nonetheless that the manservant might still be in the Holborn house. He found a shady tree in a meadow and waited beneath for the spectators to leave the road to him, so he would not be seen entering the brick house. As the daylight began to fail and the joyful people left the execution ground, church bells pealed in jubilation at the horrors. The people were in no hurry to go home. They danced and sang, and when the curfew bell rang it was ignored. A bonfire was set and lit; more appeared across the countryside. A cart trundled through the crowd distributing food and ale in celebration of the traitors' deaths. Hunger and fear of being found contemplating the darkening sky in forlorn silence, forced Arthur to join the revellers. 'And there's seven more tomorrow,' a young man laughed, slapping Arthur on the back and Arthur shuddered thinking how close he had come to being the eighth.

*

All was quiet at the brick house when it was finally safe to call, but he was let in by the same man as before after knocking several times. 'You must not dally here. Walsingham is still desirous of more arrests,' the man said when he recognised Arthur. He gave him food and drink. 'If I was you I would not be trying to leave England now. The Spanish threat has everyone on edge. All passengers embarking at any port are suspect.'

'What can be done?' Arthur trusted this man.

'My father died some time back and my mother needs a spare pair of hands. She lives at the south end of Prittlewell just beyond the Thames mouth. If you wouldst get yourself there you could stay with her awhiles. I can fit you out as a workman.'

'You are kind,' Arthur clasped the man's hand. 'I know not your name...'

'And you need not.'

'But how will I find your mother?'

'Just ask for the fisherwoman in the village. There is only the one.'

The man outfitted Arthur in a workman's clothing and gave him instructions on how to get to his mother. He would be best to leave the city by Aldgate and follow the Whitechapel Road which would eventually lead him into Essex county. Once in Prittlewell he should head towards the sea. The south end was but a half hour's walk from the village. He gave him food and half a crown in case he needed money, and if not he was to give it to the fisherwoman when he arrived. He also had a small parcel for her. 'Some iron fish hooks,' he said. 'They are bigger than the ones she uses presently. She'll be glad of them.'

It took Arthur three days to complete the journey but he was used to travelling on the byways by now. He could have paid a wherryman to carry him some of the way down the Thames but he wanted to be able to hand over the half crown intact to the fisherwoman. The weather was good and he was glad of a destination even though it was not Ireland. He would lie low for a time then make his way over to Bristol. Betimes he would be able to help out the mother of the man who had been such a help to him.

As he approached the village of Prittlewell he was stopped by a soldier. 'Whence go you?'

'To the fisherwoman at the south end of the village.'

'Strapping lad like you should be in the military.' He put out an arm to march Arthur off. 'We have a muster coming soon. We need able bodies such as yours to help protect the Queen.' Arthur pushed his arm away. 'But you must,' the man insisted. 'Or die.' He raised the musket which was leaning against his leg and Arthur remembered the two things he was taking to the fisherwoman. He held up a hand to stop the soldier's aim. He took out the packet of fish hooks first. The soldier opened the package and swore. 'What good are such?'

'They are fish hooks.'

The soldier spat. 'You think I am a fool?'

Reluctantly Arthur pulled out the half crown. 'That is all I have,' he said. He would need to make it up to the fisherwoman in hard work.

The soldier grabbed the money and let him pass, keeping the fish hooks as well. Arthur was determined not to show fear, and walked off rather than ran, even adding a jaunty swagger such as the Earl affected when he came home from Court. He could see him now, feathered hat bobbing, hips swaying as he walked through the watergate. Arthur swung his hips and strolled slowly on. The soldier did not follow and he walked beyond the village until he was close to the sea. Here he stopped a man who was walking towards him and asked for the fisherwoman. The man pointed to a cottage close to the water's edge and Arthur walked to it, all swagger gone. He was sorry he had nothing to give the woman now except his labour. He paused to look at the sea before knocking, and sniffed in the salty air. This would be a good place to bide his time. He knocked on the door somehow expecting to hear the shuffle of old feet come in response. Instead strong footsteps crossed the room, the door was flung open, almost defiantly as if the woman was expecting someone of ill-intent on the door sill. The face that greeted him was weather-worn but she looked robust, maybe two score, maybe more.

'I am Arthur,' he bowed his head slightly. 'Your son has sent me to help you. Sorry for your troubles. With your husband dead and gone.' She opened her mouth to speak and the most fearsome noise came out of it. She had no tongue.

Chapter Twenty-three

Arthur was lying on a pallet of straw beside the fire. Tired though he was he could not sleep. He wondered how the fisherwoman's husband had died; if the lack of a tongue was connected in any way. There was no asking her. Her son might have made his way in the world as a servant but she was an illiterate fisher. They could not write question and answer. He would have to wait until they went out with the other fishers to learn more.

Next morning he awoke to the door being violently opened. The woman went to slam it shut. It was the wind and what a wind it was, coming straight off the sea. He could hear the rain rattling at the thin straw of the roof and some of it came in down the clay wall.

'That's a gale a-blowing out there,' he said to the woman. She nodded. 'No fishing today?' She shook her head. 'What can I do then? I must help.' She shook her head again. 'I could try and mend the roof.' She nodded.

The fisherwoman pointed at a stool by the fire. He picked it up, but she shook her head and pointed, he was to sit on it. She put food on a trencher, placed the platter of salt fish and coarse black bread on his knees, and stood watching as he ate.

'It is most tasty.' She gave a grimace which might have passed for a smile, and went to get her own breakfast. While she ate Arthur went outside to look at the roof. The wind was whipping tufts of straw away, and they flew over his head and danced over the water. He would need something to stand on before he could get the roof fixed and he must needs wait until that vicious wind had died. He went to the corner of the cottage and looked out to sea. All that was in front of him was a sheet of sand. The sky hung low and grey. He went inside. 'Where has the sea gone?' he asked.

She smiled her odd smile, and waved her hands as if pushing the sea away.

'The tide?' She nodded. 'It goes a long way out,' Arthur said and she nodded again.

The cottage was full of smoke because there was only a small hole above as a chimney. The fire was essential for warmth but the smoke smarted Arthur's eyes and soon he was coughing. It was worse than sitting with Babington and his fellow smokers. The thought of his last sight of Babington made him feel ill, or perhaps it was the smoke. He longed to be able to talk to someone about the events that led him to Prittlewell. To have a sympathetic ear and some words of advice or comfort. Yet here he was with a woman who had had the powers of speech ripped out of her. Unless, and this was a happier thought, she had been born that way.

The fisherwoman pulled a basket into the middle of the room. It contained fishing nets. She took one out and spread it across the floor showing Arthur where the net was torn. She took a tin from the basket. Inside was a length of hemp twine which she measured before nodding at Arthur to hand her the cutting knife. She cut the twine and tied a knot at two corners to join a hole in the net. She deftly sliced off what little surplus there was and set about doing the same for another gap in the net. When she had mended about half the net she handed the task over to Arthur. He was slow at first but soon got into the rhythm. 'Haargh,' she said and he laughed with pleasure because he thought it an appropriate response.

Later when the wind died he found a rough ladder at the back of the cottage. He climbed to investigate the damage on the roof. He cast about for something with which to replenish the covering.

There was nothing outside, so he went inside and took straw from his pallet, glad that he had watched Bren O'Brennan work so many times. The fisherwoman nodded. They were both pleased with the result.

When the weather cleared completely they went out fishing. The tide was out so far that Arthur could not see where the sea began. The blue sky was reflected in the wet sand so that sky and sand became one. The fisherwoman showed him how to dig with his hands for cockles hiding beneath the surface. They worked together. Every once in a while the fisherwoman would lift the basket testing its weight, and when it was about half full and she could only just lift it she handed it to Arthur, pointing to a group also collecting cockles at the far end of the beach.

He set off, then stopped waiting for her to follow. She shook her head. The basket weighed heavy by the time he reached the people bent over the shiny sand. A man stood and came over to him.

'Look,' he called to the rest of them. 'The witch has an accomplice.'

The others laughed and stood. They sauntered over to Arthur.

'What am I to do with these?' he asked, putting the basket down.

'Didn't she tell you?' a young man laughed.

'Cat got her tongue?' asked another.

Arthur looked back at the lone figure made frail by the vastness of the sand and sky. 'What happened to her?' he asked.

'She's a witch, that's what,' said a young woman.

'Who took her tongue? What happened to her husband?'

'So many questions,' the first man said, and Arthur thought with deep longing of Morveen. Always asking questions my Arty, she would say.

'Are there no answers?' Arthur stood his ground.

An older man stepped forward. 'Jack,' he said introducing himself. He indicated that the others were to return to their work then he turned back to Arthur. 'We take these to the market for her.' Seeing that Arthur was about to ask another question he hastened to add, 'And we pay her what they are worth, less a little something for our troubles.'

'That seems fair enough.' He turned to watch the group now back at work. 'Why do they call her a witch?'

'It is unlucky for her that she survived the torture. Her husband did not.'

'Why were they tortured?'

'Her son is a ne'er-do-well. Lives in London...'

'I...' Arthur began and then realised that to mention the son in this context would not be wise. 'I'm just a vagabond and she has been kind to me.'

'You are not from these parts,' Jack observed.

'My travels have taken me far.' Before the old man could ask exactly how far, he added, 'Was this a recent event? There is much trouble about. Those London traitors...'

'Tide's a-coming in.' Jack picked up the fisherwoman's basket. 'Got to fetch our nets'. He set off back up the sand.

'What is her name?' Arthur called after him.

'Sarah.' The name was shouted into the wind, but that is what Arthur took it for.

When he got back to the woman the water was already ankle deep. It seemed to creep across the sand swallowing everything with it. 'Sarah,' Arthur called when within earshot. She turned. 'Sarah,' he said getting closer. She nodded and he smiled. At least she had her name back.

She pointed to the group again and pretended to be carrying the basket. At first Arthur did not understand and then he realised. He laughed and hit the side of his head to show her what an idiot he was. By the time he got back to the other group Sarah's basket stood empty beside a barrel filled with slowly moving cockles.

Sarah had gathered some cockles for their own dinner and they went into the cottage where she put them still alive into a pot of water boiling on the fire. When they were cooked they ate in haste. Sarah set the pace, as if the hounds of hell would take her dinner from her if she did not pick the cockles off the shells and swallow them quickly. Obviously they were working against the tide. Then it was back to work this time with the net. Sarah had hung limestone weights on the net. She gave Arthur two ends and took the others herself. They walked a long way out. The water was at calf height most of the way. When they stopped and turned the little cottage on the shore looked scarcely big enough for two to live in. They moved apart until the net was stretched almost as far as it would go. Sarah showed him how the net would scoop up the fish and thus they dragged it into shore behind them. Arthur noticed the group at the far end working several nets.

It was a good catch. Whelks, salmon, flat fish and fresh water eels swept down from the estuary. Sarah took some whole fish for themselves and they threw the rest into the basket. When the net was empty Sarah picked the seaweed off it and hung it out to dry. She nodded at the basket, then at the group still working along the beach. Arthur picked up the basket and took it to old Jack who was supervising the catch at that end.

'Tell Sarah,' Jack said when he had emptied her basket into a barrel, 'that we go to market tomorrow. Ask if she requires anything.'

Arthur nodded and turned to go.

Jack put a hand on his arm to restrain him. 'And tell her...tell her...we are not all of a mind that she is a witch.' He smiled a toothless smile. 'Some of us are glad that she lived through the torture, terrible though it must have been.' He paused as if finished, then added, 'And that she has you to help.'

'What will happen to her if this witch story persists?' Arthur asked.

'That will be up to the church.' Then he said more urgently, 'Tell her she must come to the church every Sunday as we all must. Her absence points to witchcraft. Now you are here you must bring her with you.'

That night when Arthur mentioned the matter of church Sarah shook her head. 'But that could make it more dangerous for you. I shall take you.' She shook her head again. 'Then I must consider you a witch,' Arthur said laughing.

'Aargh,' said Sarah and she laughed too.

'Shall I tell you a story?' Arthur asked. He might not get any answers from Sarah, but he could tell her his story without fear of her being tortured to drag it from her. She was no use as witness now.

Sarah nodded and so began their long winter together, fishing by day and storytelling by night. Arthur told her the stories that Morveen had filled his head with when he was a child; he told her Bridie's story and the story of the massacres at Smerwick and Mulllaghmast; he told her of his time in Bristol, of the Queen's visit there; he told her about Meadhbh and their betrothal that came to naught. At this Sarah held both her hands against her heart and nodded enquiringly at Arthur. 'Aye,' he said. 'I loved her, and I love her yet, though it be a lost cause.' One night after he had finished telling her about his time in Dublin Castle she tapped his arm to get his attention. She rocked an imaginary baby in her arms. Then she pointed to herself, then back to the baby.

'Your son?' Arthur asked. He shrugged. 'I do not know his name.

'Oorghgh,' she tried.

'George?'

She nodded enthusiastically and smiled her strange smile. So now her son had a name, but that did not help Arthur decide how much he should tell her of those events. She was looking down at her sturdy hands, and Arthur thought about her striding around the sands or wading through the water with the net. She had remarkable strength, not just physically but inwardly. 'I shall tell you what I know,' he said. 'But if any part of the sorry tale should disturb you, stop me.'

She nodded and he began.

The story took several nights and she never once flinched at it. Arthur did not go into the details of the executions of Babington and the others. And her son was safe. For now.

Sarah did go to church at Christmas and he went with her, comparing the sombre service in the candlelit church to the riotous Winter Solstice gathering at Askeaton. He saw again Meadhbh dancing as the Yule log was lit. He remembered the carol dances and the songs. Merry men and boys chasing the women around the fire. He sighed. '"And Thou, Lord, in the beginning hast laid the foundation of the earth,"' the priest read from the Book of Prayer. '"They shall perish; but thou remainest; and they shall wax old as doth a garment..."' Arthur felt the warm cloth of the new smock Sarah had made him purchase with some of the fish money. Neither went into the village and Ben, the old fisherman from the other end of the beach bought whatever they needed and carefully counted out the change when he delivered the goods. Sarah seemed to like him, but she left all the dealings in fish and goods to Arthur.

Summer came and they spent more time outside and less in the smoky cottage of a night so the stories were forgotten. They had found ways of communicating by using their hands and Sarah's vocal variations. Summer brought with it more fish than they could use, and troubles. Arthur had remembered the fish hooks and he asked Sarah about them by drawing one in the sand. She went inside and came out with a small cloth which contained some small fish hooks. Arthur took one and lay it on the sand next to the bigger hook he had drawn. 'Such were the fish hooks George sent for you but which I gave up in exchange for my life. Shall we buy some with this week's money? We have plenty of ale and enough to eat.' She nodded and when Arthur took the bucket to Jack he asked for five large fish hooks.

That night he woke suddenly. It had been warm enough when they went to sleep to leave the door open. He could see how dark it was outside. There was no moon, but he could hear movement, whispered voices. And he could smell smoke. Their own fire had been left to die to an ember. He got up quietly and by the time he was at the door the night had brightened. Flames were coming from the thatch and he saw two small figures running off down the sands. The tide was out so there was no water to dowse the roof. He woke Sarah and they both watched the roof burn down to the daub of the walls until it went out. Inside they stamped on the fallen straw to prevent its flaring up.

There was no sleep that night and next morning he made a

rough new roof with a promise that he would make it winter proof when he had time. A day or so later Sarah went to bring the net in from its drying place and the twine had been cut in several places.

Arthur left Sarah to mend the net, and walked down to the cottages at the far end. He found Jack's cottage and knocked on the door. Ben answered and invited him in. Sitting on the floor around the room were what seemed to be the entire family. Arthur explained what had happened at Sarah's cottage, and as he spoke several of the men nodded in agreement.

'We were discussing this very business, Arthur,' Jack said. 'It is our young folk and they will apologise.' He raised his hand at two boys in the far corner of the room. 'Come.'

The boys mumbled their apologies and Arthur accepted them. 'I am sure Sarah will be satisfied with that,' he said. He turned to Jack. 'Could you spare the boys for a few days?' Jack nodded and Arthur took the boys back to Sarah's. 'Now you can apologise to her yourselves.'

Again they mumbled, 'Very sorry.'

'Aaargh,' said Sarah softly and she touched each boy on the head. They made to leave, but Arthur held them back. He put them to whittling two fishing rods, and when the shape was right he got them to twirl some hemp twine into a line and attach a hook. Next came the sinker. Together they hunted for the right sized limestones and together they drilled a hole at the top so that they could tie a sinker on as well. As they worked one boy said, 'We are a-feared.'

'What of?' Arthur asked.

'The witch,' said the other boy.

'Sarah is not a witch.' Arthur was angry. 'Who tells you this nonsense?'

'The Catholic Queen Mary is beheaded,' said the first boy. Ah, Arthur thought, that was the inevitable outcome of the letters being found in the beer keg. '...and the Spanish are building a great fleet of ships for to conquer England.'

'What has that to do with Sarah?' Arthur got back to the subject at hand.

'She has the evil eye,' the second boy answered.

'Yes. She is going to draw them in at high tide. And we'll all be killed in our beds.'

Arthur laughed. ''Tis the Queen the Spanish fleet is after, not young boys such as you.'

That was the end of the boys' persecuting Sarah, but not an end to the rumours about the great Spanish fleet. When the nights set in again, Sarah asked for more stories. She enjoyed hearing some of the old ones, and when Arthur got stuck for anything more interesting to tell her he recalled the rituals he had experienced at Askeaton. He talked again about Meadhbh, at which Sarah clutched her heart with both her hands and nodded that she understood how he had felt. Then she indicated that he should run away to her, but Arthur knew that he could not. He seemed cast here, unthinkingly content. He had become weather beaten, his hands callused. He yearned not for the life of a gentleman. Fishing was honest work. They made enough to live simply. His place with Sarah saved him from being taken in as a vagrant and executed. Or worse, from being recognised as one of Babington's conspirators and a death much worse than the hanging or drowning a vagrant would suffer. And as long as he was there, Sarah could not be taken for a witch.

Spring came, then summer and the clamour about the Spanish invasion grew louder. The two lads and Jack shared news from the village when Arthur saw them, and the fleet now seemed an absolute certainty. Everybody knew that the beacon system along the coast would herald the armada's arrival. It was some time after midsummers when the nightmare became a reality. Arthur and Sarah were in front of the cottage scaling the last of the fish to be salted. 'Look,' said Arthur pointing to a light that was difficult to distinguish in the glow of the dying sun. Sarah nodded and pointed further along the coast. When dusk came they knew. The beacons were lit. The Armada had been sighted.

Chapter Twenty-four

Next morning early Arthur walked down to Jack's cottage to hear what, if any news, he had. The lads came running to them. 'The muster,' they gasped together. 'They've come for the muster. Grandad, we must go.'

'You are too young, lads.' Their grandfather put an arm around each shoulder.

'But the soldier says we must.'

'It will be an adventure.'

'I'm a-feared.'

'Stop.' Jack held up a hand. 'Where is the soldier?'

'Here he comes,' and while one boy ran away, the other ran straight into the arms of the soldier.

Arthur thought he recognised him as the soldier who had taken Sarah's hooks and halfcrown. He considered running himself, but knew that would be futile. He would plead his case, he was needed to help...his mother...that would have more weight than a friend.

There was no time for niceties. One soldier became many and they dragged all the men of fighting age off to the village. The force was unnecessary as most of the men were willing to fight, and luckily they refused to take the youngsters along with them. Initially the men were locked into the church, and allocated one of the Trained Band as their leader. There were two groups of about a hundred each. The church armoury was opened and pikes, short handled halberds and bows were handed around. Those with bows were given rough green cloaks and the rest blue. The other clothes were their own, whatever the state. When they were dressed and armed the church doors were unlocked and they were marched into the village high street. Women, old men and boys too young to fight lined the street. Arthur looked out for Jack and his grandsons but there was no sign of them. The crowd roared their encouragement, waving as the fighting men passed through. Church bells rang, small boys ran alongside them until they were almost out of sight of the village and then they fell back waving and shouting messages of good luck to their fathers and brothers.

The men marched all day and into the night, picking up untrained men as they went. The highway along which they walked had several manned turnpikes at which each soldier was scrutinised before being allowed to pass through. Some were questioned and the occasional one taken away for further questioning on some pretext or other. Arthur was pleased that his faint Irish accent had been adulterated by the local speech and he did not stand out from the rest of the soldiers by way of speech or dress. Nonetheless his heart leapt into his throat each time a turnpike came into view. He wondered at the richness of the irony. Here he was now off to fight to save the Queen when but two years before he stood in front of her with murderous intent. He knew not what he would do when the battle came.

Eventually they arrived at Tilbury Port. The Trained Band captain in charge gathered his militia men around a camp fire and handed out cold chicken, black bread and ale for their supper. 'We are outnumbered on the land,' he told them. 'But our sailors are solid men and many.'

'Are we the sum total of England's fighting force on land?' a new recruit asked nervously.

'There are three companies,' the captain explained. 'It is thought the Spanish will land on the south coast so a company is waiting in Kent.' Their own company was under the leadership of Robert Dudley, Earl of Leicester. 'One of the Queen's favourites,' the captain said with a grin. 'And there is a company stationed in London to protect the Queen.'

They settled into camp life. Provisions were short and there was much grumbling. Men fought over the rations which their leader suggested was the result of pre-battle nerves, and Arthur agreed that the waiting was fraught. Rumour and counter-rumour spread through the camp. The Spanish had landed. The Spanish were in retreat. The English fleet was done for. The Spanish fleet had been sunk. Certainly the Spaniards did not seem in a great hurry, but still the fires burnt along the cliff tops and the waiting men kept up their training.

For a week or more they threw their halberds at targets increasing the distance after each successful hit; they practised archery and ran pikes through sheaves of wheat. Then one day Arthur was at archery practice. He had been singled out by the captain to help train the other less able men. 'Like this,' he was saying as he drew the string back as far as it would go. The church bells rang and, startled, he let go the arrow. Luckily there was nobody in the way. The call to arms had come. The men ran to muster in the manner instructed and awaited orders. They were still lining up in the hundred-fold groups under their captains when a messenger came running through the ranks shouting. As he ran a cheer went up in his wake. 'The Queen is coming. Her Majesty is come to Tilbury.'

Their captain found his men and addressed them. 'It is true. The Queen, that brave monarch, is come to Tilbury to cheer her people on. The royal camp is setting up yonder.' He waved his hand into the distance. Arthur wondered if the Queen's bravery had more to do with her favourite, Leicester, being present than her desire to be with her troops, for surely if that was her aim she could have stayed with the company in London. He wondered, too, how far out of favour Tom Dubh was; if he had been forgiven and taken back to Court. He hoped not, but were they to face each other Arthur imagined he would be unrecognisable in his rough garb, and with his face burnt and lined by the sun.

The Spanish were in the English Channel at the very gate of England. Yet in defiance women, children and men above the mustering age of sixty lined up with the soldiers to greet the Queen. A trumpet heralded her entry into the camp. The crowd cheered. Banners flapped loudly in the breeze. The Queen led the way, her white steed frisky, her hand firm on the reins, her head held high. This was nothing like the woman Arthur had last seen. Behind her was obviously her current favourite, the young Earl of Leicester. Then Arthur saw him.

Black Tom Butler, Earl of Ormond was a standard bearer. Arthur pushed his way to the front leaving his captain and the other men behind. He noticed Oliver Grace walking beside the Earl's horse. Both were soon swallowed up by the rest of the entourage; the nobles in their everyday clothes, with jewelled hat pins and taffeta sashes so there was no mistaking these officers for common men. The Earl of Leicester's men followed in their yellow jerkins, helmets and ruffs. Behind came all manner of men, halberdiers with their identical peascod breastplates, the light horse in their helmets and matching pantaloons, the mounted demilancers wearing full helmet and coloured sash and the regular army of yeomen in their soft flat hats. Was there anyone left in London? But they did look magnificent as they gathered before the muster troops. Some of the militia shuffled their feet perhaps embarrassed at their raggle-taggle clothing and assorted weapons. The most astonishing personage there, though, was the Queen, not because of her usual opulence, but because she was simply dressed. Her gown was covered with a light breastplate, her head adorned simply with a scarf. No doubt the flying tassels were edged with gold, but it was an effectively simple look. She always dressed as if she was a player acting a part, and here she was being one of the people. Her people. The entourage stopped. The Queen stepped her horse forward. A trumpeter called the crowd to attention.

'My loving people.' The Queen's voice rang out. 'We have been persuaded by some that are careful of our safety to take heed how we commit ourself to armed multitudes for fear of treachery.' Exactly, Arthur thought. She was at grave risk here with so many armed men and so many recusants still about that would have her dead, albeit there was no Queen of Scots to take her place. 'But I assure you,' she was saying, 'I do not desire to live to distrust my faithful and loving people.'

A cheer went up from the crowd and calls of 'God bless you Good Queen Bess.'

'Let tyrants fear.' Her voice grew louder. An even louder cheer broke out.

Arthur turned his attention to Tom Dubh. His rapt gaze was on the Queen. Even Oliver Grace was smiling. '...I am come amongst you at this time, not for my recreation and disport, but being resolved, in the midst and heat of the battle, to live or die amongst you all.'

She had to pause again until the clamour died down. Arthur was impressed. Aye, he hated what the English were doing in Ireland, but that was not necessarily all the Queen's bidding. There was no arguing that most of the New English in Ireland were punitive and acquisitive, but he still had a grudging respect for this woman. What courage and strength was here! If Piers was indeed her son he gained his brave spirit as much from her as from the Earl. He smiled to himself at the thought of Morveen and her stories, at his naivety in believing for so long that he was the son of this Queen, and he thought of Piers.

The Queen continued, 'I know I have the body of a weak and feeble woman...' The crowd was hushed now '...but I have the heart and stomach of a king, and a king of England, too...' Another roar went forth. '...and think foul scorn that Parma or Spain or any prince of Europe should dare to invade the borders of my realm.' People clapped and shouted. The pennant bearers waved their flags and none so hard as Tom Dubh with the Queen's standard.

Arthur looked again at Tom Dubh, then at his right-hand man. Oliver Grace was staring at Arthur who looked quickly away. When he dared look again the pair had turned their attention back to the

Queen. '...by your concord in the camp, and your valour in the field, we shall shortly have a famous victory over those enemies of my God, of my kingdom and of my people.' Soldier turned to soldier and shook hands, young women of the town danced arm-in-arm. The church bells rang and in the confusion that followed her speech, the Queen rode off to her encampment to await the arrival of the enemy.

Slowly the townspeople went home and the soldiers returned to their camp. They could see the Queen's standard flying high over her tent and many men saluted it that night before going to bed in their own more humble accommodation. Next day when they were not on guard or rehearsing the battle to come many soldiers drifted toward the Queen's encampment in the hopes of seeing a glimpse of her again. Arthur stayed well away. He was on edge, half expecting Oliver Grace or his man to come striding across the camp towards him and drag him away to the Earl. He could be forgiven once, but twice was beyond even the kindness of Tom Dubh. If she were to see the two of them together perhaps the Queen would reckon what had happened that afternoon in her tent. She would be vindicated and he, Arthur, would soon be dead, hung, drawn and quartered. Perhaps if there was some political gain to be had, expediency might cause a reconciliation, but what was Arthur? A humble fisherman, and a traitorous one at that. What had he ever been? The capper son of a scullion wench.

Fortunately the Queen did not stay long at Tilbury. In a day or so her entourage packed and left, although the armed men stayed behind. Now an air of lethargy hung over the camp. It was as if the Queen's visit had been the main event. The militia had to keep practising but the heart had gone out of them. Their commander-in-chief was nowhere to be seen, perhaps he had returned to London with the Queen, in which case who was to command the battle to come? Even the captain of Arthur's men seemed to have lost his spirit. Militia talking to each other agreed, the zeal for battle came from the top. Yes, the Queen had come to share the danger with her people, but she did not stay long and her fervour was now no longer matched by her commanding officers. So in many ways they were none of them surprised when the church bells rang again and the messenger ran through the camp, this time with the news that the Armada had been defeated by the valiant English navy at Kent. 'Just as well,' Arthur observed to a young recruit from Prittlewell.

Amidst the celebrations soldiers threw down their arms and tore off their coloured cloaks, although not long after they ran back to retrieve cloak and weapon; they would not be paid for their service if they did not hand these in.

*

The Trained Band and some militia were kept in reserve, but most were sent on their way. 'Too miserable to keep us fed,' said the lad from Prittlewell as they trudged back towards the village.

The turnpikes were still in place but no longer manned, and the road was busy with militia men returning to their homes. The air was bright and spirits high; England had defeated the Spanish, duty to Queen and country had been fulfilled and now it was time to return home triumphant. It was as if each man was himself responsible for the Spaniards' downfall. They did not march at the same pace as they had kept to reach Tilbury, now the pace was more leisurely. At places along the way villagers came out of their houses to give them food and ale and bid them God's speed. At one such place Arthur and his companion had just finished a meal of soft cheese and bread when a member of the Trained Band walked by. The woman of the cottage offered him some cheese and bread which he refused. 'I had my fill at the last village, but thank you kindly,' he said. So after thanking the woman themselves Arthur and the boy fell into step beside the soldier.

'Were you at Tilbury?' Arthur asked.

'I were in Kent,' the solider replied.

'Is Kent nearby?' the boy asked.

'No,' laughed the soldier. 'It is many miles distant, across the river.'

'Then how did you get here so quickly?' asked the boy.

'After the defeat of the Spaniards?' Arthur added.

The soldier laughed again. 'They were defeated some two weeks back.'

'But...' began the boy.

'Would the Queen have known?' Arthur asked.

'Of course. Messengers were sent the minute we were out of danger.'

'Two weeks ago, you say?' Arthur was calculating the time which had elapsed since the Queen's visit to Tilbury.

'Two weeks and a day to be precise.'

'What does that mean?' the lad asked Arthur.

'It means we were duped. All that talk about risking whatever danger was nigh to be with her people! What a splendid piece of theatre.'

'I heard of her visit,' the soldier said. 'I would say she is still a-feared of the Duke of Parma. He is not done yet.' Then he lowered his voice in case any of the other men trudging their way home might hear. 'I was supposed to stay on in case the Spanish returned. But I have been in training for two years and I just want to get back to my wife and children.'

'Will you not stand out?' Arthur asked. 'It is clear you are one of the Trained Band by your uniform.'

'I have been safe so far. Everyone is too content to be thinking of deserters.' He paused. 'And not all of the Trained Band were required to stay.'

Arthur left the soldier and the lad at Prittlewell; the lad to go home to his mother, the soldier to rest for the night before travelling on down the coast.

Arthur was looking forward to seeing Sarah and his pace quickened at the thought of telling her the story of the Queen's duplicity, but he determined not to tell Jack or the other folk at the far end of the beach. He was not entirely sure how far he could trust them. He stopped outside the cottage to smell the sea air and check on the tide. It was in, but there was no sign of Sarah calf-deep in water with her rod. Further down Jack and his boys were dragging a net through the water.

He opened the cottage door, 'Sarah,' he said. 'I am back from the war.' He laughed at the exaggeration but no sound came in return. The cottage was empty. He went outside and walked around the cottage, no Sarah. He went back to the front and looked across the water again, scanning the entire beach in case she had moved along for better fishing. Jack's boys were getting close to shore now with their net, but still no sign of Sarah. He climbed the dunes calling her name, no tortured answer came. Finally he walked down to the other cottages.

Jack was in the front yard picking the winkles off the net. The boys were carting the fish barrel to the road. 'They came,' Jack said before Arthur could say a word. 'They had the boy with them.'

'George?'

Jack nodded. 'The authorities have been extra vigilant with the Spanish threat. They are imprisoning anyone for the slightest of reasons.'

Arthur looked out to sea for a long time before asking the next question. 'Where did they take them?'

'To London. My lads overheard them talking. They made the lad...George... identify his mother. As a witch.'

Arthur walked away. He went back to the cottage and took some money, but not all of it – just in case – from Sarah's hiding place. Then he walked out the door and turned his back on the sea, not caring what happened to him. He set off back to Prittlewell. Come what may now he would cross the country to Bristol and thence to Ireland. If he got killed on the way he cared not, though he did not relish the thought of a death such as Babington suffered. He was weary.

In Prittlewell he saw the Trained Band soldier again, and as he told him what had happened an idea struck him. 'Would you like to swap clothing?'It would certainly be easier to cross from Bristol if he was dressed as a soldier. He could say he had been released from the Kentish group and was on his way to fight in Ireland.

'I'll be glad to get out of this garb,' the soldier said. 'And your stockings and smock look of good quality.'

'Yes, and warm,' Arthur said. 'They should serve you well. The fisherwoman, Sarah, made a moderate living out of her fish and willingly shared it with me.' He turned away lest the soldier see the tears in his eyes. He thought of Sarah and her generosity, her humour and her acceptance of adversity. Why could folk not be left to live in peace? The soldier's clothes smelt strongly of sweat, but so, Arthur supposed, did his own. Luckily they were of a similar build although the soldier's jerkin was a bit short. Still he thought he cut a fine figure in his breeches and tin helmet. The soldier would not part with his caliver and Arthur was glad of that. He had no desire to shoot anyone.

Because there were so many militia men and redundant Trained Band men on the roads it was relatively easy to travel dressed as a soldier and Arthur managed to walk unmolested to Bristol being fed and watered along the way by villagers so there was no need to scavenge. It took days, but the sight of the ships lining the quay warmed him. Getting on board one set for Waterford or Dublin could be more difficult, he thought, but when he arrived at the Quay there was a newly-formed troop of English soldiers about to embark for Waterford. He had money for the passage and mingled with the soldiers easily.

*

He stayed with the troops until they marched out of Waterford for the plantations of Munster. He marched close to the back of the line, then walked more slowly so that he was the last man. There was no need of a rear guard. All the men were keen to get to the plantations and stake their claim to Irish soil and a new life. There was really only one place Arthur could go. In the eyes of Piers and Tom Dubh he was again a traitor. In the eyes of others he was a turn-coat. Yet to others like Bren and Orlagh O'Brennan he was a patriot. He would dearly love to go and see them, to curl up beside their fire and sleep, and sleep; to be fed on Orlagh's wholesome food; to tell them about his adventures, or to talk with Piers' kind wife about the state of political affairs in an even-handed way. He knew that was useless. There was only one matter that required immediate attention. Was Meadhbh dead or alive?

He made his way on foot by boreen and fields to Askeaton. His soldier's uniform was tattered and bedraggled by the time he reached the town so he was careful to avoid the many English strutting about in ownership of the place. He slipped into the inn and spoke quietly to the bar tender in Gaelic. He knew of Meadhbh. 'Why do you enquire of her?' the barman asked. Arthur explained who he was, looking at the men drinking around him for fear they might understand. 'She is kin to the O'Mores of Aghobe and ran to them when the English took the castle. She abides at the O'More castle at Gortnaclea.'

The castle at Gortnaclea looked empty and neglected. There was no watch on the battlements and Arthur thought he had best go back to Aghaboe. He might find Meadhbh there, but first he went to the castle gate. It was locked but when he knocked a sleepy voice said, 'Who goes there?'

'Arthur Butler,' he said.

The gate opened, the portcullis lifted and an army of men came rushing out at him. They threw him on the ground, and one said to another, 'Fetch Owney MacRory.'

Arthur was almost suffocated under the weight of men, then one took a hard look at him. 'It is you, Sir,' he said. And to the others, 'Let him be.' It was Daniel Caech. 'He is Arthur. Friend, not foe.' So it was that Arthur was standing when the young, athletic Owney MacRory O'More came out to inspect him.

Daniel explained who Arthur was, and how he defended the Desmond castle before being sent to Ard Na Caithne to fight with the Spanish. 'We thought him dead,' he said finally.

Owney put a friendly arm around Arthur's shoulder. 'You are

welcome to join the ancient sept of the O'Mores.'

'What of Meadhbh?' Arthur asked. 'And Roisin and Fainche?'

'Roisin is dead, God rest her soul,' said Daniel. 'Fainche took her chances with the English. Meadhbh and myself, we are kin and of O'More stock. This seemed the safer option.' Owney O'More was bounding up the stairs. Daniel and Arthur followed. At the top Owney stopped and waited for them to catch up with him. 'You shall see Meadhbh, so.'

When Meadhbh stepped into the hall Arthur's heart seemed to stop beating. She was beautiful and finely dressed. The years had been kind to her. From the look that passed between her and Owney, he did not doubt that they shared a bed. 'Where is that page?' Owney asked.

'I shall fetch him,' said Daniel.

Meadhbh smiled shyly at Arthur. Then she turned to Owney. 'The boy will be here shortly, so.'

There was chatter on the stairs and a child of about six ran into the room. He stopped when he saw Arthur. '*Dia duit*,' he said.

'And good day to you,' Arthur said. 'What a fine boy you are.' He looked first at Meadhbh who was smiling proudly, then at Owney. 'Congratulations.'

'Are due to you,' laughed Owney. 'This is young Arthur. Greet your father properly, young sir.'

*

At supper Meadhbh sat next to Owney O'More and they laughed together, although she glanced at Arthur all the while. They ate a roasted porker and some of the strange new vegetable imported from England; potatoes Daniel Caech said they were. Young Arthur walked in carrying a jug of meat juices. He put it on the table and as he turned to leave, Owney took him by the arm. 'Who are the seven septs of Laois?' he asked the boy. 'Your father might not be of Laois but your mother is and you will grow up to fight for these rich and fertile lands. 'So? O'More..?'

'O'Lalor, O'Dowling, O'Kelly, O'Devoy...'

'That's five.'

'I have forgotten,' the boy confessed, and Arthur wished he knew so he could help him out.

'O'Doran and McEv...' Owney coached.

'McEvoy,' shouted young Arthur.

'You are a bright lad and now with your father to give you lessons you will be even brighter.' He turned to Arthur. 'We need you here to tutor the boys. Will you stay?'

Arthur looked at Meabdh who gave a small nod of the head.

'Being a Celtic warrior is all very well...and necessary...' Owney went on, 'but we must fight the English with our brains as well as our brawn.'

It was an attractive proposition. To stay with his feet on Irish soil and away from the brutality and bloodshed was a compelling idea. To watch his son grow and help in his education. But, he thought, could he bear to live under the same roof as Meadbh and watch her consorting with Owney O'More? Could he bear to see Owney treat young Arthur as his own son? He took a deep draught of ale. If it meant fighting for Ireland with words instead of bloody deeds, he possibly could.

'What say you?' Owney turned and raised his goblet in a toast. 'It will be a hard battle, but we shall make our mark. You will see.' He looked at Arthur awaiting an answer.

'My lord...'

'Owney!'

'Could I consider it and let you know on the morrow?' He looked again at Meadbh but she was sending young Arthur back to the kitchen. She is alive, he told himself. That was all you asked for. Not fidelity. How could he have expected that? Seven years was a long time; and eternity for one as young as Meadhbh was when they first fell into bed together. She looked at him then and smiled. Owney took her hand and kissed it. It looked like a parting gesture, but still they sat at the table side by side and laughed together when the travelling minstrel, brought in for their entertainment, sang a bawdy song. It was as if Owney had forgotten his offer and Arthur's question.

Arthur waited until the minstrel stopped and the clapping died away before turning to Owney. 'Sir?'

'Of course. You have had a hard journey. You are exhausted from doing your bit for Ireland away across the sea. You sleep on it.'

Even before the revelry stopped Arthur excused himself and went to his chamber. As soon as he was undressed he snuffed the candle and rested his head on the bolster. At least Meadhbh was alive. He could hear the muffled sound of the revel and distinguish Owney's laugh above the rest. He still did not know which way he would turn in the morning. It would be hard to leave the boy behind, but that was the Irish way. Most boys of young Arthur's age would be fostered out to family by now. He lay back and enjoyed the feeling of the bolster at his head and the soft mattress beneath him. Such luxury he had not enjoyed in a long time. And yet it felt empty.

The door opened. It was dark and he could not see who it was who entered, but he could smell the scent of her skin. 'Meadhbh,' he said.

She came to the bedside and parted the curtains.

'Are you not Owney O'More's lover?' he asked.

'No longer,' she said. 'He has mistresses a-plenty and can spare me now you have returned. He cares more for the pages' education than he does for me.'

'So you are to be sacrificed? I won't be a party to that. I will leave on the morrow, happy to know that you are still alive. And that I have a fine young son.'

'Ask me, Arthur. Ask me what I desire?' She sat on the bed and took his hand. 'I missed you, so,' she went on before he could ask her the question. She lay on the bed beside him. 'Did you miss me?' She traced her finger down his scar. He did not know what to do, it had been so long. She leaned over and kissed him, and the taste of her lips was sweeter than any wine he had ever partaken of. He pulled her to him, nuzzled his face into her hair. It reminded him of Morveen when he was young and they slept together under the table. The same mix of peat smoke and cooking fat.

'I missed you beyond measure,' he said at last.

'We were betrothed before you left, and I have never stopped being betrothed to you.'

'But what about my letters? Did you not receive my letters?'

'You know I cannot read.'

'But I thought someone would read them out to you.'

She sighed. 'There were no letters. None that I saw or heard of.' She kissed him. 'What did they say?'

'Tá grá agam duit.' He unbuttoned her chemise. *'Tá grá agam duit.'*

She laughed, pleased. *'Tá mo chroí istigh ionat.* My heart is within you,' she said as he entered her.

He was home.

Chronology

1531	Thomas Butler, eldest son of James Butler, 9th Earl of Ormond, and Joan FitzGerald (daughter of the 11th Earl of Desmond) is born
1533	Elizabeth Tudor born
1544	Thomas Butler is sent to London to be raised with Henry VIII's son, Edward.
1546	James Butler is (accidently?) poisoned in London. Thomas succeeds but as he is only 15 becomes a ward of the King. His mother visits Court to make sure the estate is kept intact.
1547	Henry VIII dies. Edward succeeds aged 9. Thomas fights in the invasion of Scotland. He acquits himself with honour.
1550	Dowager Countess of Ormond, Joan FitzGerald, marries her cousin Garret Fitzgerald, 13th Earl of Desmond and arch-enemy of the Ormonds. She is 40, Desmond is 20.
1553	Edward dies. Mary succeeds.
1554	Thomas distinguishes himself in the fight against Wyatt rebels in defence of Queen Mary. He returns to Ireland.
1558	Mary dies. Elizabeth ascends the throne. She is a distant cousin though the Boleyns.
1559	Thomas is appointed Lord Treasurer of Ireland. Thomas marries Elizabeth Berkeley at Court.
1563	Thomas and Elizabeth Berkeley estranged.
1565	January - Joan, Countess of Desmond dies. Later that month Desmond marries Eleanor Butler (of a cadet branch of the Butler family). Free now of any maternal constraints Thomas goes to battle with Desmond. February - Battle of Affane, the last private battle

	in Ireland.
	Elizabeth demands an inquiry. Both Desmond and Thomas are called to London. Desmond is sent to the Tower. Thomas has to wait until Christmas Eve before he learns his own fate. He is placed under cognisance of 20,000 pounds to keep the peace, but quickly becomes favoured by Elizabeth.
	Following the results of the royal inquiry into the Battle of Affane Sir Henry Sidney is appointed Lord Deputy of Ireland.
1565-69	Thomas is at Court in London.
1565-73	Desmond in prison, London and Dublin.
1566-69	Butler brothers' rebellion.
1567-68	Sir Henry Sidney is on leave in England.
1569	Thomas returns home to control his rebellious brothers.
1570	Elizabeth is excommunicated by the Pope. The Irish rejoice.
	Butler brothers attainted by Act of Irish parliament.
1571	Henry Sidney recalled to London
1571	Sir William Fitzwilliam is appointed Lord Deputy of Ireland
1572	Butler brothers are pardoned.
	Thomas is back at Court.
1574	Queen Elizabeth visits Bristol while on summer progress.
1575	Fitzwilliam is recalled to London. Thomas expects his friend, Walter Devereux, Earl of Essex, to take his place, but Henry Sidney returns as Lord Deputy.
1576-79	Thomas at Court.
1578	Henry Sidney recalled to London.
	Sir William Drury appointed Lord Deputy. He was an ardent Protestant intent on imposing the

	Queen's religion on her subjects in Ireland.
1579	Desmond declared a traitor.
	Thomas is appointed the Queen's General in Munster. He takes to the field against Desmond.
1580	Arthur, Lord Grey appointed Lord Deputy.
	Massacre at Ard na Caithne (Smerwick).
1582	Elizabeth Berkeley dies in Bristol.
	Thomas marries Elizabeth Sheffield at Court.
1583	Dr Dermot O'Hurley, Catholic Archbishop of Cashel is taken to Carraigh by Piers' Butler.
	O'Hurley is captured and taken to Dublin Castle.
	Desmond is killed.
1584	Thomas goes to Court to plead his innocence in the O'Hurley case.
	He only learns while en route that the Queen has written forbidding his attendance. He returns home.
	O'Hurley is tortured and killed.
	Sir John Perrot becomes Lord Deputy. He is instructed to impose English rule throughout Ireland.
1586	Babington conspiracy against Elizabeth I.
	Babington and co-conspirators hung, drawn and quartered.
1587	Mary Queen of Scots beheaded.
	Perrot recalled to London.
1588	Spanish Armada threatened invasion.
	Elizabeth gives a rousing speech to the troops at Tilbury, even though the invasion threat has already been averted - more by good luck (bad weather) than good management.

Glossary

I have not translated the Gaelic from the text because the meaning is contained in the context.

aba	a cloth cover to restrain a falcon
Ard na Caithne	Gaelic for Smerwick
Beltaine	ancient Gaelic ceremony to celebrate the beginning of summer
boreen	narrow lane
brail	soft leather strap used to restrain falcon
breeches	two separate trouser legs which later were joined
cadge	portable perch for carrying falcon into field
caliver	hand gun
caparison	decorative cover laid over the horse
cavalleria	person who tends the horses
chanfron	a plate for defending a horse's head
coign and livery	payment, free quarters and food for soldiers and horses required by lords of their tenants.
copatain hat	a high-crowned hat
coronal	metal tip for lance with prongs to make it easier to catch the opponent's shield
curragh	a boat built of planks and covered with skin
deboshed	drunk
dubh	Gaelic for 'black'
galantine sauce	sauce made from bread crumbs and spices
galingale	root of – used in galantine sauce
gallowglass	elite mercenary Scottish warriors
gatch	unusual gait
groat	also known as 'fuppence', a coin worth four pence
guarde	lavatory
halberd	axe and pike mounted on six foot pole
jess	thin leather strap used to tether a falcon
kerne	lightly armed foot-soldier

kirtle	skirt or gown
Martlemas	Feast of St Martin celebrated 11 November
netherstocks	stocking covering the lower half of the leg
oubliette	place to be forgotten; prison cell with access only by trapdoor
peascod	doublet stuffed to make its wearer look well-fed
quintain	free-standing target for training or games
Ralegh	Elizabethan spelling of Sir Walter Raleigh
Rince Fada	a long dance similar to today's country dancing
Samhain	Gaelic Feast of the Dead celebrated at the same time as modern-day Halloween
secke	a dry, Spanish white wine
seneschal	steward of the household
sept	clan
sherral	offensive term for an unprincipled person
shoneen	one who puts on airs
sidh	ghosts; fairies who live under a hill or mound
Ta gra agam duit	I have love for you, pron: *taw graw uh-gum ditch*
tenter grounds	ground where dyers strung cloth to dry as taut as possible between poles – the origin of 'being on tenter hooks'
Turkey carpet	Turkish carpet – used initially as covering for walls and cupboards
varvel	a small metal ring tied to the leg of a hawk and engraved with the owner's name

About the Author

Joan Rosier-Jones lives in Whanganui, New Zealand, but she loves to travel, particularly to Ireland where her partner was born and raised. They came across Carraigh castle and manor house on one visit and the story of Black Tom Butler waiting for Elizabeth to visit him in Ireland haunted her. On a second visit she started research for this novel. She has long been active in the politics of being a writer and is a past National President of the New Zealand Society of Authors. *Author's photo: Albert Sword*

Also by Joan Rosier-Jones
Fiction:
Cast Two Shadows
Voyagers
Canterbury Tales
Mother Tongue
Yes
Crossing the Alps

Non-fiction:
Writing Your Family History
So You Want to Write
The Murder of Chow Yat

More Tangerine Titles

Can three orphans with a mysterious past unlock the meaning of a chilling 700-year-old prophecy? Three will arrive: one to give, one to die and one to live.
Secret forays from their London orphanage into the hidden world of Ammasaya reveal how their lives are entwined with blood-thirsty Spine Crawlers, secretive goblins, deadly scorpions, murderous witches, enchanting Spry and the powerful Dragons of Creation and Destruction. A genocidal war and the evil Blood Empress are lurking in the shadows, waiting to change the orphans' lives forever. Author P S Mokha enchants with this tale.

Fans of *The Windsor Conspiracy* will love this explosive sequel, while new readers of Mike Ponder will enjoy the fast-paced action of *Four Kings*, the stand-alone story of Zimbabwean, Gus McKenzie, whose land, Four Kings - won in a card game by his grandfather - is ravaged by looters and murderers after Mugabe decrees all white-owned farms will be resettled. Gus vows to destroy those responsible for ruining his life. But who was responsible? Was it Mugabe, or was Gus a mere pawn in an international plot? From fighting insurgents in the oil-soaked Niger Delta, to the cholera-ravaged slums of Harare and the searing heat of the Australian outback, the reader is treated to suspense piled on suspense.

Ginny Barnes decides to leave town for the countrside and places an advertisement in a farming newspaper. Older woman, Maureen Moffat, an Elvis Presley fan, asks for help on her farm but Ginny's notion of wearing a gingham blouse and straw hat to feed pet lambs and pick wild blackberries for pies soon wanes when she arrives at the farm and is trapped in her car by Elvis, the bull. Maureen Moffat's bachelor nephew, Mike, comes to the rescue and a series of mishaps and misunderstandings unfold. Carmel Hurdle writes with infectious humour about Ginny's country escapade in this retro, rustic romp for those who loved the 80s – and for those who wished they'd been there.

Made in the USA
Charleston, SC
23 August 2013